MORE THAN A MOM

A Journey

Margie J. Harding

This book is dedicated first to Dr. Deanna Stock for believing in me and telling me I could do this and second to all the professors who encouraged me during my tenure as student. I thank you all!

A heartfelt thank you to my daughter, Beth, who supported me, worked as a sounding board, and did first the first editing. She was a God-send!

Forward

To all Moms who question their value and worth on an everyday basis. This book is written for you and proves that we can be more. I challenge you to take the leap; step out on faith and become the person you can be. I am not suggesting it won't be hard or challenging. Life always is. And it's entirely possible, like me, life won't stop or go on hold, while you travel down this unfamiliar road. Instead it will likely be "one more thing" on your plate. But you can do it. I know; I've been there.

The following is my story. But it doesn't have to be mine alone. It can also be yours.

Disclaimer:

While this is my story, and based on facts and actual events; names and places have all been changed and some events have been fictionalized to protect privacy. Any likenesses of characters are products of the author's imagination and are not to be construed as real.

Year One
Chapter 1

Lee had traveled east certain he wanted to leave his native state in the west. His goal had been simply to see the America he had fought for in the War. Vietnam had not been kind, leaving him wounded physically and reaction to him as to most Vietnam vets on his return to the states, left him wounded emotionally. He found himself needing work to support his travels and fell into construction. It was in this environment, he met Melanie.

Although petite, and pleasant, Melanie lacked self-confidence, and was surprised when Lee showed interest in her. They met at Hannah's, Melanie's best friend in high school, who had a brother also a construction worker, who worked with Lee. After dating just two short months they knew they were meant for each other.

They were an unlikely couple since Melanie was still in high school and eight years younger than Lee. Her parents, of Amish background immediately liked the tall, hard working, Lee. His dark complexion and high cheek bones gave evidence of his Indian heritage. Right after graduation, Melanie and Lee were married in a small ceremony with only Melanie's family and a few friends.

Mingled with the joy of being newlywed, Melanie shared bittersweet good-byes to her family as she and Lee made ready to move west. Lee knew the place he wanted to raise his children with his new bride, was in his native home land in the Black Hills.

"Lee, do you think your family will like me?" Melanie asked as they pulled into the driveway of the modest home of his parents.

"Sure they will." He answered quickly, and then added. "Well, Mom will. But just remember Pop doesn't like anybody. So don't be upset. It's just his way." Nervously she took his hand as they went inside.

"Pop, Mom; this is Melanie, my bride."

"Hello, Sweetie. Welcome to the family," said Mrs. Carson, a tall, large woman, warmly giving her a squeeze. Her short, neatly cut almost white hair, rounded her face giving her a youthful look. Both her hazel eyes and her smile resonated kindness. Melanie immediately knew she and this woman would be friends.

Mr. Carson, a stout fellow, with a round face and missing teeth, looked up from the newspaper he was reading. "How ya doin' young lady? You've got your hands full there with Lee. It's a lot different out here than back East. Hope you like it all right."

"I'm fine, thank you. I'm sure I'll like it out here fine once I get used to it."

"Hope so," he said picking up his paper to resume reading.

The couple was warmly received by the rest of the Carson family who were delighted to see their wandering sibling return. As they returned to their car Lee said, "I can't believe it! Pop liked you. He really liked you. He doesn't like anybody!"

Melanie laughed. "I don't know why, but I'm glad. I like him, too."

Lee was able to find work in construction, working with a painting contractor to provide for himself and his new wife. Lee and Melanie bought forty acres of the Sweet Springs Ranch from his step father, Ike and Mother, Florence, who was affectionately known as Flo and purchased a used house trailer to begin their life together.

Just four months after their wedding Melanie discovered she was pregnant. Summer brought their first born daughter, Tara. A year later Lee lost his father to a heart attack which meant more responsibility for his mother who was still raising a teenage daughter and a young son. Making ends meet meant long hours for Lee, who was attending college and working part time in a salvage yard. His work load increased when he began work as an automotive mechanic technician.

Lee and Melanie's family continued to grow as a second daughter, Kaitlyn, was born when Tara was five, and a third daughter, Mackenzie, when Kaitlyn was two. As the family grew and expenses allowed they built a modest home on their acreage and were delighted when Luke was born three years after Mackenzie and finally had Gavin, their fifth child, when Luke was four.

Melanie spent her days making "home making" an art. She cooked and sewed, saved coupons, cleaned and took care of her family. The children were her delight and her husband the love of her life. She wondered, however, what would it have been like to go to college? She'd dreamed of college before she married, but lack of money and marrying Lee changed all that. She studied Lee's text books when she could but felt inadequate even though she had done very well in high school.

As years passed she wondered more and more of her worth. She wondered if she could do anything more than be a mom. Even if she could go to college, what would she take? What would she do with the education? Lee provided for them, so working wasn't necessary. Why go? Yet, she often felt a longing for something more. She found some success in freelance writing which gave her a sense of fulfillment since every acceptance by a publisher meant she had something worthwhile to say.

As the girls grew and ventured off to college Melanie found herself engrossed in the textbooks they brought home. She convinced them to keep their books rather than participating in book buy back. This provided the means for her to delve into subjects she had never considered before. Biology frightened her, Math terrified her, but the English and History books were treasures.

Still she was mostly content with being Mom and Gran. Tara married Brent who had three children and they lived nearby in Sweet Creek. Kaitlyn, a registered nurse, married Phil who was a Physical Education instructor and they too lived nearby in Steele. Mackenzie found love with Stephen but found themselves living with Melanie and Lee for two years before they were able to make it on their own even though Mackenzie worked at the local college Administration Office, part time, to help out.

Luke enlisted in the Marine Corps and their lives were again changed. It was different than having the girls in college or married since the military had a way of taking loved ones away. Luke was no exception. He had just left for an overseas assignment after working and training in Virginia, Florida and Arizona.

When Gavin graduated from high school and registered at the local community college, Melanie faced being alone and no longer needed. Lee still needed her, but the nurturing side of her was left empty. It was time to do something different; time to do something for herself; time to consider fulfilling her lifelong dream of going to college. She discussed her options with Lee.

This would change their lifestyle. Lee had just retired and had plans of traveling across country. They had traveled some and both Lee and Melanie knew they enjoyed seeing other parts of the country. It had been his dream to see the United States after he survived Vietnam. He nearly lost his arm and took a shot in the leg, as well, and since traveling was well beyond their means when raising the children, although vacations were taken, it had been decided traveling would be their retirement.

While Lee knew his Vietnam injuries were aggravated with cold, he agreed to withstand the winters for Melanie to take on the challenge of college. Medication and a strong sense of duty and determination had helped him cope all these years. "I'll just have to take off and go for a couple weeks at a time where it's warm," Lee said.

Melanie flinched. "I hate the sound of that," she said softly.

"Well, if this is what you really want to do, then you should do it. I just want you to know that I may need to take off for now and then."

Melanie felt a knot form in the bottom of her stomach. Her heart ached. "I really do want to go to college, but you leaving doesn't please me."

"It'll be okay. I'll only be gone for a while. This will give me something to do when you're all wrapped up in school work."

Melanie felt relief, guilt and a strange sting of anger. At dinner, with Lee's support she announced her intentions.

Gavin, who even while sitting, his six foot four inch frame towered above everyone else at the table, looked at Melanie with disbelief. "Mom, this year?" He realized instantly that they would be attending the same college at the same time. Since Gavin had been homeschooled, he graduated from high school early and had wanted to attend college in western Montana but since he was only sixteen Melanie and Lee had insisted he stay for at least the first year and attend college locally. Having his mother on campus his first year of college was less than exciting.

"I won't invade your space. I promise," she said, giggling. "Whenever I see you on campus I won't even act like I know you. And I promise not to holler at you from across campus and embarrass you."

Gavin laughed his deep throaty laugh causing his sparkling eyes to dance. He had dark hair, a defined chiseled chin and seemed much to thin for his tall frame. He enjoyed his mother and knew she meant that. But could she keep her promise? She was his mom after all. How hard would it be to not speak to him when she saw him? It was so out of character for her. She spoke to everyone, including strangers. "Well, that remains to be seen. You sure you need to do this now? Can't you wait another year, until I leave?"

"No. You know I can't. Your dad and I have agreed this is the time to do this. Think how this changes our plans. We're supposed to travel since he's retired. That means we'll be here. It'll be an adjustment for everyone. But if I don't do it now while I'm ready and have the courage, I may not talk me into it. It has to be now."

"Mom, are you sure," he asked again lightly. "Now?"

"Yes, now. It'll be okay. I promise. Trust me," she said smiling.

Despite her bravado only days before with Gavin, Melanie felt faint as she parked her car in visitor parking. Trembling fingers removed the keys from the ignition and she opened her door. Fear gripped her and she fought to keep from closing the door and driving away.

"You can do this," said Shelley, Melanie's personal cheering section. "It's just the placement tests. These tests just see where you are. It's not a big deal. You will be fine."

"You are coming with me, right? I can't do this by myself."

"I can go in and I'll wait for you. I can't go in the testing center with you. Trust me. I will be right outside and I will wait for you as long as you take. I brought a book to read and I have nothing to do for the rest of the afternoon. Take all the time you need. When we are all finished, we'll go visit Mackenzie."

Melanie appreciated Shelley's confidence. She can be confident, Melanie thought, suddenly! She's a teacher! Her friendship with Shelley, an average sized woman with nearly black, shoulder length hair that always seemed in "frizz mode," had begun in the small church they attended. Shelley led the choir and was active in other activities as well, and had a single daughter, Lorrie, the same age as Luke.

They were unlikely friends, however, since Shelley was an only child, well educated with parents as educators. Her vocabulary spoke of the eloquent, sophisticated lifestyle she had growing up. Her wealthy parents had lived in Europe for a time giving Shelley an advantage of "upper class" living Melanie knew nothing about.

Dressed in blue jeans and a soft beige sleeveless top that flattered her small, petite frame, Melanie forced one foot in front of the other toward the Administrative building. Her weakened knees climbed the staircase to the entrance.

"Let's go get you signed in and then I'll take you to the testing center."

"I don't know, Shelley. I am terrified. The English part of it doesn't bother me so much, but I know I can't do the Math. What if I fail?"

"You can't fail! These are placement tests. That is the purpose of the tests. You are placed in classes depending on your ability. Believe me there are a lot of students right out of high school who have to take non-credit, remedial classes."

"Somehow that doesn't make me feel any better."

"Well, it should," she said laughing. "It has been nearly thirty years since you've taken a math class. You have the right to not know how to do it. The kids that will be in there with you just graduated. They should know and they don't."

"But won't I be at a greater disadvantage since they at least will be familiar with the material. In Algebra, I haven't a clue! I have no background. I will be lost!"

"That's why you'll be taking the class Melanie. To learn. You will get it because you want to learn it. Most of the kids that are in there didn't get it the first time because they weren't interested. You have the advantage.

"Go on in," encouraged Shelley, softly, yet firmly when they reached the testing center. "I'll sit right here and wait. You'll do fine."

Melanie turned the knob and walked in. The well lit room was small, with ample room however, for three rows of computers. Four computers were lined up against the far wall and four more faced the door in the center of the room. A large desk filled with stacks of papers, assorted books, a telephone, and other office and educational material, was to Melanie's right. An additional four more computers lined the room on that end of the room as well. "Good afternoon," said the well dressed woman pleasantly.

"Afternoon," Melanie returned shyly.

Shaking, she handed her registration form to the waiting receptionist.

"Okay, Sweetie. Just have a seat at any one of the computers and you can get started. You are not timed, so take your time. Just follow the directions as they come up on the screen. You will be asked a question and you just have to click on the answer you believe is correct.

"You will have the English placement tests first. When you are finished with that you automatically move on to the Math. Feel free to use your calculator and here is lots of scratch paper to work on."

Melanie felt awkward at the computer. Using her own was so different from these. What if she did something to wreck the whole thing? What happens if she wants to go back and change an answer? What happens if she skips a question? Her head was spinning. Gripping the mouse more tightly than necessary she moved the arrow to the box that ushered her to begin.

Grateful that the English test was first, she read the first question and checked the box. That was easy, she thought. Maybe I can do this. She moved on. In what seemed a very short time, she answered the last question.

The computer prompted her to move to the Math section by clicking another box. Suddenly tense, she stared at the screen. She glanced at the white scrap paper glaring at her from the table. It seemed to mock her. I can't do this, she thought panicky. I'm not good enough she berated herself. "Breathe, Mom," she could hear Mackenzie say. "Breathe."

Resolutely, she moved the cursor to begin. For just a breath, Melanie bowed her head in prayer. "God, I can't do this alone. I am so frightened. Give me strength. Reign in my fear." She clicked the mouse and opened her eyes. Her first problem was before her. To her surprise, she knew the answer. She moved forward and reached for the pencil and calculator. Adamantly she forged ahead. Some questions could only be answered by a best guess. No matter how many times or ways she did the problem none of her answers matched the ones given to choose from.

Near the end of the test she was faced with both geometry and algebra problems. She fought the desire to scream "this isn't happening" and run as far away from the computer as she could run. Tears welled in her eyes.

"You okay, honey?" asked the administrator of the test. "You can take a break and get a drink or something if you like. Remember you aren't timed and you can come back when you are ready."

"I'm just having problems with some of the math questions. If I stop now and leave, I might talk myself into not coming back."

"Don't do that. Take a breath and just do the best you can. It will be fine. These are placement tests. That's all. You can't fail them. It's just to see where you are."

"Thank you," Melanie said weakly. "I'll just stay and finish." Breathing deeply Melanie looked back at the screen. She was forced to choose a best guess answer again, since she had no idea how to even begin working out the problem.

She finally reached the last problem and clicked on "finish." The computer asked her if she was sure she didn't want to go back and redo any problems. "Great," she thought. "Already the computer knows how bad I did. It wants me to go back and redo the problems." She again clicked on finish and rose from her seat. Exhausted and feeling like she had done a day's work of hard labor, Melanie walked out of the testing center.

Shelley greeted her with a smile. "How'd you do?"

"Awful. I know I did just awful!" she replied, swallowing hard to push down the lump forming in her throat as tears welled in her eyes once more.

"Now calm down. I doubt you did awful at all. We'll go visit Mackenzie and see if she can slip out of the office to walk down to the Registration office with us and see how you really did."

Mackenzie, Melanie's third born, Shelley and Melanie walked down the hall. Mackenzie's medium length, soft brown, wavy hair bounced as she walked. She was average size with a friendly face, pleasant and always neatly dressed. Melanie was grateful that she and Mackenzie seemed to have a special friendship that went beyond the mother-daughter relationship. Panic suddenly again gripped Melanie and she could barely put one foot in front of the other. "I failed. I just know I failed."

"Mom, breathe! You couldn't have failed. How many times do I have to tell you that?"

"Easy for you to say. You didn't have to take any placement tests!"

Mackenzie and Shelley laughed. "Mom, you're impossible. I'll be so glad when we get you registered!"

Mackenzie knocked on Mr. Whitmyer's door. "Come on in," came a pleasant reply.

"Hi, Mackenzie. What are you doing here? asked the fair skinned, red headed man behind the desk."

"This is my mom and her friend, Shelley. Mom just took the placement tests and we want to see how she did and then register her for classes."

"Okay, not a problem," he said typing on the keyboard. "Your full name?"

"Melanie Hope Carson."

"Oh, yes, here you are. Well, it seems you did very well on the English placement test. You will go right into a credit English."

"Really, no kidding?" asked Melanie clearly astonished.

"No kidding. You did better than most of the kids right out of high school. Your test score would almost put you past English 101."

"Wow!" said Shelley and Mackenzie in unison.

Melanie laughed. "I doubt it'll be that good on the Math side.

"Well, you are right about that, I'm afraid. But how long has it been since you were in a Math class?"

"Thirty plus years. I didn't have any Algebra in high school, so doing some of those problems was out of the question. I didn't have a clue how to even write the problem."

"I think you should being in 031 Math. That will give you the ground work for the Math classes to come. What will your major be?"

"Education."

"Then I would certainly recommend 031 since the curriculum for Education requires three separate Math's. But realize that 031 is not the lowest remedial class you can have and many of our students that come in, start in classes lower than this. So again, you did very well considering your lack of experience."

Melanie beamed, but felt tears well in her eyes again. "All I can do is cry," she said. "This is stupid!" Everyone laughed.

"Let's get you registered."

Mr. Whitmeyer smiled and handed Melanie the pink sheet from the bottom of the three layers. "You are done; ready for classes in the Fall."

Melanie looked at list of classes. She would be taking Math 031, United States History, Wellness For Life, Psychology 101 and FSC (Freshman Seminar Course), all required classes. Nearly overwhelmed, she whispered, "Thank you, Mr. Whitmeyer. I am so grateful for your help."

In the hall, Mackenzie hugged her mom. "You did good, Mom. You did good!"

"Well, I've gotten started. That's really all I've done." She replied.

"But it is a good start," chimed in Shelley. "Mackenzie's right. You did good! I knew you could. I'm proud of you."

"Me, too," said Mackenzie. "But I have to get back to work! See you both later."

"I am so excited, but I'm still scared" said Melanie climbing into bed that night.

"You'll do fine," said Lee. "You're smart and beautiful and I love you! You will do just fine!"

Chapter 2

It seemed fitting that Melanie would take a Wellness class at the same time she was experiencing health issues of her own. It began years ago when she learned she was born with a condition known as a sequestration lung. While lung surgery took care of the problem overall, there were residual effects felt for years. She was looking forward to the hiking trip up Harney Peak with Lee but apprehensive since other instances had proved problematic regarding altitude and climbing.

Melanie was just finishing filling the backpack with grapes, nuts, water and candy bars as Lee walked into the kitchen. "You ready?" he asked.

"Almost. I have to get my ski poles from the closet and then I will be!"

"Are you really going to use those?"

"Yeah!"

"Most people just use a walking stick."

"Well, these are my walking stick. We've been on hikes and have seen people use these before. I picked these up for next to nothing at the thrift shop in town. I aim to give them a try. They might look funny but they will be lighter and I can stick them into the ground if I want since there's a point on the end."

"Whatever! I'm ready. We need to get started if we're going to do this today."

Parking the car in the already filled parking lot at the trailhead at Sylvan Lake in Custer State Park, they walked to the path bearing the entrance to the hike. The cloudless sky, brilliant sunshine and early fall temperatures of 60 degrees with warm breeze swirling through the trees was inviting knowing the energy that would be required on the walk upward.

Melanie paused as she stopped to read the sign before continuing. Harney Peak, it read, highest point East of the Rockies. Starting elevation 6,250 feet, climbing to 7,242 feet in three miles. Round trip: about six miles. "You okay doing this?" Lee asked noting the concern on Melanie's face.

Melanie noted how much this mountain looked like those in Appalachia, although this place was covered with Ponderosa Pine rather than the ash, oak or giant poplar. Yet this is the highest summit, east of the Rocky Mountains. Traveling eastward, you would have to go several thousand miles away to stand on higher ground in the French Pyrenees in southwest Europe between Spain and France.

"I've got to try," she said advancing forward while noting the domes and needles in various sizes that seemed to rise through the mist from the waters of Sylvan Lake.

"Just let me know if I need to stop or slow down."

"Okay," she said resolutely.

The path, well worn by other hikers was easily negotiable from the outset. The incline was slow but steady. Mountain bluebirds, nuthatches, and Western tanagers chatted to each other, flitting from one branch to another while mountain goat trails could be seen branching off in various directions in great labyrinth style from the main hiking path.

The air thinning by 6,400 feet, caused Melanie's ears to pop and put pressure against her temples. She could also feel the added effort it took to breathe with each step she took. About a mile into the climb, the terrain began changing. The smooth path turned into rocks which got larger and demanded to be climbed on instead of stepped over. The edge of the trail had areas that allowed breathtaking views of a mile or more which then turned into walls of stone and trees. The path inclined followed by a descent before inclining again. Deer could be spotted through the thicket while always being on guard for snakes that might be near the walkway.

The gentle breeze, although refreshing, seemed more crisp and cool the higher they climbed. Melanie stopped to pull the sweater she had worn more closely around her despite the mid morning hour and the physical energy required for the hike. Lee's effort left him warm causing him to remove the long sleeve shirt he was wearing. Melanie breathed deeply of the ponderosa pine and cedar that towered above her and drank in the richness of the spruce, fir and green ash trees that were interspersed within, while marveling at the sprinkling of reds and gold from the maple trees. "This is God's country," she thought. "He must have loved this place very much to have made it so beautiful. How blessed I am to be here."

Nearing the top of the mountain, Melanie found herself struggling more to keep up. Her lungs were burning and breathing labored. Her legs felt like they were filled with concrete. Lee stopped again, and waited. "You okay?"

"I will be," she said stopping for a moment, marveling at the scene before her. The needle formations poking 100 feet or more in the air were captivating. The mica sparkling and gigantic pink and tan granite formations, along with crystal feldspar looked like diamonds reflecting in the sun. Finally when breathing returned to normal and the burning subsided, she said, "The top isn't too much further, right?"

"Right."

The pair negotiated the zigzagging, hair pinned turns as they continued their march through the woods of pine needles, dirt paths and stone. But Melanie paled when she saw the two hundred steps cut in stone that she would need to climb to reach the summit hut.

Lee reached for her hand, pulling her to aid in their progression up. Melanie held on tight to the steel gate at the summit, once they arrived. Before her stood the old fire lookout tower no longer in use that looked like a castle structure. Her knees nearly buckled beneath her as she tried to catch her breath. Collapsing to the ground, she sat for nearly five minutes waiting for her heart to stop racing, her lungs to stop burning and the ability to breathe normal.

Finally Melanie drank in what her journey and the ridge of delicately balanced granite offered. She was held breathless by the endless panorama of trees and mountains for as far as the eye could see. In ideal conditions devoted hikers willing to trek up this beautiful mountain could see Wyoming due west, Nebraska southward, Montana in the northwest and eastward stretches and stretches of South Dakotan green rolling hills intermingled with spires and great granite walls of boulders.

When Melanie felt she could stand again, she said, "Let's go out on the rocks and eat lunch."

"Are you sure you're ready?"

"Yup!" she answered emphatically as she took the forward role. Strolling until she was satisfied with the spot, she sat down and opened the bagged lunch that had been carried in Lee's backpack. The cool breeze lifted Melanie's soft, brown hair. Chipmunks scooted all around the picnickers scavenging for bread crumbs or other morsels. Melanie's gaze followed the horizon miles beyond their location.

On this day, the bare, granite summit allowed for breathtaking views. The sun was high in the clear, blue sky. Grays and dark shades of green from the Ponderosa Pine outlined the mountainous terrain aptly describing the Black Hills. The Hills named by the Native American Indians years before were sacred to the Lakota. Most traders before the gold rush avoided the area in respect of the Indians. Two hawks flew overhead, swooping down after small prey. Melanie felt chills run down her spine. Peace filled her being as she drank in the beauty and identified with the sacredness the Indians felt. It was here she belonged. There was a oneness with this place she had never experienced before. She relished the moment.

"We'd better start back," Lee said much too soon.

"Already?"

"It's a hike and I don't want to be caught up here at dusk."

"Good point. I'm ready." Melanie attempted to stand and reached for her ski poles. Awkwardly she found herself back on the ground.

"Whoa! You okay?"

"I'm not sure. My legs are shaking something awful and they just gave out. What in the world?"

"Okay, take a breath and try again."

Gingerly Melanie raised herself up while leaning on the ski poles. "Lee, I'm frightened. Why did that happen?"

"I have no clue. But we will find out. For now let's just try to make our way down."

Each step seemed more challenging than the one before. Melanie could barely keep her balance. Her hip joints began throbbing as her legs continued to tremble while she fought to control her breathing. Relief flooded her as they reached the first rest area equipped with a bench.

"Are you ready?" Lee asked with gentle urgency. "We'll stop at the next resting place. We just really can't stop long. We were too long at the top to be able to do that."

"We can go again. I'll be fine." Dusk lurked as they finally reached the bottom. The seat of the car was like resting in bed. She sank comfortably within the firm cushion with welcome relief yet fear gripped her. What caused such an occurrence? There were so many questions.

Melanie leafed through the Wellness For Life book, pausing on the chapter dedicated to the body organs, while the class waited for Dr. Kline to finish talking with the professor who entered the classroom unannounced. The incident on Harney Peak weeks before still haunted her even though a trip to the doctor revealed little except hearing him say, "Melanie, accept the fact that you just can't do the same things other people do!"

Dr. Kline's class was one of her favorites. Dr. Kline, was a big man, rising at a height of six foot seven, with a clearly defined physique indicating his dedication to health and exercise, belying his sixty-five years. He had kind eyes and likewise a kind, gentle voice. His genuineness of caring for the past forty years at Cedar Ridge Community College, was well-known and seemed to seep through his pores endearing students to him. Students clamored for his classes causing his to be filled before any others. Waiting lists until the next semester weren't uncommon. Even with the softness that seemed to envelope him, students knew he brooked no disobedience and expected total class attendance and participation.

One such example of class participation included what Dr. Kline called "creative projects" which had just begun. Each student was required to share a presentation of himself that demonstrated who they were and what they were about. Married students with young families discussed their children, while sports stars demonstrated particular moves and gave information regarding their favorite pastime. Each presentation took fifteen minutes to one half hour to complete. Dr. Kline was exceedingly patient and indulgent for each student. His goal was that each student identified their passion for life since in his view "passions" are what drive the human being. Being able to identify it would garner added energy and enthusiasm enabling the student to have a better healthful lifestyle.

Melanie's spirits were buoyed the day of her presentation with the bright sunshine and Fall temperatures. She felt conspicuous carrying her bulky burden down the hallway to the classroom. Once she arrived and took her seat, she still had the problem of where to put the visuals for her presentation. Finally, giving up on trying to get them out of the way, she left them in the isle and decided students would just have to walk around.

"Okay, "My Little," said Dr. Kline, "your turn." Melanie, grinned. "My Little" was the "passion name" Dr. Kline had given her at the beginning of the semester. He had a habit of tagging students with his own pet names as they suited him. Gavin, who had him in another class and always wore a black cowboy hat and boots, as well as a black trench coat, was simply called "Tex." Lee, whom Dr. Kline had, had nearly thirty years before had dubbed him, "Sha Na Na" after the '50's rock group because Lee combed his hair and tended to dress even in the late 1970's with the '50's look.

Picking up the items needed for her presentation, she made her way to the front of the room. "I have two passions," she explained. "I enjoy one as much as the other and couldn't decide which to bring, so I brought both," she said pulling the quilt from the large bag. Ewws and ahhs, could be heard throughout the room. "This is what I do for down time. I find quilting very relaxing and when I quilt I really don't have to think," she quipped, slightly grinning. "This is just fun.

"My other passion is what I believe God wants me to do. This does require thinking and quiet time and I absolutely love it! I freelance write. I've been writing off and on for the last twenty years and I've been moderately successful. Nothing grand, but fairly consistent. My strength seems to be in Christian material, devotionals and such, although I have written for Ranger Rick, Cobblestone and other secular magazines."

"Wow!" came a comment from the back of the room as she displayed some of the magazines which had published her material.

"Read us something of yours from one of the magazines," said Dr. Kline.

"Are you serious? Wouldn't that be illegal considering its Christian material?"

"Don't worry about that. Just read one," he insisted.

"Okay," she said shakily, completely surprised by his request.

"That is very good," remarked Dr. Kline when she finished. "Maybe you should write something about my cussing!"

"Maybe I just will!" Melanie said unable to stifle a giggle.

18

"I think you should!" he said.

Melanie felt warm as she folded her quilt and put her other materials back into their respective bags, while listening to the additional comments in the room. Slightly embarrassed, yet pleased she retreated to her seat.

"Okay, class," said Dr. Kline. "That will do us for today. Remember to keep reading your text. There is a test in two weeks. We will be finished presentations by then and we will go over the material, but there is no reason to get behind."

Even with the amount of tests Melanie had taken, they still unnerved her. She recalled the first one she'd taken in Dr. Kline's class. She was so nervous she could barely think. It was given on Thursday and knew it wouldn't be until Tuesday getting the results if he was finished grading. She found sleeping difficult and fretted about it all weekend. Mackenzie had just laughed at her and told her to calm down, it would be fine. "Breathe!" she said more than once.

On the following Monday Mackenzie happened to see Dr. Kline near her office. "Mom is so nervous about your test, she can barely stand it," she told him.

"You're kidding! She really questions how she did?"

"Mom stresses about all the tests she takes," she answered laughing.

"Well, she needn't stress. She's a good student and I'm sure she did fine. Humph," he said as in afterthought, "I should give her an A just because she worries. Most students don't."

"Mom really wants the "A" and that's in all her classes," Mackenzie added.

"That doesn't surprise me," he said. "It's nice to have students who give a care about grades and learning in general," he said. "Many of my younger students are there just because they must be. Parents tell them, go to college or get a job!"

"You sound just like dad!"

"Well, he's been around a while, just like me!" he said, with a crooked grin. "Tell your folks I said hello and tell your mom to stop worrying!"

Melanie took her seat and looked over the material in the book she would be tested on in the upcoming weeks. Some of it interested her and other material repulsed her. She hated reading about the different kinds of sexually transmitted diseases like Chlamydia, gonorrhea, syphilis, herpes and others. She had even raised her hand and asked during class one morning why they had to learn this stuff!

Patiently he explained, "My Little, your children are grown and I know have no such problems, but you will have grandchildren. And there are plenty of others in here who may have to deal with this type of situation so it's good for all of us to be informed."

"Well, Okay," she said, resigned. "I'll learn it!" Dr. Kline laughed, as did several other students.

This morning Dr. Kline arrived in the room, took roll and began addressing the class. He noticed what looked like a large oversized shoe box on his desk. He asked the owner to identify himself, which the young man did without hesitation. "That's for my presentation," he said.

"Very well, Jay" said Dr. Kline. "Are you ready to begin?"

"Sure," said the tall, fair haired, young man wearing a basketball tee shirt, walking toward the front of the room.

Dr. Kline retreated to one of the student seats toward the back of the room while Jay gently picked up the box. He took a deep breath and set the box back on the desk to take the cover off. Laying the cover beside the box he reached in and retrieved his treasure: a six foot python! Desk chairs screeched noisily across the room while gasps of fear could be also heard throughout.

"Jay! You left that thing on my desk and never told me?"

"Didn't see the need. You said we could do our presentations on anything we wanted. I like snakes. This is my favorite. I call him Slinky. He's harmless, really. I feed him and take care of him."

Melanie, whose desk was only four feet from Dr. Kline's was trembling. She had an unnatural fear of snakes. Even pictures of snakes repulsed her. Being small, she curled her feet under her with her chair pushed back as far as room allowed.   Fascination finally took over, as Jay moved the snake around without letting it out of his grasp. While she still had a fair amount of fear causing her nerves to tremble, she found the presentation interesting but relieved when Jay finally finished and put the creature securely back in the box.

"Jay, your presentation was interesting, but for any of the rest of you, if you feel the need to bring a creature of any kind in, I need to know about it first. There are restrictions about those kinds of things in a school building," he added lightly.

"I'll take him to my car now, if that's okay," said Jay.

"Thank you, I think that's a real good idea."

"Stacy, you are next on the list for presentation. Tell me you don't have any big surprises for me."

"No, I don't," she assured him.

"Good, in that case, whenever you're ready."

Stacy, a thin, dark haired girl with soft eyes, walked to the front of the room and drew a deep breath. "My creative project began about five years ago," she began while passing out a poem simply entitled *The Day I Lost You*. "We lived in Chicago then, downtown. Dad wasn't there anymore and Mom worked a lot trying to make ends meet. I was in charge of my brother, Burke who was eleven at the time, and Royce who was nine. This particular day, Royce was giving me grief. He wanted to go over to a friend's house for the afternoon, but I wouldn't let him because Mom had said she didn't want him playing with Travis, who also lived there. Mostly, Mom had issues with his mom and just didn't want Royce to go over.

"Burke went upstairs when the shouting match between Royce and I began. I told him he couldn't go and he wanted to know why. I told him I was in charge and Mom had said no, but he wasn't buying it and got angry. I told him he had to wait until Mom got home and take it up with her and until then to go upstairs and do something in his room.

"Instead of going to his room, he ran outside." Stacey fought for control. Her eyes filled with tears as she caught her breath and swallowed hard, unable to speak. "When he ran outside, he just ran and paid no mind to traffic. I heard tires squeal and I also ran outside. Royce had been struck by a car and it was all my fault. I ran out and when I got there I just cradled him in my arms. There was nothing anyone could do. He died in my arms. I've never forgiven myself for that," she said, tears streaming down her face now. "The only good that came out of it was I started writing. Since then I've written whenever I have the need to express myself. I don't know if I will ever get anything published and honestly I haven't tried. But I know it's the one way I can relieve stress, so the poem I handed out, I wrote for Royce."

The Day I Lost You

My heart's so heavy, it's on the ground,
Knowing you will never again be around.
I face each day feeling alone,
Tackling the world all on my own.
It's my fault you ran away that day
When really all you should have done is go out play.
So now I'm here, without you, sweet, little brother
Knowing they'll never again be another.

Your sister, here, has a broken heart,
I'm still crying and forever scarred.
You've got to know, sweet brother, mine,
How in my heart you are all the time.
How I regret the day we fought.

Now it all seems for naught.
I still feel your tiny hands holding mine,
When you were little and all was fine.
I look at your picture and cry myself to sleep,
My heart so heavy and pain so deep.
When I listen close to my heart and hear your voice,
I'm reminded of the times we spent together, Royce.
My heart will always long for you,
As I loathe the day that I lost you.

Silence engulfed the room. Reaching for a tissue to wipe the tears from her face, Melanie found herself empathizing with the young women who just poured her soul out to the class even though she had never been through such an ordeal. Dr. Kline stood and walked up to Stacey. He gently wrapped his arms around her and held her while she cried.

"That was incredible, my dear," he said. "If you need to leave now, you may be excused. You couldn't have changed what happened. You did not cause your brother's death. You are a wonderful girl and have suffered enough."

"Didn't you hear what I just said? He was angry with me. I'm the reason he ran out."

"Stacey, listen to me. It was not your fault."

"Whatever," she said exiting the room, still crying.

"Well," said Dr. Kline. "Remember class, what you hear in this classroom stays in this classroom. You are not at liberty to share information that may be hurtful with anyone. That is not the purpose of this activity. That being said, should someone share something that is beautiful, I wouldn't forbid such sharing. But be forewarned, I will reprimand anyone who chooses to hurt someone else who has heard something in this class.

"Okay, who is next? Blake? You are up."

"Dr. Kline, I'm not sure I can follow Stacey. That was incredible. My presentation won't hold a candle to hers."

"Do not compare your presentation to Stacey's. They are completely unrelated. I do not compare presentations. Each is graded on their own merit. I'm sure you will do fine."

Blake, a mild mannered, quiet student, walked to the front of the room. Melanie sat in a daze, still reliving Stacey's compelling story. "My presentation is on computers," Melanie heard trying hard to focus. "I want to be the head guru in catching hackers."

Melanie listened to the rest of Blake's presentation with all the effort she had. She was grateful when the class ended. As quickly as possible she exited the room, still clearly agitated, unable to shake the emotions from Stacey's presentation. She knew she couldn't share the story yet needed to find a way to express the grief she felt for Stacey.

"What is your problem tonight?" asked Lee. "You are completely distracted."

"I know and I'm sorry. I just heard this story in class today and it rattled my cage. I'm not quite sure what to do about it."

"You want to talk about it?"

"No, well yes, but I can't."

"What do you mean you can't?"

"Well, Dr. Kline told us not to share what we heard in class from someone's presentation. I don't know if that would include telling you. It's not like you're at the college or you even know the students."

"If it would make you feel better, then tell me. Otherwise I think you should shake it off and forget it. It doesn't have anything to do with you, does it?"

"No, of course not. It was just sad. Never mind. I'll be fine."

Moments later they heard a knock on the door. In the next instant, Flo let herself in. With their house just in front of Lee's parents, it wasn't unusual for Flo to visit randomly and even more so now that Ike had passed away. What became more of a problem, however, were the signs of Alzheimer's, in the once vibrant woman.

"Hey, Mom! How are you?" Melanie asked more cheerfully than she felt. "I'm just cleaning up dinner dishes. Come on in and have a seat."

"I don't want to sit down," she said, agitated. "I want to know how Luke is."

"Luke is fine," said Melanie. "He's over in Guam at the moment. We hear from him nearly every week."

"He's not in Guam," she said more irritated now. "He's in," she paused trying to compose her thoughts. "Well I don't know where he is now but I know he's been in France and Korea."

"No, Mom. Luke is in Guam. He's not been to France or Korea.

"Tell me what you've been doing today," Melanie said trying to change the subject.

"Watched my shows. I got a letter from Luke," she said, revisiting her original thought line. "He told me he's in France and he's going to China next."

"Mom," said Melanie. "Never mind Luke. Have you chatted with Kaitlyn in the last few days? Kara is growing so fast."

"No, but I have heard from Luke. He's going to France," she said. "The letter said so."

"Lee! Your mother's here. Come on out and visit. She's certain Luke has been to France and Korea and even China."

"Well," said Lee, talking to Melanie like Flo wasn't in the room, "She's probably remembering when Frank was in World War II. That would make sense given the places she's talking about."

"Mom," he said addressing his mother now, "how about walking out with me to the garden? Let's see if we can find you some turnips to take home and eat."

"I don't want turnips," she snapped. "Who's Frank? I'm talking about Luke!"

"C'mon, Mom," he said, putting his arm around her shoulders. "Let's walk outside."

Grumbling unintelligibly she consented to the redirection of her body and thoughts allowing herself to be led outside. "I'll walk her home," Lee called back over his shoulder to Melanie, "after we finish in the garden."

Lee returned about twenty minutes later completely exasperated. "I hate seeing her like that," he said. "She's lucid one minute and confused the next."

"She okay?"

"Well, she's okay for the moment."

"The other day when I was over there, I felt so bad for her. We were in the kitchen and she was chatting away and then she forgot what she was saying. She reached up with both hands on either side of her head and grabbing her hair and holding it tightly with eyes squinted shut, she said, 'sometimes I feel like I am losing my mind.'

"The truth is, she's right and might not even know it. It must be real frustrating to notice you have issues, not really know what it is and not be able to do anything about it. And the horrible thing is it's going to get worse."

Chapter 3

Melanie looked at the two large paper bags containing the grapes Lee picked from the vines! "When in the world am I going to get to those?" she said aloud although there was no one to hear her. Today would be another long day.

After her 10:15 Freshman Seminar Class, Melanie was beginning work in the financial aid office to help pay for the expenses of her new found status as "student." She was both excited and nervous which seemed to be the only way she felt these days, at least when she wasn't terrified at all the new math strategies she was learning.

"I guess they'll be there when I get back," she again verbalized.

"Who are you talking to?" asked Gavin opening the refrigerator with his over sized hands.

"Oh, no one. Me I guess. I'm just looking at all these grapes I need to put up."

"Yeah," Gavin said, smiling slightly. "You have fun with that!"

"Thanks! Now get out of here," she said grinning, belying the scolding she was trying to give.

Giving one last look at the kitchen she had just tidied and frowning at the work that awaited her return, Melanie walked out of the house.

Walking into the classroom forty-five minutes later, Melanie noted that every seat was filled with seventeen to twenty year-olds. Student Orientation, as the class was called most often by the students, was a required course and it was clear to see the students already in the classroom weren't excited to be there.

"This is a stupid class," one offered to his friend. "What a waste. I already know how to use a computer and I sure don't want to know any study skills!"

"I know but, hey, we can sleep through it."

"I have to come in for this stupid class in the middle of the day," said another. "I could be working. I don't know why it's required."

"Middle of the day?" Melanie wondered. "Middle of the morning, maybe."

Melanie took her seat near the front of the room as she waited for the professor to make her appearance. A small, heavy set woman entered the room, encumbered with an overflowing tote bag and additional folders and stapled papers. Her light brown hair was pulled back in a neat bun wrapped in a trendy scrunchie which matched the green top she wore with her tan Capri's. She dropped the folders and papers on the desk and let the tote bag rest on the floor against the desk and faced the class.

"Good morning, class. I am Ms. Hastings and I will be teaching this class," she began. Melanie was instantly fascinated with the agility and apparent nervous energy displayed despite her heavy stature. While being stern and straight faced she seemed to flit with little fast steps from one side of the room to the other while continuing. "I will not tolerate tardiness to this class. Attendance is mandatory. Realize this class is required for graduation. Not only is it required, a passing grade is required," she added, almost breathless, as she spoke quickly with only a hint of pause from one sentence to the next. "I will expect you to attend, be an active participant, and do all the required assignments," she said emphatically, demonstrating her control in the classroom.

Rumblings of discontent came from the back of the room. "Further I will not tolerate disrespect in my classroom. You in the back of the room, consider this your fair warning. I repeat, you must have a passing grade to graduate this class." The room fell silent.

"You will be given computer instruction that goes beyond email. You will learn the proper way to give a power point presentation with a partner. You will also learn how to refine your research skills by using the internet proficiently to do your research along with other important tools that will enhance your college experience. To that end, this class will meet in the media center in room 111 in the computer lab on Thursday."

Relief flooded Melanie when the class finally ended. She could email and could compose in Word processing, but after that she felt lost. She had never had reason to give a power point or do research on the computer and she was terrified. Her nerves were taunt and her head was aching. "It must be nice to be young and confident on the computer," she thought. "How am I ever going to pass this class? Partnering should make it easier, but then she'd have to admit to her younger counterpart that she is illiterate on the computer. How will that look?"

Picking up her books, she headed for the financial aid office. Melanie's pace quickened even as her heart picked up speed upon climbing the steps to the large Administrative building. This is where she will spend her time between classes. She was grateful she even got the job. Mostly, she was surprised. Lee wasn't happy about her working. Somehow he felt it demeaning that his wife would have to find work so she could do what she wanted. He should have been able to provide for her. The tension was palpable whenever the subject came up between them.

Still, Melanie liked the idea of working. She had never before held a "real" job; never had reason to. They had always gotten by; sometimes it felt paycheck to paycheck, but mostly all their needs were met. It was the "wants" in life they sometimes had to do without.

Confident on one hand about working, yet mortified she would mess things up, Melanie walked into the office. "Hi," she said shyly to the dark haired woman behind the desk who would be her immediate superior.

"Hi," said Mrs. Elliott, with recognition. "I remember you from last week. You're our new work study!"

"Yes, Ma'am."

"First rule of the house! I am not "Ma'am. Just call me Debbie."

"Yes, Ma'am." They both laughed, putting Melanie's tensions at ease.

"Your desk will be over there," she said pointing. "There's plenty of room in the work room for your books and a place to hang your coat when the time comes. Mrs. Weston is definitely the boss, but it will be me who probably will give you most of your duties. Feel free to ask questions."

Vicki Weston, her boss walked from her office just moments later. This was the same person whom she'd sat with weeks before in order to obtain scholarship money to help defray the cost of her education. This job was part of the deal.

Mrs. Weston was a small lady, though larger than herself, with a warm smile and perfect manicure. She was beautifully dressed in a lavender tailored business suit and small matching heels. "Hi, Ms. Carson. I'm glad you've come to join our team. Your jobs will be varied until you learn the ropes. Mostly from the beginning, you will be answering the phone and doing filing. Count on Debbie to help you learn what you need to know and always know that I'm here to help you, as well, so please ask questions. The sooner and better you learn the ropes, the better aid you will be to us in the office."

"Yes, Ma'am," said Melanie, completely frightened, since working in any form almost seemed like a foreign idea in itself. "I'll do my best and try not to get in the way."

"You'll do fine. Relax. We're not ogres in here. Here we just want to work as a team to accomplish what has to be done."

Melanie put her books down on her desk and turned to Debbie for instruction. "This is where the student files are, as well as, their taxes, worksheets, and personal information, known as verification documentation, which need to be filed. Confidentially is a must," she said emphatically. "What is said and seen in the Financial Aid Office must stay in the Financial Aid Office. Since it is imperative to have the student files complete in order to award them, this is where you will start."

Melanie started filing. After of couple of minutes she started to relax and found working in the office wasn't going to be as bad as she originally feared.

Thursday morning Melanie walked into the media center. Overwhelmed, she looked around frantically, trying to find room 111. Many students milled around the large room filled with rows of computers. Some were working while others were chatting with friends. The oversized windows that stretched the length of two floors on three sides of the building made the area loom even greater than it was. The open staircase added to the substantial dimensions of the already great space. Melanie weaved her way through the rows of bookcases toward the back of the room where generous classrooms were separated by more large, glass windows.

Spotting room 111 she hurried toward it, then paused. Through the glass she saw her classmates already engaged on the computers. Panicky, she checked her watch. She wasn't late, so what are they doing? Quietly, she entered the room and double checked her watch against the clock on the wall. It confirmed her first assessment: she wasn't late. Warily, she sat at an unattended computer and eyed the computer next to hers. The long, blond haired, eighteen year-old beauty next to her was actively maneuvering her way through the internet, her fingers flying furiously, while she quietly giggled.

In an effort to not appear nosy, Melanie looked away and then stared at the blank computer monitor before her. "How do you turn it on?" she asked to no one in particular, but loudly enough to be heard.

"What?"

"How do you turn it on?" She asked more timidly this time while shrugging her shoulders forward displaying a child like look she instantly hated.

"Oh, you push the button on the computer at the bottom. You've never used a computer before?" The girl beside her asked incredulously.

"Well, sure, but not set up like this. I have no clue, and feel like such an idiot."

"Oh, don't. It'll be fine. I'm pretty decent on the computer and this class is such a waste, but I'll help ya out if I can."

"Honest? And you won't think me a complete lunatic?"

"Sure. No problem."

"Thanks. I'd be really grateful!"

"Jenny! Did you see Mitch in the hall? He is so hot!"

"Oh, sorry," the girl said noticing Melanie's discomfort. "I didn't know you were talking,"

"It's okay," said Melanie. "She was just helping me."

"Cool!" said the newcomer as she took the seat on the other side of Jenny so they could continue their conversation.

As the girls continued chatting and giggling, Melanie felt her temperature rise. She couldn't decide if she was embarrassed because of the conversation or her age compared to her counterparts.

Ms. Hastings entered the room much like she had every other class, heavy laden with graded papers and hand outs emerging from her bulging tote bag. "Each student by the time we are finished will be completely fluent on the computer," she said. "You will, however, have to work with not only a partner, but you will be a team of four for your presentation. In this way you can pool not only your resources on your topic, but also your skills. Be aware that all members of the team will receive the same grade regardless of how the work is divided. That being said, each person will get two grades for the project. If there is blatant disregard for the other members of your team; that will be considered and will alter the second personal grade you are given. The teams will be counted off so you may not be able to work with the buddy you sit next to."

Melanie soon discovered she hated working with partners. She recalled the speech that came with the team work assignment. "It teaches you what it feels like to work with others in the outside world," Ms. Hastings had said. "Personalities clash and each person has their own agenda."

"I've never worked in the outside world," Melanie thought, "but it can't be as bad as this!" She enjoyed research, but didn't like feeling abandoned to all of it. She would have liked to have worked with Jenny but that didn't happen due to the count. Instead, Melanie found herself paired with students she didn't know including Rhonda.

Rhonda was pleasant enough, but clearly not organized, with homework arriving at the end of class rather than at the beginning more often than not because she placed the material loosely in her book bag and could not retrieve it until after class. Additionally, there was Thomas who really wasn't interested in doing the project at all; and Rita who was the "drama queen" of the class and while she seemed quite intelligent, preferred the "ditzy approach" when the male species were paying attention.

Reading Skills seemed like a relatively easy topic and interesting by Melanie's definition and had looked forward to the project. She found information through a variety of sources including three keys to studying, the SQ3R reading method, ways to improve memory and increasing reading ability. Still she was frustrated that the rest of the team had so little to do with the research.

"You do the research and I'll do the power point," Melanie mimicked in her anger, while her fingers typed the information she'd gleaned. "I know how to do all the fun things with it. It'll be really good," Rhonda had assured her. "I've done lots of presentations with power point and I know all the cute little bells and whistles."

True to her word, Rhonda didn't disappoint with the animated style of the presentation. There was a bell ringing, something exploding, parts dropping in or other clanging with every frame. Melanie wondered if it wasn't too much. Rita and

Thomas were present on the day of the presentation and stood behind the desk, but offered little input on the entire process. Rita had handed the forms out before the presentation that were required so that each student could critique the work of the team. It had been Thomas' sole responsibility to create the forms, hence his contribution to the presentation. It annoyed Melanie that they would receive the same grade as she, but consoled herself in the knowledge that each student would receive two grades for the same project; first as a team and the separate as Ms. Hastings had explained.

Rhonda had not only animated the power point but also moved the frames as Melanie spoke on each one. She was surprised how at ease she felt once she began. Nerves had nearly been her undoing before she started. She found her hands cold and sweaty; a strange combination, she thought. Her heart raced as she uttered her first words, but found herself in "chatting mode" since she knew the material and found it an easy presentation to deliver.

As the three students behind the desk collected their papers and removed the disk from the computer, Melanie began walking around the room collecting the critique sheets to also be handed in to their professor, waiting patiently for some to finish. Suddenly she whirled around as she heard a whistle and said. "I beg your pardon!"

"Here this is for you," a male student replied handing her a critique sheet as if she could reach it across the room.

"Excuse me," she said her eyebrows furrowed. "I am not a dog. I will not be addressed that way."

"Her name is Melanie," Rhonda piped in. "Where in the world are your manners?"

"Hey, I just wanted to get your attention."

"I can't help that. You have a voice and like I said, I am not a dog."

"Well, excuse me, Miss Melanie! If you want this sheet, come get it," he said dropping it on the table."

"I will be there directly," Melanie quipped, as she turned away, picking up others who were finished. As she continued her circle in the room, she finally arrived at the young man's desk. "I'll take that now," she said. Purposefully, Melanie walked away from the desk and handed the stack to her professor.

"Well done," Ms. Hastings said, trying to hide a smile.

Blushing, Melanie picked up her books as she exited the room. She reached in her purse and retrieved her cell phone. Hitting speed dial she waited for the voice of her best friend on the other end. "Hey, Melanie," came the familiar sound. "What's up?"

"You are not going to believe what I just did," she said giggling. "I put a young smart aleck in his place. He was rude, disrespectful and had absolutely no manners and no woman should be treated like a dog."

"Would you slow down and tell me what happened!"

"Well, it was just the weirdest thing," she began ignoring the admonition to slow down. "You know I'm not witty, but this one guy in class just irked me so bad and I let him know it! He wanted me to come to him by whistling just like you'd call a dog! And what's really neat is the professor actually told me "Well done!" How cool is that?"

"Pretty neat. Good for you!" said Shelley laughing. "Where are you headed now?"

"Work. It's my day to work in the Financial Aid Office. That's turned out a lot better than I expected. It's only been a few weeks, but I actually like working there. Course, Lee still doesn't like the idea. It is what it is!

"Hey, I gotta go. I'm at the Admin Building. I'll talk to you later!"

Lee walked into the kitchen just as Melanie was finishing preparing dinner. "Hey!" she said, greeting him cheerily. "Did you have a good day today?"

"Yup! And I need to get done eating cause I'm going away tonight."

"Where?" she asked warily.

"Over in Elk Creek. I'm starting guitar lessons."

"Who's teaching you?"

"Paige" Melanie winced. Lee had spoken of her often. He loved working at the salvage yard even before he became an Automotive Tech. Taking parts off wrecked vehicles seemed to him a fun thing to do. He had worked at Sullivan's Salvage off and on for years, even more so now that he was retired. Mostly he worked for the pure enjoyment and the friendships he'd made with the other employees there, most of which were men.

But there came a time when Paige entered the picture. She worked in the office and caught Lee's attention. More than once Paige was the center of conversation in their home. He spoke highly of the woman and indicated that there were times she just needed him for someone to talk too. Melanie just wasn't sure how to respond when the conversation went that direction.

"Well," she said slowly. "What time will you be home?

"I don't know for sure. But I'm supposed to be there by 7:00 and I don't know how long we'll work. Besides you'll be all night doing homework anyway. It won't matter that I'm not here.

"This will be good for me. I've wanted to learn for a long time. I even have the guitar sitting in the closet in the living room that I've had for I don't know how many years. I've just never been able to find anyone willing to teach me. Paige can. She says she's been playing a long time. It'll be good."

Dinner was eaten in near silence. As soon as Lee had finished, he changed his clothes and said goodbye, leaving Melanie unsure of what she felt. Was it fear? If so, fear of what? Jealousy? That'd be a new one. Who was this Paige anyway? Did she have a thing for Lee? Was she right in questioning what Lee was doing? It was something different. She was doing something different. Why shouldn't he? He has a right to enjoy himself. Right?

Questions and conflicting thoughts continued to rumble through her mind. Finally, after cleaning the kitchen, Melanie retrieved her books to begin on homework. Later she woke as she heard the door open after having fallen asleep on the sofa waiting for Lee to return. 11:00 p.m. She frowned.

Lee was in a wonderful mood and quickly explained when she walked into the kitchen, "Sorry I'm so late. We were just chatting once we finished the guitar lessons."

This was the beginning of many nights Lee would either go for lessons or would practice the instrument. Truth was, Melanie like the sound of the strumming and honestly encouraged him to continue. Yet when the call came one evening to Lee that Paige felt she was being followed and Lee went to her rescue she wondered of the wisdom of that attitude!

One such night he returned clearly unhappy. "Well, I guess my guitar lessons are done," he said without preamble.

"Why," Melanie asked, perplexed.

"Paige has decided to move back to Kentucky to be near her family."

"Really? That doesn't mean you have to stop practicing. Haven't you learned enough that you could go on without her? You could buy videos or something to keep going. I like it when you play."

"I don't know. My arm has been hurting me anyway. And be honest. You didn't really like me going over there anyway."

"Your arm?" she said ignoring the rest of his comment.

"Yeah, I guess it's the way I hold the guitar. To hold it right, hurts."

"I'm sorry. But don't quit. We both know how much you enjoy it and I think it's a good thing."

"It's not a good thing if it hurts to play," he snapped.

"I just hate to see you quit," she offered.

"We'll see," he said.

"As for you going over to spend time with Paige," Melanie began, trying to console him. "I guess I really didn't like that part. But I really do like hearing you play the guitar."

"You have to know nothing ever happened between Paige and me," he said walking over and giving her a welcome hug. "It was strictly business. I'll admit we talked a lot too. She and her boyfriend were having issues."

"I guess my head knew that, my heart wasn't so sure!" she said looking up at him.

"I love you," he said. "Don't ever doubt that."

Chapter 4

Melanie took her place at the front of the room, as she had in all her other classes. Mr. Hart, the United States History professor, a tall, well groomed man in his mid thirties sat at his desk perusing the attendance sheet, looking up occasionally as students continued to amble into the classroom.   As the students continued taking their seats, Mr. Hart rose from his chair and began writing on the blackboard. He ushered in the stragglers and closed the door.

"Good afternoon," he began as he handed out the syllabus. Melanie noted his soft brown eyes, which sparkled with excitement as he began discussing his subject, passion immediately emanating in his voice. "I will begin by telling you reading the text will be an absolute must if you plan on passing my class. On the syllabus you will see the assigned reading for the week. On the first day of class of each week you will be given a three question essay quiz that will be directly related to your assigned readings. There will be no discussion of the material before the quiz. You will choose two of the three to answer."

"Oh great," thought Melanie, suddenly stricken, looking over the syllabus. "That sure doesn't give much room for error. Three questions! No, it's only two questions and each one if 50%. That means I can fail if I get one wrong!"   Before any further thought, Mr. Hart began his lecture. In that moment, Melanie relaxed. The passion she'd heard in his voice when he first started speaking was tripled. His voice was smooth yet electric. She knew she would love this class.

One afternoon, as Melanie sat in her seat, noticed the small, fair skinned girl in the seat next to her . "Hi!" she said.   "How are you Mrs. Carson?

"Fine, thank you," she said looking at the girl standing next to her.   "Do I know you?" asked Melanie completely confused. "I mean I can see we have class together," she giggled.

"I'm Noel. I work with Gavin in the bookstore. I saw you one day when you came in to talk with him. He told me who you were. I'd love to study with you sometime. Gavin says you study all the time. In fact, he told me Friday night he took your book from you while you were working just because it was the weekend and you needed a break!"

"You're kidding me!"

"Oh dear!" said Melanie laughing. "That's funny! But my name is Melanie and I'd much rather you called me that than Mrs. Carson."

"Well, okay. If you're sure you don't mind."

"Not at all. As for studying, sure. If there is time you have free here at the college when I'm here, I'd be happy to study with you. I love this class. I take a ton of notes, but I want to be ready for the tests which scare me silly! The quizzes are bad enough!"

"I know. From what I've heard, his tests are vicious! I'll check my work and class schedule and then maybe we can work something out after we compare it to yours. Next class?"

"Okay."

"Better get back to my seat. Here comes Mr. Hart."

"Okay, class. Let's get started. I'm passing out the quiz for today. No more talking."

The days turned into weeks and while Melanie had done reasonably well on the quizzes, the thought of the tests frazzled her nerves. She and Noel had managed to squeeze out several days of studying which seemed to give them both a boost of confidence. Still on the day of the first test Melanie's hands were hot and sweaty.   There would be twenty short answer questions and five essay questions. Each student would have to choose three essays to answer. The test was on the first six chapters. Had she studied enough to be able to do essay questions? She shivered. It was not cold in the classroom. Her nerves were taunt as she pulled out her notes to study just another minute before the test was passed out.

Mr. Hart's warning about his tests was not overdone. It was just as he'd promised. The short answer questions were more like mini-essays in themselves, but were easily handled. Melanie read the five essay questions and decided on the three she would answer. Starting with the first one of her choice, she listed everything she could remember. As she started the second one, she froze. Her mind went blank. She had listed only three things on the subject and knew that wasn't going to be enough. She moved to the next question; listed all she could remember and then went back to her second choice. It wasn't happening. Frantic she re-read the other choices and decided on another question and again listed everything she could remember.

Finally, after she finished, feeling confident that she had done her best, she left her desk to take her work to Mr. Hart. As she approached she had a chilling thought. Feeling a bit foolish intuitively knowing the answer to her own question, she looked at Mr. Hart and asked, "Did this have to be in sentence and paragraph form?"

"Yes," he said, humor in his voice. "They are essay questions."

"Oh no!" she said sighing heavily, feeling heat rising in her face. "I'll be back."

Mr. Hart grinned as she walked away and sat at her desk. Looking at the list she had created for the first question, she set to the task of rewriting all she'd written in the correct format. After she had re-written all her answers she looked up to see she and Mr. Hart were the only ones left in the room. "I'm sorry I took so long," she said worriedly.

"Not a problem," he said taking her paper. "Can I ask you something?"

"Sure!"

"Does it sound to you like I ramble when I give my lectures?"

"No! I love it!"

"Me too. I could talk on the Civil War forever. I think it's my favorite time period, but I don't want to bore everyone else with it."

"Well, you're not going to bore me. I could listen to you lecture all day."

Mr. Hart grinned. "I appreciate that. You're a pleasure to have in class."

"Aw. Thanks. I enjoy it," she said, suddenly warm, but smiling both on her face and in her voice.

"It shows."

Melanie left the room feeling completely satisfied. If I ever have a classroom, she thought, I want to be able to teach just like him.

In the days that followed Melanie's love of history grew. Completely comfortable, she answered questions in class and devoured every lecture. She would quickly raise her hand to answer questions. One day when the class was particularly unresponsive, except Melanie, Mr. Hart said, "Would someone else answer my question besides just Mrs. Carson? We are not the only two in the room! There are plenty of other students in here who were supposed to read the material."

"Mrs. Carson, just put your hand down and we will wait on the rest of the class to participate." Embarrassed, putting her hand in her lap, she felt herself redden.

"Mrs. Carson please see me before you leave today," he said as the class was dismissed.

With her heart racing, not sure what she was going to be told, Melanie walked to Mr. Hart's desk. "I'm sorry if I hurt your feelings today," he said. "I really didn't mean too. You aren't the only one in here who is supposed to participate. The rest of the class expects you to answer. So for the next few classes, I'd like it if you answer questions at a minimum. I know you do the work, so there isn't an issue there. But I really want to get the rest of the class involved. Do you understand?"

Stricken, she said weakly, "Sure, okay."

"You've got a lot to offer, Melanie. Don't ever forget that. You are an excellent student. You are the kind of student professors dream of."

Melanie was both elated and devastated at the same time. She was elated at the kind words Mr. Hart had spoken, yet devastated that her participation would be minimal. The dialogue seemed to help concrete and clarify the information she had read and the material she heard in the lecture. She counted on the interaction to reinforce her memory with the information. Suddenly she felt like she was going to be hiding behind the cloud instead of standing in the sunshine that allowed the material to be fertilized once the seeds were planted. Puzzling over her latest challenge she walked to the Financial Aid office and then finally headed home.

Melanie jumped when the phone rang and then ran to get it. Lee hadn't even been gone one full week and it seemed forever. She understood his need to leave with her being in school and gone all the time, but understanding didn't diminish the loneliness his being gone brought. He had thought the perfect solution was to take their camper down to Arizona where the weather was warm and spend several weeks there before coming back for Thanksgiving. "Good evening," she answered as she did all calls coming in during the evening hours.

"Hey, Mel! How are ya?"

"Lee, it's so good to hear your voice! I miss you! How's Arizona? I had the neatest thing happen in History today! I can't wait to tell you."

"Well, I miss you too," he said. "Arizona is warm, and that's good, but they are calling for rain tonight. I don't have anything neat to tell you, but something has happened."

Melanie's heart sank both with dread and fear. "What?" was all she could manage.

"I was out on my bicycle today and wrecked."

"What do you mean you wrecked?"

"Just what I said," he snapped. "I was riding my bike and there was traffic coming up behind me and Mason, the guy I was riding with. Mason slowed down as I turned around, since I had heard it, but not seen it yet. When I turned back around, I was right on Mason's wheel. Instead of hitting him, I turned my wheel, hit the edge of the road where there is a three inch drop off and rolled the bike."

"Are you alright?"

"Well, not really," he said slowly. "I fell on my bad arm and now I can't move it. And," he added, "my bike's pretty messed up too."

"Have you been to the doctor?"

"Not yet."

"Why not?"

"I haven't been here very long and besides it's the weekend. I don't want to sit in the emergency room for three hours."

"You need to go. Promise me you'll go."

"If it's not better by Monday, then I'll see about going."

"If you can't use your arm, how are you doing cooking?"

"I'm managing. Mason's wife brought me dinner tonight and I'm going out tomorrow night with Ed and Jean from Oklahoma. You remember them?"

Melanie winced. "Yeah, I remember." Jean had unnerved her with subtle flirting whenever Ed wasn't around. Lee had really liked her and called Jean his inspiration for working out. He had met the fifty-five year-old-red headed, aerobic wonder at the onsite gym room and chatted about her incessantly. She knew nothing had ever happened between them, but sometimes something just gnawed at the pit of her stomach.

"So, for now," Lee continued, "I figure I'm in good hands and we will see what happens the beginning of the week. I probably ought to go now. It's nearly dark out and I want to take a quick walk."

"But I wanted to chat a while."

"I told you, it's getting dark," he said impatiently. "If I don't go now I won't be able to walk before it gets dark and besides that, like I told you earlier, they are calling for rain tonight."

"Okay," Melanie said sadly. "I'll talk to you later."

Tears slipped down Melanie's cheeks as a large knot hung in her throat. Her husband was miles away, enjoying the company of other people, maybe even another woman, and didn't even seem interested in her day. Putting the phone down in its cradle, she sat on the sofa and wept. What the professor had told her today seemed unimportant now. She felt empty and alone. It left her questioning the decision of going back to school. Was it the right thing to do? Was it a dream she shouldn't be chasing? Was it important? Was she even important? Did she even matter? And now he's hurt and she can't even help him. Wearily she went to bed.

The next morning, Flo was at her door early. Dressed in sweat pants, three layers of shirts, bedroom slippers and an over coat she let herself into the kitchen. She was carrying a large Tupperware container. She had already been to the mail box and was horribly upset because she hadn't received any birthday cards although this was October and her birthday was in April. Additionally she was irritated that the container she was carrying would not fit in the mail box.

Melanie opened the Tupperware container and was relieved to find only empty boxes in it. "I'll walk you home, Mom. I have classes in a couple hours so we'll just take you home so I can get back and be ready for classes on time. Judy should be home soon."

As soon as Melanie opened the door, her stomach lurched from the smell of something spoiled. Brooke, who was an Avon Consultant usually looked in on Mom first thing in the morning, but she and Kerry had gone away for the day so Melanie had already planned on visiting first thing this morning. Still she knew

Brooke would have checked on her last evening, so the smell of something awful surprised her.

Brooke, Lee's sister and brother in law, Kerry, lived just 1/8th mile away. Friends who knew about the family dynamics and relationships of the houses, made comments like "you have your own family compound." While many families could not have lived so near their relatives, this arrangement worked well for those involved, especially for Flo who needed someone nearby once she began having more and more issues with Alzheimer's.

Brooke had Power of Attorney regarding Flo and it is said you hurt the ones you love the most. The family had witnessed this first hand and sadly watched while Flo lashed out at Brooke whenever things didn't seem to go right. Yet it was she who made all the final decisions and was always around to see to Flo's needs. It was Brooke who daily checked on her, made sure meds were ready for the rest of us to administer when she was unavailable, and even bathed Flo when she was incapable. It was for this reason Lee and Melanie encouraged day getaways for her and Kerry, when Kerry's work would allow.

Lee and Brooke's brother Kent and his wife Judy lived next door to Flo. Kent, two years younger than Lee was away a lot on business trips and Judy helped out whenever she could, although Flo wasn't as receptive to her as the family would have liked. She lived the closest, but seemed to have the least amount of ability to help. Yet it was Kent who Flo seemed to need the most. It was he who Flo talked of with complete adoration. He was her favorite. Lee, the oldest sibling, Grace, Flo's third born, Brooke the youngest daughter; and Reed, the youngest son who also owned his mother's heart knew and accepted the special affection she had for Kent her second son and child.

On this particular day Judy had a doctor's appointment early and was expected to be back before Melanie would have had to leave for class. It had taken a great deal of coordinating on a weekly or daily basis to make sure there was always someone nearby so Flo would never be alone. There were times when Reed and Julie, who lived across town would come to help out when the nearby family was otherwise unavailable. Owen and Grace lived in Nebraska and were rarely able to share in the responsibility of Grace's mother.

Walking into the kitchen, Melanie discovered a pile of food on top of the table. Cookies and other baked goods were strewn about, as well as, a partly eaten sandwich, cut up vegetables and other assorted items.

Flo was now standing in front of her television set pushing the keys in her hands. "Why won't this work?" she asked angrily. "I want to see my programs and it won't work."

"Mom, you have car keys in your hands. Hold on. I'll find the remote."

"What are you talking about?" Flo snapped, looking squarely at her in an accusing tone.

Melanie continued cleaning the table without answering and found a large cookie wrapper filled with chicken and sauerkraut. Melanie reached up and covered her nose. This was the awful smell. Wrapping the entire mess in the paper towels she was using, she carried it to the trash. Coming back to the table she noticed the remote buried beneath more boxes Flo must have gathered earlier when she packed the large Tupperware container.

Finally, with the mess in the kitchen cleaned, the TV set with the shows Flo wanted to see and Flo sitting comfortably in her favorite chair, Melanie made her exit. She would be sure to check on her before she left for school, hoping Judy would return as planned before time would expire and make her late for classes.

Mid-week Melanie received another phone call from Lee. "I didn't think you were ever gonna call," said Melanie. "I miss you. I can't believe you've only been gone about two weeks. It seems like two years!

"How's your arm? Have you been to the doctor?"

"Mel, one question at a time. My arm is better, but not great. I've been exercising it like Kent did that time he tore his Rotator cuff. Honestly I think that's what I've done to mine. It's in a sling that I wear most of the time. I've seen a doctor, had X-rays which showed three torn ligaments and they wanted to do therapy. Getting all that scheduled is a mess though. I told them what I was doing and they said that's basically what I would be doing in therapy, so I'm going to deal with it until I get back and see a doctor back there."

"Are you sure? That sounds pretty serious."

"Well, it sort of is, but I've been fighting this arm for all these years. They said some of what they see is old injuries so I figure a little while longer won't matter. I use my left hand and arm to get most of what I need doing done and make my right arm work when I can."

"Oh, Lee."

"Quit fretting. I'll be fine. There are plenty of people here who have been just great about helping out. Mason feels responsible so he and Shirley have been especially helpful. I figure if I just keep exercising I'll get by. I'm even back to riding my bike again."

"You're kidding!"

"Well, I don't go too far, but I like riding my bike. I'm careful and as long as I go slow, and stay back from other bikes in case I need to stop in a hurry, it's just fine."

Melanie wondered if that was a good idea, but didn't voice any more concern. "Well, I'll just be glad when you get home."

"I've got a few more weeks down here and I plan to enjoy it the best I can," he responded.

"Well, okay. Things here are pretty normal. School is keeping me busy. I miss you."

"I miss you too. I gotta go. I'll call you either tomorrow night or the next."

"Bye," she said, sadly.

"Bye," he said much too cheerfully for Melanie.

Chapter 5

Clutching her text books, Melanie walked into the room and chose a desk close to the front. With cold, sweaty hands she retrieved her schedule and double checked to make sure she was in the right room. Math: H102. Folding it neatly, she placed it back in her purse. Looking around the room she noticed another student about her age and smiled. It felt good knowing she wouldn't be the only "old" person in the room.

While waiting for the instructor to come in the room, Melanie opened her Math book. Chills ran through her as she leafed through the first chapter. "I hope all those early hours working on this stuff helps," she thought. Melanie recalled the endless hours of trying to make sense of the math she would now be asked to master.

"If only I'd taken algebra," she mused. It wasn't a requirement back when she was in high school, however. She had taken the vocational track and one year of general math was all she needed. Ninth grade General Math. She smiled. What fun that had been. Mr. Taylor. He was great! He had made it seem so easy and she had done very well. Mr. Taylor had wanted her to continue with more math, but she had decided on Business and no amount of harassing could change her mind. She wondered now if that had been smart on her part. The placement tests showed just how far behind she was. It would take two non-credit math classes to be able to be ready for a credit class.

When Mrs. Bartlett walked into the room, Melanie smiled. She knew immediately she would like her new instructor. While Mrs. Bartlett clearly indicated she was in charge, she also radiated warmth, friendliness, and a sense of humor. "Good morning, class!" she said. "I am Mrs. Bartlett and you are in 031 Math. This is a non-credit course and you will need to work. Remember as long as you put forth the effort, you can get through this. I am here to help you. Don't wait until the last week to ask for help though. That will get you nowhere....well, unless you want to come back in be in my class in the Spring again. I suspect one semester of me will be enough!" Melanie settled in. It was going to be a good class. She just knew it. Relief swept through her.

Homework was another matter. It was one thing to be in class and watch Mrs. Bartlett do the problems and then work them out as a class. It was quite another to sit with the book before her with thirty problems to complete. There were nights when frustration turned into tears. "I can't do it," she said sobbing into the phone. "I've tried and tried. It just won't work!"

"Mom, take a breath and get your book. Tell me the problem and I'll help you." Drying her eyes, Melanie opened the book just moments after she slammed it closed. Reading the problem again, she waited while Kaitlyn worked it out. "Okay, she said, "Do you know what you need to do first?"

"I'm supposed to "foil."

"Right. Do you remember how to foil?" she asked.

"I think so. First, outside, inside and last."

"Right. Do that now." Hard as she tried, Melanie kept tripping up and Kaitlyn would stop her and have her start over. Working slowly through the problem, Kaitlyn laid out the procedure again and again until Melanie finally got the right answer. She finally completed the assignment and discovered the secret to getting through the rest of the semester. She would be doing homework over the phone!

Even though this had been their method for getting Melanie's homework completed since the semester had started, with Kaitlyn and Phil living in nearby Steele, she never expected to continue the practice long distance and certainly was not prepared for what she heard when the phone rang just six weeks before......

"Hi, sweetie. What's up?"

"We're moving, Mom."

"What do you mean, you're moving?

"Phil asked for a transfer. We're moving to Texas," said Kaitlyn stifling a sob. Melanie's heart sank as she pictured her second daughter in her kitchen talking on the phone. Her straight long hair was reminiscent of her own. There was not a curl in it. She was slightly overweight, not yet back to size from having their first born, Kara, almost a year ago. At five foot five Kara was nearly as tall as her husband, Phil.

"When?"

"In about a month. That gives us time to put the house on the market. It doesn't give us much time, but the position just came open. The coach they had has been diagnosed with cancer and since the semester has already started there, we are in hurry up mode. Phil will go on down, set up and then come back. Hopefully I can have everything packed in that time frame. Ultimately, we'll end up leaving right after Kara's birthday, between Thanksgiving and Christmas."

Melanie took a deep breath. "I didn't know you two were even considering leaving this area."

"Well, we've been going back and forth for a while. Phil wants to move on, have other challenges. He's tired of just being a PE teacher. They've offered him a position as a basketball coach, too. He loves basketball and he'd be good at coaching.

"Have you told Brianna?"

"Not yet. She's not going to be happy. It's been really stressful. Brianna is part of the reason Phil asked for a transfer. He's got to get away from her. She wants to control his life. It's like because they are twins, she should have a say in everything he does. It drives me mad and Phil just doesn't know what to do with her. He hates to tell her no."

"I'm sorry, honey. Things like that happen. I hate to see you go though."

"Are you kidding? I hate the thought of going. I know Phil has been tossing the idea around in his mind for some time, but he didn't tell me he had actually put in for the transfer until it came back that he had been."

"Does he know how you feel?"

"Sure he does. I told him! He wants to experience new horizons in another part of the country. I don't want to leave my family! I don't expect Phil's family is going to feel excited about it either. I guess we'll find out. I'm planning Kara's birthday party just before we leave. Of course Phil's Dad will be there and so will Brianna."

Melanie and Lee drove into the driveway already filling with family. He had arrived home from Arizona just a week before. Melanie was so excited she could hardly wait until he drove in the driveway once she knew he had left Arizona. He still had his arm in a sling, although he didn't wear it consistently. Once he returned, the doctor in Elk Ridge had suggested surgery and Lee wanted no part of that so he stopped going once he was in a routine with the therapy they recommend. Each day brought less pain and more movement so he was content with his progress.

Kaitlyn's house was filled with boxes piled on top of each other, each clearly marked for the room in which they belonged. The living room was the only room not littered with boxes. It clearly was decorated in early birthday party celebration. Kara squealed with delight when she saw Melanie. Extending her arms she waited for her grandmother to come to her. Picking up the baby, Melanie fought back tears. Phil, Kaitlyn and Kara would be leaving in just five days. How could she let this baby leave? They would be 1000 or more miles away with only visits several times a year at best.

Kaitlyn made the decision before they ever left to get unlimited long distance calling to be able to stay in touch. This would be an invaluable means of communication since Melanie and Kaitlyn had a close relationship and even more important now that Kaitlyn and Phil had a baby. The additional perk of being able to do homework via phone was an advantage both woman appreciated.

"Phil, could you answer the phone please? I'm kind of busy here," laughed Kaitlyn as she helped Kara open her gifts.

"Mom," Phil said, "It's Luke. It's for you."

"Luke?"

"Yeah, that's what he said."

"Lee, why would Luke call here? Something's wrong," said Melanie shaking, reaching for the phone. Luke was so much like Lee, it was eerie. He was just taller than Lee at six foot two, lean and trim. He had his dark hair, dark eyes and sometimes dark personality. He could be quiet and so reserved it was frightening. But his heart was tender like his father's, as well. In some instances with small children or older adults, he seemed like a squishy teddy bear.

"Luke, are you okay?"

"Hi, Mom," he said in a steady, low voice. "Yeah, I'm okay. I tried calling the house and when you didn't answer I figured you had to be over to Kaitlyn's since it's Kara's birthday.

"I got news today."

"News?"

"Yeah, they are sending me to Iraq."

Melanie's knees turned to jelly as she reached for Lee for support. "Luke's going to Iraq," she said while unbidden tears streamed down her face.

"Luke, what's going on?" asked Lee taking the phone from Melanie.

"Well, they're sending me to Iraq. I leave day after tomorrow and I don't know when I'm going to have a chance to talk with you again. Is Mom all right?"

"No, but she will be. Give her time. We both knew this could happen when you signed up for the Corps. It'll be hard on her for a while. I'm proud of you, son. Let us hear from you as soon as you can. Be safe. Here's your mom again."

"Luke, promise me you'll email or write or call or something as soon as you can to let me know you're okay."

"You know I will, but you also know I won't be able to give you any details about where I am or what I'm doing."

"I know that, and that's fine. I just want to know that you are okay."

"I know. Like I said, I'll let you know something as soon as I can. I love you, Mom. I gotta go now. There are other guys here waiting to use the phone."

"What's up?" Asked Kaitlyn, sensing the tension between her parents.

"Luke is headed for Iraq in two days," answered a shaking, tear filled Melanie. "I know I shouldn't cry, but I just can't help it."

Tears welled up in Kaitlyn's eyes as she embraced her mother. "It's okay to cry, Mom. We all miss him and worry with you."

"At least he's doing something good for his country," said Brianna. "Kaitlyn and Phil are moving to Texas, a God forsaken place, just because."

"Brianna, what a thing to say. That's cruel. One has nothing to do with the other," said Phil. "We're moving to Texas because it's the right thing for us to do."

"It's the right thing for you to do, but it sure isn't good for the rest of us."

"Chill, Brianna. I don't want a scene."

"You don't want a scene? So who's creating a scene anyway? I just think your leaving is selfish and wrong."

"Brianna, not now! It's Kara's birthday party for goodness sake."

"Okay, okay!" she said storming out of the room.

"Alrighty then!" said Kaitlyn, forcing a smile, "Back to the party. We're still opening gifts here. Kara, look at what Aunt Susan gave you," she added sounding more cheerful than she felt.

Brianna, a tall, dark haired beauty, slipped back into the room but no less agitated. Phil moved next to his sister and placed his arm around her tiny waist. Melanie knew he understood her pain, yet also knew his decision had been right. How many times had they tried to visit when her unannounced arrivals would create an upheaval he didn't desire? He could no longer have her interfering with his life. He needed the break. Yet, Melanie knew he would miss her. How could he not, she after all was his twin. They had been through much together.

Their mother had passed away when they were just fourteen and their dad now lived in Florida. Brianna had convinced her husband, Alan, a wealthy investor to move to the Black Hills after their father chose to move to Florida from Kentucky after Kaitlyn and Phil were married. She had been stunned when Phil had chosen to move west after the wedding and resented Kaitlyn for it. There had even been some cross words and unkind things spoken to Kaitlyn over the matter. But Brianna and Kaitlyn had seemed to work out their differences and had become at least cordial. Now here she was again losing Phil to another move and she knew it wasn't Kaitlyn's idea, but Phil's.

Two days later Melanie responded to the familiar ring of her telephone.

"Mom?"

"Hey, Luke! Where are you?"

"I'm still in Guam. They canceled my orders."

"You're kidding. Why?"

"Bureaucratic stuff. Our entire unit is on hold. So for at least now, I'll be here for a little while longer. Quite honestly, I'm disappointed. I'm ready to take care of business. That's part of the reason I joined the Marines. We all want to go take care of the garbage over in Iraq. We want to go kick some butt!"

"Oh, Luke. I know. But do you mind if I'm delighted it didn't work out just now? I was horribly upset with the news."

"No. I expected you to be happy about the change.

"You do realize, though, there will come a time when I will go. It is part of being a Marine."

"I know. You already said that. I understand, and certainly your dad does. I'm a mom. I worry!"

"I know and when I can I will let you know where I am and that I am fine."

Melanie's heart sang with joy with the news from Luke but filled with pain at the thought of Kaitlyn moving so far away. As the days passed and Melanie and Lee spent time with their daughter she swung between happiness for them and sadness for herself. The day of leaving came much sooner than she wanted. Kaitlyn, Phil and Kara came over for dinner as their last stop before heading south. The truck was loaded, followed by an overfilled U-Haul trailer.

Melanie couldn't stop the flow of tears. She knew it would be months before she saw her daughter and the granddaughter she cherished. Even knowing they were leaving, as they saw it, for the right reasons, her chest hurt as she swallowed the lump in her throat. She watched them pull out the driveway and followed the vehicles for as long as her eyes would allow. Finally she forced herself to re-enter the house. She already missed them and they hadn't even left town.

Despite her best effort of preparation and the countless hours on the phone with Kaitlyn working out the different math problems, the first test of the semester proved to be almost more than Melanie could bear. Her nerves were on edge and to make it worse she hadn't slept well. Dreams of red ink marks all over the paper had created havoc with sleep. Tired and feeling a sense of dread, Melanie took her seat.

"You ready for this?" Mrs. Bartlett asked kindly.

"I don't know. I've studied, but I'm not sure."

"If you have a question just raise your hand," she assured me. "You'll be okay."

With a fragment of confidence Melanie dove into the test. She made it through the first page and then into the second. Melanie heard shuffling and noticed students were leaving. She looked at her next problem. "Oh, man! How do I do this?" Panic began to set in. She moved to the next one. She looked at her watch. Only fifteen minutes left? She'd never finish. She felt hot and then shivered with cold. More students left. Soon she was the last one in the room and there were still one and one half pages to go. Ten problems and she'd get them all wrong. She didn't finish.

Standing, she picked up her paper and handed it to Mrs. Bartlett while tears came unbidden. "What's wrong?" She asked.

"I didn't finish."

"Can you stay and work on it longer?"

"I have another class. I can't."

"Baby, it's not worth tears."

It was all Melanie could do to not cry when the test was returned the next class. Just like in her dreams, red ink claimed the pages. She didn't fail, but it wasn't good. She was stricken. After class she approached Mrs. Bartlett. "I did awful on the test."

"You didn't do as well as I expected."

"I heard everyone leave and I panicked and made it worse. I couldn't think. I couldn't do it."

"Would you be more comfortable taking the test in the Learning Resource Center?"

"I don't know. That doesn't seem fair to anyone else. I just have to get used to people moving around me."

"Well, you think about it and if you'd rather on the next test, just let me know. Write me a note on your test if you don't finish you can finish it over there. I don't have a problem with that."

"Thanks. I appreciate that," Melanie said somberly clutching her book. "I'm trying. I'd like to do as well in Math as my kids."

"But you're doing the best you can. That's all you can do. And that's plenty. Who will even know if you get an A or B? Remember this is a non-credit course."

"No. It's not enough. I want that A." Mrs. Bartlett smiled. She didn't look surprised. That said Melanie walked out of the room a new resolve in her heart. I will get Math. I just will and that's all there is to it!

While doing homework over the phone eased much of the agony of math, there were still instances where it wouldn't work. When there were graphs involved, Kaitlyn was unable to aid her mother. It was here, Mackenzie came to her aid. Tears were rolling down Melanie's face as Mackenzie walked into the room as she struggled again with the problems before her. "Mom, what is wrong?"

"I can't get it and Kaitlyn can't help me. She can't see what I'm doing."

"That's okay. I'll help you." Mackenzie sat beside Melanie on the sofa and gave her mother a squeeze. "Let's see what you're doing. Ummm.....Getting the slope."

"Something about rise over run," Melanie said. "It doesn't make sense and I can't make it work."

"Yes, you can. I'll show you." Much like her sister, Mackenzie slowly and deliberately went step by step through the process.

"How am I ever going to remember this?"

"It takes practice. You'll get it. Just don't let it upset you."

"But it does upset me when I can't get it."

"Mom! Breathe! You will get it and if Kaitlyn can't help you, then I will. You will get through this."

"But you've got your own classes. After work all day and then driving to Elk Creek. You don't have time for mine too."

"Mom, hear what I'm saying. My classes are under control. I will help you and you will be fine. Trust me. FOIL!"

Melanie went through the process: "F, first, O, outside; I inside; L, last." I did it! But it takes so long. You just look at it and you get the answer."

"But I've been doing it for a long while. Don't worry, just do the process and you'll get it too!"   Melanie doubted her daughter's words.

With continued effort and sleepless nights Melanie fought for understanding. Mrs. Bartlett proved to be the kind, considerate, patient math professor she needed. By the end of the term Melanie had a clear handle on the concepts presented. By the final classes, Mrs. Bartlett was not just a professor, but a friend.

Chapter 6

Melanie walked into the room filled with students. Some, already seated were young, just out of high school, but she was pleasantly surprised to see several older students in the room, although if she guessed right, she would still be senior. There was an empty seat in the front of the room. Instead of individual desks, there was what looked like black marble tables which accommodated three students at a time.

The two girls already seated obviously knew each other considering their similar ages, animation and conversation. Melanie took her seat on the end and retrieved her book. She looked at the clock. Three till nine. Where is the professor, she wondered?

Just after the clock struck nine a small, bony, middle aged woman barged in. Her gray streaked hair dangled about her face. Her faded, red polo shirt with obvious breakfast leftovers covered her just too large, blue Dockers. "Sorry I'm late class," she said breathlessly as she came in. "There was an accident out on Route 90 and since I'm still new to the area I didn't know any alternate routes, so I had to wait it out. Thankfully, I'm told, no one was seriously hurt. But you wouldn't know that from the tangled mess of the vehicles involved. It was rather ugly."

Placing her things on the desk and pausing she said, "Okay, this is Psychology I and I need to tell you a little about myself." Melanie was amused at her animation yet concerned about her apparent lack of respect for the position she held. "I am Dr. Gilmer. I am from the Denver area and moved to this area just about a month ago. It's a change, but I think I will like it. My major is obviously Psychology, but not in teaching. I have worked at a variety of different levels of psychology in hospitals throughout Colorado, Wyoming and Montana but received my doctorate in Denver."

"I would like you each to say your name, give your town and major so we all get to know each other," she continued. Each student did as requested and then they moved to the syllabus. "Ahhh..." Dr. Gilmer started as she stared at the syllabus. "Did everyone pick up the reader that goes with this course? It wasn't listed as a book you needed before class started."

No's reverberated throughout the room. "Okay, class is over for today." Melanie looked at the clock. There was still thirty minutes left. "I need everyone to make their way to the bookstore to get the additional book and read chapters one through three in your book and do the first case study in the reader you pick up today before coming to class next time."

Some students rose and exited quickly, excited at having class end early. Melanie hoped classes would be a bit more productive the rest of the year. This first class was disappointing.

Just three classes into Psychology and Melanie saw a trend. Dr. Gilmer's inclination for arriving to class late carried precedence over being early or even on time. She was disorganized and her teaching methods less than desired. What Melanie had hoped would be an interesting class appeared like it would create tension and worry since Dr. Gilmer never seemed quite sure what she was doing. Instead of teaching the material, she created slides right from the book and read them to the class, rarely elaborating or explaining. Understanding of an idea would come solely from reading the text or independent research. It seemed odd to Melanie that Dr. Gilmer would use this method of teaching since she obviously knew her field. Her speech and casual discussion of psychology indicated her education. Her difficulty came in the presentation of the textbook and what the students would eventually be tested on. In this regard Melanie was horribly disappointed.

Melanie breathed a sigh of relief when she entered her home. This day had been stressful and she was glad it was over.

"Great, now I have homework. Psychology. Lots of reading. And Dr. Gilmer gives us these papers to write, but what she wants is so vague. I've only had three classes and I feel like it's already been a whole semester!" she said to Mackenzie, who was willing to be Melanie's sounding board.

As the year wore on, frustration in the class continued and reached its peak when the class was doing debates over controversial issues. Melanie's team was given "On Spanking Children." This topic gave Melanie pause because she was the only mother on the team of two eighteen year old females and two eighteen year old males. Her team was designated as having to prove it was not a legitimate form of discipline. Three teams were to debate each day, each having twenty minutes of timed debate, followed by five minutes of rebuttal on both sides and then a class critique. Time was crucial to their grade. By the time the third team debated and finished, class time left was barely ten minutes.

On the day of Melanie's team's presentation Dr. Gilmer hadn't arrived after ten minutes of the scheduled class time. A staff member came into the room to tell the class that Dr. Gilmer had phoned; she would be there in about ten minutes and she expected everyone to wait. Several students who had previously presented left the room after the staff member exited.

In addition to Dr. Gilmer being late, Melanie noticed that both the young men on their team were also not in the room. Panic filled her. They had been told the team would debate when scheduled whether all the team was present or not.

Melanie had practiced her part since she knew debating on the side of not using spanking as discipline went against her own beliefs. While she opposed abuse of any kind, open handed spanking was how she and Lee had always raised their children. She felt she was speaking a non-truth with every word she spoke and she was afraid she wouldn't sound as convincing as she knew she needed to be to win the debate.

Twelve minutes later Dr. Gilmer bolted into the room in normal fashion, flustered and out of breath. "We really have to get started," she said. We have three debates to do today."

"No kidding," said Melanie under her breath. Raising her hand and waiting to be acknowledged she asked, "What if there isn't enough time for the last team?"

"Don't worry. We'll get them all done today. You'll see."

As the two teams before her debated, Melanie became more and more agitated. Her heart raced and body temperature rose with each second the clock ticked closer to their debate. The two absent members of the debate team still had not arrived. Finally it was time for her team to take their places in the front of the room. Jayden, a tall, thin, well dressed young woman and Claire, a young woman of average height donning a short, blunt hair cut, looked at Melanie displaying as much fear as she felt. "Can you believe the guys haven't shown up? What are we going to do?" said Claire as she stood, pushing her chair in loudly.

"I don't know. They have part of the visuals we are supposed to use. I have no clue, but to attempt to pull it off. I am so upset I could cry!"

"Don't do that," said Jayden picking up her papers. "We won't ever be able to debate if you do that."

"Just remember like I told you before, I really should be on the opposite side of this debate. I don't agree with this. You two are going to have to pull the weight here. I feel like I'm lying with everything I'm trying to prove." Slowly they took their places, both girls seated to Melanie's left. Just as they seated, both boys waltzed in the room as if they had arrived at the beginning of the class. Braden, a tall blonde wearing a sky blue dress shirt dangling over his jeans ambled to the chair next to Melanie as if nothing was irregular. Seth, a tall brown haired athletic young man, whose muscular physique was exposed through his taunt grey tee shirt sauntered to the chair beside Braden on the outside of the table.

Melanie looked at her watch and spoke quietly to the team. "We only have thirty minutes before the end of class. I have no idea how Dr. Gilmer will handle the end."

To her great relief, the team was everything she had hoped for. While she had to speak up and share her part of the debate, the bulk of the debate was with Jayden and Claire and the male members of the team had brought their visual aides and were prepared to debate, as well. The class had been required to remain in the class until the presentation was finished. The critiques of the class had been abbreviated and lent itself to their favor since most were in a hurry to leave the classroom.

The phone was ringing when she unlocked the door, finally home after a long day at school. "Good afternoon," she said hurrying in before the call went to the answering machine.

"Hey Melanie. It's Brooke. Today has been unreal. I need to talk with Lee. We need to discuss Mom. When I went to check on her this morning, she had locked herself in the bathroom. Her bathroom door knob won't allow you to unlock it from the outside. I tried and tried to talk to her and all she would do is scream at me and wouldn't unlock the door. Kent is on the road and Judy was at work. I ended up calling Reed and Shari and they came over and finally talked her out of the bathroom.

I tried calling up there, but Lee never answered the phone.

"No, he went with Zach Wilson up to Belle Fourche to pick up cars today. He hasn't gotten back yet. He should be here between 8:00 and 9:00."

"Well, I need to talk with him, and soon. I'm worried about Mom. I don't know how much more I can take."

"Okay. I'll tell him you called. Do you want him to call you after he gets back?"

"No, wait until morning. Judy is going to be around and she said she would keep an eye on Mom tonight. Kerry and I are going out and won't be back till 11:00 or so."

The next morning Brooke knocked on Melanie and Lee's door rather than phoning. "Hi Brooke," said Melanie cheerfully.

"You are way to cheery first thing in the morning. Lee is still here isn't he?"

"Yeah. I told him you wanted to talk with him." As she spoke Lee entered the room.

"Lee, what do you think about maybe putting Mom in an assisted living home?"

"Do you think it's time for that?" he asked.

"I don't know. I just know that I worry about her every day in that house alone. Her Alzheimer's isn't bad yet, but there are sure signs of it. She's doing some wandering now and we just can't keep wondering where she might go. I had Kerry turn off the gas to her stove last week. We've been making the meals, along with Kent and Judy to make sure she gets her meals."

"I know you've done it before but I'd hoped you would be willing to help with meals until we get this settled. I have done some checking and I know a representative from the nursing home has to come out and talk with Mom just to verify she is qualified to be there."

"Well," said Lee slowly. "I guess if that's what we need to do, then I'll support it."

A week later, Brooke drove Flo to the Peaceful Haven Assisted Living facility just barely in town. On her way home, Brooke stopped by to see Lee and Melanie. "Mom doesn't like it one bit," said Brooke, worried. "I don't know how long it will last. If this doesn't work I can't imagine what we will do. I am nowhere near ready to put her in a nursing home."

"Me either," agreed Lee emphatically. "How are Kent and Judy with all this?"

"I don't know. They are having issues of their own. Kent has been offered a promotion in Minnesota and Judy doesn't want to go. She doesn't want to leave her family. Kent is even suggesting he'd like to sell the place."

"Sell? You're kidding! I never expected that."

Three days later when the phone rang, Melanie was stricken by the sobs she heard.

"Brooke, is that you? Brooke, what's wrong?" asked Melanie.

"Peaceful Haven just called," she choked between sobs. "They told me to come get Mom. She's hitting the staff with her food tray and being completely disagreeable. I want Lee to go with me."

"Okay, I'll get him, but calm down."

"But, you don't understand. I don't want to put her in a nursing home," she said, sounding suddenly angry.

"I know. Me either. We'll work this out."

"I don't know how," she spat. "Why is it me who has to make all the decisions? Why do I have to be the bad guy?"

"Brooke, you're not the bad guy. Lee will help you and I'm sure if you ask, Kent will help, too."

"Sure they may give their opinions, but I'm the one who has to sign the papers. Melanie, I don't know if I can do it."

"Brooke, we'll get through this. God will get us through it."

"Easy for you to say. I don't see God in this at all."

"Sometimes we can't. I won't claim to understand. I just know He's there when things are good or bad. It's what we have to cling to. He's where I have to draw my strength."

Melanie could only hear sniffling through the phone. Wondering what to say next to soothe her sister-in-law, she said. "I'm going to hang up now and pray before I call Lee. This isn't going to be an easy time for us, but we will get through it. I have to believe that."

"Well, you can believe all you want. I'm going to wait and see."

Two hours later Lee and Brooke had Flo once again settled in her home. They would alternate taking food and watching her to make sure she was taken care of. Kent and Judy agreed to take on more of the responsibility and Reed and Shari offered their help even knowing they would have to drive across town to be of service. "I'll just come spend the day with her, if nothing else," said Shari. "It won't always work, but on the days I can, I will. That will give you guys who take care of her every day a break."

The sobering truth was they would all have a full time job monitoring Flo. None wanted the nursing home.

It seemed like stressful news just wouldn't stop coming. Melanie was sitting on the sofa when the phone rang. "Mrs. Carson?"

"This is she," she answered, clearly confused.

"This is Brent Phillips, the local EMT at Cedar Ridge Community College. We have Gavin here in the office. He has collapsed. His heart rate is extremely high and his blood pressure is extremely low. He is complaining of chest pains. We are sending him via ambulance to Elk Ridge Medical Center."

"What?" exclaimed Melanie. "Why? What's wrong with him?"

"Mrs. Carson, I really don't know what is wrong with him. But I would suggest that you meet us at the hospital."

"I'll call Mr. Carson and we'll be there as soon as we can."

With trembling fingers she dialed the number to reach Lee. After filling him in on her most recent phone call, Lee came home and they were en-route to the hospital. Melanie's cell phone rang.

Mackenzie was crying on the other end and could hardly talk. "Mom," she sobbed. "They've taken Gavin to the hospital in Elk Ridge. I was following the ambulance and I lost it. Where have they gone?" she cried in desperation.

"Calm down, Mac. Where are you so I can tell your dad so we can figure out how to get you to the hospital? Dad and I are on our way too." Gavin had always been Mackenzie's favorite sibling. She was six years older than he and they had a relationship that rivaled the best of best friends. She doted on him like no other. When he was hurting, she felt his pain. She was frightened first because she didn't understand like the rest of us what was wrong with "her" Gavin, as she often called him. And to compound that fear, she had no clue where she was in town since she had never had reason to visit the hospital there.

"Steven is coming too," she said, catching her breath.

In the moments that followed directions were clarified and everyone met at Cedar Ridge Medical Center to be with Gavin. Once into the Emergency Room and with identification everyone was ushered into the cubicle where Gavin was hooked up to machines monitoring his heart and lungs. He was resting comfortably and seemed free of pain.

"Gavin!" exclaimed Melanie. "What in the world?"

"I don't know, Mom. I just know that I felt really weird and I collapsed."

Moments later the doctor on call came in and spoke candidly. "Mr. and Mrs. Carson, we aren't completely sure what Gavin's issues are. Our first thought was a collapsed lung and then we considered heart issues. Currently everything has returned to normal and there, at the moment, doesn't seem to be anything wrong. That being said, I can tell you, something definitely caused his issues and I recommend you have it checked out as soon as possible by your regular attending physician."

The next weeks were trying with doctor's appointments at both heart and lung specialists being juggled between classes for both Melanie and Gavin. Lee was the strength that carried Melanie through, as well as, her faith. After many tests they learned Gavin may be dealing with Marfan's Syndrome.

His symptoms of this disease included his very tall, slender loose jointed frame, his over sized hands, his protruding sternum and he had exceedingly flat feet, to name a few. Additionally the rapid heart beat and heart palpitations further meant the likelihood of this disease. Confirmation of this terrified Melanie. The prognosis would not be good.

Finally they were sent to an eye specialist to determine if there was deterioration behind Gavin's eyes. "We can't tell you what is wrong with him, Mrs. Carson, but it does not seem to be Marfan's. Even though he fits nearly every other criterion, the final one with the eyes doesn't fit." While relieved it was decided Gavin didn't have the dreaded Marfan's disease, they were left with many unanswered questions and could only wait and hope the episode at the college was just a fluke.

Melanie was glad when the semester neared its end. It had been challenging in many regards. Math had been stressful because she felt so far behind. With Mackenzie and Kaitlyn's help she had muddled through it and it looked like she might even earn an A. That depended entirely on how she did on the final. Fitness For Life had been a warm, friendly class. She attributed that largely to Dr. Kline while Student Orientation had proven worthy of the effort she'd given since she learned so much, especially regarding the computer. Melanie had loved History class. Mr. Hart's passion permeated his lectures making it easy to declare this class as one of her favorites. Psychology, on the other hand, had been stressful, due largely to Dr. Gilmer. This instructor had also made an impression upon her, but not one that made Melanie particularly happy. This is a professor she would never want to emulate.

Early December found Melanie preparing for finals. She was both excited and terrified. The very thought of sitting for three hours working on a test that could bring her grade down or raise it to the next level gave her chills. She had studied hard all semester and had given 110%. All finals were finished except this last one: psychology.

Melanie entered the room for the last time completely comfortable with who she had become in this environment. The students here, as in her other classes, had accepted her and seemed to respect her opinion. One last final and it would be finished. She turned her paper over and generally perused it. Her eyebrows furrowed as she noticed one large section on schizophrenia. "What in the world?" she wondered. Not only had they not discussed this in class, it was not in the reading material. "Oh well," she decided. "There was no turning back. All I can do is answer the best I can."

Melanie turned in her paper and left the room. Outside the building Rachel called to her. "What in the world was all the schizophrenia questions about?"

"I haven't a clue; no idea where those came from!"

Rusty echoed his surprise. "Did I miss something in class?"

"I didn't miss any days, and I'm sure we never discussed it. It wasn't even part of the syllabus. Go figure! All we can do now is wait to get our final grades. Dr. Gilmer said she wouldn't even give us our grade from the final until Spring, even if we emailed or called. So I'll probably never know how I did on her final. I just hope my final grade is good."

Chapter 7

Melanie headed for the phone. It's going to be one of those days, she thought. The phone's not going to stop ringing. The first two so far were solicitors and it wasn't even lunch time yet. Here we go again. "Mom!" came the lively voice on the other end.

"Hey, Kaitlyn! What's up?"

"Hold on. I have someone on the line who wants to talk with you."

"Hi Mom!" came a deep voice.

"Luke! Oh my goodness," Melanie said, suddenly torn between laughing and crying. "How are you able to call? How are you? Oh my goodness! I miss you! Are you okay? Oh no! Is something wrong! Where are you?"

"Mom!" Luke interrupted, laughing. "One question at a time! I was able to call because Phil has connections through a military friend he knows. I am fine, and no, there is nothing wrong! And, I'm in Saudi Arabia now.   I got here two days ago.   Just wanted to call to say hey!"

Melanie's mind was racing. It was all she could do to keep calm. She had so many questions; so many things she wanted to say. Finally sighing she said, "Oh Luke, I miss you so much. I just want to have you home again and safe."

"It's okay, Mom.   I can't talk long. We have about three minutes and then I'll have to get off. I just wanted to let you and Dad know that things here are fine and I miss you guys, too."

Moments later, exhilarated, Melanie hung up the phone and tried to continue with the domestic duties she had attempted all morning to complete. In frustration Melanie reached for the ringing telephone again.

"Good afternoon," said Melanie in her normal telephone salutation.

"Hi, Mel. It's Wendy. I have some news I need to share with you and then I have a few questions."

"Okay," she responded warily.   It had been ten months or more since she'd heard from her and their last conversation was less than pleasant as they discussed the state of affairs regarding their mother who passed away two years ago.

"Dad's not well," she stated simply. "He's been in the hospital again and he was supposed to get released, but they've changed their minds and are running more tests. He might even need heart surgery."

"Oh, my!" Melanie cut in taking a ragged breath.

"The doctors say his lungs are shot and his heart is only working at forty percent. He also has swelling around his brain and some internal bleeding. It doesn't look good.

"You know Dad has been staying with me and I've been talking with Patti and basically we want your input on what to do with Dad after he leaves the hospital. With my work schedule, I can't take care of him 24/7."

"What does Patti think we should do?" Melanie asked. She hadn't had any contact with her sister just a year older than her for over a year. Patti always seemed to need more from her than she was able to give.

Once in a telephone call several years before Patti wanted to know why they couldn't be best friends. *"We're supposed to be," she had insisted. "We're sisters."*

"Patti," Melanie said, "you will always be my sister and we can always be friends, but I'm afraid we probably will never be best friends. We have way too many differences. We look at life differently, our faiths are similar but you insist if I don't believe just like you then I'm not even saved. I keep trying to tell you I accepted Jesus as my Savior years ago and that doesn't seem to be enough for you. So, all we can be, as I see it for now, is sisters and friends who don't agree on everything. And that's okay. I can still love you. That's what's important." The call ended with Patti angry and in tears.

"Well, Patti wants Dad taken care of and thinks a nursing home might be the answer.

"You know Dad wants to be cremated when he passes," Wendy continued. "And before that gets done he wants to donate his body to Science."

"You're kidding."

"Nope. And I intend to make sure that happens. The only thing is he wants his ashes in the VA cemetery over there in Sturgis, SD."

"Really?" said Melanie, clearly surprised. "I didn't expect that."

"He fell in love with that area after he came out there right after you and Lee got married. So, if that is what he wants, I'll tend to that part of it. I just want some input on the time remaining."

"How 'bout if I think on it, talk with Lee and I'll get back with ya?"

"Okay. Just don't take too long."

"I won't," she reassured her. "I'll call you back either later today, or sometime tomorrow."

The next morning was filled with bright sunshine, but cold with a brisk wind. Just as Melanie was ready to head out the door, the phone rang. "I should let the answering machine get it," she said aloud, but pausing, decided she'd answer.

"Good Morning," came her cheerful greeting.

"Hey, Melanie. It's Wendy."

"I told you I was going to call you back today," she laughed. "I just had some things to get done today. They're calling for more bad weather tomorrow. Glad classes don't start till the end of the month.

"Good news or bad news first?" Wendy asked.

"Let's go for the good news," Melanie replied.

"I found a notebook that was actually Mom's which she made that has names, birth dates and other information about her side of the family and even some of Dad's. And a composition book filled with obituaries from newspapers from family and friends Mom and Dad both knew from years ago. I also came across an old Bible that Granddad had given Dad back when he was a child. I thought you might like that."

"Oh wow! That'd be great! Thanks! But is Dad ready to part with that yet?"

"Well, that's the bad news. The nursing home question is no longer an issue. Dad passed away last night."

"Oh, Wendy!"

"With the Science folks getting Dad's body and such and then the cremation, it'll be a while before we get Dad's body back. Our next issue will be the funeral."

Another semester was beginning. It still didn't seem possible to Melanie she'd completed one already. Tentatively she walked into Communications class. She looked around the room to see if there was anyone she recognized. She'd been nearly the last one arriving and had had to sit with a boy that couldn't be over eighteen toward the back of the room. She hated the back of the room. Being small made it difficult to see around other students. Melanie's hands were cold and clammy. The instructor, a tall, robust woman, was at the front desk.

"My name is Mrs. Kaimana. Since my name is hard to pronounce and friends, as well as, students for years have completely decimated it, I am totally comfortable being called Mrs. K, as long as you don't do that in front of Administration. My husband is a native Hawaiian. I went to college there, fell in love and married. After I graduated we lived on the island of Kauai, an incredibly beautiful place, for six years before moving to the mainland. Kaimana in Hawaiian means "power of the ocean" and it also stands for the English word diamond.

"I will ask each of you to share about yourself over the coming days, but for now I will share a bit more about me," Mrs. K said as she walked to the overhead projector placing a photograph in view. "This is me when I was a child; here's one as a teenager and I liked sports, particularly kayaking, so here is one of that."

She placed a photograph of her graduation and as quickly removed it. Several more were placed in view and removed more quickly than the one before.

"Okay, now you know a little about me. Let's talk about this class everyone so cheerfully signed up for and more importantly, my expectations."

Melanie was fascinated with Mrs. K's energy and enthusiasm. She embodied confidence and for a woman her size seemed bigger than life as she continued her narrative. "I generally take off up to ten points for missing any of my classes. So, if you're going to miss my class, come see me. But don't come to me with some lame excuse. You'd better be dying! I've heard all the excuses like the dog ate my home work or my car broke down. Find another ride. Don't say you need to attend a funeral especially on a Monday. Nobody has funerals on a Monday. People want them before the weekend so that family can attend and go back to where ever they came from; so not even that one will work. I'm always amazed at how often kids try that."

The rest of what Mrs. K said was lost as Melanie squirmed in her seat feeling flushed. It had been nine long months since her father had died. He had donated his body to Science which was followed by the desired cremation. The ashes had finally been returned to the family. Her heart still ached for the man she had long cherished. Unbidden tears stung her eyes as she swallowed a lump in her throat. It would have been so much easier if that snow storm hadn't hit last weekend and closed everything. The funeral had been set for that Monday, but the only ones who could get out were those with snow mobiles. The entire area was paralyzed beneath the three foot white blanket. Classes hadn't started yet for the Spring and timing seemed perfect. Now there were going to be issues.

At the end of class, Melanie collected her things and waited until all the other students had left and then went to the instructor's desk. "Can I help you?" asked Mrs. K without looking up.

"I have to talk to you," she said softly. "I have to miss your class on Monday, for my Dad's funeral."

Mrs. K's head jerked up. "What? Did you not just hear what I said in class?"

"Yes, ma'am. The funeral was actually planned for last Monday, but because of the blizzard we had last week." Melanie choked on the words, unable to finish the sentence or stop the flow of silent tears.

"You're serious, aren't you?" asked Mrs. K showing a glimpse of genuine sympathy.

"Yes, ma'am. We lost Dad about nine months ago," she said, allowing her tears to go unchecked. "It was really hard. Not completely unexpected. He had been sick, but we all thought he'd come through it like he's always done. No one was ready, but Dad donated his body to Science and had long wanted cremation.

Then we had the blizzard last week. I don't want to miss your class, but I won't miss the chance to tell my Dad good-bye."

"Don't you worry about," said Mrs. K standing and then giving Melanie a quick, unexpected hug. "It's the beginning of the semester. You'll be fine. You can make up any missed work. Just get the notes from another student and I won't dock you the ten points either," she added, smiling slightly.

"Thank you. I appreciate it," Melanie responded before turning to leave.

"There is just one thing," Mrs. K said. Melanie stopped in her tracks and turned around. "I'd rather you didn't share with the other students just now about having to miss my class and not being penalized for it. It would wreck havoc with my reputation," she added with a lopsided grin.

"No, problem!" Melanie said, smiling at her new friend.

Melanie woke to a gentle snow outside her window. It didn't look like the beginning of another blizzard, rather a soothing kind of day. It seemed fitting somehow that the day of the funeral it would snow again after all the issues of the previous week. She was glad Mackenzie and Steven were always nearby. It was helpful to have Mackenzie to talk and cry with given her own fragile state of emotions. Who would have thought? She certainly didn't expect her own flood of feelings. It didn't seem to matter what was said, Melanie found herself constantly fighting the overwhelming need to cry.

Phil and Kaitlyn had arrived the night before from Texas. It had been a happy reunion even if under unhappy circumstances. Melanie had been sure Kara would forget her with her tender age, but was relieved when her precious granddaughter reached out her arms to her the instant she came in sight.

Melanie looked at the clock. Tara and Brent would arrive in just over two hours. They would all travel together, albeit in separate vehicles to the Veteran's Cemetery, except Mackenzie and Stephen who would ride with Lee and Melanie. She needed to get up and get started. Lee, still sleeping, was undisturbed by Melanie's departure from the bedroom. She knew he would arise shortly by his own internal alarm clock.

Lee and Melanie traveled the miles in silence, but as they turned into the roadway leading to the cemetery, Melanie spoke softly. "A Veteran's Cemetery somehow always seems like an unfriendly, lonely place; don't you think, Lee?" Without allowing time for a response she continued. "I know this is where Dad wanted to be as a final resting place: among other veterans who had served their country." She paused. "I guess he's not really alone. He has friends here."

Melanie stiffened when she saw both her sisters had already arrived. She hadn't seen either in years and had only minimal conversations on the telephone.

Patti, her older sister, had married rich and moved to Chicago. Once in Chicago, Patti made it plain she wanted separation from her sisters. Her lifestyle was incompatible with theirs. Patti lost her husband to cancer four years before and had met someone new whom Melanie was yet to meet.

Wendy, her younger sister had moved to Sioux Falls and lived with their father for many years after her marriage failed. Before he became ill, however, there were cross words spoken between them and they went their separate ways, although they stayed in the same town. Due to proximity it was she, however, who came to his rescue when he became ill. She saw to his needs in the hospital, and his wishes which followed his death. It was also she who approached the urn with their father's ashes and picked it up. In an instant Wendy violently shook the ashes.

"What are you doing?" asked Melanie mortified.

"Well," she said laughing, "I don't know just where his bottom is so I couldn't kick his 'kiester' so I figured I just give him a good shake!"

"Why?"

"I figure he deserves it. He got aggravated with me and sent me on my way when I was just trying to help him and then he up and died. What was he thinking? I never did get to make things right with him."

"I understand what you're saying, but shaking him? Somehow that seems irreverent."

"I can't help that," said Wendy with a laugh. "I needed to do it!"

"I declare after he and Mom split up things really went weird, didn't they?" said Melanie, more to herself than her sister. "I know Mom and Dad had issues all the while they were married, but both of their lives were just bizarre after their divorce. Mom remarrying a couple times and Dad and his significant others. It's sad really. I hope they both found what they were searching for before they passed away."

"I can't believe Mom has been gone for nearly two years now."

"I know. But Dad found a church he was comfortable with and stopped the searching you were talking about. That was good. I just wish he and I hadn't had words before I left."

"Well, I know you can't say anything to him now and have the same effect it would have if he was still living, but I hope in your heart you find peace."

"Hi, Patti. How have you been?" asked Melanie as her older sister approached. She was always amazed at their differences. Patti was much larger than Melanie. She had a distinguished look, probably from all those years in the city, Melanie decided. As children, they had been close, just over a year apart. Even as far back as their early high school years, many friends and the occasional teacher had asked if they were twins. It wasn't that they looked at all alike, although they were similar enough to tell they were related to each other. But they seemed inseparable.

Then came tenth grade and everything seemed to change. Melanie was outgoing and energetic, while Patti seemed to withdraw into herself and often felt left out when it came to making and even keeping friends. They eventually went different directions to the point of hardly speaking to each other to where they were today, nearly strangers.

"I'm fine, thank you," Patti replied. "I'd like you to meet Glendon Franklin."

"Hi, I'm Melanie. How are you?" she said extending her hand while making quick observations. He was over six foot, bald, wearing an expensive suit and shoes, with a pleasant smile and soft blue eyes. "Guess our weather here is a lot different than you deal with in Chicago."

"I'm fine thank you. It's nice to finally meet you. Patti has shared a good deal about you." Melanie shot Patti a look. "And yes, your weather is different than in Chicago, but sometimes different is nice."

Melanie found herself liking him, in spite of herself.

"I'm Wendy. Guess Patti and Melanie forgot I was here. I'm their younger sister," she added lightly while extending her hand.

"It's nice to meet you." Glendon said sincerely. "I've heard plenty about you, as well."

"That could be interesting, and I'd love to know what all you know, but for now we need to see to the funeral-memorial service for Dad. Here comes the director."

In the moments that passed, Melanie found her thoughts racing between her childhood memories of her father and her sisters. She longed for a relationship with them, but she knew it wasn't likely. Patti and Glendon would leave later this afternoon and fly back to Chicago and Wendy was leaving in the morning for her return trip to Sioux Falls. Why do families do this she wondered? All we have are each other, yet it seemed impossible to even consider a real relationship with either of her sisters since they live so far apart and their differences seem larger by the moment.

She was relieved when the service ended. They walked in silence out to the "Wall" where her father's remains would be placed. The grounds were still covered in two feet of snow from the recent blizzards. Paths were dug so they would know where to walk. The air was brisk and cold. She caught her breath in an abrupt gust of wind.

"This is odd," she thought; "not at all what I expected." There were rows and rows of metal boxes that reminded her of mailboxes in front of apartment complexes. "Wouldn't it be awful if this was really a mailbox," Melanie thought? "Where did that come from, she berated herself? This is stupid. This is where Dad is going to be buried and where he will stay."

Melanie clung to Lee even tighter, equaling the tightness in her throat. She realized tears were falling down her cheeks, unbidden. "This isn't real, it can't be," she thought. Yet as she watched, the director placed the box holding her father's ashes inside the Wall. It is finished. Dad is gone.

The next class in Communications on Wednesday proved interesting to Melanie. Mrs. K began as soon as the door was closed. "First impressions are important especially when you have the need to present yourself in another situation particularly in a business setting. People respond to how you project yourself. We're going to determine what other people see in you after only a couple of meetings. You will go around the class and write two things you consider probable about that person. In about ten minutes you will each share some of your thoughts regarding your peers in this classroom. The person receiving the thoughts will tell the class if this assumption is correct."

Melanie was terrified at what the much younger class would think of her. "I think Melanie probably makes good cookies," one student said, to which Melanie said, "My kids think so!"

Another, "I see Melanie as competitive."

"Only sometimes," said Melanie. "Mostly I like to do well, but not at the expense of others," she said candidly.

One other comment really surprised Melanie. "I think you were a prom queen in high school," one young man said.

"You're kidding," said Melanie blushing. "Hardly. I didn't even go to the prom. But thanks. What a nice thing to say."

Gratefully, Melanie found the comments of the class reassuring in who she was. There were times when doubt crept in, stealing the joy of being the wife, mother and student she had become. With observations such as these, she felt she just might have what it takes to finish her dream of graduation successfully.

Ms. K was serious about presentations and Melanie found herself continually preparing for another speech in front of the class. There were conversation starters, interview presentations, group and informative presentations, persuasive and video presentations, all of which took Melanie out of her comfort zone.

The group presentation was the most difficult for Melanie, just as she found in her The Freshman Seminar class the first semester. Working within the parameters of a group dynamics was in Melanie's mind, frustrating and suffocating!

The group had chosen an informative presentation on show horses. While she knew a little about the large, beautiful animals and knew she would do thorough research, she was terrified at the thought of the question session at the end of each presentation.

Dana, who was serious and quiet, covered grooming, showmanship and competitor wear. Melanie was delighted with her thorough and responsible attitude.

Tiffany who researched rules of the horse show and exhibitor information tried Melanie's nerves with her outspoken criticism of the members of the group and her need to be leader even when her views were quite different than the others.

Melanie appreciated Jake whose personality most resembled her own. He was friendly and focused, action oriented but different from Melanie since he was a risk taker and preferred a fast passed lifestyle. Jake explored Sport horse disciplines of sporting events including dressage, show jumping and combined driving, conformation, movement and temperament; while Melanie, examined the different horse breeds including stock, action, Arabian, draft and gaited.

Nervous as she was, Melanie forged ahead when it was her turn at the podium for her share of the presentation. Sharing the information regarding gaited tendencies of each of the breeds and the difference between the trot and an amble and which horse would be more likely to gait, cantor or amble, trot or do more than one, seemingly interested her audience. Finally finished, since she spoke last she said, "You have been an excellent and fun audience. I hope everyone enjoyed listening to this presentation as much as we enjoyed doing the research. Thank you."

"Good job," said Mrs. K. "Any questions?"

No one responded to the question so Mrs. K looked at the group and said, "I was a little confused on the whole idea of the gait of a horse. Could you explain it a little bit more?"

Melanie took a deep breath, trying to draw the information from her mind to give a clear answer to the question. Without warning, Trent, a tall, lanky blond haired young man, raised his hand from four rows back.

"Trent, you have a question?" asked Mrs. K.

"No, but Melanie said it right. The gaited horses have natural gaited predispositions which means they have the ability to perform four main gaits which are to walk, trot, canter and gallop. All combined are called ambling gaits."

"Thank you, Trent," said Mrs. K grinning. "Good job."

"No one has any more questions for the group?"

After class Melanie found Trent before he left the room. "Trent!" she called.

Turning, he said, "Hey! What's up?"

"Thanks for rescuing me," she said. "I really think I did mess that up when I gave the presentation and I think I even had me confused as to just what it was I was trying to say."

"No problem!" he said. "It's something I know. We have a horse farm. I knew what you meant even if you didn't say it right!"

"Cool! And again" pausing to take a deep breath, she repeated, "thank you! I think you just saved my grade!"

Chapter 8

Another math class. Melanie felt herself tense even as she entered the room. She was only the second student to arrive and as usual, took a seat in the front near the center of the room. She wanted full view of the blackboard although it looked like this professor was going to use the overhead projector, instead. That seems to be the more favorable way of teaching now, she thought to herself. It just made sense. The instructor didn't need to move around much and could use different color dry erase pens for emphasis. Melanie was grateful for the extra colors since emphasis was really needed in this subject. How she wished she had taken more Math in high school.

Drifting back thirty years she remembered the friendly face of Mr. Taylor, who passed away, she learned about five years ago. He enjoyed his students and encouraged each of them to do their best without a lot of pressure. Smiling she remembered what he'd written in her yearbook at the end of her Freshman year. "Let this red ink be reminiscent of the mistakes you caught me in!" She had re-read that note many times and smiled when she pictured in her mind his patience of her finishing a test before grading any others. He would grade hers first and if any answers were different from his own, he would re-work the problem. On several occasions it was he who was wrong. He had consistently urged her to continue in the math field, certain she had the ability to advance in this subject. She had remained adamant that she really wasn't interested in math and remained in the "business track" as it was known back then.

Her reverie was broken when a small, well dressed, sickly woman walked into the room. It seemed odd to see this little, middle aged woman looking frail and frazzled being her instructor for the next semester in a class that she dreaded. There was nothing about her that reminded her of Mr. Taylor.

The little woman with every hair in place and fierce eyes contrasting the paleness of her face smiled weakly and took her place behind the desk. As she sat on the stool near the overhead projector she reached over and flicked on the switch. The bright light shone up on the screen already in place in front of the chalk board. "I am Ms. Reston," she said softly. "You signed up for this class; therefore I will believe you want to be here. You need to pass my class to move up to a credit math class. Understand, if you are taking this 032 Math, it will not net you a credit. However, you can with effort, progress successfully and move on.

"That being said," my expectations are that every person arrive on time and give one hundred percent in class. This is the best way we learn. Do your homework, which you will have every night and bring your questions with you to class. I am very willing to help those who are willing to help themselves.

"My method of teaching includes using the overhead projector which you see here. Let's begin with a refresher on what you should already know." With that she began placing figures and equations on the board and Melanie began writing. "I'm going to be alright in here," she thought confidently. "I think I like her!"

The days passed and Melanie found herself frustrated time and again. It seemed no matter how hard she tried the equations she needed to know were just beyond her memory and grasp. Determined, she did her homework and fought the tears that threatened time and again to overwhelm her.

Concentrating, Melanie jumped when the phone rang. She wiped the wet from her face and reached for the phone.

"Hey Mom. How are ya?"

"Awful, just awful," Melanie said beginning to cry again. "I've got a test tomorrow in Math and I just don't get it. I have done and redone the problems, and they just aren't coming out right."

"Calm down," said Kaitlyn, like she had said a hundred times before. "Get your Math book and let's figure out what you're doing wrong." The next hour was spent working and re-working the problems until Melanie felt like she had a handle on the newest concepts of the class: Algebra and Absolute Value.

"You are actually dealing with a two step problem," Kaitlyn, explained. "After you isolate expression within the absolute value brackets, you must also solve the equation outside the brackets. What is your first problem?"

$|x + 2| = 6$. Solve for x.

"Okay, since x + 2 has the absolute value brackets around it, for the expression to equal 6, the expression x + 2 when outside of the absolute value brackets can equal either +6 or −6. So you're actually dealing with two equations:

$$x + 2 = 6$$
$$x + 2 = -6$$

To solve the problem, you need to solve both of them. First, solve for x in the equation $x + 2 = 6$. In this case, $x = 4$. Then, solve for x in the equation $x + 2 = -6$. In this case, $x = -8$ So the solutions to the equation $|x + 2| = 6$ are $x = \{-8, 4\}$.

Finally Melanie said, "I'm done. I think I have it. I'll go over these again before the test. I can't believe how hard this is for me. Math wasn't this difficult in high school."

"Mom, this math is different. Algebra concepts can be tricky. You didn't have it when you were young and face it, you're not a math person. You prefer the

English side of things! Now, let me tell you what Kara did today!" said Kaitlyn to change the subject.

"I wish you guys still lived here."

"Me too, but it's not the case. Phil is getting more and more involved with the school and he likes what he's doing. I don't see us coming back any time soon."

The next day Melanie walked into Math class with a worried knot in the bottom of her stomach. Hard as she tried she couldn't shake the fear of taking this test. Turning her paper over after having been given directions she began. "I've got this," she thought. When she reached page four she began having doubts. "I can't remember how to do this," she thought getting more and more irritated erasing the problem again. For a fifth time she redid the problem and for the fifth time, she got another answer. She moved on to the next question but the one before her kept interfering with her focus. Finally finishing, she realized she was the only student left and Ms. Reston was waiting. In frustration she walked up to her desk and turned in her paper. "I'm sorry I took so long," she said.

"It's not a problem," Ms. Reston said kindly.

Feeling like the world sat on her shoulders, Melanie walked out the door.

On the way to work at the Financial Aid Office, Melanie saw Martin, a small, wiry boy from her Math class. "I didn't see you in class today," she said off handedly. "You missed our test."

"That's cause I wasn't there," he said. "I told Ms. Reston I had a doctor's appointment and had to be excused."

"Did you?" she asked, not quite sure how to respond.

"No," he laughed nervously. "I wasn't ready for that test and didn't feel like being in class."

"You lied to her?" she asked incredulously, not believing what she was hearing.

"Yeah! Why not?"

"That's horrible," she scolded, her eyes furrowing. "You should be ashamed of yourself. That's downright rude and wrong," she continued.

"It's nobody's business but mine," he retorted.

"Well, I know and I don't have to like it," she quipped, walking away.

Melanie was working on homework when the telephone rang. "Mel, this is Judy. Kent isn't here and I really need Lee's help. I've tried calling Brooke and Kerry and they're not home."

"What's wrong?"

"Flo is standing on her porch in her nightgown screaming at someone she thinks she sees in the woods. She's been at it for an hour. I've tried talking to her, but whenever I go out there she just waves her cane at me and tells me I don't belong there. And then she asks me if I see them. She says there are people in the trees and can't understand when I tell her there is no one there."

"Oh, dear. I'll get Lee. We'll be there as soon as we can."

"Mom," said Lee, after they arrived.

"What are you doing here?" she asked angrily. "Tell those people to leave."

"Mom, there are no people. It's just Melanie and me."

"There's people in those trees. Can't you see them? There's three of them."

"It's shadows, Mom. There's no one there. Let's go inside and get you settled."

"I don't want to go inside."

"I know, but let's go see what's on TV and maybe get you a snack."

"What about those people in the trees?"

"I'll tell you what. Let's go in and I will take care of the people in the trees."

"Well, you better. I don't like them up there watching me."

"I will, now come on," he urged taking her arm and leading her back into the house.

"Wow," said Melanie, after they finally exited the house. "That's awful. She is getting worse by the week!"

"I know and I don't like it at all, but I don't know what we're going to do. I still don't want a nursing home. I wish she would agree to have someone come stay with her."

"Well, we both know that's not going to happen. All we can do is run interference as long as we can, and hope we're doing the right thing."

Melanie woke as tired as when she went to bed the night before. It seemed forever since she had gotten a good night's sleep. Between the stress of helping take care of Flo, classes, Lee who seemed to not be feeling well lately, as well as, the issues between Kent and Judy and the threat of their moving along with the possibility of she and Lee purchasing the property owned by his mother, brother and sister-in-law and the lack of solid sleeping, she was beginning to feel drug out.

She considered all that would be involved in the purchase of the property. She hated the thought of Kent and Judy leaving. Ten year old Caroline, the only child of Kent and Judy, was selfish and spoiled to the point of being unbearable and while they didn't have the best sister to sister relationship, Judy, quite the contrast of

Caroline, always seemed pleasant. Judy and Kent seemed suited to each other on one hand, but on another completely mismatched.

Judy a creative and complex, olive skinned buxom woman, came from a well to do family and liked nice things. She often wore her blonde hair high atop her head and had a gift for decorating. While she didn't do it for a living, her home always looked like it came right out of a home catalogue. Every room had a unique style in modern Victorian ornamentation. She kept the look modern and fresh by using lighter colors which enhanced the crown molding and chair railing throughout the house. The long delicate curtains added a romantic flair to each room without being too feminine.

Kent, a rugged, handsome man, on the other hand grew up on the farm, working hard. He decided not to go to college but instead went to a trade school and became an electrician. He enjoyed his work and was delighted when he was offered the opportunity to be head electrician for the company in Minneapolis, Minnesota. His work kept him busy as he tried to keep up with the lifestyle Judy expected, and accepted all the over time they would allow.

Judy was horribly unhappy with the possibility of a move. Her family lived in Brockett Springs where Cedar Ridge Community College was located. Her grandparents were some of the original investors of the college when it was first built. Her father had been a prominent medical doctor in the community before he retired and her mother was involved in all the social political circles. Her siblings lived in nearby towns along with a long list of nieces and nephews. The very mention of leaving left her in tears.

The night Kent knocked on the door of Melanie and Lee's home, they were just finishing dinner. "Come on in Kent," Lee said. "We have some food left over. Would you like to join us?"

"Oh, no. I do need to talk with you though."

"Where's Judy?"

"She didn't want to come and I understand why, but I have to press this.

"Minnesota Electric has asked me if I'd be interested in becoming head electrician in Minneapolis. It would be a nice pay raise."

"We heard that."

"Well, I have accepted the position, but it means selling the house and moving. Judy does not want to go and has been really upset about the whole thing. Because Mom has life time living rights in her home, we can't sell to outsiders. It has to be in the family. I know we've talked about it before and I'm absolutely certain I need to do this.

"I hate the thought of leaving Mom and I feel like I'm leaving at the worst time. I know Mom's Alzheimer's is getting worse. That is hard on everyone and I know this move is making Judy angry and she's fearful. She's leaving her family too. But we're only about six to seven hours away.

On the other hand, Caroline is happy about moving. Judy and she are going to stay at Judy's parents until school is finished for the year. There's only about six weeks left before summer starts. For her, it's an adventure. Mom makes her crazy. But what does she know? She's only a kid. But if I don't go now, I never will.

"All that being said, would you and Melanie be willing to buy the place?"

"Kent, I hate the thought of you leaving. I'm not sure Mom is going to understand you not being here. She absolutely cherishes you. Having you live next to her has been the highlight of her old age. I know right now you'd never know it when you consider her illness, but if you two really go through with this, it's going to be really hard on her," Melanie offered.

"I know that, but like I said, I really need to do this."

"Let us talk about it," said Lee, "and we'll get back to you in a few days."

"Okay, that'll work. That's all I can ask. Honestly, if you don't buy the place, we'll still leave. It will just leave Mom alone there. It'll be hard with two mortgages. I've already put a down payment on a house there."

"I don't know if I want another mortgage," Melanie said when she and Lee discussed it later. "I love Kent and Judy's house but what on earth would we do with it? We live here. I can't imagine leaving the house we built together and raised the kids in. That just doesn't compute in my brain or heart!"

"I know. I feel the same way," Lee said, "but I don't want to leave Mom with no one to look after her. If they are really leaving, then I feel like it's my responsibility to look after her. It would be a lot, but we could handle it. It would mean a change in our spending for a while. But," he paused. "We could do it.

"I guess we could let Mackenzie and Steven live there. I'm sure they would love having their own place. It's been a little crowded here, since we've all lived together. But once they start having children, we are going to run out of room.

"Besides, Mackenzie seems to have a special relationship with Mom. She seems to be able to talk with her even when she doesn't make sense."

"That would be an option," Melanie agreed. "Does that mean you really want to buy it?"

"Let's go to the bank and see what we can find out. And we should talk with Mackenzie and Steven and get their feel for the whole idea."

She looked at the dark circles forming under her eyes. Adding a little more make up around her eyes, she picked up her books and headed to class.

The return trip to Math class proved no less stressful than the last few days. Melanie, nerves taunt over the grade she was afraid of receiving walked into the classroom. Ms. Reston was nowhere to be seen. While the class waited the students discussed the test and no one seemed comfortable with what the results would be. Finally a tall, middle aged, dark haired man came into the room. He was dressed casually but neat. "I'm Mr. Davis, and today I'm standing in for Ms. Reston because she is ill. Before you ask, I do not have the results of the test you took last class. We are going to begin the next chapter and see how far we get."

Melanie liked the substitute. Ms. Reston's style was steady, while Mr. Davis's seemed slow and steady. She left the classroom feeling like she had a handle on the material. Melanie couldn't have known, however, that this first absenteeism was only the beginning of a seemingly stream of absentees for this math class. It did prove to be helpful in a manner in which she didn't expect however.

One day as she entered the classroom after Ms. Reston had been absent several days in a row due to her own illness and then her mother taking ill and being in the hospital. She was surprised that only about five students of the twenty-five were present. "Take out a blank sheet of paper," Ms. Reston said. "We are going to have a quiz."

Panic swept through Melanie. First she's been absent and now we're going to have a quiz?

"Write these problems on your paper," she said matter of factly as she began writing on the over head projector. 36/6; 21*5; 105+918; 1986-52; and 99/3. "You will have five minutes to complete the quiz."

Moments later she said, "Hand your papers forward, please." Melanie could hardly believe what had just happened, and discovered as the semester continued, on those days when only a few students would come to class, she could count on a 100% for a pop quiz grade.

"I haven't had the time to grade your papers yet," said Ms. Reston after she collected the papers. "I will get to them as soon as I can." Reaching down she picked up a blank sheet of paper and placed it on the overhead projector.

As the days passed, Melanie struggled with the different concepts. "Melanie, are you okay?" asked Ms. Reston one day as the class was leaving the room. "You didn't do as well on the test, as I expected, although you are clearly passing."

"I'm not doing all right," she said clearly agitated, while fighting the overwhelming desire to sit down and cry. "I am frustrated and wish I could get the Math. I feel so stupid most of the time."

"First of all, you are not stupid. Some of this just takes time. You will get it. Just keep plugging at it. You are doing fine. And believe it or not, your expressions let me know when you aren't getting the material. And that is not only helpful for me, but also your classmates. You are not the only one who is struggling. Almost everyone in here has some difficulty so when you react I know you are not likely the only one not getting the material and it's time for me to go over it again."

"Thank you, but most of the time I really do feel stupid. As for my expressions, that is not deliberate, I just respond to what I am hearing."

"Remember, this is a non-credit course. You do not have to get an A in here. You need to pass, that is all."

"Mrs. Bartlett told me the same thing last semester."

"She's a smart lady. If you want extra help, you can go to the Library. They have tutors in there that would certainly be willing to work with you."

"Thank you, I'd like that, but right now I just don't have the extra time. But that being said, if I get too frustrated, I might. For now I am relying heavily on my daughters who do really well in Math."

"However you choose to do it is fine. Just don't let this class get the best of you. You really are doing fine."

"I appreciate the pep talk. It's been a tough last few weeks. Between classes, my mother-in-law who has Alzheimer's, my brother-in-law and sister-in-law moving and we're buying their place, I feel a bit overwhelmed. We go to settlement at the end of the month."

"I wish you well. Just remember, when it comes to lawyers and those kinds of things, it usually doesn't happen in the time frame you expect."

"Thank you, I'll try to keep that in mind."

The next weeks were trying for everyone involved. Judy had begun packing. With each item she placed in a box, she would shed more tears. Papers were signed in the time frame designated while Flo was clearly confused about all the busy-ness around her.

Finally moving day came. The large moving truck backed up to the expansive porch to accommodate the loading. Brooke and Kerry came over to help in whatever way they could and Lee and Melanie were also nearby in case Judy or Kent needed them. Flo kept walking around the truck with hands on her hips barking orders on which box should be loaded first and then fussed when her instructions were not carried out.

"That's it," said Kent. "We're all loaded."

"I don't understand," said Melanie. "You left furniture in the house and what about all the stuff in the basement?"

"Well, mostly it's just stuff and we decided that whatever is left in the house is yours to do with whatever you choose."

"Judy, all your decorating stuff. Are you sure you want to leave all this?"

"It's fine," she said, swallowing a lump in her throat. "Use it or give it away. I don't care. I'll replace it. That's easier than packing it and trying to figure out what to do with it in the meantime. The house we're moving into isn't as big as this one. We'll eventually build onto it and then I'll work on getting the things I need for decorating."

"Be careful traveling," said Melanie after hugs were given.

"We're not going to be that far away," said Kent as he readied to drive away from the house. "We'll be back to visit before you know it!"

Chapter 9

The day was cold with a bitter wind. Melanie was glad for the refuge of the Humanities building where she would attend her English class. This was a favorite subject for her, even though the thought of grammar itself, could cause a slight shudder. She remembered sentence formation and strategies in elementary grade school, but since that time, writing had become second nature and she dreaded the thought of being asked to break down sentence diagramming. She could easily identify the subject of a sentence, the verb or the adjective, pronoun and prepositional phrase, but past that it became confusing. She'd heard and probably even learned about direct objects, participles, adverbs or interjections but she hoped the class requirements wouldn't include being able to label a sentence correctly with its English construction piece.

The room seemed friendly enough, upon entering. A few of the students she even recognized from other classes, even though she wasn't sure of names. Mrs. Jansen, sitting behind her desk, organizing papers and perusing the new attendance sheet was a pretty lady, in her mid fifties, well dressed in navy dress pants with a light blue blouse and vest which matched the dress pants. She wore cropped, shoulder length, dark brown hair and bangs that nearly reached her soft green eyes. Her smile showed off her perfectly formed white teeth.

Melanie was pleased to see the first seat of the third row was still available and quickly took her seat. Perfect, she thought! I'll be able to see!

Silence filled the room for another five minutes as students continued to come in, filling all but two seats in the entire room. "Good morning, class," Mrs. Jansen began. "This is English 101 and for those of you who do not know, in this class there is much writing; so be prepared. You will be demonstrating the writing process by using prewriting, drafting and revising strategies, including analytical essays, and writing a research paper among other writings. Additionally you will be learning about the evolution of the English language.

"That being said, you should immediately begin thinking about what your research paper will be about. Once you choose your topic, it will need to be approved. But I encourage you to have fun with it. Work with a subject that interests you. This will make the research easier, because you will not become bored with your subject.

"You will be turning in all note cards and a very specific bibliography. Be careful of plagiarism. If you choose to plagiarize, you will not only find yourself getting a zero for the class, but the potential to be expelled from the college."

"Wow, that tough," thought Melanie. "What on earth am I going to write about?"

As the days passed, Melanie found she completely enjoyed her English class. She learned about Mrs. Jansen's daughters who lived in Tennessee on houseboats. One morning, without preamble she offered, "My daughter, Lindsay called last evening and shared they are using a generator for electric on their houseboat! How bizarre is that?" She laughed and said, "I have the funniest daughters.

"They both live down on the Tennessee River near each other and like to live next to nature. Did you know there are 10,000 miles of navigable rivers there, and they never even have to take their boat out of the water? When they first moved out there, Lindsay, the youngest and most extroverted was the only one married. Dana went with her and she's married now too and even has a little one. They travel back and forth along the 650 miles of river, dock at a marina when they need to and buy only the items they need because there isn't a lot of room on the boat. They have telephone and internet access when they need it.

"It amazes me and I'm just never sure how to respond to any of it. Who would of thought?" No one in the room commented or asked a question regarding the comments and after just a brief pause, she said, "Okay class, let's get started. I need to begin checking research paper topics and I need to know what word you will be using for the English evolution project."

"I would like the word 'pandemonium' Mrs. Jansen," said Melanie.

"Okay, that one will be fine. I'm looking forward to your presentation."

"Do you know what your research topic will be?"

"Yes! I would like to do Home Schooling."

"That would be a topic no one has done before. Are you sure you can find enough material to adequately support the subject subjectively?"

"Yes, I have plenty of material. When my husband and I decided to home school we did a lot of research. I have lots to pull from."

"Very well, then. I'm looking forward to your paper."

Melanie answered the ringing phone. "Good afternoon."

"Mrs. Carson?"

"Speaking.

"This is Dr. Hayes office calling from Elk Creek. Dr. Hayes would like you to come into his office this afternoon."

"Is something wrong?"

"Well, I can't really discuss that with you. I just need you to come in."

"Okay. I'll be there as soon as I can."

Shaking, Melanie dialed Lee's number knowing she was going to need his support. "Dr. Hayes asked me to come into his office today and the nurse wouldn't tell me why. Can you come with me?"

"Sure. Give me a few minutes to get things straight here and I'll be right home."

Melanie walked into his office and signed in. "The doctor will be with you in just a few minutes, Mrs. Carson."

"Thank you."

"Melanie," began Dr. Hayes, "I sent the tissues from the spot on the back of your leg to our research center and to my surprise it came back cancerous. It's amazing that it has been there for as long as you describe and it never spread. It was like all the cancer cells were caught in a sealed envelope and were never allowed to go any further. You were very lucky. It could have been ugly."

"How long did you tell me it was there?"

"I haven't a clue. It's always been there!"

"Like I said, you were lucky."

"I was blessed. But why did you call me in then?"

"Because I didn't get all the cancer when I removed the spot. I honestly didn't expect it to be cancer. There is still tissue around the area that needs to be removed, and promptly."

"How promptly?" Lee asked cautiously, reaching for Melanie's hand.

"I'd like to have it taken care of within the next two weeks."

"Will they get it all this time?"

"Oh I'm sure they will. The doctor is a specialist in this area and you shouldn't have any more issues except that you will need to keep a close eye on any other spots that you see."

"Okay," said Melanie calmly.

For as calm as Melanie was, her daughters fell apart. Kaitlyn could not be consoled and Mackenzie mirrored her sister's fear. "I'm fine," she assured them. "Relax. God didn't let it get any worse than it is after all these years. It'll be fine."

"But, Mom, it's cancer!" the girls wailed.

"Would you stop! I am fine. You are both getting yourself into a state before you have to. I'm going to have the surgery and it'll just be gone. So stop crying and worrying like that!"

After only a week of finding the cancer, it was removed. Two weeks later the doctor's office called and said she was cancer free. Relieved, Melanie relaxed on the sofa as she and Gavin chatted. "I'm glad it all went so well," she commented.

"As long as nothing goes wrong, now."

"Gavin!"

"Well, they didn't get it the first time," he countered.

"They didn't know it was cancer!"

"I know. I guess I'm not much different than the girls. I just want everything to be all right."

"I am fine," she assured him.

The phone rang. "I'll get it."

"Here, mom, it's Adam."

"Melanie, are you doing okay?

"Fine thanks. I got the call from the doctor's office just today and they told me they got all the cancer. I'm good." With the ensuing silence Melanie finally asked,   "Adam, what's wrong?"

"You need to know Shelley has lung cancer and it's not good."

"How long does she have?"

"They are saying she might not make it to Lorrie's graduation.'

"You're kidding me. That can't be right. Shelley's fine. I was just talking with her and I know she's felt bad, but cancer?" How can this be? Melanie wondered without saying a word. "On the same day I find out I'm going to be just fine, my best friend finds out she's going to die." Melanie hung up the phone as tears streamed down her face.

"Shelley, how are you?" asked Melanie just a few evenings later when she had a chance to visit.

"I'm okay. It's been a tough day. It was my first chemo treatment."

"Oh, Shelley. I'm so sorry! Should I go?"

"No. Please stay."

"Why didn't you tell me?"

"I couldn't. I was in denial. But I can't anymore."

"Are you okay talking about it?"

"I'm okay. It was just hard and long day! I was at the hospital for seven hours. Most of my time was spent sitting and waiting. They gave me eight kinds of different drugs. I didn't have any horrible reactions yet from the meds, but I expect eventually I will lose my hair and that thought really scares me.

"I was drowsy when I left, but I feel better now, but I'm told that won't last. In fact he told me I'd actually feel better for a few days before the treatment really would kick my tail and make me feel bad.

"They tell me that chemo affects everyone different, but if it means I can hold on for a while longer, then I'll deal. I'm told, though, that I probably won't be around," Shelley choked back a sob, "for Lorrie's graduation."

Melanie felt hot tears wetting her own cheeks. Putting her arm around her friend, she held her until she could continue.

"Thanks for helping me through this. Adam has been great. Lorrie is scared to death and can't talk about it at all. She just cries. I'm grateful for the concern, love and humor that has gotten me through all this, this far. I know there is more yucky stuff to come."

"You have to know that there are lots of prayers being lifted up, too. You are on a good many prayer lists across the country."

"I'm not sure I want to bring God into this," said Shelley, solemnly. "I have a real hard time praying at all right now. It doesn't seem fair."

"Oh, I agree, it's not fair. But God is in control. I know bad things happen to good people," replied Melanie, while tears continued to fall. "My faith in God is the only way I can cope with what you are going through. All I can do is keep praying that He will heal you and if that is not his will, then that the chemo will get the cancer. I'm not ready to give you up yet. You are my dearest friend."

"Let's change the subject. If we keep talking about this, I'll never stop crying! Tell me about your classes."

"It's been interesting," she began. "I completely enjoy English, but it has been challenging!

"I had to go to the library where the English class was meeting to do research for the word evolution project today. I was searching the pages of the Old English Dictionary and recoiled at the word I chose!"

"What word did you choose?"

Pandemonium. As a noun it means "the abode of all demons; hell, the infernal regions." Specifically: a place represented by Milton in _Paradise Lost_ as the capital of hell, containing the council chamber of Evil Spirits."

"As I was sitting there staring at it, all I could say is, 'I don't like my word! That's horrible! That's not how I pictured that word at all!'

"Mrs. Jansen came by and said remember, the project is to learn the evolution of words. It's part of learning about the English language which we will get into after presentations."

"I told her I still don't like the word, and that it's going to be an interesting project!

"Mrs. Jansen laughed and said, I'm sure it will!"

When the day arrived for Melanie's presentation on her word, she began with her feelings about the word. "I discovered as I did my research that this is an awful word! Well," she clarified, "It started out as an awful word. It was created by Milton in 1667 for his story _Paradise Lost_. It is the center of wickedness, evil and utter confusion. It was used even as late as 1993 in the New York Times Magazine as demonically possessed."

After she finished with the particulars about the word, she presented photos on a large poster board. She said, "That was Milton's pandemonium, this is mine! Christmas at the Carson home when all five of my children are home and the grand babies are there! Gifts are opened and paper strung all around with everyone talking at once. It is chaos, but it's a good kind of chaos and not demonic or wicked at all. I like my version much better than Milton's," she concluded laughing.

Surprised, she blushed as the class applauded. Collecting her things she made her way to her seat. "Well done," said Mrs. Jansen. "You gave a really interesting presentation. Thank you."

The next week proved to be more stressful than Melanie expected. She arrived in English class and learned that Mrs. Jansen would not be in the classroom for the next two weeks. She had just learned her best friend, Violet, who lived in Illinois, had suffered a heart attack and died while driving with her young teenage daughter in the car. Mrs. Jansen had gone to Illinois for both the funeral and to accept guardianship of Eden.

On the same day this news arrived, Mrs. Sullivan who worked in the business office right next to the financial aid office, passed away suddenly. Cedar Ridge staff was stunned. It seemed inconceivable that someone as young, who had no apparent illness could just die, yet it happened. The week was spent with sad, soft conversations and the occasional teary eye, even for students who had come to know her.

Melanie and Lee made another visit to Shelley and Adam's. The chemo had taken her hair as Shelly had feared and she found herself more and more fatigued. The medication gave blessed relief to the pain. She was awake and alert when Melanie and Lee arrived, but dozed several times during the visit. On one such occasion, she woke and pointed at Lee. "He's the one who messed up my life," she said accusingly. "I'll give you a dollar to put him in jail!" she said mockingly before drifting back to sleep.

Adam laughed good naturedly while Lee sat stunned. "What was that all about?" he asked.

"I have no clue! She must have had something on her mind and you were handy," Adam said.

"Well considering the way you and she have always sparred," Melanie said laugh, "I'm not at all surprised she said that! Looks like she gets the last word in after all!"

Days later Shelley sent Melanie an email. "I declare they are "frying my brain" with all
the radiation. They are trying to reduce the swelling. I can't seem to think clearly any more. I just had another test on an expensive high-tech medical machine when

the fire alarm went off. It scared me silly but the nurse told me "No need to be concerned." My heart rate must have gone absolutely crazy!"

It was mid-February and Luke was coming home from his latest assignment: Saudi Arabia in early March and it was time to get started on preparations. There was going to be a Christmas celebration at the Carson home. Luke would only be home two weeks and the family intended to make the most of it. Kaitlyn, Phil and Kara along with the newest member of their family, three month old Jackson would be coming up from Texas, Tara and Brent, Ariana, Dylan and Ethan would be over and with Mackenzie and Steven and Gavin all in attendance, Melanie could barely contain her excitement. There were cookies to be baked, gifts to be wrapped, decorations to be found and a tree to be decorated.

"I want the tree up by the time your dad and Luke get home," said Melanie.

"Got it covered, Mom," said Gavin. "It's up and as soon as Mackenzie and Steven get here, we'll get it decorated. I put up the lights on the porch like you asked."

"I can't wait till the turkey is done. Why don't we fix turkey besides Christmas and Thanksgiving, anyway?"

"I don't know. I guess just tradition."

"Can we open presents first?" asked six year old Ariana as soon as they walked in the door.

"Ariana!" scolded Tara.

"Please?" chimed in Dylan wrapping his arms around Melanie's legs.

"I don't see why not," said Melanie, returning her grandson's hug, while speaking to Tara and the other adults in the room. "Dinner won't be ready for a couple hours. We can do presents first and then there will be plenty of visiting time. Kerry and Brooke along with Travis, Trista and Troy are supposed to be here later. I hope they'll stay for dessert."

"Dad and Uncle Luke are here!" called Ariana from the kitchen. "Ohhhh! I can't wait!"

"You are not the only one," Melanie said hugging the child who looked so much like her mother.

As Luke walked into the house he was surrounded by family who had missed him and each wanted to welcome him with hugs and heartfelt affection. Melanie looked at her son. He was the reflection of his father both in looks and personality. The picture of Lee at age twenty hanging proudly on the hallway wall, when he went into the Marine Corps all those years ago, could have been the image of Luke.

Melanie was always surprised to see how very much alike the two men really were. Both were independent, strong willed and exceedingly masculine. While both were quick to help a person in need, neither was comfortable in large groups of people, especially in a party celebration. Both felt the Marine Corps defined who they were and who they would become.

"Uncle Luke, Gran said we could open presents first. Are you ready? We got you something really neat."

"Ariana," Tara cautioned.

"But Momma said I couldn't tell you," she finished sheepishly, causing everyone to laugh.

"Okay, everyone. To the living room. Let's get the important stuff for the little ones over with! Let's do gifts and then we'll do dinner and we adults can catch up!"

After dinner, Mackenzie said, "As long as everyone's here, Steven and I have an announcement to make. Steven and I are expecting!"

"What? That's fantastic," said Melanie.

"Well, it's about time!" said Kaitlyn.

"We've only been married a couple years!"

"Congratulations," said Luke. "That's good news. It'll be good to see another new baby when I get back."

Hugs and well wishes warmed the hearts of everyone there making the Christmas celebration even more special. Even the Christmas lights seem to celebrate the news with their blinking colors of red, yellow, blue, green and white.

Before the evening was finished the family sat around the Christmas tree and shared the Christmas story from Luke 2. As the family sang Silent Night and It Came Upon A Midnight Clear and other traditional carols, Melanie's heart warmed. This was her family and she cherished each one of them.

Monday morning Melanie waited for Luke to come back from his run. "I am so sorry I won't be here today," she said. "I have class, though and can't afford to miss it."

"Mom, it's fine. I'm going to help Dad with some yard work before we go down to the VFW for a while. I'm just glad I get to be home. You go on to school and I'll see you tonight."

"Well, okay. I love you," she said sighing, giving his arm a squeeze. "I'll see you tonight."

Mrs. Jansen's return to the classroom was welcomed by all students, especially Melanie who appreciated the kindness and sincerity of her professor. Looking at Melanie as if she was the only one in the room, yet seemingly addressing everyone, she said "It's been a rough couple weeks." Choking back the tears, she continued. "I don't know how much any of you know about my absence, but I lost my dearest friend in a car accident and I now have guardianship of a teenager. I will tell you I haven't had teenagers in my home for a lot of years. I never expected to have Eden come live with me. It should be an interesting next few years!"

Turning her gaze to the rest of the class she said, "I need to get caught up with research papers. I have read the rough drafts and while you are working on a writing assignment which I will give you in a moment, I will be calling each of you, one at a time to my desk to go over research papers."

Later in the day Melanie made her way to the Financial Aid office to work. She was quite comfortable in the office now and was surprised when Mrs. Jansen stopped by. "Melanie," she said, "have you ever thought about working in the writing center in the library? Many people can write well but have a difficult time talking to others well. You do both remarkably well!"

"Thank you," said Melanie, clearly surprised. "That's very kind of you. But no, I have not considered working there. That's an interesting option."

"Well, just so you know, I plan to give them your name and I expect they will be in touch with you."

"Thank you, I appreciate that."

As quickly as Mrs. Jansen came in, she exited.

"That was quite nice," said Debbie who had heard the entire conversation. "But I don't think Vicki is going to want you to think about leaving in here. You're doing a good job. Vicki has commented on that several times."

"Wow! That's pretty cool. I'll have to thank her!"

"I can't believe you have to leave already," said Melanie as Lee and Luke finished packing the car. "It's been a good two weeks, but it seems so short. Luke, be careful. I hate having you so far away from home."

"I'll be fine, Mom. I'm a Marine! We are well trained and I have some real good buddies that I work with. They cover my back and I cover theirs. In fact, do you know what I'm called by the rest of the squadron?" he said as they embraced.

"No clue. What?" she asked looking up at her son a full foot taller than she.

"Killer!"

"What?"

"Killer! They call me Killer cause I don't take any stuff from anybody!"

"Be careful," she said again as seriously as she could, shaking her head. "Just be careful!"

As hot tears dripped down her face she watched Lee drive out the driveway headed for the airport. She re-ran the past two weeks events through her memory not wanting to forget a single moment. The Christmas celebration was a colossal success and brought a few comments from neighbors and church family since it's unusual to see a home decorated with Christmas lights this time of year or to see a Christmas tree shining through the large living room window.

Melanie knew the ache in her heart would ease as the days passed and she again acclimated to the absence of her oldest son while waiting with anticipation for any short note she might receive to let her know he was doing fine and was safe. All she could do for now is cherish this time they had together.

Chapter 10

Melanie dreaded her next class. Science. She enjoyed General Science the only science requirement for graduation over thirty years ago in ninth grade. This was going to challenge her perhaps even more than Math.

The room was nearly full when she walked in. Rather than individual desks, there were large black laminate topped tables that allowed three people to sit on either side. Each table had its own sink and spigot. Melanie saw a spot in the center of the room and made her way around the other students and sat down. She didn't recognize anyone sitting near her. Finally she recognized Rani, a blonde haired beauty her own daughter had babysat many years ago.

Dr. Vasser walked up to the black board. His graying hair in slight disarray matched his weathered face. Dressed in a suit and tie he picked up the chalk and began writing math equations and scientific formulas on the board writing from right to left. Melanie picked up her own writing instrument and began writing, as well, trying to write every word Dr. Vasser was saying, especially since she immediately recognized she hadn't a clue what he was talking about.

While he continued writing and talking he suddenly stopped, looked at what he wrote, mumbled to himself and wiped what he'd written with the bottom of the sleeve of his jacket smearing the white chalk from the wrist to elbow. Then in another breath wrote the correct number he wanted before moving to the next problem. In just moments he had the entire black board covered with so many math problems and formulas Melanie was completely confused.

Melanie fought the urge to run from the room. She was suddenly warm and wiped the moisture from her forehead. Her heart raced as panic filled her. What was she doing here? Terrified she knew in an instant she would never be able to get through the math required for this class, even if she thought she could get a handle on the science. Fear was etched on her face.

To her surprise Dr. Vasser pointed at her and said, "You're not going to bail on me are you? You look like you want to run away!"

Embarrassed, she said, "I am terrified."

"You look it!"

But in that moment she also liked and respected this man who could read her so quickly with so many other students around her, and added, "I won't bail."

"Good! Talk to me after class."

"Okay," she said, not quite sure what to expect.

After class, Melanie quietly walked up to Dr. Vasser. "You wanted to see me?"

"Yes, Melanie. How much math have you had?"

"Well, I'm in 032 Math."

"I'll be honest with you. I don't usually allow students who haven't passed at least one credit math to stay in my class."

"Well, I'm not there. Does that mean you want me to leave?"

"I can't believe I'm saying this, but no I don't. It's going to mean a lot of work on your part, but if you're willing to work hard, I'd like you to stay in my class."

"Thank you. I'd like that. And I promise you, I am frightened but I will give it all I've got."

"I know you will. If you have questions, come see me. I'll be happy to help you."

"Thank you, thank you," she repeated, finally feeling a sense of calm.

"Where did you go?" asked Melanie, clearly concerned. "I woke up and you weren't there! I checked the house and I couldn't find you!"

"I couldn't sleep so I went for a ride," Lee stated simply.

"What's the deal? What's up? I don't understand."

"I think it's all these medications the doctor has put me on. Some to help me sleep, others to help me get going, some to ease pain, another for indigestion. The list is ridiculous. In fact, I've made a decision. I'm just going to take myself off some. All these meds together are just fighting each other. I'm done! I quit. Starting right now, I'm only going to take my blood pressure medicine and one pain medication, and the medicine for the Hiatal hernia. That's it!"

"Lee, you can't be serious! If you really want to do this, at least cut back a little at a time and shouldn't you talk with the doctor first?"

"He's just going to tell me to keep taking them!"

"Oh, but Lee," Melanie cautioned again.

"I mean it. That's all the meds I will take. We'll see how it works. I'll bet I feel better in just a few days!"

Four nights later, lights out with Melanie asleep, Lee woke wanting a drink of water. Slipping out of bed quietly, he headed for the door. Suddenly, Melanie heard a crashing sound and reaching for the light said, "What in the world?"

To her surprise and terror, she saw Lee sprawled on the floor. Jumping out of bed, she ran to him. Leaning over him, she called to him, "Lee? Lee, can you hear me?"

"What happened?" he mumbled.

"I don't know for sure. You obviously fell."

"Oh my hip," he moaned.

"Can you get up?"

"I don't remember falling, but I remember not being able to feel my legs."

"Not at all?" she asked trying to reign in her fear.

"I think it's better now. They tingle, so let me try to get up."

"Should I call 911? Maybe you had a heart attack or something"

"No! And I didn't have a heart attack! I am fine. Just let me get myself up and get my bearings. I'll be fine."

With Melanie's help, he pulled himself up and got him seated on the bed. In the next instant, Lee was covered with sweat. "I am so hot!" he said.

Before Melanie returned with a cool cloth, he said, "I'm freezing! I am so cold."

"Let me call 911," Melanie pleaded.

"I said no! I will be fine! I just need to lie down."

The night continued to be stressful as Lee became violently ill before finally leveling out allowing for sleep.

The next morning Melanie placed all Lee's prescribed pills before him. "Take them," she insisted. "I'd lay odds that your issue last night was not taking your meds. Take these, I'll make an appointment and see what the doctor says. Tell him you want to cut back, but do it right!"

"I'm not ready to go back to the doctor. I'll take my pills again for now and see if that helps."

"I don't like that you won't go back to the doctor."

"They don't know what they're doing! I feel like a guinea pig! They're always experimenting with something. All they're doing is guessing! But for now I'll take the meds."

The next few weeks were harrowing for Melanie as she worried about Lee and her classes. She had learned to enjoy Science class, even though she wasn't entirely sure of what she was doing much of the time. She often felt lost or at least three steps behind. She was grateful for Rani, Alyssa, a Science major and Trista whom she'd learn to count on for help in this subject.

The Science labs, however, still had a way of rattling her nerves and on one particular day, she was forced to sit next to Myra who sat in Trista's normal seat since seating wasn't assigned and students had the freedom to sit where they desired, although most often, students returned to the same seat every day. The change in seating arrangements, however, meant Melanie was paired up with her for the day. The day had primarily been lecture and Myra seemed to chat the entire time Dr. Vasser was speaking. To make matters worse, when it came time to do some Math calculations Myra discovered she had forgotten her calculator and decided Melanie's would be a good substitute and helped herself to the instrument which was automatically placed on the table since it was used nearly every day. "You're calculator needs to be re-calibrated," she said in a hushed voice near the end of class, but loud enough for Melanie to hear.

"Shh! My calculator is just fine." said Melanie trying hard to understand the directions.

"I'm telling you, it needs to be re-calibrated," she said again.

"Shh!" she said again more forcefully this time.

"On Monday you will be investigating if an object's average velocity remains constant regardless of distance when it moves on the air rail," said Dr. Vasser. "You will need to list the variables, decide on a hypothesis, rationale, list your materials used, procedures for controlling your variables and your equipment, and create a conclusion. There is a written report required and I expect all data to be in graph or table form.

"Are there any questions?"

Melanie rushed to class on Monday wanting to be certain she could team with Rani, Trista and Alyssa. She was pleased to find the girls had made certain her spot was available so they could work together. Melanie watched as Dr. Vasser went to the chalk board. She admired the late fifty year-old for his amazing intelligence. She smiled to herself as she compared him to Einstein when he would be fitfully writing on the board, suddenly lose his train of thought, reach up with both hands and grab his head deep in thought. After a short pause, when he removed his hands, he often would cause his hair to look like it had been electrified and stuck out at the sides, or occasionally on top.

She also admired his kindness. It was a side of him most students didn't see, either by their choice or his. Students seemed to either love him, or hate him. He seemed to prefer that students considered him hard and mean. It suited his character in the classroom and he didn't want anyone to know he was really a kind, gentle person.

Dr. Vasser was a dedicated Scientist and shared stories of when he was a child. "I remember one time," he said in the middle of a classroom lecture, "I put my ear to a railroad track to feel the vibrations and make an estimate of where the train was and when it would pass by that way. I used to drive my mother nuts," he said with glee. His love for Science was projected in his teaching and wanted each student to understand and retain as much information as possible. This was translated in his tests, as well, which was one of the most difficult parts for Melanie.

Melanie waited anxiously for the doctor to return. Lee had been in for his IPV test for three and a half hours, which seemed horribly longer than she expected. One of the nurses came out and asked if she was waiting for someone, making the waiting more intense. After another half hour, which she learned was the average time for the test for most patients she was finally permitted to join him in the examination room.

The doctor was reassuring saying that while there were obvious issues with his swollen kidneys, he didn't see anything that could be causing the pain and discomfort Lee had been feeling. "I guess we don't know anything more now than we did before!" he said angrily.

"I know and I'm sorry," Melanie said sympathetically. "I hope your new blood pressure medication will help. It seems like if it's not one thing it's another. We still have the gall bladder issues to deal with too."

"I'm just going to go away and then maybe I'll feel better," he stated simply.

"I don't want you to go away, though," she said, suddenly sad.

"Oh, it'll be fine. I only plan on being gone about three weeks or so."

"Last time you went away you wrecked your bike!"

"Well, I won't this time, but I've got to go. I'm glad you're going to school. I know how much you enjoy it and you're a good student. I'm restless and the cold is killing me. The doctors have all kinds of theories and medications, most of which I think is making things worse rather than better."

"When do you plan on leaving?" she asked resigned to his announcement.

"Probably late next week."

Melanie swallowed the lump in her throat but held her tongue. "It's going to be a long three weeks," she thought.

Just as predicted Lee pulled out of the driveway, the car loaded with his suitcase, fishing pole, pool stick and a cooler full of food. He was headed for Arizona once again, to pass the time while Melanie was in class. This was the one thing about being a student that broke her heart. She waved to him as he left and then forced herself to get ready for her class in just two hours. With a heavy heart she returned to the college. The days passed slowly and each night Melanie waited for the telephone to ring.

When the phone rang one morning after Lee had been gone five days, she was completely unprepared for what she heard on the other end. It was only 8:20 in the morning and all she heard was deep sobbing.

"Brooke? Brooke is that you? What on earth is wrong?"

"We've got to do something about Mom," she said in ragged breaths. "I was just over there and she's sitting there holding her jaw, crying saying it hurts. If we don't do something she's going to sit in that chair and die."

"Calm down. We'll figure this out. What do you want me to do?" asked Melanie. "I wish Lee was still here."

"Where did he go?"

"He's gone to Arizona. He'll be gone another two weeks. He's only been gone for five days."

"I can't do this alone," said Brooke, sobbing deeply again.

"You won't. Hold on. Let me gather my thoughts. Do you want me to go back to see if I can talk to her?"

"Would you? See if you can talk her into going to the doctor. She won't even let me talk to her about it. It just makes her cry."

Melanie walked back to see Flo. Just as Brooke had described, she was sitting in her favorite chair, a well worn recliner, holding her jaw crying and repeating, "Oh, it hurts. My mouth hurts. Someone make my mouth stop hurting."

Walking over and kneeling down in front of her, Melanie said, "Mom, I'm sorry your mouth hurts. If I take you to the doctor so someone can look at your mouth, will you go with me?"

"Uh huh," she answered still crying.

"You realize Brooke will have to drive. She knows the way."

"Uh huh," she said again.

"Mom," she said cautiously. "I'm going to go see Brooke and I'll be right back."

As quickly as she could she ran to Brooke's. Reed and Shari had come over and the two girls were in deep conversation. "She says she'll go to the doctor. I'd do it now, though. I don't know how long she'll be agreeable. I told her you would have to drive. I just told her we were going to the doctor. I never mentioned the nursing home and that is what you have planned, right?"

"I think it's the best thing. Don't you?"

"I don't know what I think. I just know I don't like how much pain she's in. They will look at her mouth once we get there, won't they? I promised her someone would."

"I'm sure someone will," said Shari.

After getting Flo into the car, Brooke, Shari and Melanie headed for Peaceful Pines Nursing Home. Arrangements had been made weeks before that should the family decide that Flo would be best cared for there, she could be brought at any time with just a telephone call advising they would be there.

Pulling up to the entrance, Shari quickly retrieved a wheel chair while Melanie and Brooke got Flo out of the car. Flo, a large woman, was very agile while her health was good. Once her mind began failing, her agility did, as well. To compound that issue was her distress with the pain.

Once in the wheelchair, Shari parked the car while Brooke and Melanie went inside. Brooke had power of attorney so she had the responsibility of filling out all the forms. Melanie waited with Flo, scratching her back and chatting with her even though dialogue was sketchy at best. The most Flo would say reaffirmed her pain.

The smell of food drifted down the hallway. It was a blend of so many scents it was hard to distinguish just what the smell was. Then the strong tangy smell of sauerkraut assaulted Melanie's stomach causing it to flip flop. It wasn't that she opposed sauerkraut, but that smell intermingled with smells of ammonia, bleach, disinfectants, iodine and other hospital odors just didn't mix.

"I hate nursing homes," she thought to herself as she watched the nurses go to and fro seemingly completely busy while ignoring the occasional outbursts of the residents in nearby wheelchairs. Some would sound like they were singing, while others were in complete hysteria. Others were having conversations with themselves or the stuffed animal or doll they were holding. These sounds would sometimes be drowned out by the patient trying to lift himself out of his wheelchair causing an alarm to scream. Then there was the patient who shuffled their way toward them, totally confused as to who you were, why you were there and who they were themselves. "What an awful place," she said aloud, before she realized it.

Melanie tried time and again to telephone Lee. Reception was poor and when she finally did get through, Lee's phone went directly to voicemail. She waited patiently while they took Flo to get chest x-rays, a requirement before becoming a resident of the nursing home. She was returned to her spot once again, where Melanie held her hand and stroked her back until finally the nurse came to wheel her into her room.

As the small, red headed nurse pushed the wheel chair around the corner and out of sight Melanie was suddenly overcome with emotion and sobbed uncontrollably. She turned around from Flo's direction and held her hands over her face as the tears streamed down her face. Another nurse, a middle aged, brown eyed and brown haired woman came over and wrapped her arms around Melanie's shoulders. "Let's go into the chapel," she said softly. "This is always the hardest part."

"It's all my fault," Melanie stammered while still trying unsuccessfully to control her tears. "She came here because I told her a doctor would look at her mouth."

"It's going to be all right," the nurse reassured her. "It's the best thing for Miss Flo."

"I know. It's just I feel like I deceived her," Melanie said, tears starting anew. "Someone will look at her mouth. Won't they?" she asked desperately.

"I'm sure someone will."

"Promise me someone will look at her mouth," she insisted. "I don't want to have lied to her. I would never want to do that. She was always so kind to me. I hate to see her like this. She was always such a vibrant woman, busy, and fun. Alzheimer's stole her life. It's not fair."

"I agree with you, honey, it's not fair. But it is what it is and we'll take care of her. You can call here any time night or day to check on her."

"Thank you and I'm sorry for my outburst."

"Oh honey, don't be sorry. It just shows how much you care."

"There you are," said Brooke. "We were wondering what happened to you. Shari and I think we should all go out to lunch. There is no way I want to go back home right now."

"Me either," agreed Melanie. "I don't know that I'm hungry, but I will go with you."

Once Melanie returned home, she called her children and again tried calling Lee. Every time she spoke of the incident, tears would fall again. Tara, Kaitlyn and Mackenzie were as emotional as Melanie, while Gavin gently said, "You did what you had to do, Mom. I know it hurts you, but Grandma is where she needs to be."

Melanie was unprepared for Lee's reaction: anger. "I'm going to get her out of there as soon as I get back," he said adamantly. "I'll take care of Mom myself if I have to."

"Well, we'll just wait until you get home and see how things are then," Melanie said choking back the tears that were threatening again. Rather than receiving the comfort she expected from the man she loved, she felt lonely and horribly sad. It had been a long, emotionally draining day. Exhausted, fatigue overpowered her senses and Melanie never even picked herself up off the sofa. She slept right where she was, relieved she no longer had to think or feel.

Melanie was glad to have classes to attend. The weeks were passing agonizingly slow with Lee gone. She felt so alone and guilty having Flo in the nursing home. Her heart ached after each visit.

Medicine was being administered to keep Flo calm. She hugged the large stuffed rabbit Brooke had brought like it was her very last possession. There were occasional bursts of lucidity when she knew the family as they visited. Flo was especially happy when Mackenzie came in the room. She would giggle and often acted like a child, picking at and playing with her food. "I like your red finger nail polish, Grandma," Mackenzie said on one visit. "You going out on a date?"

Flo giggled again and said, "Uh huh!"

"You go girl," Mackenzie said laughing, causing Flo to belly laugh and then immediately look like a child caught misbehaving.

Melanie was delighted to see Flo laugh. Pointing at Melanie, Flo said, "This is my grandmother." It was Mackenzie's turn to belly laugh.

As days passed news from the facility seemed to be changing. The family was disturbed to find the staff at the nursing home had somehow lost Flo's teeth. The room failed to stay clean and sterile as it had been when she first arrived. Smells began to emanate from the room that were less than appealing.

To make matters worse, Brooke, through tears phoned to ask Melanie to make sure Lee called her as soon as he returned. "Melanie, we have to decide whether or not to resuscitate Mom should something happen regarding her health. I can't decide this alone," she sobbed. "I've spoken to Reed and he won't even talk about it and I haven't been able to talk with Kent.

"I let Grace and Owen know about Mom and Grace is angry that we didn't consult her before we put her in the nursing home in the first place. When I asked her to give her opinion about the resuscitation issue she just screamed and hollered about how her opinion didn't matter anyway and hung up on me! She hung up on me! Can you believe that? As if I don't have enough on my plate," she said sobbing hysterically now.

"Oh, Brooke, I'm sorry. We'll get through this, I promise. You didn't deserve that. I'm sure Grace is not really upset with you. It's probably misdirected anger. She is likely angry that she couldn't be here when all this happened."

"Yeah, well I'm hard pressed to believe that. She only calls when she wants something or has a fight with Owen. She keeps saying she's going to come home and how long has it been?" she asked angrily. "It's been years since we've even seen her."

Sighing, Melanie said, "Brooke I can't speak for Grace, but I know that we did the right thing. I hate it as much you do. But we didn't have a choice. I don't feel like I have the right to offer my opinion about the resuscitation issue. That has to be between you, Lee, Kent, Reed and it should include Grace, but if she's not going to be willing, you just won't include her. And truthfully, if the others won't offer their opinion, then it's going to have to be between you and Lee."

"Somehow that just doesn't seem fair."

"I will tell you that Lee was real unhappy that Mom is in the nursing home. I'm sure once he gets home and sees her, he will remember what all we've been through and know we did what we had to do. He's probably, like Grace, just unhappy that he wasn't here when we put her in.

"Melanie, I will tell you now, if Lee doesn't support all this, I'm done. I can't handle all this. I'm a wreck. I can't even think anymore. Kerry says I'm cranky all the time and just tries to stay out of my way. He's even been taking on more work just so he doesn't have to be home."

"I'm sorry. This is really hard on everybody."

"Like I said, it's not fair."

"I know, but it is what it is. Just wait to even think about making more decisions for now, if you're able, until Lee gets back. It won't be that long now. Maybe it'll even be long enough that your siblings will be willing to see they should be part of the decision making process."

"I'll try, but I'm not sure it'll work," she said sadly, but no longer crying.

"Do you think Lee will talk to me?"

"Brooke, it's not like we haven't discussed putting Mom in a nursing home before. It's been a topic of conversation long before now. Like I said, he's likely upset that we made the decision while he was gone. He'll be fine," she added sounding more confident than she felt given their recent conversation on the telephone.

Melanie was relieved when Lee finally came home. It had been a long three weeks. Lee had the opportunity to relax and enjoy life in a less stressful situation while Melanie had remained home and dealt with issues as they presented themselves. Melanie and Lee rode in to see Flo. A slight degree of recognition came to Flo as Melanie walked into her room. They sat and chatted for a bit, although it could not be called conversation since Flo's words couldn't even be formed into a complete sentence. "Mom, look," said Melanie. "Lee is here."

"Who's that?" she asked. Lee looked stricken. It was the beginning of many visits that left Melanie and Lee trying hard to fill the hole in their hearts.

As they left from their first visit with her and re-entered their car, Lee placed his hands on the steering wheel and stared straight ahead. "You know," he said, "I hate seeing her in here, but I know you and Brooke did the right thing."

"It's been real hard on Brooke and with all the new issues, she feels overwhelmed sometimes. The family has to make a decision about resuscitating Mom should something happen regarding her health. I don't know the details and like I told Brooke, I don't have the right to even offer my thoughts. She's your mom, not mine. It has to be between you kids and that's been challenging too."

"You need to talk to her."

"I will. I'll call her first thing in the morning."

As winter turned into spring, Melanie found her world again turning upside down. Sitting working on homework, one cloudy, rainy afternoon, the telephone rang. "Hey, Melanie," came Adam's familiar voice.

"Hi," she responded cheerfully. "How's Shelley?" she continued without pause.

"Well, Shelley's troubles are all gone now. She passed away about an hour ago."

Melanie felt her knees go weak as a lump came in her throat that refused to go down and tears streamed down her face unbidden. Unable to speak she leaned against the wall for support as she fought for control.

The next few days completed in a blur as Melanie dealt with classes that were nearing their end and the funeral of her best friend. When she, Lee and the family arrived at the church on a cold blustery day, she was surprised at the line that extended out of the church and along the sidewalk for two city blocks.

The staff of Sweet Creek Elementary School turned out in number for the devoted and loved fourth grade teacher. She was credited for her continued work in preserving the wetlands of the area near the school and making it a genuine place where her young students could learn first hand about the plants, bugs, frogs and birds that inhabited the special place that was simply named Shelley's Space in her honor.

The attendees received comfort from the minister who had an amazing voice and sang several hymns and gave a heartfelt message of hope. He gave a picture of Shelley free from pain and being carried by angels to heaven and into the arms of God.

Melanie was glad the semester was coming to an end. It meant finals and she dreaded that but she felt reasonably prepared for at least two of her classes. Mrs. K's final in Communications was one Melanie expected to do well. Once finished, she was confident she had done well. She had enjoyed Mrs. K and the material, learned how to give impromptu speeches, as well as, speeches that demonstrated her knowledge in a subject and in teamwork.

Mrs. Reston's Math class had proved more stressful than Melanie would have liked. While she had come to appreciate the diminutive instructor, it didn't seem to improve her ability to consume and digest correctly the material presented. She had struggled and feared the final even though she knew her grade was good enough that even should she fail the test, she would still pass. As she completed this exam she felt she had done reasonably well, and therefore not end the class without at least a solid B for a final grade.

Mrs. Jansen had become a friend and Melanie had completely enjoyed her time in English. There was nothing that Melanie could even name that she didn't like about the class. She enjoyed research, writing and the stories Mrs. Jansen shared about her daughters making the class often feel like a time of fun conversation, even though it was almost always a monologue by Mrs. Jansen. She had no doubts she would complete this final well without much effort.

Melanie was terrified about the upcoming final in Mr. Vasser's Science class. The last three weeks of the semester before final week, focused on the element table. The material was presented with the idea that each student knew the different elements and their representative numbers. Melanie had not dealt with the elements since early in her ninth grade General Science class.

Mr. Vasser presented assignments combining the elements to create other elements and hard as she tried, she couldn't make sense of it. Her memory seemed on overload and every time she would try to memorize the table, she got completely confused. This section of the class curriculum was worse than her Math class. It left her frustrated and fearful, especially once she learned that at least one third of the final would be on the elements.

Melanie sat down at the desk that had become hers for the past weeks and turned over her paper. The beginning of the test Melanie struggled, but felt she had the material under control. She reached the section on elements and the ensuing combinations she was expected to know and knew she was "done." "It's not happening," she thought. "All I can do is guess and hope for the best." With effort she read every single question at least twice and as best she could make an educated guess.

Turning in her paper, Mr. Vasser looked at her. "Well, what do you think?"

"I was fine until the elements," she said.

"Don't worry about," he said kindly. "I know you were at a disadvantage. You did well in class. That will count for something."

"I appreciate your kindness," she said.

"Well, that's just fine. But don't share that with anyone," he cautioned. "I'd deny everything," he said grinning.

"Got it," she said smiling, turning to walk away. "Enjoy your break."

"Thanks, you too!"

Year Two
Chapter 11

"Will I ever get finished Math classes," Melanie thought looking for the classroom. Peering into the room before entering, Melanie was pleased and surprised to see Natalie, whom she'd had another class during first semester. Slipping into the seat next to her, which was near the front, she took the time to really look at the room.

This room was different than her other classrooms because it was set up auditorium style, with each row of seats higher than the one before it. She liked the visibility it offered, but was surprised and wondered what the room originally was for. She turned as an attractive, auburn haired lady dressed in a business suit came into the doorway pulling a luggage cart. A robust, bald headed man came in behind her and she moved away. Picking up the cart, the man took it down the steps of the elevated room and placed it near the desk. The woman, slightly smiling, followed him. She turned to him, spoke something unheard and he exited the room.

"Good morning, class," the woman said, softly. "My name is Mrs. Anderson and I will assume you are here for Statistics class. If not, I suggest you check your schedule because you are probably in the wrong class."

Melanie was both pleased and surprised by the attention this soft spoken woman received from the class. It was necessary to truly listen in order for her to be heard. She also liked the kindness that flowed through her voice; kindness with authority, she thought.

After the introduction to the math called, Statistics, Melanie was again struggling to get a handle on this subject that seem to mock her lack of expertise. Still, she seemed to be doing reasonably well and the project before her offered an opportunity to bring her grade up from the B she was holding.

"Each student will be required to do a computer project that shows some of the basic ways a researcher might collect and record a collection of mathematical results," Mrs. Anderson said. "You will find the mean, mode, range, frequency of distribution, variance, standard deviation, and specifics we will cover today and you will need to create a histogram with all your information, as well. I do not care what data you choose to collect, just record and tabulate your information correctly. You may choose to collect height, weight, temperatures, incomes, test scores, or how many licks you and others can get from a single lollipop! You will have two weeks to complete the project. Be creative!"

Melanie tried to think of something different and unique for her Math project as she absently went into her closet before leaving for class to retrieve a pair of shoes. "Where are my hiking boots?" She asked herself pulling through the several different kinds and colors. Moving two black pairs of string tie shoes, a brown slip on pair, she noticed she owned two pairs of green heels, a pair of maroon heels and a pair of blue ones. She had three pairs of white dress shoes and a pair of white sandals and a brown pair, as well as, a pair of black sandals; plus, two pairs of black dress boots, tan sandals, red sneakers, white sneakers and a pair of black flats. "Wouldn't that be something?" thought Melanie. "I could do my project on how many different pairs of shoes people have. I can do both men and women!"

Musing over her idea, she approached Mackenzie. "How many pairs of shoes do you have?"

"I have no clue!" she laughed. "But I will count them and get back with you!" she said after hearing Melanie's idea for her project.   "That's a pretty cool idea!"

With that beginning, she approached 29 different people so she could to make her project both fair and interesting. Melanie discovered people in general owned a fair amount of shoes. The question brought giggles and a small amount of embarrassment as the people disclosed how many pairs of shoes they actually owned. One person totaled theirs at 120 pairs, which was the highest, while the fewest pairs were four. As she sat in front of the computer, however, Melanie could not make the Excel spreadsheet work the way she wanted. Frustrated she called Mackenzie. "I can't get it to work," she said. "My totals don't work and it doesn't look right!" she added, disgust in her voice.

"Mom, breathe! I will help you. I'll be up in a few minutes and we'll get it all straight."

With relief an hour later Melanie looked at her paper. "We did it!" she exclaimed. "It worked! How cool is that?!"

Mackenzie laughed. "Mom, you try too hard and make something that isn't difficult, hard for you."

"I don't mean to," she said defensively.

"I know," Mack said giving her a hug. "Gotta run. I'll talk with you later."

"Mack's right," she thought. "I feel like such an idiot on the computer. I wonder if Gavin is right. Should I take a computer class? That would really make me look stupid," she berated herself. "Maybe though," she thought again. I'd love to be able to do my projects without always needing help!

Hearing the knock on the door Melanie left her reverie to answer it. "Tara, what's wrong?" she asked noting the tears and distress on her daughter's face.

"I'm really, really angry with Brent right now and just need to vent."

"Ariana, Dylan, how about you two going into the play room and finding something to do for a little while, while your momma and I chat. Take Ethan with you, but watch him and if you need help, just call us," Melanie instructed the children.

"What on earth is this about?" asked Melanie when the children were out of ear shot.

"I think Brent is cheating on me."

"What?"

"He's been acting strange, and really secretive. He stays out a lot and we've been running short on money for bills."

"I'm sure it's just a misunderstanding."

"I'm not sure it is."

Melanie hugged her daughter. "Let's pray about it and see what happens."

"Pray? What good is that going to do?"

"Well, we'll pray that whatever Brent is having issues with, the Holy Spirit will convict him."

"You pray. I'm going to confront him about it."

"Well, if you're sure you want to do that, then I'll pray he's honest with you. At least then you can deal with whatever "it" is."

"I've got to get home," Tara said rising and going to the play room. "Ariana, Dylan, it's time to go. Ethan, you ready to go home? It's your nap time!" she added scooping up her youngest son.

Melanie fell to her knees after Tara and the children left. "Please, God," she said, "Intercede between Brent and Tara. Whatever is coming between them, please, please help them work it out."

The next afternoon Melanie walked into her Math class. Sitting at her desk, she had a hard time concentrating. It had been a restless night. As the projects were being handed forward, she absently pulled hers out of the folder she had neatly tucked it into.

"Class, remember there will be a test next week so let's go over your homework and today's new concept so you will be ready."

Trying hard to focus, Melanie looked at Mrs. Anderson. Even though she smiled, Melanie noticed how frail Mrs. Anderson had been looking lately. She had been hearing whispers that she had some type of cancer. That would explain why the bald headed gentleman always brought Mrs. Anderson's books so she didn't have to carry them down the steps of the math class room. Melanie's heart went out to the kind lady.

Before she realized it, Mrs. Anderson excused the class. She had written furiously all the formulas and notes written on the board with as much explanation as she could. The book was helpful, but it was better explained in person. "Remember. You have my telephone number. It is my home phone, but if you really need help, call me. My goal is that everyone in here not only passes my class, but does well."

Punching in the numbers in the calculator again, Melanie pushed the enter button. "Errr!" she said her hands and arms stiffening in front of her. "Why isn't this working?" One more time, carefully and deliberately pushed each numbers for the problem. Again she saw "error" come up on the screen.

"Gavin! Help! It's not working. Why isn't it working? What am I doing wrong? We've got that test coming up on Monday and I can't get the calculator to do what I want!"

Gavin plopped down on the sofa beside her. They shared the same professor, Mrs. Anderson, for their Math classes but since they had the same class on different days, Mrs. Anderson didn't seem to make the connection of son and daughter. Melanie had promised she wouldn't tell as soon as it was discovered, having made their separate schedules at different times. She had kept her promise and was grateful he felt comfortable sitting next to her in the privacy of their own home. "Show me what you're doing so I can see if it's you or the calculator," he instructed.

Patiently Gavin watched while Melanie slowly again punched in the numbers for the equation for population standard deviation: $\sigma = \mathrm{sqrt}\,[\,\Sigma\,(\,X_i - \mu\,)^2\,/\,N\,]$. "You're putting it in wrong," Gavin said. You have to put the parenthesis in at the right place or you'll never get the right answer."

"I'm glad Mrs. Anderson is letting us bring the formulas to class for the test," Melanie said. "But what good is it if I can't remember how to put it in the calculator?"

"Write down the order you are supposed to put it in the calculator so you won't get confused," he offered.

"Do you think that would be alright?"

"Well, she told us to bring the calculator and our formulas, so I can't imagine it being an issue to write the order the formula goes into the thing!"

"Good idea!" she said looking at her son with great admiration. "I appreciate your help. I might even do okay on this test!"

"No problem," he said, laughing at her.

On the day of the test, Melanie nervously made her way to her seat. She had studied and felt prepared until she saw the test. Feeling the color drain from her face she flipped the pages. Placing the sheet with the formulas before her and then deliberately blotting everyone and everything out she took a deep breath and plowed in. The moments passed and before Melanie realized it, it was time for class to end. Looking around Melanie noticed there were still four other students left in the room. Filled with immediate panic, Melanie burst, "Mrs. Anderson, I'm not finished."

"Do others still need time to finish?"

"I do," said Paige

"Me, too," added Mary

"I'm almost finished," said Eddie

"I need just a little more time," chimed in Taylor.

"Well, I hadn't prepared for it, but I'm sure we can find a place to continue working over in the library. This room has another class coming in, so we can't stay here. Pick up your things and for those who want to, we'll all move over there together."

Forty five minutes passed before Melanie finally turned her paper in. She was the last student finished. Mrs. Anderson had patiently waited, working on other material near by. Handing Mrs. Anderson her paper, Melanie said, "I'm grateful you let us finish, but I'm sorry it took so long."

"Don't be. It's just fine. I was able to continue working while you did. It's not a problem.

"Tell me, Melanie. What are your plans once you graduate?"

"I don't know for sure," Melanie admitted. "I just know I want to be productive and do something good. I've known people who retire and then because they don't stay active they in effect die.

"We had to put Lee's mom with Alzheimer's in a nursing home not long ago and I honestly believe that while the disease would have attacked her anyway, I believe her lack of interest in anything and her inability and choice to be non-productive she withered and died. I know that isn't what gave her Alzheimer's but I sure believe it made it progress more quickly.

"She was an amazing lady and I miss having her around."

"You sound like you really love her."

"Oh, I do. She was always kind, busy and such a vital part of our lives, until she retired. It's just so sad."

"Well, whatever you choose to do, I think you'll be successful. You work hard and professors like myself really appreciate that."

"How kind. Thank you."

Melanie looked at her watch. "I can't believe how long I took to finish the test. I've got to run. I'm supposed to be in the financial aid office in five minutes or I'm going to be late!"

"Well, don't worry about the time it took for the test. Like I said it wasn't a problem. Have a great rest of the day!"

"Thanks," she said, smiling broadly. "I will try!"

Melanie got to the Financial Aid Office just in time to answer the phone. Debbie was on the other line and Vicki was in a meeting.

"Financial Aid Office, this is Melanie, how may I help you?"

"When will our checks be mailed out?" came the voice across the line.

"Refund checks get mailed out about six weeks after classes start, so when the Business office finishes processing them they will mail them out to you," answered Melanie, a little annoyed.

After Melanie got off the phone with the student she looked to Debbie and said, "Can I tell the next student who calls that we ran out of money and we aren't mailing them this semester."

Debbie laughed. "No, we can't."

"I know," said Melanie, "I just wish when people called they didn't act like the money was owed to them. It's such a blessing to get free money from the government. Doesn't anyone call and think you guys made a mistake sending them a check?"

"Yes and those few phone calls make it worth it!"

Lee opened the door for Melanie as they neared the nursing home facility. "Thanks," she said. "I hope Mom is in a good mood today."

"Hi, Mom! How are you?" asked Melanie as they greeted her among all the other patients in the dining area. Each table held a minimum of two patients, most often three and sometimes four. Each had a tray filled with a plate of pureed meat, vegetable and potatoes, although the plates were not identical. They also had a slice of bread, soup, pie or cake and ice cream, as well as, a glass of water, juice or milk. Some had coffee or hot chocolate.

Each patient wore an oversized bib. Some simply stared at their platter with complete disregard for the nourishment before them. Others toyed with their food by mashing and re-mashing what lay before them, while others found pleasure in stirring. Occasionally a patient would heartily devour the feast before them while others required feeding by nurses or family members.

Flo seemed to fit all categories. There were occasions she had no interest in her food and simply stared at it as if trying to figure out just what it was. Yet there were times when she would feed herself and nearly finish everything on her tray. Other times she would require feeding by the nurses or visiting family because she would only play with the food by mixing it all together, which was particularly unappealing to Melanie. Today she stared at her food in apparent disgust.

"What are you doing here?" she growled, pointing her fork at them.

"Mom, it's Lee and Melanie. We've come to visit."

"Hey, Mom!" said Lee bending on one knee beside her so he was at her eye level.

Turning her head toward him a flicker of recognition crossed her face. "Hi!" she responded. "Where have you been?"

"We've been around," he assured her. "We've come today to visit with you! Are you behaving yourself?"

Melanie and Lee watched as the curtain fell over her face blinding her from all recognition. "What are you doing here?" she snapped.

"Oh dear," said Melanie.

"I'm going to go check her room," said Lee.

"Okay, I'll chat with her a bit," Melanie said as Lee strode away.

Suddenly filled with rage, Flo began shouting at Melanie. "You left me!" she accused. "You were supposed to come back and get me, but you left me in the house to do all the work. You and that friend of yours," she added pointing her fork at her for emphasis. "How was I supposed to get back to town when you took the car? You left me to clean up! I had the whole house to clean. You knew we were getting company. Momma told you!"

"Mom, calm down. It's Melanie," she said slowly and clearly. "It'll be okay. Look you have your dinner to eat," she added trying to change the direction of the conversation.

"You're a mean somebody!" Flo started again, her eyes flicking fire. "You tried to take him from me. You and that girl. You knew he was my husband. You had no business being there. You left me!" Flo continued while adding expletives between every two or three words.

"Mom, it's Melanie," she tried again, fighting back the tears.

Hearing his mother down the hall, Lee hurried back to the dining room. "Mom, look at me. That's Melanie."

"Hi," she said, suddenly smiling and just as quickly turning angry again. "What did you bring her here for? She's a mean somebody! She knew we were getting company. Momma told her. She left me to clean the whole place up. She's mean," she added squinting her eyes.

Melanie's face burned with tears. She loved Flo, and knew Flo wasn't herself and even knew she didn't mean any of the things she had just said. She clearly had Melanie mixed up with someone else from her youth, yet the accusations caused an emotional overload. "I can't stay any longer," she said. "I need to get some air," she said as she fled the room.

The ride home was tense with not a word spoken between Lee and Melanie, until Melanie finally broke the silence. "I love your mom and I know she's not really angry with me but those kinds of outbursts just break my heart."

"I know. I'm sorry. I don't know what to do."

"Me either. I'll adjust. We can't stop going to see her. That would be just wrong. She needs to know, if she's able at all, that we still love her and haven't abandoned her. Even knowing she doesn't seem to remember one moment to the next."

"I love you for that," Lee said, reaching over, placing his hand on her shoulder.

She smiled but said nothing.

"Brent came home last night with a ticket," Tara said angrily before she had even taken her coat off. "He'd been to Deadwood and of all things got pulled over for an illegal lane change! Then to add insult to injury he hit a deer coming off the mountain and broke a headlight.

"What am I going to do? I'm beginning to think it's not another woman at all. He's got a gambling problem."

"You really think so?"

"I do and it scares me."

"And my problem with Brent is just not going away. You keep saying to pray. It's not working. I'm done. I've had it. He works overtime and then instead of coming home he's off to Deadwood gambling. He stays for hours and ends up coming home about five o'clock a.m. and then has to go to work at seven. It doesn't make sense!

"I had no idea. Whenever you two are here, you'd never know you had any issues."

"That's cause we tried to hide we were having problems.

"I think the gambling thing started innocently enough," Tara continued almost to herself. "He went to play the slots every once in a while. Then it went to once a month, to once a week, and now it's several times a week. He drinks while he's there. He's not coming home drunk, but you can't win at those things and he keeps thinking you can. All he's doing is wasting our money. Money we need for groceries and our mortgage payment."

"How long has this been going on?"

"I don't know. It's been close to a year. It runs in phases. There were times, like I said, when he only went once a month. He even stopped for a while and then it went to once a week. Again, I guess he tried to stop and he did for a while. I've been trying to ignore it, but I'm done."

"What do you mean 'you are done'?"

"I'm leaving him."

"Tara, you don't mean that. That's a strong statement. Surely there is something we can do. There's got to be a way you can work through this."

"When you came over that time and told me you thought Brent was cheating on you and that you were going to confront him, what did he say?"

"He denied it. And he was right. It's not another woman. It's gambling. He's obsessed! He doesn't have any desire to do anything around the house when he is home. He just watches TV and sleeps; and most of the time that's on the sofa. He doesn't do anything with the kids anymore. I declare they don't even know their daddy anymore!

"All we do is fight and most of the time it's about nothing. And sometimes in front of the kids, no less. How awful is that? And sometimes the kids even hear it and that makes it worse. Ariana hasn't been sleeping nights. She wakes up from nightmares. And Dylan has been having behavior issues. His teacher even sent a note home with him last week saying he's been acting out in class. Ethan just clings to me"

I'm fed up. I'm absolutely done. All I do is cry. I don't want my marriage to fail, but I don't know how to solve the problem. Brent won't even consider that he has a problem. We can't pay our bills even with me working. We're about to lose the house and my life is an absolute mess."

Melanie hugged her daughter. She was at a complete loss with any way to comfort her. "This is going to take nothing less than a miracle," she thought. "God, I know you're able. It's up to you."

As the days turned into weeks, Math still managed to add another thorn to her already stressed and strained days, but today Melanie could barely contain her excitement. She looked at the grade again on her test paper. There it was: 100%. She recalled the class period before. She finished the test in only half an hour and that alone frightened her. Carrying the paper up to Mrs. Anderson, she cautiously handed the paper to her and then began retreating to her seat. "Melanie could you come back here for just a moment?"

"Okay," she said clearly concerned.

"I need you to put these three answers in proper form, and you might want to redo this part of this problem," she said quietly, pointing with her pen."

"Okay."

Taking her seat, Melanie checked the problems before her and then remembered the "form" Mrs. Anderson was speaking of and made the change. After redoing the other noted problem, Melanie again went to Mrs. Anderson's desk. "I got it!" she said, confidently smiling.

"Yes you did!" she replied with a friendly smile.

Holding her graded paper firmly in her hand, she walked to Mrs. Anderson's desk after class. "Thank you," she said as students were exiting the class.

"No problem," she said, "You clearly knew how to do the problem."

"It was still kind to catch my mistakes. I am grateful."

"You are quite welcome."

As Melanie turned to leave, another student entered the room. "Hey Gavin! What are you doing here?"

"Gavin Carson, Melanie Carson." She carefully looked at the two students before her. "Are you?" Mrs. Anderson didn't finish her question before both Gavin and Melanie started laughing.

"Mother and son?"

"Guilty as charged!" Melanie replied smiling broadly.

"I should have known. Your Gavin is a good student and a nice young man," she said to Melanie.

"Thank you. I kind of enjoy him myself!"

"And your mom is also a good student who works very hard."

"Thank you," he said with the deep chuckle that Melanie loved to hear. "She does okay, at least when she can figure out how to use the calculator!"

All three laughed in unison.

"Did you need to see me?" she asked Gavin.

"Yes, Ma'am."

"I'll see you both later," Melanie interjected while exiting the room. "I have another class, and another stop before I get there!"

Chapter 12

Melanie looked at her schedule again, as she made her way through the maze of students, most of which seemed as lost as she. Although she had been in this building before, the classroom seemed to evade her as the hallway took more than one turn. She had never had reason to come down this way before and she found herself a little intimidated.

Finding the room number she entered slowly, hoping to see at least one person whom she knew. No one yet, but then the room was only half full. She would have to take her seat and wait and see if someone familiar would walk through those doors, as she had moments ago.

IDC; Interdisciplinary Course, better known as "The Nature of Knowledge" she remembered from the blurb in the catalogue, "wonder just how it all fits in? It's supposed to be how we acquired knowledge in different cultures and disciplines. What in the world does that mean?" she wondered. "How do you fit in humanities, science, and social science all together? It should certainly be interesting! The introduction promised discussion, analyzing, projects and understanding. Wonder if I really will," she thought. "It'll be my luck I'll say something dumb and just embarrass myself."

The second hand on the clock continued to countdown as more students entered, taking available seats. It looked like it was going to be a full house and still there was no one she knew. Just then Amber walked in. She was an unusually pretty girl, with a full head of long, auburn hair. She wore provocative clothes and while she was clearly beautiful she completely knew she made heads turn.

In some bizarre way, Melanie found herself irritated with the way the girl drew attention to herself because of her remarkable beauty. She would giggle, bat her eyes and toss her long locks back with a shake of her head and cut her eyes across the room to which ever young man would take notice.

Before she had any more time to berate herself for her less than young, flirty look, a tall, fifty-ish, well dressed, blonde haired lady, pulling a cart loaded with a crate filled with papers, a lap top computer, an assortment of books, and a drink entered the room. Stopping beside the desk she began removing the items from the cart and carefully placing her load in specific piles.

Melanie knew immediately she was going to like this professor. Her kind eyes and genuine smile instantly put her at ease. "Good morning, class" she began. "I am Mrs. Simon. You are in IDC which means we have the next twelve weeks to get to know one another. The goal of this class is to among other things, help you recognize the need for knowledge in the different perspectives available, why you should find it, and then how to use it."

Continuing she said, "You will be required to keep a journal," which instantaneously brought the sound of moaning and mumbling in the room. "No need to get upset about the journal. It is what it is," she said emphatically, "and it's worth about 20% of your grade, so I encourage you to be diligent. The purpose of the journal is that I can know you have understanding of your readings, theories and issues presented and it provides a source to write your ideas on paper before you present them in class. This will enable you to be a valued participant in the dialogues we have in class.

"Which brings me to class participation. This is very important and also 20% of your grade. Ideas and theories are as different as the people we are. Your religious beliefs, value systems, ethics are all about whom you have become and who you will grow into. There aren't any real wrong answers, but certainly there are different answers. In this class we will discuss some of these very different ideas with the knowledge that you or your neighbor can have a completely different idea and not be wrong.

"Nearer to the end of the semester your will do team projects which will tie science, social science and humanities all together. It is my desire that when you begin these projects you will be able to present an understanding of how all these different perspectives come together so there is an appreciation of the nature of knowledge.

"All that being said, your next class will include a debate regarding your reading. I will not tell you specifically what the debate will be about, but come prepared to discuss it."

An hour later, Melanie left the room with excited nervousness. The class sounded challenging, but intimidating if it was going to include debates. Unless she was on the side she believed in she had already learned she was fighting a losing battle.

Melanie could hear the phone ringing as she turned the key to the door. "I'm coming, I'm coming," she said aloud. "Just let me get in the door!" Hurrying she ran to answer the phone. "Good afternoon!" she said cheerily.

"What a pleasant way to answer the phone," said the caller. "This is Rebecca Hollister from Cedar Ridge Community College. I am trying to reach Gavin Carson."

"Well, you've reached the right residence, but at the moment, Gavin isn't here. Is anything wrong?"

"Oh no! I actually would like to offer him what I think might be an interesting employment opportunity."

"Really?"

"Yes, I am the Media Specialist here at the college and am prepared to begin a local television station from the college. I'd like Gavin to be part of it. He has been recommended very highly by his communications instructor and from everything I have seen and heard of Gavin, he seems like the perfect candidate to help me get the program off the ground."

"Wow! That would be amazing!

"Can I have him call you or get in contact with you in some other way."

"Phoning would be fine. My number here is 605-555-7458. I'll be here until about 8:00 tonight. I have a 5:00 class that ends at 6:15, so any time after that would be great."

"I'll make sure he gets the message. Thank you for calling."

"Wow," thought Melanie. "This is perfect. Maybe Gavin will consider staying in South Dakota instead of leaving for Montana." Her thoughts went back to a conversation she and Gavin had not long ago.

"Mom," he had said, "Can I talk with you a minute."

"Sure, what's up?" she asked drying her hands and turning from the sink to see her son with a very serious look on his face.

"What's wrong?" she asked suddenly concerned.

"Well, you know how I feel about Montana. Ever since we visited there when I was a kid, I knew it is where I'm supposed to be. I just feel it, but I'm not sure I can explain it."

"I know," she said sadly. "I've expected you to say something before now."

"I'm not ready to talk to Dad about it yet, but you have got to know I plan to transfer out there, maybe after next semester."

Melanie's heart sank. "You're serious, aren't you?"

"I am. I know you don't want me to leave, but I have to. I have to leave to become the man God means me to be."

Tears welled up unbidden in her eyes. "Don't cry Mom. That just makes me sad and feel guilty."

"I don't mean to cry. It just breaks my heart to think of you leaving. Can't you wait until after you graduate from here and then decide if you want to go?"

He sighed heavily. "I don't want to wait. You told me that when I turned eighteen you wouldn't stop me if I wanted to leave. I know you don't want me to go and I don't want to hurt you but do you understand why I have to do this?

"Honestly, I do and I don't fault you for it. It's just going to take some time to get used to the idea and I want you to pray about it and be absolutely sure of what you're doing before you make the final decision."

"I will and you know I will only do it if I feel God has opened the doors."

Melanie's mind closed in on the most recent conversation with Ms. Hollister and the possibility she presented. "Maybe God is closing the door," she thought hopefully and then immediately ashamed of herself. "Maybe, though, God will help him find his place here in this TV station thing rather than going away." Still, she doubted her own hope. It was highly unlikely that Gavin would decide not to leave. He's had leaving on his mind for a long time.

Melanie walked into class confident with the knowledge she had read the material assigned and would be able to participate in a class discussion. The class divided into two groups and when she heard the topic, she immediately doubted herself. Science versus religion. She felt strong in her faith, but wondered where that would leave her in a discussion filled with young people.

The question itself, made Melanie nervous: If the world declared only one could exist, either science or religion, which one would win? She was immediately relieved, however, to discover she, at least, was on the side of the room that would debate on the side of religion. She wondered, however, how strong the rest of the team would be regarding this stance.

The other started: "Science would win, hands down," said Matthew. "Science provides the means to prove ideas through scientific methods."

"Matthew's right," added Tara. "Science begins with a problem and then there is set before the scientists or whomever is doing the study, a method of testing the idea as true or untrue. Your Bible says the universe is created by God. Science can describe in great detail the universe from a scientific perspective. It can name all the stars, galaxies and when phenomenon is going to occur long before it does.

"I don't believe there even is a God," said Dale, clearly agitated. "A person who believes in God and a Creator believes in very constricting ideas and limitations. Science gives the world great things like space travel and simple things like electricity and information regarding disease and weather issues and information about the earth and plants that simply doesn't exist in your world of religion."

"Science is just smart" said Amber, as she ran her fingers through her long auburn locks. "Religion is fake. It's all made up!" she added smiling sweetly, exposing her perfect white teeth.

It was all Melanie could do to keep quiet until it was their turn to speak in the debate. Her heart was racing and she found herself trembling with unexplained anxiety. "Religion is not fake! It's all about faith!" she said adamantly

"How can you say there is no God?" she added quickly, clearly appalled. Then taking a breath plunged ahead stating the question with her thoughts in the strongest manner she could muster.

"I believe if the world declared only one could exist, clearly religion would win because a person's faith goes far beyond what is earthly. It is true that science gives the world great things. You're right there is the study of medicine, geology, astronomy, physics, chemistry and all the other sciences I can't even remember. But it has to have started somewhere."

"With all the scientific information out there," said Brandon when Melanie stopped to collect her thoughts on how she should proceed, clearly not expecting her team to support her views. "You will not find contentment and peace no matter what is invented, studied or created by man," he continued. "Clearly this comes from a Higher Power, and I tend to agree with Melanie, that ultimately religion would win because people would still have a void that could not be filled except through their faith."

As the discussion continued, Melanie felt herself relax when she discovered there were like minded people in her class. She hadn't expected anyone, especially young people to help support their side of the debate.

"Science brings satisfaction in a job well done when accomplishments are accepted and worthwhile" said Natalie.

"Science brings much, but it cannot fill the inner soul and will leave a person haunted with emptiness until it is filled with the Holy Spirit and given a faith and peace that can only be found by God," Melanie interjected.

"I think you are completely wrong," Matthew said when it came their turn to speak again. "Religion is a crutch, a tool people use to support their superstition and fears. Education in the sciences is more important. If people are undereducated they are easily controlled. That's why people believe in the Bible."

"I respectfully disagree," said Melanie, "and it makes me sad you feel this way. I will admit Science has a place in our world. I still hold, however, that God's truths are the foundation on which we exist and live. It is by His grace, not science, that we are here. That may sound like too much religion for you, but then I do believe in the Bible and I think Science compliments the world that God has made!"

"I agree," said Brandon. "God has given humans curiosity and the ability to use all the different sciences for our good, but God is at the root of it all."

"Good discussion," said Mrs. Simon. "I will admit I hadn't expected the debate to be that personal, but that is good. That is what this class is about. It is important that we share our feelings, be willing to debate them without becoming angry or intimidated when someone disagrees. Everyone has feelings and they won't necessarily be the same as yours.

"I commend both groups on participation and on the level of intelligent discussion. Well done!

"That is all for class today. Continue reading and journaling."

"Mrs. Simon, I am so sorry for talking so much today. I didn't mean to get so upset."

"No apology needed. Your comments were valid and I commend your stand."

"I like it when you talk," said Stewart a mid-twenties young man who was standing behind her waiting to talk with Mrs. Simon, like she. "Even if I didn't agree, and I do, with what you said, you spoke like you believed it and you spoke well. I enjoyed it, even if I didn't say a whole lot.

"Actually, I think I learned a lot. I don't think I'd ever thought about science versus religion. I've thought about all kinds of stuff I haven't ever before! It's at least been interesting," he added laughing.

Melanie immediately liked the young man, whom she'd never spoken to before and joined him in easy laughter. "I agree. This class has been if nothing else, enlightening!"

"Don't ever think you can talk too much in this class, Melanie. Your thoughts are as important as anyone else. And your journal writings confirm you think about what you are writing and have serious convictions and I commend that. You write well. You might even consider holding on to your work. You might want to refer to them one day on other projects."

"Okay," she said. I hadn't thought of that. But thanks. I think I will."

"I need to answer Stewart's question and then I have a question for you. So don't leave yet if you have a minute."

"Sure."

Moments later Stewart walked out of the room and only Mrs. Simon, Melanie and Hope were left. "Is that tall young fella that wears the cowboy hat, long black trench coat and cowboy boots your son?"

"Probably!" laughed Melanie. "Most guys wear the cowboy boots and hat, but Gavin likes the trench coat too, and that kind of sets him apart in a crowd."

"Why?"

"No reason, really. He's a nice looking young man."

"Yes, he is," chimed in Hope, a shy, pretty girl with long blonde hair that curled just on the ends. "He's your son? You don't look old enough to have a son that old."

"You're kidding right!? Gavin is the youngest of five. But thank you! You are very kind to say that and I am grateful!"

"I wasn't being nice. It's true."

"Well, thank you!"

"I have Statistics with him. He's smart too! Course he doesn't know I'm alive."

"Hmmmm" said Melanie. "I don't believe that! He seems to have a sense for pretty blonde haired girls and believe me when I say, you qualify! Just say something to him. He's friendly enough. He'll be a gentleman and chat with you."

"You think?"

"Absolutely!"

"There you go!" said Mrs. Simon laughing. "Next time you see him, strike up a conversation! Don't be shy!"

"Hey, Mom! I finally called Mrs. Hollister. I'm going to be working with her on the new TV station at the college she told you about," said Gavin coming into the kitchen later that day.

"Good deal! Do you think this opportunity might cause you to re-think leaving in the Fall?" she asked hopefully.

"Sorry, Mom. Not happening. I'm delighted I get this chance and I'm grateful. This might be just what I need to open doors in Montana."

"Aw Gavin," she said sadly. "I sure wish you'd change your mind."

"You know, there was a time when after we chatted, I really considered staying. Your arguments are good, not to mention your emotions, but I have to go where I believe the Lord is leading me. This is something I must do."

"I know, I know," she sighed. "You can't blame me for hoping."

"No, I give you that!" he said, grinning. "But I'm determined. I will not change my mind."

As the week began winding down, Melanie became more and more apprehensive about the final project. Near the end of class one day, Mrs. Simon shared the details. "Your final project will be 30% of their total grade." Mrs. Simon began. "You will be required to incorporate all the disciplines we have discussed in class to complete the assignment correctly. Each group will be assigned an unknown object to examine. While the actual identity of the object is not important, what is, is that you investigate your particular object as though you are a physical scientist, social scientist or a scholar in the humanities. You will be required to write a five page report from the perspective you have chosen.

"Each group will have five to six people, so ideally, each group will have two people per team. There will be occasions where one member may have to do his part of the project writing on his own. Choose your parts wisely. I am providing questions you can use that will help you in your research.

"During the last several classes of the semester, each group will present its findings. Understand that you are expected to present your object to your audience from the three different perspectives. Since the presentations, which should be about twenty minutes long, are designed to cover all three disciplines I encourage you to use visual aids.

"What in the world!" thought Melanie. "I hope I have a good group!"

"Amber!" Melanie thought looking at her group members. You might know I would end up working with the girl who is beautiful and knows it! This is going to be interesting! Raeanne and Faith, should be okay," Melanie thought. "Kevin could be interesting and Naneth acts like she's mad at the world most of the time!"

"What do you think this thing is?" asked Naneth.

"I don't have a clue," said Melanie.

"Remember, we're not supposed to know," said Kevin. "We have to come up with our own conclusions."

"This is stupid," said Amber.

"I don't think stupid, but certainly challenging," countered Melanie.

"Well, we have the weekend to give it some thought and we're going to meet as a group next class period, so we'll discuss it. Let's see what we come up with!" said Faith. Agreeing, the group left the classroom.

"I have no idea what I even think about this project," Melanie said to Lee at dinner that night. "I feel clueless!"

"I'm sure you'll figure it out," he said.

"I hope so," she answered sounding doubtful.

Even after thinking all weekend about how the project should be handled, Melanie was still without a single idea when she walked in the classroom. Holding the heavy metal object, without a name in her hands, Raeanne turned it over again and again. "Any ideas, anyone?"

"It looks like it could be a piece of machinery of some kind," said Kevin. "Maybe from a wheel or something."

"Could we make it part of something that causes some kind of accident?" asked Faith.

"That's it! Even if we don't know what the piece is specifically we could make it cause a car wreck or something," said Kevin.

"No, how about a train wreck? That, whatever it is, doesn't look like a car part. It looks like something that's bigger," said Naneth.

"Well, if we did something like that," said Melanie slowly, "we could certainly cover all three disciplines. We would have the physical scientist side because we would need to discuss the accident itself. The Social Scientist would deal with how people dealt with the accident. The scholar in humanities would research the project through history and writing."

"We could make it a terrible tragedy," quipped Raeanne.

"What about making a video of it?" asked Naneth.

"A video?" asked Melanie.

"Sure," said Kevin. "That would be perfect!"

"Hey, that would fun!" agreed Faith.

"Okay, let's talk about who's doing what then," said Melanie. "I'd be happy to do the Humanities side of it."

"I'll help you with that," said Faith.

"I'd like to do the Social Science part," said Kevin. "And I'd love to work on the video," he added.

"I'll pair up with you," said Raeanne. "And I'll help with the video, too."

"That leaves you, Naneth. Are you good with the physical science part?"

"Sure. I'm good with that."

"And, since Amber isn't here, I guess she'll be working with you."

"No! No, way! I will not work with her! I'd rather work alone than work with her. She's unreliable, always trying to be cute and I don't believe for one minute she'll pull her weight. I will not do it!"

"Hold on," said Melanie, suddenly feeling like the "mom" in the group rather than just another student. "Let's see if we have another option."

"Okay," Melanie said returning. "Mrs. Simon says there are several people absent today and since we have our project well in hand, and others are working on their projects too, she's going to group all of them together and let them do their own project. Everyone good with that?"

"Yes!" the group answered.

"And I'll just do my part on my own," said Naneth. "And I want to help with the video too."

The next several weeks were spent answering the questions and making sure all the bases were covered before their presentation. As with all groups, Melanie knew that not all things would go smoothly. It had rained horribly over the weekend. Raeanne came to class completely upset. "I couldn't get my part of the video done," she said, wringing her hands together. "I just know everyone's going to be mad, but the weather was awful. There was no way I could shoot it."

"Are you still going to get it done?" asked Naneth. "It sure doesn't give us much time to get it back to do the editing."

"It'll be okay, Naneth," said Kevin. "If Raeanne can get it to us by the middle of the week, we'll still have a few days to do the editing."

"Are you sure?"

"Yes, I'm sure. It might mean working right up to the time we turn it in," he said laughing. "But we'll get it done."

"I'll get it done so we can do the editing on time. I promise," said Raeanne apologetically.

Each member of the group worked diligently to complete the project with only minor bumps in the road. They practiced their presentation and finally finished their video which included pictures of a train accident that happened decades before.

"Since everyone else is working on the video," said Melanie, "I'm willing to pull the group paper together if everyone will write their part of the report. I'll make sure the transitions work from one section to the next, grammar is right, write the end so every discipline is explained and tied in, have it printed and everything is ready to turn in."

"Are you sure?" asked Naneth.

"Absolutely certain," said Melanie. "This is at least something I do reasonably well. I'd love to."

The day of the presentation, Kevin looked at the members of the group. "I think we should go first," he said. "I want to get this done and over with. At least then we can relax and watch the others. What do the rest of you think?"

"I agree," they all said in unison."

"Then let's find out if we can," Kevin said. "I'll be right back."

Glad to be the first group to go, Melanie handed out the newspaper article she had created to each student in the class room, which covered the train accident due to the malfunctioning piece of equipment. Then she took her seat at the front of the room and waited while the video of the tragic train accident rolled before their eyes.

Melanie and Faith took their places to be interviewed in a television setting as Social Scientists to demonstrate how the accident will affect the community with regard to hospital care, jobs, and other relevant community issues.

Feeling completely out of her comfort zone, Melanie answered the questions as planned, fighting the urge to giggle all the way through by deliberately taking deep breaths. She was glad Faith was beside her seemingly as nervous as she. Both ladies, smiling and clearly satisfied with the results breathed an audible sigh of relief when their twenty minutes were completed. The rest of the group gathered around them, all with relief and satisfaction reflecting through their eyes. Taking a deep breath and looking at the waiting students, Kevin said, "On behalf of the entire group, we thank you for your time and attention."

To the surprise of the entire group, the entire class applauded with genuine appreciation. "How in the world are we supposed to follow that?" someone in the back of the room asked.

"No kidding!" said someone else.

"Well, I guess the standard has been set," laughed Mrs. Simon. "Let's see what the rest of you have!"

Melanie was glad the class was coming to an end although it had turned out to be one of her favorites. She looked over her last journal. "What is the definition of an educated person?" This is one of the first questions she addressed in her journal at the beginning of the semester. She had written simply: "a person who can understand, reflect and communicate what he has read, seen or heard in a manner which demonstrates logic and reasoning skills."

She amended her definition with: …which demonstrates logic and reasoning skills using all the disciplines available: the humanities, natural sciences and social sciences. Further an educated person is one who continues to learn and search for knowledge; not being content with the easy answer to any question that can be approached from a variety of angles depending on the interest of the person asking the question or the one being asked."

"I have learned much," she thought, "and I've grown from having a narrow view of an educated person to a broader perspective of what such a person is. This is good," she concluded with a smile.

Chapter 13

Melanie learned early to expect the unexpected from her classmates. This especially rang true in her Human Development class. Much of the semester was spent on relationships, families and children as well as the development of the human body. One afternoon while discussing adolescence and the changes encountered through the teen years, Jennifer, a small, blonde, vivacious student raised her hand with a question.

"Ms. Spiker, I've been wondering about something. It keeps popping up and I keep hearing about it. Well," she hesitated, "what are wet dreams?"

Hush fell over the classroom.

Without missing a beat, Ms. Spiker, a confident, well spoken woman who moved about the classroom as she taught, turned to one of the male students in the classroom and said, "Wilson, would you like to answer that?"

For a moment Wilson could only stare. Blushing he finally said, "Ms. Spiker, I really don't feel comfortable talking about that."

"Okay. Well, Jennifer, it's a very normal occurrence that can't be controlled and is most apparent in boys although girls can also have wet dreams. One way to think of it is it's when boys start washing their own sheets."

"Oh," Jennifer responded with apparent understanding. "It's kind of like a giant squirt gun. It just goes everywhere!"

Cocking her head sideways, Ms. Spiker contemplated the analogy. "Well, something like that."

The class erupted into laughter that could no longer be contained.

"Why is everybody laughing at me? I just didn't know," Jennifer said defensively.

"There was nothing wrong with your question," Ms. Spiker, assured her. "It's just a little unusual to hear it asked in a classroom.

"Okay, class, let's move on," she said, heading back to the front of the room. "I have mentioned several times you will be given a group project to work on. Your group will consist of four people and we will count off to form these groups. I will be giving you a four page handout to aid you in topic selection."

Groans reverberated throughout the room. Melanie completely understood their feelings because she shared the emotion of instant frustration at the mention of group work in general not to mention the added aggravation of a group not of your choosing. Counting began at the back of the room and she cringed when she had to say "two" when Haley had already voiced that number. It seemed somehow that whenever there were groups, and they were in the same class, they ended up on the same team. It wasn't that she disliked Haley since she didn't know her well and didn't feel justified in coming to that conclusion, but their ideas were so far apart. She seemed highly intelligent although she was known for overpowering and usurping a conversation with her highly controversial views. Generally Melanie avoided the larger girl who reminded her of a "punk rock star" who often dressed in either white or black skin tight jersey pants that did little to hide any of her larger than average body. She wore her long hair straight and wore makeup that seemed to reach the room before her face made the entrance. Her black knee boots and tops that revealed a large cleavage, completed her outfit.

"Break into your groups for the last fifteen minutes of class and begin to discuss your topic ideas and a name for your group," said Ms. Spiker. "I want good ideas! Choose from the list of ideas I've given. There are plenty and once you have an idea, you may expound on it in any manner you choose."

The students rose to join with their groups. Melanie moved to the middle of the room where Haley, Constance, and Rebecca had already met. Haley immediately took the lead and said "I have the neatest idea for the name of our group!"

"What's that?" asked Constance, a well dressed, evenly tanned, twenty-year-old.

"Well, I don't have the entire name yet, but it needs to have something with "estrogen" in it."

"You are kidding," said Melanie her brows furrowed. "There is no way I want that to be our group name."

"Me either," echoed Constance and Rebecca.

"Why not? Don't you think it'd be cool?"

"No, I don't and the name we all need to agree on, so let's come back to that after we decide on topics that at least interest us. We can narrow it down later. We'll at least have something to work with over the weekend. We can each do some research and see if there's enough material to give a good presentation on our topic."

"Sounds good to me," said the pony-tailed, red-headed, Rebecca already perusing the list.

"Well before we go any further then," Haley said, "I want to know something. Who in the group is an A student?"

"What difference does it make?" asked Constance.

"I just want to know what I'm working with."

"That's just wrong!" said Melanie. "It doesn't matter who is or who isn't."

"Well, I'm not an A student," said Rebecca looking down. "I get mostly B's and I work very hard to get that."

"I'm borderline," said Constance, "and I'm happy there."

"I am an A student," said Melanie more firmly than she felt, "but Rebecca and Constance, you have as much to offer as any of us here. So it doesn't matter! What does matter is we choose a topic. Where do our interests lie?"

"I like these cult topics and the gay and lesbian issues listed here," said Haley.

"Not me," said Rebecca. "That stuff scares me."

"I'm right there with you," chimed Constance.

"Me too!" said Melanie.

"Sounds like you guys are just going to be hard to work with," pouted Haley.

"I'm sure we'll find something we can all agree on," Melanie replied none too confidently.

As the class time ended, each of the girls had two topics they were to research and bring to class early in the week although three of the four girls leaned toward a psychological creativity topic. Haley was the only dissenting voice. Some of the topics to be considered challenged Melanie's beliefs, morals and ethics. "Perhaps there is something to be learned here," she thought.

Making her way to the car, Melanie placed the ringing phone to her ear as she fished for her keys. "Mom can you take care of Ariana, Dylan and Ethan tonight," asked Tara without preamble.

"Sure, what's up?"

"Oh, nothing, really. I'm just going out."

"What do you mean?"

"I'm going out. Brent's had his life and it's messed up ours so now, I'm going to go find my life."

"Are you sure you want to do that? It sounds like you're up for a party. Where are you going?"

"It doesn't matter," she said defensively. "I'm going out. Will you watch the kids for me or not?"

"Of course I will. I told you that already."

"I have no idea what time I'll be back."

"Well, do you just want them to stay the night? They can go with me to church in the morning and then go home with you afterward."

"Sure, that'd be great. I'll bring them over about 6:00."

"Okay," replied Melanie, still wondering what "going out" meant.

"Where in the world is Tara?" she asked Lee after church clearly knowing he didn't know either. "Guess we'll just take the kids back home with us and she'll get them later."

This was the beginning of a spiral Melanie felt completely inept to handle. "God," she pleaded, "please turn Tara's heart around. She's destroying herself and her children. Help her to see that her behavior is not going to change Brent's. Give them each a heart of forgiveness and the determination to work things out," she continued to pray even as they drove home.

On the day of the presentation the girls in Psychology class, ultimately called "Haley's Comet" were apprehensive of their capability even knowing each had prepared as planned. The group name was Haley's idea and gave her the feeling of leadership, although the other three agreed this absolutely was not the case. The project required a minimum of three different visuals and at minimum of five points made with each, a combined four page paper describing each individual's part and how it tied in with each of the others. Additionally, the presentation could last only a maximum of fifteen minutes. Grading would be by the professor, the class and each group would grade each other individually at the end of the presentation. Haley had agreed the creativity project might be interesting and even offered to do a video clip of her section.

The group was instructed to demonstrate at least one the four "Ps" in creativity: process, product, person and place as related to creative thinking in the different kinds of art. Choosing to focus on the nature of the creative person relative to her creative interest, Melanie described intellectual habits, which include attention levels, concentration abilities, accuracy of whatever process is before them and reflection among others. It also required relating to levels of autonomy which is the degree of ability to schedule the time necessary to complete a project as well as, determining how it is to be completed. Melanie would also need to explain her level of expertise, skill and proficiency as well as, investigative behavior, again relative to her creative ability.

Rebecca chose to focus on the process in creativity in cartooning and used several posters for her visuals. Haley focused on product in creativity through visual arts by creating a video clip, while Constance dealt with place in creativity relative to landscapes, seascapes and cityscapes with the use of an overhead projector. Each of the participants discussed their part of the project adequately and Melanie had to give Haley a lot of credit for the video clip especially since the very thought of trying to speak while operating something mechanical made Melanie shiver.

To be what seemed routine to Melanie, working with groups certainly added a different dimension to completing a project successfully. One day, upon arrival to the classroom during the time period allotted for work on the projects, Rebecca was absent. Haley completely outraged said, "I believe we should take ten points right off the top of Rebecca's grade for being absent."

"We can't do that!" said Constance.

"She's supposed to be here!" Haley stated adamantly.

"She could be sick or anything. We'll do our work, call her or otherwise meet up with her so she can catch up and it'll be fine," said Melanie. "It's not fair to penalize her for not being here unless it became a habit and really wrecked the group. I don't see that happening."

"Well, I think when I grade her, she's still getting ten points taken off her grade for not being here."

Melanie shook her head in dismay, while Constance rolled her eyes and said, "Whatever!"

On the day of the presentation, the time element was the only part that nearly hurt them. So much information was gleaned; it was difficult to stay within the time frame. She was glad she opted to display her creative art through quilting. "I am so grateful for the down time quilting allows when I am stressed since "thinking" isn't required to sew and my knowledge about quilting has come through years of experience," she said, finishing her part of the presentation.

Melanie was surprised with the questions the class had for them at the end of their presentation. She was even more surprised at the response she received from her most recent quilt project. Despite the positive reaction she had received the first semester in the Fitness For Life class when she used a quilt for her presentation, she still worried that quilting would dub her old and out of touch with the current "real" world. Instead of being considered old fashioned, many of the young girls suggested they might like one day to learn the craft themselves.

Stopping by the mail box at the end of the driveway, Melanie pulled out the envelopes carefully, not wanting any to drop or get blown out of her hands from the strong winds that always seemed to blow in South Dakota! Noting the familiar handwriting, she quickly placed the one from Luke on top. Quickly driving into the driveway, she hurried inside to read her latest letter from her son so far away.

As characteristic of Luke's letter writing style, it was brief, barely a half page long.

Hi, Mom and Dad, it read.

Leaving Saudi and headed for Australia. How cool is that?

Don't know how long the deployment will last. Dad I know you'd like

to go there. I'll take pictures and make sure you see what it looks

like. Mom, don't worry, I'm fine. Will try to send a message via email

when I get there. Gotta run. Know that I miss you.

Love,

Luke

She placed the letter against her chest and prayed yet again. "God keep him safe. He's so far away. Keep him out of harm's way and bring him home soon." Placing the letter on the counter where she knew Lee would find it as soon as he came in, she began preparing dinner.

"Dinner's ready, Lee" she called from the kitchen, that same evening, as she heard the door bell ring.

"Be right there," he said, "I'm going to get the door."

"Hey, Tara. What's up? We're getting ready to eat. Want to join us?"

"Maybe," she said. "I've got so much stuff on my mind."

"Well, you could join us for dinner and then go with us to church."

"Actually, that might not be a bad idea. Something's got to give and it might have to be me."

Quietly, Lee and Melanie remained by Tara's side during the church service, each saying a prayer that lives would be changed before any more damage was done. "God, only you can repair this marriage," prayed Melanie. "It's gone so far from where it started. Change Tara's heart to recognize her need for you. And, Lord, touch Brent's heart, too. Help him to recognize his gambling problem and the problems it's creating for himself and his family. Amen."

Tara made her way to the altar and as tears flowed with a repentant heart, she gave her heart and life back to God. With happy hearts Lee and Melanie hugged their daughter. "We'll keep praying for Brent," Melanie said.

"Thanks," said Tara. "We've got quite a road to travel yet. If Brent does choose to work things out, he's going to have to admit he's got a gambling problem. That might be really hard for him."

"Nothing is too hard for God," Melanie reminded her. "Our job now is pray."

Ms. Spiker walked around the room placing papers on individual tables. She handed Melanie hers and said, "I wrote a note at the end of yours but I don't want you to read it until after class."

"Am I going to be upset?" Melanie asked, clearly concerned.

"Oh no," she replied, "It's personal."

"Melanie," it said, *"I would like to request a favor from you as a Christian sister. We've shared concerns over Ian's anger issues he has displayed in our classroom. Would you consider adding him to your prayer list? Pray that his anger is directed in a way that does not hurt himself or anyone else. While I am very concerned about this, I don't believe I have the right to share my concerns with any professional since he is an adult and hasn't really done anything that*

would warrant my expressing my concern except what he has said in this classroom. That being said, while I normally would not even consider sharing this with another student, I believe you will keep our prayer request personal; just between you, me and God."

The next class period, Melanie, approached Ms. Spiker after class. "Just so you know, "he" was already on my list," she said smiling.

"I thought maybe, but wanted to be sure we approached God together on this. I would hate to see anything happen to destroy that young man's life."

As the semester began winding down and the holidays drew closer, Melanie was surprised by a copy of a letter she received from the Office of Student Activities that was addressed to Luke.

Dear Luke,

Although we have never met, I have known your sister Mackenzie for many years. I have also had the pleasure of meeting your Mom and brother as they are both taking courses at Cedar Ridge. As a part of our Veterans Week celebration of honoring those who have served and those who are currently serving, Cedar Ridge's Student Government Association asked members of our College community to sign the enclosed banner as a holiday greeting to you and your unit.

Please accept this banner on behalf of your unit as a thank you for your dedication, bravery, and service to our country. As I believe you will see as you scan the banner, we are very grateful for your service and wish you all many blessings for a successful mission and safe return home.

A very happy holiday to you all, along with a community wish of prayers and blessings. You will be in our hearts and minds.

Sincerely,

Ria Sparks

Counselor/Director of Student Activities

As Melanie read the letter, tears flowed down her face from both pride and sadness. She missed her eldest son and wanted him home safe and sound this Christmas but knew it wasn't happening.

Three days later Lee said, "Hey, we just heard from Luke again."

"What did he say?

In Australia now. We've been real busy and I can't go into any details, but at least I am well. We had one issue where we had the day off and our squadron went to the beach. The rip tide was horrible and we lost one of our guys there. It was awful. Not a good way to start!

Melanie found herself overcome with tears again. "All I do is cry," she thought!

Digging in her purse to find the ringing phone, Melanie bumped into Dr. Vasser. "Oh, I am so sorry!" she said completely flustered. "I wasn't watching where I was going."

"You're fine," he said, "Don't worry. No harm done.

Lee uncomfortable and he welcomed his trips to Arizona to soak in some of the warm sunshine.

"Hey, Melanie. You doin' alright?"

"I'm okay," she said, "but I sure miss you, Lee."

"I miss you too."

"Ready to come home yet?"

"I just got here!"

"You are not going to believe what came in the mail yesterday," she said, suddenly animated and excited.

"What?"

"I got an invitation to join PTK!"

"PTK?"

"Yeah! It's Phi Thetta Kappa! It's college honor society. How cool is that? I didn't even know I was qualified! I have this form I have to fill out and get taken care of to say I accept it and then there's this induction ceremony they do at the college. I am so excited. Who would have thought?"

"Good job!"

"And, what else is neat, Mackenzie also is going to be inducted to her honor society, Alpha Chi, at Rushmore State!   Her induction is the first week in November and mine will be the second week. You will be back then, right?"

"Should be."

"Should be?" she asked clearly annoyed.

"Yes, Melanie. You know I'll be back for both inductions. I'm proud of you. I proud of both of you."

"Thanks!" she said, again wearing the smile of accomplishment. "I really am excited."

As she entered the room and took her seat, Lacy, a beautiful brown girl with long silky curls, called her name. "Melanie, what did you think of "The Bluest Eye?"

"Ugh!" she said just before Mrs. Thayer walked into the room. "But, it wasn't Gothic," she added laughing.

"I heard that!" Mrs. Thayer said, amused.

"I can tell that at least Melanie and Lacy have read the book I assigned over the weekend. Let's get some input about it. Melanie, what did you think?"

"The truth is, honestly, there hasn't been very much I've liked that we've had to read," Melanie responded. "But like I said, at least it wasn't Gothic. The story was interesting, but way too explicit in parts. That whole section on the little girl's mother's sex life. Horrors! I did not need the details. I could have created my own images without the description!"

"I agree," said Lacy. "Sometimes you need to be able to read in between the lines. This is a college class. We're not stupid."

"And the flip side of that," Melanie added thoughtfully, "is I wouldn't want a child to read that."

"Yes, Emmi?" said Mrs. Thayer

"Not to pick on Melanie," she paused.

"Go ahead. I'm not offended," Melanie offered, laughing.

"Melanie's proper. I didn't mind the details. I don't know that the story needed it, but it didn't gross me out either."

"Different people require different things and it's good that each of you have your personal views. That's what makes literature so interesting. While the author may have had one thing in mind, sometimes it's not what the reader has at all because the reader relates what is being read, to his life experiences. A reader's perceptions are also contingent on upbringing, religious and moral beliefs. Each of these brings different ideas to what you are reading.

"Perhaps, as Emmi suggested, Melanie is proper. That's okay. Her perception of the story is based on her moral beliefs that graphic material need not be included in a reading. On the other hand, much of our media today includes material such as was included in the story and much more."

Mrs. Thayer ended the class saying, "Begin reading Othello through act three. Before you go, I have an announcement to make. Our Melanie has made PTK, our honor society here at the college.

"Congratulations, Melanie. That is quite an accomplishment and you have every reason to be proud of yourself."

"Thank you," Melanie responded. "I'm just surprised and really grateful. I honestly had no idea that I would be eligible for anything like this."

"Well, you work very hard and you deserve it!"

"Thank you," Melanie said modestly, a bit embarrassed.

Melanie drove to Peaceful Pines nursing home. Having been there so many times, some of the patients recognized her and responded even if she didn't know their name or they hers. "It is so cold in here," said one of the patients as she passed by. "Need to turn the heat up."

As Melanie continued to the Alzheimer's ward another patient in a wheel chair grabbed her arm and held on tight. She pulled Melanie to herself and Melanie found herself hugging the lonely old lady. The lady smiled sweetly and said, "I love you."

Flo was just finishing her lunch when Melanie reached her. "Hey, Flo," Melanie said easily, kissing her on the cheek. "You doing alright?"

Flo stared straight ahead while clutching the doll in her arms. "She's just babysitting," said Miss Amanda, another patient sitting nearby. Abruptly Flo handed the doll to Melanie who took the doll by the arm and then held the doll more like a real child when Flo looked at her with hurt filled eyes.

"I'm sorry," said Melanie. "I didn't mean to hurt your baby. She's all right," Melanie assured her. Flo never responded with words but her countenance softened when she saw Melanie hold the doll gently.

"Lee will be home soon," Melanie said. "I'm sure ready. It's seems like it's been forever. He should be back in another week or so."

"I want to go home," said Flo suddenly. "I want to see Momma and Celia Rose."

Melanie was at a loss. Even after all this time she still wasn't sure how to respond properly to these kinds of requests. She certainly had no power to make the requests come true and further even if she could, she knew no one outside the nursing home would be able to handle the woman before her who once was vibrant and full of life.

"It'll be okay," she said as reassuring as possible. "I need to go now. I have so much to do."

"Go!" said Flo suddenly bitter and staring straight ahead again in apparent defiance.

Melanie placed a kiss on the now unresponsive cheek of the woman she cherished and made her way off the ward. "I hate this place," she said angrily once she was outside and away from anyone who could hear her. "I hate Alzheimers. It's not fair! Mom didn't deserve that!"

The beginning of November arrived with more snow and cold wind. Lee arrived two days before Mackenzie's induction into Alpha Chi, at Rushmore State. As they made their way into the auditorium, Melanie's phone rang. "Hey, Mom," said Tara. "We're on our way, just running a little late."

"Okay," she said surprised her daughter would call to tell her that. "We're going to dinner afterward. Want to come?"

"That would be perfect!" Tara replied.

"What do you mean, perfect?

"It just would," she said.

As the family sat eating their meal several hours later, Lee said, "Great job there on your awards, Mack. You did good!"

"Hey, Dad," said Tara, grinning broadly at Brent. "You want more good news?"

"Sure," he said, reaching for his coffee.

"You're going to be a grandfather again."

"What?" Lee said hitting his cup and spilling its contents all over the table.

"Oh my goodness! That's wonderful," said Melanie laughing as she sopped up the mess Lee had made.

"Another little one," said Lee reflectively, enjoying the prospect of being a grandfather again. "God is good!"

"Yes, he is," Tara affirmed reaching for Brent's hand.

Melanie looked at herself once more in the mirror. Her dark blue, A line skirt with a soft blue top complemented her small frame. Her hair hung loosely around her shoulders. "It's as good as it gets," she said to Lee. "Do I look alright?"

"You look great!" he said but as soon as they entered the auditorium, she knew something was wrong.

Every former member of the organization and most of the new inductees were dressed in black and white. Only she and two other inductees were not. As quickly as possible she searched out Mr. Parnell. "Why is everyone in black and white?" Melanie asked completely agitated. "No one told me to wear black and white."

"I sent an email out to all the new inductees," he answered. "But I will admit my email has been doing strange things recently. It's possible it didn't reach you."

"What do I do?"

"Nothing. Don't worry about it. You look fine. You look very nice. It isn't a problem."

"But everyone else, well almost, is dressed right. I'm just wrong."

"Believe me. If your colors and the way you dress were the only problems I encounter tonight, I will consider myself blessed!"

Mr. Parnell no sooner had the words out of his mouth when a young man wearing a green dress shirt and jeans with holes in the knees passed by. "You look fine! Don't worry about it," he said again sternly yet with a smile.

"Well, all right," she said resolutely. "If you're sure!"

"I am, now go. You need to be in room 211 just down the hall."

As the evening progressed, Melanie was surprised by the selection of role models the students had included in their brief biography to be shared with the friends and family in attendance. Colleen's choice made Melanie catch her breath. "Jesus," she said, her long blonde hair accentuating the genuine smile on her tanned, oval face. "He's the perfect role model. I want very much to be who he wants me to be!"

"Wow, that was great!" said Melanie later to Lee and the children gathered around while enjoying the hors d'oeuvres prepared for guests and inductees. "I like my role model choice, but I sure wish I'd have put Jesus down. That was amazing. It didn't occur to me to even consider that in a public college and I certainly didn't expect that from a young person, especially one who is so pretty and apparently quite popular."

"The presentation was beautiful," said Mackenzie. "And the white rose a nice touch!"

"Hello, Mackenzie," said a tall, well dressed woman, walking up to them.

"Hi, Dr. Teator. How are you?"

"Very well, thank you. Are you related to this inductee?" she asked smiling and nodding toward Melanie.

"Actually, yes. This is my mom, Melanie. Mom this is Dr. Gina Teator, Vice President of Academic Affairs.

"It's nice to have you. Congratulations on your achievements."

"Thank you," said Melanie nervously.

"We've met before," Dr. Teator said, "just not formally. From what I have seen and heard about you, you are a welcome addition to our college."

"Oh my. Thank you," said Melanie now feeling very warm.

"I like it here. It's wonderful being a student. Everyone has been very kind."

"Well, like I said, it is good to have you. Enjoy your evening."

Three weeks later, Melanie was again to feel abundant joy when she received a telephone call from Phil early one morning before she left for class. "You're a grandmother again," he said proudly. "Kaitlyn just gave birth to a brand new baby boy. We've named him Jackson."

"Just in time for Christmas!" laughed Melanie. "Congratulations. Lee and I are so excited. I don't know exactly what our plans are, but hopefully we can get down to see all of you right after finals."

"That would be great, Mom," he said. "I'll let Kaitlyn know. I'm sure she'll be calling you later today.

As the semester was coming to a close, Melanie studied for finals. This was the one thing she really didn't care for, even though she usually did quite well on the tests. Still they left her on edge. Even knowing finals were close, there were still regular assignments due. She was delighted when she finally found a reading assignment she actually liked. "A Doll's House", a social drama, by Henrik Ibsen was a perfect assignment for the end of a semester filled with horror and ugly things.

"I finally found a story I liked!" said Melanie excitedly when Mrs. Thayer came into the room.

"Good!" laughed Mrs. Thayer. "Why did you like this one?"

"I could relate to it," she said, honestly. "Women still live in a man's world. You really have to search for options that aren't readily available. Especially for women like me who are older, have hardly ever worked outside the home, but want more out of life. It's a struggle and it's hard sometimes to know what are good choices.

"And you have to remember that your choices don't just affect you. They affect, if you're a family, every member of that family. The story just resonated with me."

"Well, I'm glad," said Mrs. Thayer, laughing. "I'd hate to think you spent an entire semester in here and never liked anything you read!"

English and the last day of finals were finally over. This final had not been nearly as taxing as the Statistic final which had clearly been the most difficult, probably because Melanie felt most inadequate in that class. She studied hard, and asked Gavin to clarify some of her questions and then plowed into the exam with a fair share of confidence.

IDC was completed with the final project involving the "object" which she and her team decided was a malfunctioning piece of equipment that caused a tragic train accident. She was delighted with the results and considered herself fortunate to have been required to take a class many students considered unnecessary.

The Human Development final hadn't been particularly difficult, but it was Mrs. Spiker who would remain steadfast in Melanie's heart since she entrusted her prayer of another student to her. She cherished the professor's kindness and confidence in her and she trusted God to touch the young man's heart.

It had been a good semester, but she was glad it was ending since the Christmas season was upon them and that meant some travel and general household chaos. How she loved this time of year.

"Dad and I are going down to see Phil, Kaitlyn, Kara and Jackson next weekend," Melanie said to Tara one evening as they were visiting and trimming the Christmas tree. "Their church is having their Christmas Pageant and Jackson gets to play baby Jesus! Do you and Brent want to come along? We could buddy up in the cars."

"Steven and I are going, too," Mackenzie chimed in. "It would be great if we could all go!"

"Well," said Tara, turning to look at Brent, "that would be nice, but I don't think we'll be able to, we already have plans for next weekend. But we have some news of our own."

"What's that?" asked Lee.

"Brent and I are going to have another baby!"

"But we already knew that!"

"No, we really are going to have another baby," Tara said again, more slowly.

"Oh my goodness!" said Melanie as the news of their revelation finally made sense. "Are you saying what I think you're saying?"

"Well, if you're thinking we're having twins, then you are thinking right! We just found out this week. We are so excited and I am scared to death!"

"Wow! God is so good! What a blessing! Congratulations!" said Melanie as she hugged her daughter. "It's going to be another good year!"

Chapter 15

Melanie looked up, smiled and returned the "hi!" she had just received from another student as she walked down the hallway looking for the room 117. She had been told that Mr. Leadbetter's Geography class was going to be interesting and challenging. It seemed students either liked the professor or disliked him completely. He had a reputation for doing things out of what was considered normal.

Walking into the room, she was immediately surprised by the negative responses she had heard since students were crowding around his desk. It seemed everyone there liked this particular professor. Taking a seat near the front as was her custom, she watched as other students continued to file in and those around Mr. Leadbetter's desk also took a seat seemingly on a silent queue.

The medium height, blonde haired, well dressed man rose. Walking to the door, he looked up and down the hall way, then purposely closed the door and faced the room. "I expect that those who have arrived are here for Geography class," he said. "If not, then may I suggest you are in the wrong room, and urge you to leave and find the class you meant to be in."

A few giggles could be heard near the back of the room, but no one said a word. "Now that, that is settled," he began again while picking up a stack of papers, "this is the syllabus we will be using this semester and I want everyone to be sure to pay attention to the material because near the end of class we will be having a ten question quiz to see just how well you have paid attention. Melanie could feel her eyebrows immediately furrow in a slight case of panic. A quiz already? She wondered.

"Note the second item underneath the basic information regarding this class," Mr. Leadbetter continued. "You will see that all cell phones are to be placed in this basket upon entering the classroom," he said reaching across his desk for the desired object. "I absolutely loathe hearing a phone ring, ding or sing while I am teaching. Therefore all said electronic paraphernalia will be collected and you can pick it up on your way out of class."

"No way," a voice was heard saying from the back.

"Those are my rules," Mr. Leadbetter said.

"Is that legal?" asked another student.

"My classroom, my rules. Just be sure you don't forget it before you leave. And I have a feeling the relationship many students, maybe even most students have with their phone, iPods, etc. you'll not likely forget. Just be sure you pick up your own and not someone else's. Okay, everyone that has a phone, bring it on up."

A girl in the far back corner of the room stood. Walking slowly, with slumped shoulders she dropped her phone in the basket. Another girl came forward until almost all the students laid their technological communication in the basket.

Melanie hesitated. She considered her options. Her phone was either off or on vibrate during class and in her purse which sat on the floor. She couldn't hear it even if it should have vibrated and would have been mortified to even think of being disrespectful enough to respond to a message of any sort during class.

She'd seen students use them to text in almost every class regardless of what else was going on. Teachers could often tell a student was texting even when the phone wasn't visible. They would hold their phones under the desk or table but their intensity clearly gave them away. Many used the calculator on their phones in math class. Melanie didn't even have a clue how to find the calculator on her phone, much less use it!

Confident knowing she could never be charged with using a phone during class she remained in her seat as did several other students. Mr. Leadbetter never questioned their decision, but continued class.

She found herself liking Mr. Leadbetter's easy style of teaching. He was very different than Mr. Hart, her U.S. History professor she had several semesters ago. Mr. Hart had very obvious passion and love for his subject. Mr. Leadbetter was more of the attitude, "I like it, it's okay if you don't." Even upon introduction on this first day it was clear he knew his subject. His perspectives seemed to come from one who had been to the area he was talking about, despite the generality and global view he was taking.

"Remember to keep an eye on the syllabus," he said, twenty minutes before class ended. "You will need to be able to identify and correctly name the listed countries on the quiz you will have the first class period of each week. If that changes or needs to be altered in any way I will tell you.

"Now, everyone put their syllabus away and take out a pencil or other writing object. Circle the correct answer on the quiz. You may not discuss it with your neighbor."

Melanie glanced at the questions before her. This is just weird Melanie thought, as she glanced at the questions before her. "Oh well, at least I can get a good grade on the first day."

Quiz #1

Circle the correct answer:

1. What is the subject of this class?

   English   Math   Geography

2. What time is this class?

   6pm-8pm   9:45-11:00   5am-4pm

3. Did immigration only occur in the US?

   Yes   no   maybe

4. Does religion and culture have an impact on global space?

   Yes   no   maybe

5. Is there ethnic competition throughout the world?

   Yes   no   maybe

6. What countries will you learn about in this class?

   US   none   duh!

7. Has there always been global discontent among peoples?

   Yes   no   maybe

8. Does development vary among nations?

   Yes   no   maybe

9. Who teaches this Geography 101 class?

   Mr. Leadbetter   Ms. Ray   Charlie

10. Do changes and new ideas affect other places?

   Yes   no   maybe

Number one was Geography, that was a no brainer, number two 9:45-11:00, no to number three; yes, number four; yes, number five; What? She read number six a second time and a third. That doesn't make sense, she thought. Of course we'll learn about the United States and "none" isn't the right answer, but neither is "duh!" She moved on to number seven, yes; eight, yes; nine, Mr. Leadbetter and ten, yes. Again, Melanie read number six: What countries will you learn about in this class? It's more than just the United States, she reasoned, so US is a wrong answer too. There are no right answers for that one. I know I'm not being stupid. Frustrated she thought, how in the world do I answer that?

"It's time to pass your papers forward," Mr. Leadbetter said. Melanie looked at the question one more time and circled US, even though she knew the answer was going to be wrong. It seemed the only option available. Maybe it was a typo, she hoped, but even that didn't ring true.

After placing her paper on top of the ones from the students behind her, she handed the stack to Mr. Leadbetter and starting gathering her books. Before leaving the room, she walked up to his desk and asked "What was the answer to number six? That didn't make sense to me."

"That's easy," he said off-handedly. "Duh!"

"Duh!?"

"I don't understand," she said completely confused. "That's not an answer."

"Sure it is," he responded. "If you know the answer "none" is wrong; this is a Geography class," he insisted, "and you know it's going to be more than just the United States, then "Duh!" has to be the answer."

"That's not fair. That's not an answer."

"So you got one wrong. Don't worry about it. It's just a quiz and if you got the others right then you get a 90%. That's not a bad way to start the semester."

"It's awful," she countered. "I did get it wrong, because to me "Duh!" is still not the right answer."

"It was the right answer," he argued. "Deal. You'll do fine in here. If you are that concerned about that question being right or wrong, you should have little difficulty passing."

"It's more than just passing your class that I'm worried about."

"Melanie, relax. You'll be fine. Trust me."

"I don't know," she said not sure where to take the conversation from here. Turning, she walked away.

Tired from a long day at school, Melanie pulled the mail from the mail box and tossed it on the seat. Parking the car she reached over and picked up the envelopes she had just moments before tossed aside and immediately noticed the small, block lettered hand writing she recognized as Luke's. Ripping it open she pulled out its contents with urgency. Luke rarely used the Postal Service; normally his messages came email. She read:

"Hi Mom and Dad!

Thought I'd sit down and write you a real letter this time. Just so you know I'm fine. Things here have been crazy and the hours on the flight line even crazier.

I don't want you guys to worry, but you should know I'm getting ready to head for Iraq. Mom, don't be upset. I'll be fine. Dad, I know you'll be there for Mom and I'm glad. I don't know how writing will be once I get there. I will still try to send a quick email when I can, but I can't promise anything. Remember to not ask about the particulars of where I am or what I'm doing 'cause I just can't share that kind of stuff. You know, security and all that.

Know that I love you both. Will write when I can.

Luke."

Melanie felt the hot tears roll down her face. Iraq? He's going to Iraq? Laying the letter against her chest, she allowed herself a good cry before even attempting to get out of the car. Once she opened the door, she was reminded the weather forecast had been for snow. She hoped Lee would be home soon from a trip he had taken to Belle Fourche earlier in the day. She wanted desperately to be held and reassured that her son would be just fine. She wanted to hear him say again that the training he'd received in the Marine Corps was the finest in the country and the skills he learned there would keep him as safe as anyone could be in that situation. She wanted the support that only Lee could provide.

Three hours later, through nearly white out conditions, Melanie was grateful to see headlights in the driveway. It could only be Lee. She had been upset about Luke's news and then the delay due to the weather of Lee's arrival home made her nearly frantic. Her eyes were red and puffy from crying, and she found herself shaking like she was cold, even though she was standing in a very warm room. She ran to the door and opened it as soon as she saw her husband emerge from the car.

"Melanie, what on earth? What in the world is wrong?"

"Luke. Luke is going to Iraq."

"Is he really?" Lee asked softly reaching to hold her before he even removed his coat.

"We got a letter from him today. Look," she said trembling with tears threatening to fall again.

"I will," he said taking it from her. "Shhh. It'll be alright. This is what he was trained for. God will keep him safe. If he's got to fight, at least he's had the best training out there. You stay strong and believe he'll be just fine. That'll keep both of us sane. I fought over in Vietnam. He'll be okay. He'll come back just like I did. You'll see."

Melanie rested against him calming her shivering body in spite of his cold, wet coat. She felt safe and secure and confident in her husband's assurance of the well being of their son. She thanked God for both of them.

The snow storm brought six inches of snow overnight and then temperatures in the 50's the very next day. Roads were completely passable so Lee and Melanie decided to visit Flo. It was always disheartening to witness the decline of not only their beloved but also the other patients that had at times reached out for a mere touch or tender smile from even strangers. Today Miss Adela who just a week ago had been walking around with incessant chatter now was in a wheel chair almost unable to eat or at least swallow. The nurse at her side was trying desperately to encourage her to open her mouth to take food and then persuading her to swallow it. Ultimately, Melanie noted, most of the food just dribbled back out.

Recalling a conversation with a friend of hers some years before she said absently, assuming Lee was listening. "I couldn't work in a place like this. Remember when Mrs. Thurman told me she thought I'd be just perfect working in a nursing home. She said she thought my upbeat personality would be a pleasant change for the patients. I don't know, but I think if I worked in a place like this, keeping happy, upbeat and pleasant would be a really tough job. Kudos to those who do this day after day."

"I have to agree with that," Lee said. "It sure is a tough place to even visit for me."

"And I think what makes a nursing home even worse is knowing that these poor old folks you take care of day after day are just one day going to be gone. I think my heart would just break. It would be like losing your mom or dad over and over again."

On this day, as on previous ones as they continued down the hallway, Miss Georgette, a tiny framed woman, walked up to Lee. "Are you a preacher?" she asked desperately. Pulling on his sleeve she continued, "I love my Jesus. I'm going home soon. I just know I'm going home soon."

"Yes, ma'am!" he said, while continuing his effort to reach his mother in the lunch room sitting near the window in her chair staring into space, seemingly lost in another world.

"Flo, it's Lee and Melanie. How are you?" Melanie said. "You're looking good today. Are you enjoying your lunch?" With hardly any reaction Melanie looked at the food in front of her mother-in-law.

"It does look kind of awful? Doesn't it?" she asked Lee. "I'm not sure I'd like it."

"What Mom would really like is a hot bowl of chicken soup Pop used to make and watermelon. Why she used to sit down and eat half a watermelon all by herself. She'd shake a little salt on it and she'd go to town. She liked that almost as much as she liked ice cream," he said slowly relishing the memory.

"You need to be somewhere," Flo said suddenly. Reaching for Melanie, she said it again. "You need to be somewhere."

"Where do I need to be, Mom?

"Somewhere," she said softly. "Somewhere," she said again before fading and being lost completely in her thoughts.

Melanie sat down in the chair and opened her Geography textbook. She knew there would be a quiz today and she wanted just a few more minutes of study time before Mr. Leadbetter started class. She was startled when a beautiful girl who sat in the back of the class squatted next to her desk.

Melanie looked at her long straight jet black hair, soft brown eyes, perpetual tanned skin, tiny frame, slim and delicate features. She looks like a Hawaiian princess, Melanie thought. Even her name sounds like royalty, Victoria Kamaka.

"Hi," she said cheerily. Are you Gavin's Mom?"

"Yes," she answered cautiously.

"I work with Gavin in the TV room and I've see him talk with you. So it made me wonder. I just wanted to say hi. Do you like this class?"

"I do, mostly," Melanie offered. I don't like the idea of all the quizzes, especially the ones on the countries. I've been studying and he hasn't said any more about it, but it's hard to remember which one is which!"

"Me too. We won't have time today, but maybe next week we could quiz each other a little before class starts. If it's fresh in our minds, maybe it'll help us remember.

"That sounds great. I'll get here as soon as I can and even if it's only a few minutes, that's better than not at all!"

"Thanks, 'Mrs. Gavin's mom' she said, hurrying back to her seat as Mr. Leadbetter closed the door. Melanie giggled.

"Today's quiz has two pages," he said.   "The first is on the reading you were assigned and the second is a map you need to fill in," he continued passing out the papers to the first person in each row. "Pass them on back," he commanded.

Melanie's stomach lurched. Not one word had been spoken about the countries except on that first day when Mr. Leadbetter had told them they would need to know them. The text they had been reading didn't correlate with the list, so she had set aside the need to study them intently, even while she did try to at least get a general idea of places in Europe. She had looked over the first list, found them on the globe, but was certain that at some point there would be discussion about them in class. Berating herself for not being prepared she remembered the first quiz. That had seemed irrational too. She should have expected the unexpected.

Melanie answered the first page of questions and then nervously flipped over to the second page of the quiz. Her panic turned a moderate relief when she saw the map. It was of the Middle East and since Luke was there, she and Lee had spent some time looking at the area where he was stationed. Confidently she filled in the spaces with the names of the various countries. She wasn't certain all of them were correct, but she knew she was close, resolving to know from then on she would be prepared for the rest of the "country quizzes" by memorizing each of the lists and their placement on the maps.

"I can't believe we haven't heard from Luke," said Melanie after coming home from a long day of school and work.

"He told us he'd try to stay in touch. Don't start worrying yet," Lee reprimanded.

"I can't help it. It's been too long. What if something's happened?"

"If something had happened, then we'd know. This is a "no news is good news" situation," Lee said, sounding more confident than he felt.

"You just don't understand. Every day that goes by without hearing from him just makes me more and more nervous."

"I do understand, but you can't let it rattle you like that," Lee retorted beginning to get annoyed.

"But it does," she said angrily. "It just does," she repeated sighing. "And it scares me to death."

"We have plenty of other things to think about right now. Let's not think anything horrible about Luke."

"What's more important than Luke?"

"I didn't say more important, just other things."

"Like what?" she asked firing up again.

"Well, we have medical decisions to make regarding my rotator cuff, which car to fix for which child next. We need to decide what our mission project is going to be this year. I need to buy a new tractor and a back hoe would be really great. Should we build on to our house now, or wait another year?"

"None of that really seems important right now," she said turning her back to him and immediately wished she hadn't. "I didn't mean that the way it sounded. Honest. I'm just so worried. We do need to make decisions and I know you're right. We'll hear from Luke soon enough. He'll write when he can."

"Look, I'm worried about him, too," Lee said as he came up behind her and put his arms around her. "We really will get through this. We've got to trust God. That's all we have."

"This is why I've said so many times I'm glad I didn't know you while you were in Vietnam. I don't believe I would have been able to deal with it. And when the news came that you were hurt. I can't imagine the pain and heartache your mom and grandmother must have had."

"It's taken me a long time to understand that," Lee admitted. "It used to hurt my feelings knowing you were glad you didn't know me then."

"I'm sorry."

"Don't be. At least I understand now."

A week later Melanie absently checked her email before she left for class like she did every day and shook with relief when she saw the message. "Lee," she screamed. "Luke's okay," she said crying. "He's really okay. He sent an email. Look!" she said again unable to stop crying or shaking. Clicking on "open" she read:

"Dear Mom and Dad,

Sorry for the delay in writing. It's been a tough month. Wanted you to know I'm okay. Like I told you before I can't give details. Just thankful for being alive. Thanks for all the prayers. I love you, Luke"

Melanie melted in Lee's arms and cried tears of relief and gratitude. "He's really okay," she said. "He's really okay. Thank you, Jesus!"

Chapter 16

Melanie looked at the clock. 9 a.m.   Lee wouldn't be in for at least two hours. This might be a good time to check this online class out. "It's kind of neat not having to be in class for class," she thought smiling. "I like not having to leave as early for school a couple days a week. This could be good! Maybe I can get some other stuff done before I do have to leave."

Melanie looked at the disk in her hand.   The only thing on the cover said, "Instructor: Dr. Alexandra Hayden, Education Professor Cedar Ridge Community College. According to the directions that had come with her packet, she was supposed to get the information for the class off the disk. She wasn't at all sure she was going to like this. Apprehensive she put the disk in the computer and let it load. The power point's first frame said, "This CD will give you the basics for your Education 214 class." Clicking the arrow key, she continued: "Once you hear the introduction go to the WebCT site on the College Home Page, click on it for your first assignment. She continued clicking until she read each frame: "Each assignment will be two-fold. There will be Chapter readings and after each one you will be expected to comment thoroughly on what you have read. Because it is an online class and I, as instructor want class participation, everyone's comments will be posted. Please comment, also, on other people's comments. This dialogue is how we learn. We must listen to other people's ideas.

"Secondly, you will listen to the first video session and again complete comments are a requirement. As before, all comments will be available for everyone to read, as well as myself. This is largely where I will be able to tell you understand the material.

Before you begin, however, you will find an area where you should type an introduction about yourself. Include your professional status, family hobbies, where you live, etc. It would be great if you would share anything about yourself you would like us to know so we can get acquainted with each other. Remember, we don't meet face-to-face, so this is everyone's opportunity to get to know each other a little. Please don't be shy."

Melanie closed the window for the CD. "Dr. Hayden sounds nice enough." And in the next instant, noted again the passage about everyone being able to read everyone else's post. "Great!" She thought. "If I say something stupid, everyone will know it. This is worse than being in class," she thought. "What if I have a question for the professor? The CD didn't say anything about that. It's all online. I don't even know what Dr. Hayden looks like! I hope I get this!"

Melanie spoke to her computer like it was a human. "Okay, you! Let's see how this works. She went to the college home page and clicked on "WebCt." Just as promised she found the class and the area to write about herself. She was more interested, however, in learning about her professor, and read, "I am Alexandra Hayden, married to Kent for 12 years and have three adorable children: Logan, 8 years old, Amber 6 and Natalie 4. We moved here from Wyoming and I have been a professor at Cedar Ridge for ten years. I love to ski and ride horses."

She pulled out the Video cassette. "Good thing I've got a VCR," she said aloud even though she was alone.

Shoving the cassette into its compartment, she settled back for the first segment on background knowledge and its role in reading. As soon as it was finished she went back to the computer, "I can do this," she thought while carefully clicking on WebCt for a second time in the same day. "Maybe this won't be so bad after all," she said aloud, again talking to herself as she began typing.

"Background knowledge is not only important but crucial in getting understanding of what you are reading. It helps the reader gain insight to what he is reading. I remember when we had visitors from the east with young boys a few years ago. Like most boys, they enjoyed watching cowboy and Indian movies and reading books of "how the West was won." The only problem is, the stories depicted the Indians as savages, people who had little respect for others, lacking compassion, and a whole host of other negative attributes. On one of our day trips together we visited Wounded Knee. They were pleasantly surprised when a true live, old Indian was caring for the burial ground. This old Indian was wonderful! He chatted with the boys and showed them that Indians are people too, much unlike the way they were depicted in stories in books and on TV. The boys were "wowed" by this. It shattered their current incorrect "base knowledge" about Indians and replaced it with what was real."

"Learning about the brain isn't nearly as interesting as the videos," Melanie ventured to add in her posts for the reading segment of the assignments. "That being said, "I agree with Jan and Holly about the "scientific" way we learn….."

Melanie looked at the clock. 11:15 a.m. "Wow," she thought, "I've been at it a while. Lee should be in any time. Got to get his lunch ready before I head out of here. It was going to be a long day. This would be the first time for a class that didn't start until evening: 6:15 p.m. Lee wasn't a bit happy about it, but it's the only time the class was available.

"Lee," she said, pleasantly as he walked in the door. "I was beginning to think you wouldn't get here before I have to leave."

"What's special about today?" he asked, suddenly suspicious.

"It's my first late in the day class. Remember? It doesn't start until 6:15. That means you either have to eat dinner without me, or wait until I get home which won't be until about 8:30. I have to leave here at 12:30 for my Fundamentals of Math class. Then I have a break until my EDU 102 class at 4:00 which actually goes with my EDU 101 class that I take on Monday's and Wednesday's when I have Geography. I'll work at the Financial Aid office during the break."

"Anybody who would schedule a class that late in the day doesn't have a lick of sense," he said.

"It has nothing to do with having sense," she said exasperated. "It's when it's available. It's a required class and I have to take it. I'm sorry."

"Right!" he said disgustedly.

Disheartened Melanie cleaned up the table and counter from lunch and got ready to leave. Lee was still sitting at the table as she walked out the door sipping on a cup of coffee. "It's gonna be a long day," she thought.

Gavin had been quiet for days. Melanie knew it was coming and with each passing day her heart grew heavier. She had seen him place the prayer request sheet a few Sunday's earlier in the church offering plate. Even though he had never spoken of it, she knew what it was.

Lee and Melanie were sitting in the living room watching television when he walked in the room and handed each of his parents an envelope. Tears came unbidden as trembling fingers received it. "Gavin," she cried as she opened it, "please don't do this. Please, not now. Rethink what you're doing."

Lee opened his, looked at it and tossed his into the floor without saying a word. Gavin looked at his mother and simply said, "I have to. I've prayed about it. It's time and I'm going. I know you don't want me to, but it's time I got out on my own. I told you I wouldn't make the move until I was certain of financial aid from the school I went to and you know Glacier Falls University offers everything I required. Trust me on this. I have to do it." Resolutely, saying nothing more, he walked out of the room.

Sobbing Melanie read the letter he had written. *Dear Mom, You have taught me much. I will never forget all you have given me: life, love, guidance and more. I love you and I know I haven't told you that nearly enough. I know you don't want me to leave, but it is time.*

You've known for a long time of my love for Montana, it is something I know we both share. While I love the Black Hills, Montana is part of who I am. When I am there I am at peace; I am at home. Please understand. You know I've prayed about this and believe it is God's will in my life. I've saved my money and am ready to make the move.

You worry too much, Mom, we both know that. I will be fine. I have the teaching that both you and Dad gave me. How can I go wrong? I won't forget all you have taught. This is the biggest decision I have ever made. But let me trust my heart. One day I hope you will understand."

Melanie held the letter close to her as if it could mend the break in her heart. She did know of his love for Montana. The family had visited there many years and summered there for the last four years and he had spoken often of his desire to live there. It was as Gavin said, it was something he and she shared.

Montana seemed to be almost magical and mystical in its ability to draw Gavin in. It was ironic that the place she enjoyed so much would be the place that would steal him away. The rugged terrain claimed him, it was where he belonged. When time was over from summer vacation and they began the drive back, Melanie would find Gavin quiet and removed as if overcome with grief. She noted at how physical the attachment had become and hoped desperately the deep desire for him to be there would leave. But after all the years, the shroud of dark heaviness that seemed to claim Gavin since childhood when they would begin their drive back to their home remained.

Melanie really did understand Gavin's need to be there. It was the way she felt about the Black Hills when she and Lee first arrived so many years ago. It was beyond understanding or describing when the feeling is so intense you feel consumed by it. But that knowledge did not ease Melanie's grief. In a bazaar way, she felt like she was losing him. My "baby." How he hated that, yet she could see him smile whenever it was said, in spite of himself. They had been close a long time. Perhaps partly because he was the baby, but also because he was the "easy" one. Gavin was real mellow and easy going, not real chatty, but a thinker and mother and son often had "deep" conversations about life, love, happiness, who they were and what they wanted to be.

Melanie found herself unable to speak without tears the rest of the evening and for the next three days. She couldn't say a word to Gavin without crying. "Bear with me," she pleaded. "I know you're going, but you've got to let me cry. It's the only way I'm ever going to get through this. I'm not angry, but I feel this terrible loss. It's seems so far away; 800 miles. I know it's only a long day's drive, but we both know weather plays a huge part in travel. There isn't even an airport close by we could use. That means I will go months without seeing you." She laughed at her words and added. "I'm sure that must not bother you nearly as much as it bothers me."

"Probably not," he agreed chuckling.

Lee felt the same as Melanie although he expressed it much differently. He didn't want Gavin to go. Melanie responded with tears, his was anger. A required trip to the Motor Vehicle Department offered the opportunity for Lee and Gavin to finally chat. Gavin shared with Melanie later that while his dad didn't want him to go, he would support him but Lee told him he'd better be home for Christmas. "You promise?" Melanie asked even knowing the answer but needing to hear him say it.

"Yes, Mom, I will be home for Christmas."

Melanie was glad for the holiday coming up. Easter was early this year and she was looking forward to the quick trip down to Texas to visit with Kaitlyn, Phil, Kara and Jackson. She had not seen them since soon after Jackson's birth and she knew her grandson would have grown much in that time.

"I wish we could go with you," said Mackenzie. "I'd love to get away for a while."

"It'd be great if you could," Melanie agreed. "I'm looking forward to going, but I have this paper I have to do for my EDU 214 class. I have no clue when I'm going to get it done or how!"

"Why? What is it?"

"I have to interview, chat with, observe a child of my choice to determine what stage of language acquisition they have. Dr. Hayden suggested a library, church setting, or even a pre-school to observe a child. I don't want to go somewhere and just get some child to chat with. The parents would think I'm nuts!"

"Does it matter how old they are?"

"No, they just need to be able to communicate so you can chat with them and observe and record their answers."

"Mom! Why not use Kara? You're going to be right there. She's young, but that shouldn't matter. It might make it really interesting!

"It is so good to have you and Dad here," Kaitlyn said. "I have so much to share with you."

"It's good to be here; thanks!"

"So what kind of news do you have to share?" asked Melanie completely interested.

"Well, you know I've been working at the Grassley Regional Hospital two days a week since we've been down here."

"Yeah."

"Well, I've met a mid-wife and I want to become one!"

"What? You're kidding?"

"No! It'd be great. And I'm growing herbs because I've found that herbs make great natural remedies and I've got a huge vegetable garden planted because we're going vegetarian; well mostly vegetarian anyway! We're not going to eat meat but we will still eat eggs and other dairy products."

"No way. Okay. Stop! Start from the beginning. First tell me about being a mid-wife."

"Well, Texas has a mid-wife board which I've already checked into and I've got to take some classes, or work as apprentice, but in some places being a mid-wife is considered a "calling." I'm sure I want to do this and while I didn't have a mid-wife to help me with Kara or Jackson, I certainly will when we have more children."

"Wow!" Melanie said softly. "That's interesting," she added taking in the information just shared. "I think I can see you doing that. I remember you used to like working in Pediatrics before you and Phil got married.

"But what does that have to do with being a vegetarian and growing herbs for medicine and such? That's not a requirement, is it?"

"Oh, no!" laughed Kaitlyn. "I have done a lot of research and it's where I think we should be as a family. Come look at the gardens I've started; one for herbs and one for veggies. I don't have nearly all the herbs I'd like but I've got Ginseng for a fever reducer and respiratory tract disorders, Wild Yam Roots for nausea and menstrual cramps, peppermint for indigestions, rhubarb for an anti-inflammatory agent, rosemary for upset stomachs and headaches, thyme for indigestion, garlic for colds and flu and some others. This doesn't touch what I could have and I've learned that some of the herbs are actually trees! I am so excited!

As for being a vegetarian we would be in the "lacto-ovo vegetarian" class because while we would not eat meat, fish or poultry we would still allow eggs and other dairy products. Kara loves cheese and milk and she'll eat eggs too."

"What on earth got you interested in all this?"

"Well I want to be a Proverbs 31 woman. I want to eat organic, do as much sewing as I can for our clothes, garden, can and eventually even home school.

"Mom, there is so much scientific research that eating organic and following a vegetarian lifestyle really has many benefits. It reduces the risk of obesity, high blood pressure, diabetes and can even deter different kinds of cancers."

"Well, I hope you know what you're doing. It sounds interesting and I admit, I can see merit in at least part of it. It seems like it would take a lot of energy. Just be careful to keep your focus on your family and not on what other people expect you to do if you show interest in something like this.

"I can certainly see you home schooling the children. In fact I'd be surprised if you didn't. I love the garden and canning. I've done that for years. Not sure about going vegetarian. I don't think it'd be for your father and me. As for your herbs, that's fascinating but I hope you won't rule out regular doctor visits and that kind of thing."

"I'll be careful Mom, and I'll use good sense when it comes to seeing doctors and that sort of thing. Stop worrying. This whole idea is amazing and I am so excited and looking forward to the adventure."

"I guess it would be an adventure, wouldn't it?" Melanie mused.

"Oh, I hear Jackson. Time for his feeding."

"Would now be a good time to do my Language observation assignment with Kara?"

"Sure, that'd be great!"

"Kara," Melanie said as she went into her bedroom. "Is it okay if I come in?"

"Uh, huh!" she responded. "Come look at my play house," she added pulling on Melanie's hand. Melanie drank in the scene reminding her of her own little ones so many years ago. She loved the time spent with Kara. Her room was filled with blocks, dolls, containers with toys, a large basket with play food and a fish tank. Kara was quick to share and demonstrate just how her large play house with a play phone operated. They used building blocks, picked up and put away items in her room, and identified food from her kitchen set and discussed the colors of each. Kara and Melanie counted, played dress up and named letters.

Melanie smiled when she observed her granddaughter chatted with herself while doing something alone and had quite complex telephone conversations, using infections in her voice and hand motions! Her own hand motions during conversations had often been a source for teasing and amusement through her lifetime. It looked like her granddaughter was going to have the same issue!

When Melanie sat down with her notes after their return trip she smiled even as tears ran down her face while she breathed a prayer. "God, I sure wish Kaitlyn and Phil didn't live so far away. How I miss them and those sweet babies."

Proof reading her assignment one more time, Melanie logged onto WebCT. She was ready to upload the paper on Language Development. As she did she saw the newest assignment posted. "Create a Graphic Organizer on the history of language." What in the world? Thought Melanie. She read the assignment again and was more confused than when she began.

"Mackenzie," said Melanie, "I don't get this assignment at all and I don't even know what Dr. Hayden looks like to search her out on campus."

"Try asking some of the other students in the class."

"Will that make me look stupid?"

"No! If you're having issues with it, it is completely likely someone else is too!"

Melanie hit the send button and hoped someone would respond. Leaving her computer she went to find Lee. It was Saturday and they had an afternoon of shopping to do. Just as they reached the door to leave, the phone rang. "I'll get it," said Melanie.

"Good afternoon. I am trying to reach Mrs. Melanie Carson."

"Speaking."

" Ma'am, I have been trying to locate Steve Rigby, but so far he isn't answering his telephone. Mackenzie keeps asking for you."

"What do you mean?"

"Mrs. Carson there's been an accident."

Melanie felt her knees weaken as she reached for anything to hold onto to keep her from falling. "Lee," she screamed. "Lee!"

"What is it?" he said, immediately noting her distress.

"Mackenzie has been in an accident."

Taking the telephone from Melanie, Lee completed the call saying, "We'll be right there."

Moments later they were at the accident scene. Melanie shook all over as she took in the scene. Fire trucks, ambulance, police cars, and Mackenzie's car on its side. Fear gripped her as she wanted desperately to know if Mackenzie was going to be alright. A fireman walked up to them and asked, "Are you this young woman's parents?"

"Yes," Melanie answered, swallowing hard, fighting the tears that threatened to overtake her. "Is she going to be alright? She's pregnant you know. Please make sure the baby is alright too."

"We'll do our best. Right now we are trying to get her out of the car. Mrs. Carson, you might want to wait over there away from the car. What we are doing is covering your daughter so when we break the glass and use the "jaws" we can extricate her."

Just then, Tim, a man her husband had known for years, walked up. His long, shaggy hair and tattered clothes made him look well beyond his 35 years. Placing his arm around her tenderly, he led her away while signaling to Lee he could go on over to the car.

"Now, Melanie. She'll be okay. Just let them get her out of the car. She's talking. She wanted you."

Melanie relaxed a little while Tim spoke, yet all the while allowing the tears to fall freely down her cheeks. Just then she heard the metal creak and groan against the pawing of the "jaws" and the sound of a helicopter approaching. She jerked her head around to see. "What is that helicopter doing here?"

"Now Melanie, I told you she's gonna be all right. It's just a noisy process. They will come get you just as soon as they get her out. As for the helicopter, that is just routine. Mackenzie's car is so wrecked, it doesn't matter that she seems okay. The car damage alone warrants a visit to shock trauma down in Rapid."

"You're sure?"

"I'm sure," he told her again, feeling her body tense again.

The minutes seemed like hours before a fireman walked up to her. "Mrs. Carson, your daughter is out of the car now. She's ready to see you. She seems to be all right. In fact it looks like she came out of the accident with only a sprained wrist. We have a monitor on her and the baby and everything seems amazingly fine."

Melanie allowed herself to be led over to the helicopter. "Mackenzie?" she said as soon as she saw her.

"Hey Mom. I'm okay. Honest. And they tell me the baby is okay, too. That poor deer I hit sure isn't okay, though, is he? Looks like I get a ride in a helicopter."

"Do you need me to come with you? Or is it okay if your dad and I come down in just a little while?"

"Come down later with Dad. Honestly, I'm going to be sore tomorrow, but I'm all right. God is good!"

Melanie watched as the helicopter lifted into the air and moved away. She saw Lee walk along the edge of the road picking up debris; there was the bumper, large shards of glass, rubber pieces and mangled pieces of metal that no longer held the shape intended. Walking over to the mangled car, to Melanie's surprise he opened the driver's door and closed it. He opened the back door on the driver's side and then the passenger's side followed by the front passenger door. "What are you doing?" she asked completely confused.

"Angles were in this car with her," he said matter-of-factly. "The top is pushed in and the car is a mess, but look; all four doors still open and close. It didn't crush her and as bad as this looks, it should have."

"Thank the Lord," Melanie said as she shivered from the realization of what could have been. "God is indeed good!"

As the days passed Melanie found herself fighting to stay caught up. Frustrated with the assignment, she sought out Mackenzie's help. "Send Dr. Hayden a message and ask if you can come to her office. At least that way you'll be able to meet her and then ask her what she wants you to do. My guess is you're making this much harder than it needs to be."

Melanie rounded the corner of the hall. It had been a nice walk over to the Spotted Eagle Building although it was completely across campus. The sun was shining and it seemed remarkably warm for the time of year. Seeing Dr. Hayden's nameplate on the door, she knocked.

"Come in," said a friendly voice.

"Hi, Dr. Hayden," said Melanie smiling at the tall, brunette. "I am Melanie Carson, part of your EDU 214 online class. I emailed you about visiting for clarification regarding the Language graphic organizer. I don't get what it is you want us to do."

"You're making it too hard, Melanie. The graphic organizer is nothing more than a Venn diagram." She reached for a pencil and piece of paper. Drawing a center circle and adding more circle around it, she said, "You start with a center and go out from it. Some items you include will overlap. Use this information to demonstrate where words come from."

"Oh," said Melanie feeling a bit foolish. "You're right. I was making it way to difficult. I'll get started and upload it as soon as I finish."

"No problem. And I'll say, it's nice to be able to put a face with the name. You're doing a good job."

"Thanks," Melanie responded suddenly warm. She hadn't expected the compliment.

With clarification Melanie was able to finish the graphic organizer required for the class. Once she had it figured out, she discovered it was more time consuming than difficult. When she uploaded her finished product she added this to her post.

> *My "graphic organizer" shows where different words started and the direction they traveled to be the words as we know them today. Note that a line is highlighted in Old English, Middle English, Early Modern English, and finally in Modern English. This is the first line in "The Lord's Prayer. In addition to the "Organizer" is a brief history time line and summary at the end.*

> *I would like to add: The Language Organizer was quite a challenge to upload! I don't think I'm the only one who thought so! I was the first one and have enjoyed the responses on it! It is a helpful thing to do, though. A person doesn't generally think about just where our words come from. I think the thing that amazes me most though are the words (weird ones like ain't) that make it into the dictionary. Just because it's become an accepted word I'm not sure that qualifies it for the dictionary....but then what do I know?!*

As the class wound down she decided that if all on-line classes were like this one, she would like to try another. The students had interesting conversations via WebCT even though she had never met them. Dr. Hayden had responded whenever there was a question and added notes to many of the discussions. This had definitely been a good experience and she was happy to have participated.

Chapter 17

"Another math class," Melanie thought, heading in the direction of room number H202. She heard a familiar hello and someone calling her name.

"Hey Rosa. How are you?"

"Good, where you headed?"

"Fundamentals of Math with Wilton."

"Oh yeah? Me, too! I hope this class isn't horribly stressful, but you know, I have my doubts. Do you like math?"

"Not really, but I need it for my major."

"Me too. I need three Math's for Education! Three!" she added for emphasis.

Rosa, a small, bronze skinned, 25 year-old with curly jet black hair, laughed. "This is my last required one and I am glad. Know much about Mr. Wilton?"

"No. Hope he's good."

"And patient!" Melanie added laughing as they entered the room. Scanning the room she noted several students she'd had in other classes. Taking a seat near the front she opened her Math book and looked at the Table of Contents.

"Addition and Subtraction of Whole Numbers and Multiplication and Division of Whole Numbers; those at least I can handle," she thought. "Not sure about the exponents, roots and factorization of whole numbers." She grimaced. "I hate factorization! I like fractions, so that part should be all right; decimals aren't bad but ratios and rates don't sound like fun. Estimation might be okay but oh no, I'm not going to like geometry and what in the world is signed numbers? And Algebraic Expressions and Equations that's going to be hard."

Melanie turned to Rosa sitting behind her. "I don't know about this," she said frowning with her eyebrows furrowed. "This might be kind of tough. Not all of it, but enough. I might be calling on you for a hand every now again. You good with that?"

"Sure," Rosa laughed. "We'll muddle through it together!"

Mr. Wilton, a ruddy looking man with skin that looked slightly sunburned, white hair and matching white mustache and beard made him look years older than Melanie thought he probably was. She immediately liked his warm smile and soft blue eyes. "Maybe I'll like this class after all," she thought smiling.

Melanie made her way to the basement to retrieve the Christmas tree. Luke was coming home and another Christmas celebration was on. She'd been working on the preparations for weeks. The gifts had been wrapped for December's celebration and even placed under the tree but had been set aside when they'd learned he wouldn't make it home. Melanie had been horribly disappointed but knew it couldn't be avoided.

Seeing the box she desired, she pulled it off the shelf, nearly dropping the bulky prize. Gathering as much coordination as she could muster, she carried her treasure up the stairs. After several more trips downstairs she had all she needed, the tree, the decorations, the nativity, and Christmas wreath. "Luke is going to have Christmas just like he had before he left," she said aloud with determination. Two hours later she stood back to admire her work. The lights and ornaments had carefully been hung, the angel set on top of the tree and the tree skirt beneath. The packages of red and green paper with bright colorful ribbons and bows finished the display.

A week later Melanie was at the door when Lee and Luke arrived from the airport. His 6'1" frame stood erect, giving more definition to the fine lines in his chin and close "high and tight" hair cut. "It is so good to see you," she beamed hugging him tightly. "It seems like it's been forever!"

"It's good to see you, Mom. It does seem like it's been forever and a lifetime ago." Melanie noted a slight sadness in his eyes.

"You okay? You look like you've lost weight."

"Aw, Mom, maybe a little, but not enough to fuss about. I'm okay, just tired. It's been a while since I've been able to relax."

"Gran....," said Ariana, "Hey everybody, "Uncle Luke is home!" she squealed, running up to give him a hug.

"Hey, Luke! It's good to have you home!" came excited echoes of each his siblings in turn all hugging him tightly. Taking a moment he addressed each one.

"Tara, you look good! I hear we're expecting twins!"

"Believe me, it's beginning to really feel like it, too!" she said, laughing, giving Luke a hug. "And I already feel like a tugboat and I have four more months to go!"

"Hey Brent! Kaitlyn, Phil, I understand I have a new nephew. I need an official introduction! And Mackenzie, look at you! Looks like Steven is treating you right! And I hear you're going to have a baby, too!"

"True, true!" she said, smiling broadly.

"Gavin. You have gotten taller, brother. What's Mom been feeding you?"

"I don't know. But I'm ready for turkey now!" he responded laughing. And I hope it's almost ready. I'm starved!"

"It does smell good," he said walking into the living room. "Wow! The tree is beautiful. You really did set up for Christmas again. I'm not sure I thought you'd really do that. Wait till I tell the guys when I get back! They are absolutely not going to believe it!"

"We even put a few lights on the outside of the house," giggled Melanie. "Dad thought that was a little much, but hey….it is Christmas!"

"It is indeed!" said Luke visibly relaxing.

"Well, you chat for a few minutes while I go put dinner on the table. How 'bout if you girls give me a hand."

When the family was gathered all around the table, Lee spoke as he reached for Melanie's hand and Luke's on either side of him, initiating the long custom of holding hands while grace was spoken. "We have much to be thankful for." Bowing his head he continued. "Lord, we are a blessed family. Thank you for once again for bringing Luke home to us out of harm's way. We are grateful our family sits around this table at this special time to enjoy this time of celebration. Bless this food, we ask in your Son's holy name. Amen."

Luke looked at the table spread with food. There was turkey, mashed potatoes, gravy, sweet potatoes, green beans, cranberry sauce, fresh baked biscuits and tea. This is a feast!" said Luke. "It's been a while since I've eaten like this. "

"You know Mom when it comes to Christmas. She's got this meal down pat. Now," Gavin said, looking around, "where's the mayo?"

"Right here," laughed Melanie. "And here's the bread, for your sandwich."

"You still do that?" asked Kaitlyn.

"Are you kidding? This is the best way to eat turkey," Gavin laughed while piling food on his plate beside his bread. "Hey, I need a saucer. My plate is too small!"

Gathering around the tree, the children could hardly contain themselves. "Do we get to open gifts too?" they asked.

"Sure," said Lee. "You don't think we'd have Christmas and not have any gifts for you to open, do you?"

The next moments were spent with each person opening gifts, followed by an evening sitting around the fireplace drinking cider and coffee, eating pecan and pumpkin pie, cookies, and brownies. The little ones were finally tucked in bed and even some of the adults had given in to the events of the day and called it a night. Melanie walked to the kitchen to begin clean up of the rest of the dishes. Half an hour later putting the last things away, and drying her hands she finally headed back to the living room where conversation continued.

As she rounded the corner Melanie heard Luke speaking and on impulse stopped not wanting to interrupt what sounded like more than idle conversation. "Gavin, can I talk with you a minute?"

"Sure. What's up?"

"Look, Gavin, I know you want to leave. I understand that, but I think you need to wait until after you finish college."

"What do you care when I leave, Luke? You enlisted in the Marines when you turned seventeen. What makes it right for you to leave but not me?"

"That's just it, little brother. I left and I won't say I have any regrets about going in the Corps, but I missed out on a lot. You have a chance to do stuff with Mom and Dad and once you leave all that is gone. I missed Thanksgiving and Christmas and other family gatherings. I missed Tara's kids growing up and little Kara forgot who I was the first time I came back home. Can you imagine what that felt like? It was awful. Yeah, I traveled a lot and I enjoyed it. But I left too soon. I don't blame you for wanting to go; I just think you should wait a while. You don't ever get this time back."

"I appreciate what you're saying, Luke. But, I'm going. I don't want to hurt anyone and I know I'll miss things. But this is important to me. I have to do this and I have to do it now."

"Would you at least give it some more thought?"

"Well, I think about it all the time and I might even second guess myself sometimes, but this feels right."

"Hey, guys," she said when the conversation seemed to have ended. "I'm headed for bed, but Luke, did you have any specific plans during the next week?

"Nope! I just want to spend it with you and Dad and the family for as long as they are here. I've missed being home. This is great!"

"Okay. You know I have class and for that matter so does Gavin until Friday. We have the weekend and we'll have to do something special then."

"Sounds good!"

Melanie cautiously entered the room seeing it was filled with other students around a large table eating pizza and drinking sodas. Seeing Mr. Parnell, she immediately went to chat with him.

"Melanie! How nice to see you. I'm glad you could come."

"Thank you for inviting me," she said.

"You're part of this. You should be here. Go find some food. There's plenty!"

Taking a seat at the long table, she chatted with Colleen, the young woman who had used Jesus as her role model at the induction ceremony. "I'm part of the Campus Crusade," she shared. "I went to Europe last year and it was amazing."

"You're kidding. How old are you?"

"I just turned twenty. I've been part of the Campus Crusade for three years now. I love it! What a great opportunity to witness for Jesus!"

"That is absolutely fantastic! Where did you go and what did you do?" Melanie responded beaming with interest.

"Our group visited Thailand. It's a Buddhist country and the goal is to increase harmony between the religious communities. It's not always easy. We evangelize and disciple in different universities and campuses in the region. Our goal is to teach that Jesus is the One True God. It's amazing to see those young people come to Christ."

"I am impressed. You just seem so young."

"I love it. It's what I'm supposed to do."

"What's your major?"

"Humanities."

"Ladies and Gentlemen," interrupted Mr. Parnell. "I'd like to thank everyone for coming. This is your club. You've earned the right to be here. I'd like to have a roster of club officers. Is anyone willing to be President?"

Silence was his only answer.

"Melanie, what about you? I think you'd make a wonderful president. Would you consider it?"

"Sure, I think," she laughed. I'd like to talk it over with my husband first, if that's okay."

"No problem. I'm counting on you," he said matter-of-factly.

"Okay," she said cautiously. "I hope I don't disappoint you."

"You want to do what?" asked Lee.

"Run for President of PTK."

"I think Mom would make a great president," said Luke as he entered the kitchen. "That'd be kind of cool!"

"It would take a lot of time if you're going to do it well," Luke said.

"I know and that's why I wanted to talk to you first. I'd need your support and willingness to work around schedules if I'm busy."

"If it's what you want to do, then by all means, go for it."

"Hey, Gavin," Luke shouted, "Mom's running for PTK president!"

"Running is the operative word," Melanie said. "There was this other girl who right before we left the meeting told Mr. Parnell she might be interested, too. And she's beautiful and dresses very professional. She's tall, probably 5'6"; has long auburn hair with sea blue eyes."

"You'll get it," said Luke confidently.

"Well, we'll see. I've got to get some kind of plan together of goals and projects to present to Mr. Parnell the beginning of the week. We'll see what happens. There's a really nice girl, named Vanessa who is running for Vice President. I like her. I heard her dad is even a minister. That's pretty cool. I think I'd like to work with her."

"Well," said Lee. "Do what you need to do and see how it turns out."

"I love you," Melanie said, kissing his cheek. "I'm grateful for your support!"

Cautiously Melanie walked into Mr. Parnell's office. "Hi, Melanie, how are you?"

"Fine, thank you. I brought you my ideas for this next year's PTK activities. I hope you approve."

"Wow!" he said. "I appreciate your initiative. This is great. There's a Leader's Convention in June. I'd love to see you attend."

"Interesting. Maybe. I'd have to work that out with Lee."

"Okay."

"Have you heard anything from Tristen?"

"Not a word. What I think I'm going to do, is call her and see what she has in mind, and attempt to steer her in another direction. Are you good with working with her?"

"Sure. I don't see a problem. I don't know her at all. But that should be all right."

"I'll call Tristen, and then have her call you and we'll see where it goes from there. You okay with that?"

"Okay," she said nodding, not sure why it seemed to put her nerves on edge.

A week later Melanie's cell phone rang. "What do you think? Should I answer it?" asked Melanie. "I don't recognize the number."

"That's up to you," said Lee.

"Good afternoon," Melanie said.

"Hello. I'd like to speak with Melanie, please."

"Speaking."

"Melanie, this is Tristen Cadby."

"Hi, Tristen. How are you?"

"It doesn't matter how I am," she said curtly. "You and I need to talk!"

"Excuse me?"

"Look," she said matter-of-factly, "I want you to know that I am running for PTK president too. I think you need to back down. And I will tell you I will not be strong armed by anyone. Besides I have all the right qualifications for this position. My major is Business with a focus on accounting, my mother is in politics, my father is a top executive in the Phillips, Cadby, and Hastings Law Firm and I've been working for him as an intern for the past three years in Minneapolis.

"Furthermore I feel like I have the most to offer because of my experience in a big city. Kids here don't think college is important. I can change that. I'm a realist and know how to get college kids involved. Besides, why should we have an election no one cares about anyway?"

"What?"

"Tristen, I am not backing down. I may not be as experienced as you since you come from a big city. I am not nearly as young as you, and I don't have your attitude. But that doesn't make me any less qualified. I may not win, but I will not just walk away from this opportunity.

"And the next time you call or talk to me, I would be very grateful if you minded your manners and not be rude. I certainly haven't given you any reason to speak to me the way you just did. I didn't deserve that kind of attack. I told Mr. Parnell I would be willing to work with you. I now think that could be challenging!

"I need to go now. You have a nice day. And I'm sure we'll be chatting again." Melanie placed the phone on the counter and for a moment just stood there seemingly unable to make her feet move, yet feeling her entire body tremble.

"What was that?" asked Lee.

"That was Tristen. You would not believe what all she just said to me! It was awful!"

"It sounded it!"

"She wants to be president of PTK. I told her I'm not backing down, but I have a feeling she's the stronger candidate. After talking to her, well, listening to her, I kind of feel like a backwoods dumb smuck! I guess I should call Mr. Parnell and let him know that she felt threatened by whatever it was he said to her, and see what he thinks I should do."

"I'd like to do something!" Lee said clearly agitated.

"You can't," she said hugging him, "and I love you for it. But I have to work this out. If God wants me to be president, then I guess he'll make it happen. I've got the feeling it's going to be an interesting ride!"

Still shaking, Melanie dialed the number to Mr. Parnell's office. She wasn't surprised when she only got a voice mail box to leave her message about the conversation with Tristen. All she could do now was wait.

The wait lasted only a few hours. "Melanie," the email from Mr. Parnell said, "It looks like Tristen may end up being a formidable candidate. She has made it clear she wants the office of president. Therefore, I am asking you both to write a two hundred word paragraph to let the PTK members know who they'd be voting for. Voting will take place during the week of finals. I will let you both know the results of the election which will be done via computer. I wish you well. Mr. Parnell."

As April turned into May, it seemed things just kept getting more complicated. Luke had spent his two weeks home and had gone to Florida for more specialized training before he would be sent overseas again and Melanie missed him. It had been such a special time having him home and she wondered if she would ever get used to her children leaving.

Melanie twisted in her seat again trying to get comfortable. Sitting had become more and more problematic. She finally made a visit to the doctor. "I have what?" she asked.

"Degenerative disc disease in the lumbar spine or better known as the lower back. For you it's basically a tail bone issue. Because of your size, you sit right on your tail bone with very little cushioning. You'd be surprised how many women would love to have your problem."

"You are kidding me."

"No, I'm not."

"What can you do for it?"

"Largely, besides medication to ease the pain, especially since in college you have the need to sit a lot, avoid hard chairs and sit on a pillow."

"A pillow? You are suggesting I carry a pillow on campus, to class?" she asked aghast.

"Well, yes. That's really all we can do. There is nothing we can do for the tail bone, except attempt to make you more comfortable. Sorry."

"Are you taking your pillow to church with you?" asked Lee.

"No! At least there the seats have cushions. It's not like I have to sit on a hard chair. I absolutely refuse! It's bad enough I have to carry the thing to class. The remarks sometimes are downright offensive. One person suggested that it looked like my very own personal toilet seat. That's just rude. I have even had a professor I don't know well question why I carry it. It's embarrassing. It is better now that I just carry it in my bag and pull it out long enough to sit on it."

"Okay, I was just asking."

Lee and Melanie took their usual seats near the front. Just before the morning worship service began, Gavin was approached by Brock, the church Youth Pastor. They spoke privately a few moments and then Gavin said in hushed tones. "I will need to get up during the service."

"Okay." Melanie responded with a puzzled look on her face.

Prayer opened the service for the two hundred gathered, followed by several hymns and special music. "Would those persons I spoke with before the service, please make their way here to the podium?" Pastor Brock began. "Mother's Day is a special time to honor those ladies we often take for granted," he continued. "Today we are going to recognize some of these mothers and find out what makes them so special."

Gavin rose to his feet and walked to the podium along with four other parishioners; two gentlemen in their fifties, a lady in her forties and a lady in her thirties. Gavin stood on the end and waited while each person shared a little about his or her mother and what made her so special.

Lee put his arm around his wife as Gavin took the mike. At once Melanie's eyes filled with tears. "My mom," he said, "reminds me of the dandelion." The congregation rippled with giggles. "Not that they're ugly," he quickly amended his thought while shaking his head. "It's just that you can never get rid of them. Think about it. It doesn't matter what you do to your lawn, the dandelions keep coming back. Weed killers don't work. Pulling them out doesn't work. Cutting them off doesn't work. They are always there. Mom is like that. It doesn't matter what I do, she is always there. She loves me when I make mistakes and I've made a lot of them, helps me when I don't believe I need her help, and listens when I need her to listen. She is always there."

"Mom," he said speaking now directly to her, "I know I don't say it enough, but I love you." Tears streamed down Melanie's face as Bryce the older gentlemen in the pew in front of her reached back and clasped her hands. How she cherished that moment. Knowing Gavin would be leaving soon, the moment now meant more than ever.

Melanie made her way into the classroom. Mr. Wilton had proved to be a good Math professor even if she wasn't crazy about the subject. He allowed time for questions and didn't mind going over material until he was sure everyone in the class room understood the concept. He also arranged for a review and study time before tests. With finals just around the corner, Melanie was grateful for another opportunity to go over the material.

"Today we're going to pair off into groups of three or four for studying purposes," Mr. Wilton said after everyone had taken their seats. "You can choose your partners as long as there aren't any issues and you promise to study and not socialize."

"I want Miss Melanie for my partner," said Ian.

"Me, too," said Harmony.

"You're popular," said Mr. Wilton turning to Melanie, laughing.

"Is it okay?" she asked

"Sure, have a good time!" he said laughing again.

Moving desks together; then pulling out notes, the three tediously went over the material. All three had goals of an A on the upcoming final. Working together, Melanie felt confident she would do well.

Chapter 18

Melanie was excited and hurried to what she felt was her first real education class. She had the Reading and Acquisition class on line and technically that could be included in the Education curriculum, but this one was specifically about the teaching profession, with emphasis on teaching methodology, curriculum and how it all ties in to parents, society, as well as, the students. "This is where it really starts," thought Melanie as she walked into the room.

A petite, bronze skinned woman sat at the desk. Part of her jet black hair was pinned to the top of her head with long locks cascading down out of the mass. Her dark eyes seemed kind and warm. Standing, she wrote on the board: Kimimela Rackard.

"Hello, everyone," she said. This is EDU 101, Foundation of Education. I hope you are in here because this is where you wanted to be. We have much to learn. It will be a busy semester.

"My name is Dr. Kimimela Rackard. Kimimela is a Sioux name which means "butterfly." Most people just call me Kim since pronouncing Kimimela can be a little tongue tying.   Since this is an education class we will be doing presentations throughout the semester and your peers will be critiquing you. It's important that you get a feel for being in front of a classroom. It's also important that you are prepared when you face your class. So while you may at first be uncomfortable with the process, you'll become more at ease as the semester continues.

"Before all of that, however, let's get to know one another a little better. We have a small class and that lends itself well to dialogue and community. I'll begin and then we will go around the room and allow everyone to share a little. I was born and raised here in South Dakota. I love the Hills and enjoy hiking with my husband of two years. We've hiked both the Centennial and Mickelson Trails and the Harney Peak-Sylvan Lake Trail. Harney Peak is a place of wonder and one of my favorite local places to visit. Of course there are many places up in Spearfish Canyon and down in the Custer State Park area too and that is only a few of the places we like to hike.

"I come from a family of four children, two brothers and a sister, who all, like me try to keep to the traditional Indian heritage as much as possible, but I don't let that stop me from visiting other cultures.

"Okay, enough about me. I want everyone to give their name, share something about yourself, where you're from, live or a favorite place you like to visit."

By the end of class time, Melanie felt overwhelmed with the information she had gleaned from her class mates. One was from South Carolina, another from somewhere near Washington, D.C. and other from Texas and one from California. There were only two boys in the class and both seemed a little awe struck by the females.

They were instructed to visit the bookstore and purchase "Savage Inequalities" by Jonathan Kozol. She learned they would be studying about the inequities of education in different parts of our world, particularly in the larger cites as viewed by Jonathan Kozal, they would have to visit a school board meeting and report their findings and even create a personal philosophy of education. "Shew," thought Melanie. "How in the world am I going to do that? I have no idea how in the world I would put that on paper!"

"Wow, I really like my education classes. I can't believe we've been at it two months already," said Melanie as she put dinner on the table one night. "It takes a lot of work, but so far, it's interesting.

"There's this one girl, though, Crystal. I can't figure her. She's got an attitude I just can't put my finger on. I know she's had a rough time. She's young, divorced and has a brother that lives with her that has some kind of medical issue and her four small children, a set of twin boys and two older girls. How awful is that?" she asked without waiting for an answer. "She told the class she moved here recently from Chicago. I can't imagine living there! She takes her brother to Denver every once in a while for some kind of treatment for whatever is wrong with him. That's got to be hard."

Lee sat down, but said nothing.

"You okay?"

"I'm just feeling out of sorts," he said vaguely.

"I have to give a presentation in two weeks," she continued. "I'm not crazy about that, but it'll be okay."

"Could you just stop talking about school for a while?"

"What?"

"Just stop! School is all you talk about."

"I'm sorry. I thought you'd be interested."

"Don't you get it? School doesn't have anything to do with me."

"Lee! What a thing to say! What are you saying?"

"I'm saying I might need to get away for a while, again. I think I'll go to Arizona for a couple weeks, just to get my head straight. It was good having Luke home for a while. He's gone now and I'm just ready to do something different."

"Because of me?"

"Because of me. I just need to get my head straight, that's all."

Surprised by his outburst, Melanie sat transfixed, not sure what to say next. Finally she asked, "When do you plan on going?"

"I'll go the end of the week. That will get me out of here while you do your school stuff and I can go relax where it's warm. I'm tired of the cold, I'm tired of not feeling good. I'm just tired."

"Oh," was all she could say. The rest of dinner was eaten in silence. Neither offering consolation to the other.

The next morning seemed to go as badly as the night before had started. Moments after Melanie entered the Financial Aid office to work, a tall, robust girl stomped into the office. Melanie put on her nicest smile and said, "Hello, can I help you?"

"Only if you can tell me why you took my money away." Courtney replied. She had more than enough attitude, that said she looked ready to pick a fight, but Melanie replied calmly, "Let me see what I can find out. What's your student ID?"

Courtney looked at her like she was stupid, "My what?"

"Never mind," Melanie said, "What's your name?"

"Courtney Ramsey."

"Ok, Courtney, it says here that your instructor has reported you as not attending classes. If you don't go to….."

"What? I do go to my classes. Well most of them. At least I did until I got bored with them." Courtney interrupted.

"Your instructors for all your classes said you quit coming after the first week of classes," Melanie continued.

Courtney was getting more irritated, "No one said I had to go to every class all the time. I'm entitled to that money. I'm not paying for this bill you sent me in the mail. I can't afford that!"

"I'm sorry, but your award letter, that you signed, said if you didn't go to class we would take the money and you would owe the bill. I really am sorry, but that's the Federal regulation. You can set up a payment plan with the Business Office to get that paid off, but you won't be able to sign up for classes for the Fall until it's paid."

Courtney gave her a funny look.

"I know it's a little early to be thinking about Fall classes when our semester just started six weeks ago, but you owe most of your bill from this semester and you've already said you can't afford it. I just wanted to make sure you gave yourself enough time to pay it off."

Looking defeated, Courtney headed for the door, stopped and turned around. "I'll be back," she said. "And when I do, I want to talk to the director!"

Melanie sat back in her chair shaking her head. "That was awful!" she said clearly rattled.

"Actually, you handled that very well," said Debbie. "I'm proud of you. It's hard to stand up to someone like that. You were completely calm and you gave all the right answers. Good for you!"

"I needed to hear that just now. It's been a tough week!"

"You know," Debbie added thoughtfully, "you did forget to tell her that if she isn't going to her classes then she needs to drop them."

"Oh man! Well then, I guess it's a good thing she's coming back," she quipped, then surprised at her own remark.

Melanie watched Lee drive the truck pulling the travel trailer out the drive way. He was only going to be gone for two weeks, but the ache in her heart made it feel like two years. He loved Arizona. It was his favorite place to be when it was cold. He appreciated the dry warmth on his aching joints, as well as, the opportunity to play pool.

The various camping resorts had pool tournaments several times a week. The senior men would get together and play each other, as well as, other resorts. It had become the highlight of Lee's visits to the area. The camaraderie between the men seemed to grow stronger with every visit. They often had much in common like automobiles, and numbers revolving around miles per gallon or engine size; Veteran discussions, describing places and events the men had been and fought; and travel itineraries detailing routes and hot spots to tantalize the visitor. It was in this place Lee was happiest when cold winds prevailed in the North.

It was finally the beginning of presentations and Ben, one of the boys in the class offered to go first. Setting up his power point, he began, "The history of education is important and I think education keeps changing. Children are capable of learning, but I wonder about the time stolen from them that would allow them to be children. I believe they are being robbed of exploring, questioning and just enjoying life from the perspective of a small child. Children seem to be entering the world of "conditioned learning" earlier and earlier.

"With all that being said, I want to present the history of education through a musical piece I created." Picking up his guitar, he strummed a tune and sang for the class room. Finishing, he said, "Thank you!" and the class applauded.

"Thank you," said Miss Rackard.

"Class, now it's time for you to critique Ben's presentation. I open the floor to comments, both good and not so good and suggestions."

Melanie raised her hand. "I thought it was great. I would never have thought to present an education lesson using music."

Molly, a soft spoken, golden haired girl, raised her hand and said, "Melanie's right. That was good."

"What are your thoughts?" asked Miss Rackard, noting Crystal's hand.

"It was different," she said annoyed. "I don't think children learn that way. And I believe you should get a child into a school environment as soon as possible. Otherwise they get spoiled and want no part of a classroom. They stay tied to their mothers for much too long, or their mothers to them."

"Furthermore, your Power Point left much to be desired. Haven't you ever given one before? Don't you know how to set one up properly?" she scolded. "Don't you know you're not supposed to write what you want to say on your slides? Wouldn't it have helped to have pictures or something else on it?"

Ben was stunned as was the rest of the class. Silence at that moment was so loud a pin could have dropped in the room and it be heard.

"Thank you, Crystal," said Miss Rickard. "Any other comments?"

No one said a word, but rather fingers could be seen toying with the corners of their papers on their desk and others just looked down pretending to be reading.

"Okay. Who wants to be next?"

"I'll go, said Randi, an overweight girl of nineteen. Walking confidently to the computer she slipped in her USB and attempted to pull up her power point. Try as she might, she couldn't find it in her list of documents. "I know it's here," she said. "I'm just nervous." "Take your time," said Miss Rickard.

"Oh, there it is," she said finally, clicking on the desired document.

"I'm doing my presentation on making a difference. I read in the "Kozal" book about the teacher who made a difference by including a volunteer mother who brought her baby to class and allowed others to help take care of the baby. It's fascinating how much impact you really have on a child. I think further that your attitude and disposition has a direct reflection on your student.

"There was another situation discussed about the monotone and lack of enthusiasm the teacher had and how it carried over into the classroom. It's frustrating for a student to go in a class room and have people be in a bad mood, especially if it's the instructor and it's a daily occurrence! That kind of thing has undercurrents you can't see. People generally want to avoid that kind of environment. I think older kids, when they can, would skip a class rather than deal with a teacher in a perpetual bad mood.

"It's my goal that when I work with children, I care enough about the children and the impact my attitude and personality has on them to make them excited about being with me in a learning environment, excited about the subject they are studying and, excited and happy with themselves and hopefully be able to see the bright side of life no matter how frustrated life may make them.

"Thank you for your time and attention."

"Thank you, Randi."

"Comments class?"

"I think you are right," said Staci. "It's hard to learn when you have a teacher in a bad mood all the time."

"I can't believe someone would actually bring their baby to a classroom and have other people help take care of it. That's just lazy on the mother's part," said Crystal. "I know I wouldn't take my children into a place like that."

"A place like what?" asked Miss Rickard.

"A classroom. I wouldn't want my children handled by other people, especially a baby. Suppose they get sick from other people's germs. It's just sick!"

"Well, I suppose it would depend on what was being taught. And apparently this mother thought a real child might be better than a plastic doll which would have no emotion. She was there to handle things if she thought necessary. So I think maybe it wasn't a bad idea, even if I would recommend being careful in such a situation."

"Besides the fact that I disagree with your ideas, you've got to be better prepared. Your inability to find your presentation is unacceptable. If you are going to be in front of a classroom, you have to know where your information is. You're not in high school anymore."

"Thank you for your thoughts, Crystal. Anyone else?"

Again the silence was deafening and the sense of defeat was palpable from the remaining students. "Okay, that will end class for today. Melanie, you are up first when we return."

"Yes, Ma'am. I will be ready," she said even as she was putting her things away.

Melanie walked into the empty house and collapsed on the sofa. What a day! Emotionally drained she wanted nothing more than to sleep. Leaning back, she tried to relax and then jumped, startled by the clanging sound. "The phone!" she said aloud, realizing she had dozed off.

"Good evening," she said, not fully awake.

"Hey, Mel! What are you doing?"

"Lee!" She said. "I was taking a nap. How are you?" she asked suddenly alert.

"I'm good. The weather is perfect as is the company and I'm having a good time."

"Are you playing a lot of pool?"

"Oh, yeah!" he said, clearly excited. "I've won a couple of tournaments already. And I've had steak dinner at the club house and even had some time lying around the pool. The water is wonderful!"

"Good," she said, trying hard to include sincere joy in her tone. "Things here are going okay. I miss you."

"I miss you, too," he said. "I can't talk long, though. I'm getting ready to go out to eat with the gang."

"The gang?"

"Well, there's about four or five couples who are going out to celebrate Russell's birthday. You know how they do that."

"Yeah, I do. Okay. Hope you have a good time," she said lamely.

"I will! I'll talk to you later. Bye!"

Putting the receiver back in its place, she felt alone and horribly sad. Returning to her spot on the sofa, she allowed the tears to fall freely. What is happening? What is wrong with me? Am I just supposed to stop what is important to me? Am I being selfish for wanting to go to school?

Walking into the classroom prepared for her presentation, Melanie took her seat but was distracted by Leslie fidgeting with her papers. "Melanie," she said, "Do you think Crystal will attack us like she did the others?"

"Possibly," she said matter of factly. "All we can do is the best we can and accept the fact that Crystal probably will not be happy with it," she said more confidently than she felt.

"I don't know," she replied. "I am scared to death."

"Don't let her do that to you. Remember that she is only one in this classroom and I am in your corner! It'll be okay. Focus on me while you speak and never mind her criticism at the end."

"Thanks, I'll try!"

As the class was coming to order Melanie gathered her things and went to the front of the room. Like Leslie she wondered how Crystal would attack her rather than if. Pulling up her power point, she began:

"My presentation will be on the evolutions of schools. I think the evolution of schools has come a long way. I'll admit to having mixed feelings about some of it. I believe that our schools have become so social and focused on extra curricular activities that the main thrust of learning is often overlooked. I don't mean to suggest that extra curricular activities aren't important, but I believe they are way over emphasized. Reading, writing and

Math are vital to any child's growth. It is here they learn the fundamental knowledge to be able to communicate and function in a very busy and complicated world. Often, even in grade school, our little ones are so wrapped up in other stuff, real learning is put on the back burner. In addition to this issue is the issue of the slower learner. There isn't a child alive who cannot learn. They learn differently, including their abilities to communicate. It's important that instructors take the time (and I know that is in scarce supply) to watch for indicators that would show where a child would excel. It's these children and those so involved in outside activities, that get lost through the cracks without the proper education that is available to them. That's sad...."

Finally she said, "Thank you for your time and attention."

"Thank you, Melanie," said Miss Rickard. "Comments, class?"

"I thought it was interesting," offered Leslie.

"Me, too," said Sandi.

The class waited with all eyes on Crystal. "Why's everyone looking at me?" she finally asked. "Melanie did fine. She at least did her power point right."

Leslie walked to the podium after Melanie took her seat. Locking directly on Melanie, she began. "I am going to address Thomas Jefferson's views on how integrating social studies, which includes history and the sciences, in curriculum is important in enabling a person to be not only a good citizen but a vital and functional one. An educated person's life is enhanced because it enables a person to make intelligent decisions based on what is already learned. When educated, he has a wide range of knowledge to draw from enabling him to have an intelligent conversation no matter what the subject matter, despite socio-economic status….."

"Thank you," she said finishing.

"Okay, class. Again, I welcome critique's of Leslie's presentation," Miss Ricard, said. This is important because it gives us a degree of understanding how we are sharing our knowledge with those we are teaching."

"I think she did a nice job," said Melanie. "I like the subject matter, as well!"

Again the class waited. When no response came from Crystal, Leslie looked at Melanie and smiled. "I'll echo, Melanie's comment," said Randi. "Good job!"

"Anyone else? Okay, I agree with the class that both presentations deserve the status of nice job. Let's see if we can keep that going. Who's next?"

Melanie was glad when the class ended. Crystal had been quiet the rest of the day and while Melanie was relieved, she was also perplexed. It seemed out of character for her not to say something negative. She was grateful, however, and dismissed the question from her mind.

Hearing Lee's voice over the phone made Melanie's heart beat faster. "When are you coming home?" she asked.

"In the next few days," he said. "But you'll never guess where we had a pool tournament. It was unusual cause the resort was over an hour away, but it was great!"

"Where?"

"A really cool town, called Bisbee. It was a huge Copper camp back in the 1800's and the houses would just blow your mind. They are all painted in so many different colors. It's wild. There may be a green house with the shutters and trim all done in dark purple and pink, or a lavender house trimmed in orange and green. It's bizarre. The whole town is painted like that!"

"It sounds awful."

"It isn't though. It's interesting. It makes me think of an Asian country, maybe China or Thailand. They have some really cool Bed and Breakfast places and lots of shops that you might like and oh, they have Ghost hunting weekends. I'm not sure how you'd like that, but it might be an exciting change if you're up for it when we come down together sometime."

"Ghost hunting? You're kidding! You'd like to do that?"

"Well, maybe."

"I also found out they have tours from here. There are a couple I'm sure you'd like. One called "All About Hummingbirds and there is one on the historic churches of Bisbee."

"That does sound nice. I'm just ready for you to come home."

"In just a few days I'll be headed up. You doing all right?"

"Yeah, I'm okay. Did you win the tournament?" she added quickly.

"Actually, we did! It was great!

"Good deal!"

"All right then. I'm out of here. Talk to you soon."

Much too soon, Melanie replaced the receiver. "He never wants to chat on the phone," she thought. "He talks to other people for a half hour easy. What is it about me?"

Chapter 19

Melanie walked into her Field Experience class. "I wonder how this works?" Melanie mused while waiting for Ms. Bradley to come in. The class was small with only eight other students in the attendance. Moments later the sound of high heels clicking across the floor broke her reverie.

"Good afternoon, class. Sorry I'm late. I'm doing fifty things at once. So let's get down to business," she said speaking rapidly with just the slightest lisp.

Calling roll, each student's name was called, followed with "present or here." "I'm glad everyone made it," she said, her eyes glancing over the students momentarily. Silence filled the room for several moments while she appeared to be making notes in her roll book and then she began again.

"You each are required to spend a total of twenty hours in the classroom observing other instructors outside the college setting on your own time. You would be advised to try to set up something in the grade you would like to work in. It is your responsibility to set things up with the principal of the school you wish to do your field experience in. You must fill out these forms with the information as soon as you have it and turn in a written report after each session in your school. Remember that the teacher who agrees to allow you in his or her classroom is not to be responsible for you. Remember you are a guest and in no way will assume any responsibility in the classroom.

"I recommend you begin as quickly as you can because time has a way of creeping up on you and if you don't complete the allotted hours you will not pass my class, regardless of how well the instructor tells me you shadow.

"Additionally you will be required to put together a report with a partner on a topic you can choose, but must be approved, regarding the public school system. Find the person you choose to partner with today and I want your chosen topic available at our next class meeting. I have handouts regarding the particulars on the presentation. Any questions?"

Everyone just looked at the tall, well dressed professor, stunned at the amount of information given without seeming to even breathe or any hint of social grace. Her hair pulled high atop her head in a bun and glasses that hung around her neck, and darting, dark brown fidgeting eyes gave the impression she was nervous and in a hurry. Her presentation was straight forward with little or no emotion and hardly any indication she even cared about the students seated before her.

Melanie shuddered. "This was going to be a trying class," she thought. "What a professor!"

"Okay, since there are no questions, I will leave you to decide who you will partner with.   Make sure you pick up the handout regarding the required presentation."

Melanie looked around the room to see other students looking as dazed as she. "You want to work with me on this presentation?" said the girl to her left.

"Okay," she replied hesitantly. "I'm Melanie. Do you have any ideas on what you'd like to present on?"

"I'm Malinda and not a clue. Let's exchange email addresses and do some searching, and plan to get together to figure it out. What do you think?"

"Sounds like a plan."

"Okay, then. Here's my email. Let's see what we can do!"

Leaving the room, Melanie headed for the library. It seemed like the best place to get ideas for the presentation.   She still had an hour before she was expected at the Financial Aid office and then she'd finally head for home and try to get things in order for the following morning to make connections with Sweet Creek Elementary.

"It's all set," she told Mackenzie. "I'm going to work in Kindergarten with Mrs. Ryan. I am so excited!"

"Why Kindergarten? I expected you to take an older class."

"Well, I'm not sure what I want so I figured I'd start here and work my way up. Course, that isn't what we're supposed to do. Ms. Bradley said we should work in the grade we want to be in. I'm just not sure yet."

"When do you start?"

"Well, I've chosen Wednesday's from 1:00 p.m. to 3:00 for now. So that means tomorrow.   I have a class early, then work for two hours before going to Sweet Creek Elementary. So I'll be busy trying to get this all in."

"You'll get it done."

"I know," she responded with a sigh. "It's hard on your dad, though. He really doesn't like all the hours I put in. Between school, work and now this, he's feeling really left out, even "put" out."

"After all these years, he should be able to handle some time on his own."

"He does. But this is why he likes to go to Arizona and other places to do what he likes to do."

"Mom, Dad is a big boy. He can handle this. He was supportive of you going to school. I wouldn't think he'd have issues with it now."

"I just feel bad for him. I feel like I leave him alone all the time and that makes me feel guilty."

"Deal, Mom! It'll be okay," Mackenzie said laughing.

Hugging her daughter, Melanie set about getting things ready for dinner. She still had homework and she needed to contact Malinda about the presentation and then she had to get ready for her first day in the classroom!

Melanie woke to a fifteen degree drop from the day before and a steady rain. Checking the mirror one more time to make sure she was professionally attired, she headed for her newest adventure. When she walked into the classroom filled with kindergarteners, the children were having indoor recess. Mrs. Fagan, the Kindergarten assistant, was having the children hide their eyes on their desks except for four who stood with her. The ones remaining had to walk as quietly as possible to another student who had their head down, disguise his voice and in nearly a whisper say hello. When Mrs. Fagan said, "Heads up" the children had to guess who had said hello to them. The goal, Melanie learned, was to *not* be recognized and remain standing the longest amount of time teaching the children to use both auditory and verbal strategies, encouraging good listening and voice control skills.

Later, Melanie walked with the children to their "special" for the day which was music. She was amazed how different the children were in this class than when they were with Mrs. Ryan. They were noisy, busy, and non-attentive much of the time, even unruly. The children were crawling on the floor under the chairs, hitting each other with the instruments and shouting at each other across the room. Clearly the music teacher had little or no control. It was all Melanie could do to not intercede. Surely the bad manners were not acceptable. She held her tongue, however, since she had clearly been given the directive that she was only there to observe. So she watched as they played instruments, sang, danced and did a clapping song. "This is not how I want my class to be," thought Melanie, resolutely.

Having decided on the Learning Disabilities as their topic for presentation, Melanie began her research. She and Malinda had agreed to meet to begin work on the project. Looking at the clock one more time, Melanie tried calling Malinda's phone number. "Hello."

"Hi, I'm trying to reach Malinda," said Melanie.

"She's not here right now. Can I give her a message?

"We were supposed to work on our presentation today, and she's 45 minutes late."

"Oh, I'm sorry. I guess she wasn't able to contact you. She had to work and won't be there."

"Oh," said Melanie completely frustrated. "She has my cell phone number. I wonder why she didn't call."

"She must have forgotten."

"Okay, thank you," she said before hanging up.

Driving home, Melanie was so angry she could barely think. "That is so rude," she thought! "I hate working in groups or with a partner," she said out loud.

Opening her email, later that evening, Melanie found one from Malinda, "I don't know why I agree to meet you during the day when I don't know if I will have to work or not. Sorry I couldn't make it to the time we had set. We'll have to do it another time. I really am sorry."

Scheduling continued to be a problem for Melanie and Malinda. What worked for one never seemed to work for the other. Using the internet and email, however, Melanie felt confident the presentation could be given adequately. Finally the report was finished and they were scheduled to present the following Monday. And then Melanie received another email that completely enraged her.

It read: *"I talked with Ms. Bradley. I think the presentation is too long and she thinks it is too. We have to pare down out list to gender, ethnicity, socio economic status and learning/medical needs. So basically we have to cut out culture, gifted and talented, age and emotional and focus on the other ones. Malinda"*

"I am not pleased!" Melanie responded. "I disagree with what you think we should cut out. Ms. Bradley told us to do the report on what we wanted. So I think it's unfair now that we have it finished that she's going to adjust it. Why did you even go to her about it? The report is good just like it is."

"I think the presentation is too, long," Malinda responded. *"I went to Ms. Bradley and she agreed with me. I didn't mean to upset you."*

"It's fine," Melanie wrote in her next email, although she was still frustrated. "No hard feelings. We just needed to be honest with each other from the beginning about how we felt about it. Let's just go forward and do the best we can. I hope it's not too short now since we pulled so much out. We have a good bit of time to share with the class."

On the day of the presentation, Melanie and Malinda walked to the front of the class. Taking turns with the power point, each spoke about their respect topics. Finishing five minutes early, Melanie looked at the classroom. "We are open to questions," she said.

The class looked at them blankly. "Well, there are some factors we didn't include here," offered Malinda. "Other hindrances to education for the disabled include culture, gifted and talented and emotional issues."

"Culture can be a big issue depending on where you live," joined Melanie. "For instance if you lived on the East Coast rather than here in the mid-west, you wouldn't learn very much about Native American Indians and their way of life. So if there were Indian students there in the classroom, the instructor would have to be sensitive to their needs, and differences, as well as, everyone else's."

"The gifted and talented offer their own set of differences to a classroom," Malinda picked up. "The teacher has to be sensitive to them, as well."

A student in the back raised her hand. "Yes?" Malinda asked and then followed with an answer that for the moment was lost on Melanie which related to the medical needs of physically impaired students.

"I have worked with students with that kind of problem," she said. "I work with disabled children as an aid in Elk Creek. I'd like it to be my specialty."

Malinda glanced at the clock and stopped. They had been warned they could not go over time, but neither could their presentation be too short. "Thank you for being such a good audience," she said backing away from the podium and ending the dialogue.

Picking up their papers, the ladies went to their seats and sat down. "Nicely done," said Ms. Bradley. "You both offered a lot of material, and presented it well."

Relief flooded Melanie while she hoped Ms. Bradley was not just being kind in front of the other students. It hadn't gone as planned, but at least it was over!

Melanie stared at the email as her heart sank. *"Melanie—I just tabulated the results, and I'm really sorry, but Tristen received a higher percentage of the votes: 57.5% to your 42.5%. Will you please stay as a VP along with Vanessa?   --Mr. Parnell"*

Walking to the living room, she said, "I didn't win, Lee. I didn't win."

"You didn't win what?"

"I didn't make PTK president. Tristen did."

"I'm sorry. I didn't know you wanted it that much."

"I'm not sure I realized how much I really did want it. Tristen has more connections. She's a lot younger and I'm certain she used "influence" when it came to getting votes."

"What do you mean?"

"Well, I'm not sure I can put my finger on it, but her family has money and is political and that creates a certain amount of influence I just don't have."

"Well, God's got other plans. So don't worry about it."

"Mr. Parnell wants me to be VP."

"You're kidding! Are you considering it?"

"I think I am. I'm not sure about working with Tristen, but besides having a voice too, I'd like to work with Vanessa. She's the one whose father is a minister. So I'd like to tell him yes. Do you mind?"

"I think it's a mistake, but if you want to, go ahead!"

Confused with Lee's remark, Melanie retreated to her computer. She wrote: "I'll admit I'm really bummed but I'd love to work with Vanessa, and be part of the team. I hope things work so I can still be useful. So yes, I'll stay on as VP.... Thanks for asking."

Moments later a return email: *"Melanie --I'd be concerned if you weren't bummed. I'm sorry about the way things turned out. Thanks for agreeing to stick around. Hopefully we can still work together! Don't think that any of your ideas become invalid or subordinate just because of the election results. We're still an honors student group; we still traffic in ideas; and we will still need leadership from within the organization!"*

"Well, that's done," Melanie announced. "It's official. Tristen is President and Vanessa and I are co-vice presidents. It should be interesting," she said with an edge to her voice.

"That's one way to put it," said Lee with disgust in his voice.

Turning, Melanie walked away.

Melanie and Lee quietly walked into the large open room and immediately spotted Gavin, despite the other students who were dressed just as he: white pants and white jacket held closed with a long black tied belt. Gavin was moving smoothly and rhythmically while holding the five foot staff in various directions for balance. Tai Chi had become his favorite out of school activity . He practiced several times a day on his movements. Tonight was to be an exhibition of what he'd learned about the centuries-old Chinese martial art. It was designed for self-defense and a promoter of inner peace and calm, but has been discovered to have wonderful health benefits besides.

More than once Gavin had tried to talk Melanie into taking classes with him, but she'd always declined. But tonight she was excited to see her son in action before his peers and instructor. Taking their seats along the side lines, they watched. In a single moment, Melanie knew something was wrong. Gavin was seated on the floor, legs twisted beneath him in obvious pain. "Lei," she heard Gavin say. "Something's wrong. I can't get up."

In less time than it took to say it, Lei, Gavin's Asian instructor was by his side. Using obviously skilled hands, he noted the site of the injured knee. The knee cap had lodged itself to the inside of the knee area, completely away from the front of the leg. Swiftly removing his own sash from around his waist he wrapped a figure eight around the dislodged knee cap and then spoke to Melanie and Lee. "We're going to have to take him to the hospital. This needs immediate attention."

"Certainly," said Melanie.

"I'll take him in my truck; it's probably bigger than your car."

"Okay. We'll follow," said Lee.

Three able bodied men picked up the injured Gavin and carried him to the truck as painlessly as they could. Once in, Lei was behind the wheel and racing to the hospital. Melanie and Lee were close behind. Pulling into the circle before the emergency room, Lei quickly went inside, leaving Gavin in the truck. Melanie and Lee stood nearby feeling particularly helpless. Moments later he. along with medical staff pushing a wheel chair came out of the building. It was then Melanie noticed the badge Lei was wearing, although she wasn't sure of all it designated. "I put a call in on the way down," he said, noting her observation. "They were waiting."

Trying to extricate Gavin from the truck without pain was more difficult than getting him inside. Noting Gavin's apparent agony, Melanie walked away, swallowing the lump in her throat and blinking away tears. In the next instant the scream of excruciating pain that came from Gavin sent Melanie into sobs. She was tortured knowing she could not help him in any way. Knowing his great pain made her heart ache.

Once in the wheelchair, Gavin was taken inside and placed on a gurney. Gavin, having regained his composure said, "Mom, come look. It popped back into place!"

"Do you want to go back with him, or would you like me to?" asked Lei while they were waiting. "It shouldn't take them too long to get him back there."

"You seem to have everything under control along with knowing what to say and who to say it to! I'd be pleased if you went back with him to make sure everything is done properly," Melanie said.

"I'd be happy to. I'm so sorry this happened."

"It's not your fault," Gavin interjected.

"No, it's not." Added Lee, "I just hope there's not very much damage done."

Melanie and Lee watched as just moments later Gavin was taken back into the treatment room with Lei close behind. Waiting for the doctor to come out with information made both Melanie and Lee's nerves tight.

An hour later, Gavin, Lei and the doctor were coming out of the examination room. Gavin was sporting crutches and a full leg brace but he was smiling. "He's going to be okay," said the doctor. "It's amazing. There are no tears and nothing is broken. How that happened is beyond me. Given the location of where the knee cap lodged, there should be a good deal of damage; at least tears in the ligaments. There is absolutely no sign of that."

"Thank the Lord," said Melanie.

"Gavin tells me you are leaving for Montana for a few months, in just a few days."

"Yes."

"I would suggest he stay off the leg for the duration of the trip, and once you get there, have him checked and x-rayed again. I think he should be just fine."

Turning to Lei, the doctor continued, "Your quick thinking to wrap the knee probably really aided the limited damage. Good job!"

"Thank you, doctor. I just hate to see this young man hurt. He's a good student."

Relief flooded Melanie as they exited the hospital. "It's all good," Gavin said, leaning on his crutches. "I'm just sorry you didn't get to see me do my thing in Tai Chi!"

"We saw enough!" laughed Melanie, "Believe me!"

"Yeah, but you didn't see the right thing," he scolded, before laughing.

"I'm curious," said Melanie, pausing. "What's the badge Lei had on?"

"Oh, I never told you? He's a DEA agent. How cool is that?"

Melanie and Lee exchanged glances but neither spoke. Secretly Melanie was glad Gavin had befriended this kind, Drug Enforcement agent. He had given Gavin confidence in ways he had never had before and she was grateful beyond words for the wonder he had just performed before their eyes. "God is good," she thought, giving Gavin's arm a squeeze.

Year Three
Chapter 20

The drive to the college had been tense and stressed as they all tried to make small talk while dancing all around where they were going and why. "Are you sure your knee is okay?" asked Melanie.

"Mom, you've asked me that a dozen times over the summer. Honestly it's fine."

They had been amazed at how quickly Gavin's knee had healed from the twisted mangled thing it had become during the last Tai Chi class. As instructed Gavin had worn the brace out to Montana and as soon as they'd arrived he was taken to a local doctor to have it checked. He had been instructed to wear the brace for an additional week, do exercises and then remove it.

The knee, having popped back into place upon extrication from the vehicle had no further damage, short term or long term. Gavin had gone through the entire summer with only tenderness around the area. Still, given the horrific sight and amount of pain Gavin endured, Melanie worried that issues would resurface.

Lee pulled the car as near the outer door as he could and put it in park. "This is it," Melanie thought. "This is where we leave Gavin." Getting out of the car she looked at the massive building and grounds. The two story brick building looked no different than the other thousand college dorms she'd seen over the years. The year 1964 was embedded in one of its corner blocks sitting just above a well-landscaped walk area.

It was the backdrop of the Rocky Mountains that stirred Melanie's heart. The snow-covered peaks reminded her of her home in the Black Hills during the winter. The college was nestled within the mountains and offered a sense of security in this beautiful place. The ferns mingled with the wildflowers gave the area striking colors of russet orange, rose, yellow, indigo blue, lavender and white contrasting with the deep forest green of the cedars and hemlocks, spruce and fir trees. In the distance Melanie spotted a mountain goat and two deer leisurely enjoying the flavor of the breathtaking meadow for their afternoon snack. Looking closely she could make out a natural waterfall that splashed down the side of the mountain between the trees and over the rocks into a nearby stream. Listening she heard the familiar call of a dove and saw a hawk perched high overhead in a cedar tree. A western meadowlark flitted by and settled on the tall grass in the meadow beyond the parking area and a swift resembling a boomerang darted by to some unknown destination.

"You helping to carry this stuff upstairs?" asked Lee interrupting her thoughts.

"Oh, yeah. I guess I should," she said, swallowing the lump forming in her throat. Turning she picked up a box holding some of Gavin's things and followed Lee. Each step climbed seemed more difficult than the one before. Without free hands, Melanie could not wipe the tears suddenly streaming down her face. Finally reaching the room that would house her son for the next year, Melanie placed her burden on the table and walked into the bathroom. There she let her tears flow into the sobbing she could no longer contain.

"Mom, don't do this," said Gavin sadly. "I'm not trying to hurt you," he said wrapping his arms around her from the back. "It's just time."

"I know," she said between sobs. "I just hate the thought of leaving you here. I can't imagine what it's going to be like not having you at the house. I love you so much."

"I know. I love you too. But your crying makes this that much harder. Please don't cry anymore."

Breathing deep, Melanie stopped her tears even while her heart continued to break. "I'll try not to cry," she said. "I'll go get some more things."

Without saying another word, she turned and headed out the door. "I won't cry anymore," she kept telling herself. "I just won't!"

When all of Gavin's belongings were in his room, Melanie fought her emotions while Lee and Gavin did an inspection of the room itself. He would be sharing a room with an unknown roommate who had not yet arrived at the college. There were bunk beds, two dressers, two desks and two chairs. Closet space was especially limited, but Gavin was sure he'd have enough room since most of his things were folded and put in a dresser anyway. One large window gave light to the room and overlooked the parking lot, but also gave an amazing view of the towering snow covered mountain peaks. Melanie could have stood at the window for the rest of the day just drinking in the beauty if the pain of leaving Gavin hadn't been so great marring the joy of this beautiful place.

"Well, I guess we should head out," Lee said.

"I know," said Melanie looking at her son deeply.

Walking over to her, Gavin wrapped his long arms around her and held her tight. His six foot four frame stood more than a foot over Melanie's head. She buried her face in his chest. "Mom, it's okay," he said kindly as he could tell she was crying again. "I'm going to be fine. I promise I will not forget to call you. You're making this so hard on both of us."

"I'm sorry," she said. "I'm fine," she added abruptly swallowing hard. "I'm done crying. I'm just done," she said again, all the while knowing she was lying.

Giving Gavin one last squeeze she looked up at him and said, "I love you. Stay well and stay safe. Call if you need us."

"I will. I promise."

"You'd better!" she said making her way to the door.

"Take care of yourself, son," said Lee reaching for Gavin's hand.

"Thanks, Dad. I will," he said returning the hand shake and then hugging each other firmly.

Without another word, Melanie and Lee walked out the door and made their way to the car. Pulling out of the parking lot, Melanie chanced a look up at Gavin's window and saw him sitting on the window ledge. "He's so content here," she said softly.

"Yes, he is," Lee agreed and then noticed the silent tears streaming down Melanie's face again. Reaching over he squeezed her hand but said nothing allowing the tears to run their course.

One week later Melanie walked into class. Another semester, but now it would different not seeing Gavin on campus. She grinned to herself as she pictured seeing her tall son coming toward her with a cute female at his side. They'd locked eyes, half smiled and then passed each other on the sidewalk.

Once when Gavin and Lauren came toward her, she looked past her son and headed straight for Lauren. She'd known Lauren since she'd been five years old, but hadn't seen her in years. They were headed her way and she wasn't about to miss the opportunity to hug the beautiful young woman. Sandy brown curls bounced around an impish face with a perfect set of white teeth set behind a welcoming smile. "Lauren!" said Melanie when she reached her.

"Miss Melanie! How are you?"

"I'm good!" she replied looking at Gavin and then laughing while hugging the pretty girl. "How's your mom?"

"She's good. She's still teaching at the elementary school. What are you doing here?"

"Gavin didn't tell you?"

"Nope!" came her quick reply, while smacking him lightly on the arm.

"I'm taking classes."

"That's fantastic! I'm proud of you!"

"You're kind. Thank you. It's been interesting!"

Turning to Gavin, she'd said grinning, "Now Gavin, you can't get mad at me for talking to you on campus. I came to talk with Lauren."

"You leave your mom alone," commanded Lauren, giving Melanie another hug while Gavin giggled and rolled his eyes.

"Women!" he said as the two of them went on their way.

"I will miss him," thought Melanie. "Oh well, he's gone and I have to deal. It is what it is," she scolded herself, picking up the pace to make it to her Earth Science class.

Walking in the room she remembered her last encounter with Science. It had been challenging and she wasn't sure she was up to this class, although this would surely not be any more difficult than Physical Science, and it was bound to be more interesting!

Mr. Mallory, a distinguished looking man sat at his desk leafing through a mound of papers. His well groomed, graying hair framed a kind face with gentle smile. For a fleeting moment Melanie was sure she'd seen sadness in the soft green eyes. "Perhaps he's just tired," she thought absently while taking her usual seat in the front row next to a diminutive figure whose legs where in braces.

Moments later another female student nearly her age sat on her other side. "Interesting mix of students," she thought pleasantly. "Hi, I'm Melanie!" she said to the older student pleasantly. "It's nice to have someone near my age in a class for a change!"

"I am right there with you," she said, laughing. "I'm JoyAnn. I'm so excited about taking this class. I really want a Geology class, but I have to wait until I go to the University for that."

"Are you kidding me? You're really going on after you finish here?"

"Well, I think so. I'm a little old to be a Geologist and my kids think I'm nuts. My husband was killed in a farming accident three years ago and I'm still getting my feet wet in this brand new world."

"I'm sorry about your husband," Melanie said sincerely. "That has to be tough."

"It was. But you have to move on. I still live on the farm. My oldest son runs it now and that's a blessing. But I can't just sit there and not do anything. This is a great area for Geology students. I'm interested in rocks and dirt and all that kind of thing, so I figure I'll go for as far as it'll take me.

"College has been challenging. I was behind in a lot of subjects, but I've kept plugging and in another year I should graduate, barring anything weird happening. I'm not an A student, but I do well and that makes me feel good. What will I do with it? I'm not sure," she said pausing. "I think working at the Bureau of Mines would be interesting or doing research. This place is an amazing area with all the history in the Black Hills. Worst case scenario maybe I could work in a museum. I just know I've got to do something."

"I'm inspired," said Melanie. "I'm going to college just because I've never been. I like my major in Education, but haven't a clue what I'll do with it yet. My real interests are in History and English. Who knows! Maybe we'll work in a museum together," she said laughing.

"I'm Annette," said the girl with the crutches. "This is my second time taking this class. It's not really hard, but can be confusing and I really didn't do too well last time I took it, so I'm taking it again."

"Well, we'll all get through it together," said Melanie kindly.

"We'll be a team," chimed in JoyAnn.

"Sounds good to me," replied Annette thoughtfully. "I didn't fail, but I did get behind and a C on the report card just isn't as good as I want. I'd like to come out of here with at least a B."

"Is Science your major?"

"Oh, good grief no!" she said, apparently appalled at the idea. "It's a requirement, that's all. My major is general college studies, but you need a Science and I figured this would be the easiest one."

"Well, we'll see!" said Melanie as she watched Mr. Mallory rise from his desk.

"Ok, class. Let's get started. We're going to be studying the Earth from the inside out," he began. "You will have labs, so make sure you have a least one good partner, preferably two so the work can be divided evenly. At the end of the semester you will have a large, in-depth report you will turn in as a team; we will be studying different kinds of rocks and you will be tested on the rocks, so don't take the material lightly. We will be studying earthquakes and other matters that relate to the earth's surface and we will be dealing with weather matters.

"This need not be a difficult class, but we do move along so you need to stay caught up."

Melanie chanced a look at Annette who was squirming in her seat. Sounds like Annette had a point, she thought. "I've got to stay focused!"

At the end of class as Melanie stood up to gather her things, she noticed the full class room. There wasn't an empty seat left. "I'm looking forward to this," said JoyAnn as she readied to leave. "I think it's gonna be good!"

"Can we work as a team," asked Annette. "We three?"

"Sounds good!" replied JoyAnn.

"It's okay with me," agreed Melanie as she began walking to the door. "Gotta run. I've got to get to the Financial Aid office to work."

Later that week Melanie felt her phone vibrate. Opening it she saw a text from Tristen. "1st PKT meeting tomorrow at 4 in the Spotted Eagle Building, room 212."

"Great!" she thought. "That means I'll be late getting home. Sure hope Lee doesn't mind!"

The next afternoon Melanie heard her phone vibrate on her desk. "Who in the world would be sending me a text now? Everyone knows I'm at work," she commented to Debbie, sitting at the desk across from her, while picking it up and flipping it open.

"Oh my gosh! It's from Brooke, Lee's sister. Mom has fallen out of bed and broke her hip and they've taken her to Elk Creek Regional Hospital. What in the world? How do you fall out of bed at a nursing home?"

"You're kidding!"

"Okay, I've got to think. I finish here at one; I have a class at 1:15, so I can get there about 2:30. And then I can come back for the PTK meeting Tristen called.

"You're going to come back for that?

"Well, I think I should. I am officially co-Vice President. Vanessa Wagner is the other one. I'd hate to shirk my duties from the get go."

"Good luck with that," said Debbie laughing. "I think Tristen might be a challenge to work with. I've seen her on campus. She has an interesting personality!"

"That's a fair description. We shall see. I just don't want to make a bad impression. So, yes, I will be back, although I don't know how Lee is going to feel about that. He already doesn't have very nice feelings about her, and he's never even met her!"

"Well, that's just because of the way the voting thing went."

"I know. He loves me!"

Melanie hurried to her car. She was still stunned and confused at how a patient could fall out of a bed in the nursing home. She quietly entered the room of her mother-in-law.   The strong smell of ammonia, alcohol and unnamed disinfectants accosted her nose. The once robust woman looked tiny and frail in the large bed under white sheets and a blanket and bed rails holding her secure. The steady beep of the heart monitor gave little solace to Melanie's anxiety. "A little late for bed rails, now," said Melanie a bit sarcastic, to Brooke and Lee who were already there.

"How did this happen?"

"Well according to the nurse, it happens all the time," said Brooke.

"What do you mean?"

"According to her, between half and three-quarters of nursing home residents fall every year. And sometimes the fall even causes death. I think Mom's issues will be a reduced quality of life, as if it wasn't bad enough."

"But how do they fall out of bed?" Melanie persisted.

"Well, apparently that isn't all that uncommon either. The bed height could be wrong and when they roll over they just fall out."

"That just amazes me," said Melanie shaking her head. "We pay good money to have her taken care of there. It doesn't make good sense to me. They are supposed to be watching her," she continued completely agitated.

"Mel, calm down," said Lee. "Nobody likes what has happened. We'll deal. We have to pray that this broken hip heals quickly without any complications so she can at least get out of here."

"I guess," she responded sullenly taking a seat in the green vinyl chair in the corner. Sitting she stared at the sight before her, while melancholy threatened to overwhelm her. "I've got to get back to the college," she said, after an hour had passed. "Tristen called a meeting for PTK at 4:00.

"Sorry, I'm late," she said as she entered the room. "I was at the hospital with my mother-in-law and then there was an accident out on Route 90 and I couldn't go anywhere for a while."

"Try to be on time next time," said Tristen, tersely. "We need to get things rolling. I've got a million things to do too. So being on time is a necessity."

"I said I was sorry," replied Melanie sharply. "I was at the hospital."

"Never mind," said Tristen. "Let's just get on with it. Before you got here, we decided we need a newsletter. Do you think you could handle that? Everyone else has an assigned task already."

"Sure," said Melanie. "I have a program on my computer that would make a nice newsletter. Just tell me what you want in it.

"Are we mailing it?"

"No, I think we're agreed, that mailing would be too costly, so we'll have it available at different areas on campus. We need it done by next Tuesday, a week from today. You okay with that?"

"I should be able to handle that."

"Okay, here's a list of what should be included. If you think of anything else, add it and then we can always edit if it doesn't suit the group. And with that being done, I have a political meeting to attend for mother before heading to my father's law office." Tristen said, running her hand through her thick auburn locks in apparent conclusion.

"Okay, then," Melanie said sighing. "I'll do the best I can."

"That's why you're here," Tristen quipped.

"If you say so," Melanie retorted, gathering her things.

"If I'd known this was all that was happening today, I'd have stayed at the hospital longer," Melanie said to Vanessa after Tristen walked out the door.

"It's going to be an interesting year," Vanessa said. "I hope we can keep pace. You'd be surprised all the talk that's going around."

"What do you mean?"

"Just whispers about Tristen's "other" life. I mean she's wealthy, her mom's in politics and her dad a big, fat lawyer. And to make it worse, Tristen is apparently at least socially involved in both things. She just comes off snobby and well to do, with attitude!"

"Well, it is what it is. I guess she'll always feel like she's above us."

"I expect your right."

"Mr. Mallory, are you okay?" Melanie asked as she entered the room early for class.

"I'll be fine," he said looking up at her, trying to smile while holding on to the cabinet in an effort to come out of the squatting position. "I'm an old man in an older body," he added, grimacing as he rose.

Melanie stood for a moment holding her books without going to her seat. That same sadness she'd noticed the first day of class was apparent again in his soft green eyes. "So what's really wrong?" she pressed.

"Nothing I haven't dealt with for a lot of years," he said simply. "I have Lyme's disease. It pains me sometimes and some days more than others and causes my joints to stiffen which is why it causes pain," he said, trying to laugh.

"I'm sorry," she said softly.

"I'm fine," he said again. "Don't you worry about me."

"Hey, Mr. Mallory," said Kevin as he entered the room followed by three more students. "What are we doing today?"

"Science!" he retorted. "What did you expect to do in Science class today?"

Mr. Mallory looked directly into Melanie's eyes. "I'm okay," he said again. "Thanks for your kindness."

Melanie smiled and without a word went to her seat.

"Our next unit will be on Meteorology," Mr. Mallory said after all the students had filed in. "It's the study of changes in our atmosphere in temperature, moisture or water vapor, wind and air pressure. Much of this begins with the sun's energy.

"Weather forecasting has become a much relied science since the latter half of the 20th century. Computers have enabled Meteorologists to make fairly accurate predictions based on data gathered from the use of satellites, instruments on weather stations, buoys, environmental observations from the surface of the sun to the bottom of the oceans, as well as climate history in all parts of the earth."

Melanie focused on his words completely engrossed until time for class ended. "Lee," she said excitedly, "everyone has always laughed at me because I get so excited about the unusual cloud formations in this part of the world. I absolutely love them," she went on. "Did you know that "dinner roll clouds" that I like so much are actually Mamatus clouds? How cool is that? They just look like perfect white dinner rolls. Remember that day when it looked like the entire sky was a huge pan of rolls? From the way they were shaped it looked like they had been taken right out of the oven!"

Lee laughed. "You're a lunatic!"

"Yeah, but it's really cool! And I found out those really neat clouds with different layers are shelf clouds. But they're dangerous ones. They usually bring horrible storms," she said a little calmer.

"I just really like this unit! It's fantastic. It's interesting! I think I'd like to do my big project at the end of the semester on weather and maybe even on clouds specifically. But we'll see. The other girls have to agree on it too."

"Well, good luck with that," Lee said, still laughing at her. "I'm glad you're at least enjoying it! It sure sounds a lot better than that whole Tristen deal you had the other day."

"I know. Speaking of which, I need to get back to that, too. I'm not finished. I at least have the weekend. Course we still need to go back and see your Mom, too. Any word on how she's doing?"

"Brooke says she's not doing as well as they expected. She's been running a low grade fever."

"Uh, oh,"

"Yeah, it's not good and I can tell you I am concerned."

Melanie walked into the room and laid the folder in front of her. After spending several hours each day over the past three in an effort to get the newsletter in proper form, she commented, while collapsing in the chair nearest her, "I think you'll like the newsletter." "It's been a rough weekend, but I got it finished."

"What happened?" asked Vanessa.

"Remember I was late getting here at the last meeting because I was at the hospital because my mother-in-law had fallen?"

"Yeah."

"Well, she now has pneumonia. She's not doing well at all and everyone is really concerned. So we've spent a lot of time at the hospital this weekend, too."

"I'm so sorry," said Vanessa.

"Yeah, me, too," said Tristen offhandedly reaching for the folder. "We have got to get this done and out!"

Melanie looked at her and frowned.

"Hmm," said Tristen. "It looks all right," she said condescendingly. "You at least have the components in it we need, our mission, goals, events, contact information, some nice pictures of the new officers. Not too bad.

"Wait a minute," she said with a long pause. "What program did you use to create this?"

"I have Print Shop on my computer."

"We should have thought about this sooner. We're not going to be able to use this after all."

"Why?"

"Because I don't have that program and if I want to add something or make changes, I won't be able to."

"You're kidding me!" said Melanie feeling her temperature rise.

"No. Guess I'll just have to do it myself."

"That's just wrong," said Melanie. "I gotta go."

"We've just started the meeting."

"You'll do it without me this afternoon. I'm headed for the hospital." Picking up her things, Melanie walked out the door in total disgust.

Melanie found working on the project for class exhilarating. The team decided to create a "Wild Weather Scrapbook for the Black Hills of SD," give a presentation on "Ways to Survive Wicked Weather," and "Weather Prediction Through the Years." She would create the scrapbook, JoyAnn the power point on surviving the weather and Annette would present on the changes of weather prediction and weather instruments through the years.

"Lee," said Melanie louder than she meant to. "Look at this! Did you know that fastest temperature rise recorded was in Spearfish? It happened on January 22, 1943 at 7:30 in the morning. It involved Chinook winds and within two minutes the temperature went from -4 degrees Fahrenheit to 45 degrees Fahrenheit. That's a 49 degree spread!

"And," she continued without allow a response time, "the fastest temperature drop was in Rapid City."

"Now, I think that's unlikely," Lee said clearly doubting her findings.

"I'll show you," she said, defiantly. "Look! It says it right here and here are the dates. The cool down in Rapid City was the same date as the warm up in Spearfish! The article doesn't give the time, but it says the temperature dropped 47 degrees in just five minutes. It went from 60 degrees Fahrenheit down to 13 degrees Fahrenheit!"

"Well, I'll be," was all Lee could say. "I wouldn't have thought that possible!"

"This project has been amazing. There are other weather stories I've found and even eye witness accounts and interviews on the events. It's been great!"

"Well, it does sound like you're having a good time, at least. Are you doing this alone?"

"No, I told you, there are three of us and honestly, this may be the best group project I've given so far. At least they seem interested in the topic, too. I'm hoping for a good grade. My grade right now is good in Mr. Mallory's class and all we have left is this and the final. I just want to make sure my grade's an A and I think this will push me over the edge, as long as I do reasonably well on his final.

"I've really liked his class. It's a shame he's sick."

"What do you mean sick?"

"He's been battling Lyme's disease and there are times it really shows. He's a great instructor, though and I sure hope it doesn't ever get him completely down. That'd be a real shame."

Chapter 21

Melanie leafed through the Humanities book. "It looks interesting enough," she said to the small girl beside her who couldn't be more than sixteen years old. "I love the pictures of the art work."

"Me too" she said, while continuing to work on the pencil drawing she was working on before her.

"Your work is beautiful," Melanie said.

"Oh, thanks," she replied smiling. "Someday I'd like to be a professional artist."

"How old are you?"

"I'll be seventeen in two months," said the petite, red head.

"So how are you in here?"

"Dual enrollment."

"Really? That's fantastic!"

"It's great because I can get some of my core credits out of the way and it's about half the cost while I'm still in high school."

"Good job. So this is a required course for you?"

"Yeah, and it should be fine. But I hear Dr. Jamison is a little weird and his class is hard."

"Really?"

"Yeah, something about most of the instruction actually comes from the students."

"What do you mean? That doesn't make sense."

"Well, here he comes, I guess we'll find out!"

"Good Afternoon class," said the well groomed, gray haired, 40 year old man as he entered the room and immediately began placing papers on desks. "We're going to get started right away. You'll notice I have placed a sign up sheet at the beginning of each row. Each person must look at the list and write your name beside one of the titles. You will be expected to use the material in the book and any other resource material you choose to expound on your topic and present the class with your findings on a scheduled date, which will be chosen next week."

"I don't understand," said Kevin, one of only three boys in the class.

"Hang with me, and you will," quipped Dr. Jamison. "This assignment is only one of several presentations you will give. This class is not only an art requirement, but also a teaching requirement. As teaching students, this class will enable you to present from a teaching standpoint to your peers on your subject."

"Your right," said Melanie quietly to the red head next to her. "This is a little weird!"

Looking carefully at the list, Melanie finally saw a topic she considered and it wasn't yet taken. Literature! Quickly she wrote her name beside the topic and noted the date beside it. She would have one month to prepare. "This is going to be interesting," she said to the thirty something student on the other side of her.

"I think so, too," she replied as she took the paper Melanie handed her. "I hope I can find something on here I like and that isn't taken already."

Melanie watched for a moment as the woman studied the list. She had dull, brown hair pulled back in a bun, an oversized shirt on a medium sized body, with stretch pants and sneakers without socks. Melanie found herself smiling in spite of herself. She sensed a kinship to the slightly disheveled lady next to her. Looking up, Melanie saw she had kind, soft eyes to accompany her soft voice. Looking up, she smiled. "Got it!" she said.

"Good deal!" Melanie responded quickly. "I'm Melanie."

"I'm Laurel. I'm going to love this class. Art is one of my favorite things although I can't draw or create art at all. I love looking at it. That's the one thing I miss about being back East. Our family often visited the Smithsonian and the Museum of History. But my favorite was always the National Museum of Women in the Arts."

"Wow! I don't believe, even when I lived in the East when I was young, that we ever visited the art museums. I know very little about art but I think it's beautiful. My favorite art is Thomas Kincaid paintings."

"Well, you won't find those in any of the museums in DC," laughed Laurel.

"Oh!" said Melanie, clearly disappointed.

"Okay, class. Let's continue with more housekeeping."

Before the end of the semester you will need to visit a museum and since we don't have a Smithsonian nearby, I will be giving a handout of the museums which will qualify for this course: The National Museum of Woodcarving in Custer, The Indian Museum of North America found in Crazy Horse, The Journey Museum in Rapid City, The Historical School and Museum in Keystone among others. There are criteria you must follow, which is also identified in the handout and a paper will be written by you regarding the art work you find there.

Additionally, near the end of the semester you will be required to take a test which will be taken at your convenience out of class time in the testing center on art work of the world. It will contain sculpture identification, architecture for a given time period, famous paintings and more. You will need to know who created the art, where it can be found, the type of art and in some cases even the medium used to create the art. It is quite comprehensive. You will find most of the pieces described in your book and those we discuss in class which are not in the text; so it is imperative that you do not miss class and that you take good notes."

Melanie winced. "Ugh," she said. "I didn't know I signed up for this!"

Laurel laughed. "You'll be fine," she assured her.

Later that day Melanie pulled out the catalogue and searched for the description of Arts and Humanities. "There it is," she said to Lee sitting on the sofa.

"What?"

"The description of my Humanities class! It includes connections between all the disciplines: art, languages, literature, music, philosophy and religion. Apparently Dr. Jameson is really into the "art" side of it in all the forms. We may learn about the languages, literature, music, philosophy and religion side of it, but his focus looks like it's definitely going to be art."

"Is that a bad thing?"

"No. Just difficult, I think."

"You'll be okay. You've gotten this far. There's no reason to give up now."

"Who said anything about giving up?" she quipped. "I just think it's going to be hard!"

Walking into the PTK office Melanie observed Tristen at the desk, who without looking up, or preamble, said, "I'm glad you're here. We're doing some fund raising projects and I need your help."

"Okay," said Melanie cautiously remember the last time she was asked for help.

"I need you to organize the food drive first of all."

"That's not a fund raiser, is it?"

"No, of course not," she said condescendingly. "I just need you to do that. We are selling tee shirts, and we've got to get a raffle going too. Vanessa is contacting local businesses to see who we can get to give prizes for that and I'm working on some other projects, as well."

"Well, I should be able to handle the food drive without too much issue. What are we doing with the food once we get it?"

"The PTK society has a food bank already set up so all the goods will go there. It'll be your responsibility for advertising the need, collection, boxing and making sure someone is here when the truck comes to get it."

"Okay. I can do that."

"Oh, and I also need you to set a block of time aside to come man the phone a couple times this week. We are calling all the new potential inductees with a personal invitation."

"I don't know about that one," she said.

"Why?"

"Well, I do have a family, I work and I have class. Not to mention my mother-in-law is not well."

"You need to find the time. This is important."

"Tristen, I will do the best I can, but right now I can't promise you that."

"Work on it," she said disgustedly.

Melanie turned and walked out of the room.

"So what did the doctor tell you, today?" asked Melanie.

"They want to operate on my shoulder. The x-rays show my rotator cuff has at least two tears in it, one that is five centimeters and I have tendonitis. Part of the area has wasted away and there is other degeneration too. You might know it'd be my right arm. I swore no one would ever take a knife to that arm again."

"I know," said Melanie. "But this is different. Your elbow and arm issues from Vietnam won't be affected by it, will it?"

"Course it will be," he snapped. "You don't think surgery on my shoulder will affect the rest of me, especially as tender as that area is?"

"I'm sorry. I didn't mean it that way. It's just that if you need to have shoulder surgery so you can move your arm right again, then you should probably get it done. Do you know the process and recovery time?"

"I'm told it's a one day thing if they can do it through arthroscopic surgery. You come in early, have it done, go home and mend from there. They make tiny cuts in your shoulder, go in with a tiny camera, fix it and then stitch you up. Healing time depends on how bad it is, my age, and how I do in rehabilitation."

"So are you going to get it done?"

"Yes," he said sighing. "It's scheduled to be done in two weeks."

"Wow, that's quick."

"I thought so, too, but the time slot just happens to be available. So I agreed."

Melanie looked at the list of museums that qualified one more time. "I think I'd like to go to The Historical School and Museum in Keystone," she said to Mackenzie one afternoon. "Want to come with me?"

"Sure, that'd be fun!"

That Saturday, mother and daughter were off on their adventure. Driving up the winding road to the school, Melanie was at first surprised at the size of the building. On one hand she expected it to be a one room school house like most of the pioneer schools she had visited in the past, but was equally surprised at how large it was. The two story building which Melanie learned served the area until 1988, sitting at the top of the hill was host to a half a football field playground that held a large swing set, a picnic table, teeter totter and monkey bars.

Walking inside the double entry doors they were greeted by a series of steps into the upper level where each classroom held a display of early Americana. Paintings on the wall gave clear indication of the growth of the area over the years. Portraits of the presidents hung on the walls, huge dictionaries were displayed on pedestals so you could turn the delicate pages, desks from another era filled the room and a chalk board with the alphabet sitting high above it and surrounded by photo collections depicting various history data from the region.

Mackenzie and Melanie walked slowly through the museum admiring the history. Melanie found herself touching the desktops as if reliving a time past. "Somehow I feel completely home, here," she said. "It doesn't make sense. I feel like I could have taught here. How bizarre."

"Well, sometimes people do feel like they fit in another time period. Maybe this one is yours.

"Check this out," said Mackenzie. "There's a whole room of just the Ingalls."

"Mackenzie look! I didn't know Carrie Ingalls ended up living in Keystone! It says she even was involved in the town management. She was a newspaper manager. Imagine. We hear so much about Laura, you don't think about the rest of the family being famous!"

"Wow, that was fun," said Mackenzie as they were leaving.

"No kidding! I'm going to use the Victorian architecture of the building for my art piece presentation, but the best part about being here was learning about Carrie Ingalls. I just didn't expect that!"

The morning of the shoulder surgery came much more quickly than Melanie felt possible. They had to be early for pre-op which included the EKG, x-rays, blood work and other tests required before surgery. While they waited for the next round of procedures an older gentleman in his seventies who was pushing an even older man in a wheelchair, joined them in the waiting area. Beside him stood a woman who Melanie decided was probably the wife of the seventy year old. She was hunchbacked, medium build with thin gray hair, wearing gray sweatpants and a loose blue top, and red slip on sneakers without socks.

"My Dad is having surgery today," the woman simply stated in an attempt to start a conversation.

"I'm sorry," Melanie offered.

"It's not your fault," she said. "He's being tested for cancer."

"That's horrible! So they're doing a biopsy?"

"Yeah, that's what they called it. A biopsy."

"Well, I hope things go well."

"Mr. Carson, you want to come on back?" asked the nurse.

Rising to follow the nurse Melanie stopped when the woman began to speak, "Good luck," she said, "You just never know what can happen on the operating table!"

"Thanks, I think," said Melanie slowly. "We'll take the Lord's hands instead of luck though. Hope everything works out for you."

Without missing a beat, she said, "It'll be fine. I'm just not worried about it."

When Lee was taken back to the pre-op room on the gurney, Melanie was asked to wait in the waiting room until he was hooked up to IV and other medical apparatus. She was delighted friends, Valorie and Jake, from church, were there to offer support.

An audible sigh of relief escaped Melanie's lips when the doctor came to her in the waiting room. "The surgery went well," he said. "I'm surprised he did as well as he did considering the damage that was done and the length of time he put off getting it repaired. His shoulder was really a massive mess. We've cleaned out the inflammation, filed down the bone and pulled the tendons over and screwed everything in place.

"The healing process does concern me," he continued. "It's going to take a long time and may never ever completely heal due to his age and mess his arm was in."

"May I see him?" Melanie asked.

"Sure, but be advised he isn't awake yet."

"Okay," she said following him. Three hours later Melanie finally saw Lee begin to stir. He was groggy and thirsty so Melanie kept giving him ice chips as the nurse indicated. Once he finally awakened enough to walk, Melanie and Mackenzie who came later in the day, helped him to the car and made their way home.

"I think the doctor was right," Lee said that night. "I'm not moving out of this chair. I'm staying right here!"

"Well, the doctor said you might want to sleep in that chair for a couple weeks. Didn't your brother Kent sleep in his for a while when he had his shoulder surgery?"

"Kent slept in his chair for about six weeks. I hope it doesn't take me that long to get back in my bed."

Melanie gave him his medication and helped get him comfortable for the night in his oversized recliner. Even reclined, the pain at times was more than Lee could bear and preferred to have himself in a just slightly reclined position, but the next morning Lee made another announcement. "I will sleep in my bed tonight! I didn't sleep worth two cents!"

"Let's wait and see how you feel tonight."

"Nope, it's settled!"

"Well, we'll see," Melanie said not trying to agitate him. "It looks like we're in for some snow. They're calling for ten to sixteen inches. It seems early to get that much."

The weather forecast was on target and the next morning sixteen inches of the cold white stuff covered the hills. Melanie loved it when it snowed; everything pristine white, with the air crisp and clean. There was hardly a sound to be heard when she stepped out on the porch, only the clean silence. And this was a welcome respite considering fitful rest she had had during the night. On top of this, due to the amount of snow received, classes would be canceled for the day. She was scheduled to give her presentation in Humanities class but that would have to wait a couple days. She was glad she had the time to spend with Lee.

True to his word Lee had spent the night in their bed, but it was erratic at best. Getting comfortable was nearly impossible and the sling he was instructed to wear twenty-four hours a day made it even more difficult for Lee to find a comfortable position. And with every movement Lee made or moan that escaped Lee's lips, Melanie found herself worrying that she had caused his discomfort by unintentionally hitting the wounded shoulder.

The following morning Melanie asked, even as she helped Lee with his coat, "You're not really going outside in this are you?"

"I am," he said. "I don't feel that bad and I can run the tractor, even if I can't shovel! And if I have to shovel, I can do it with my left hand. I need to move some of this snow so we can at least get out. It's not supposed to warm up much over the next week and you're going to need to get out, to be able to go to class."

"But, Lee," she countered. "Do you think that's wise?"

"Time will tell," he said with a slight grin. "I'm not going to sit in here all day. I'll go positively nuts!"

Two hours later, the drive way was cleared and Lee came in triumphantly tired. "I got it done!" he announced completely pleased with himself.

"Yes, you did! You're amazing!" she said, giving him a hug. "How do you feel?"

"Like I need a long nap!" he admitted allowing her to help him remove his winter garments.

"Well then, let's see to that!" she said. "But first have some warm soup so you can thaw!"

When class resumed, Melanie found herself nervous even though she felt totally prepared. Walking to the front of the room she found her hands cold, but face flushed and stomach in knots. Looking at her notes one more time she began:

"Good Afternoon," she said, "For the next twenty minutes we will be discussing the evolution of word meanings as related to culture and time period. Words travel…country to country, adding and subtracting, combining, being created.

Calming down with a boost of energy and confidence, noting the class participation she said, "Question: How many people have heard the song by Tim McGraw, "Remember When?" Two thirds of the hands in the class went up. "Listen to a few lines of the song, for those of you who do not listen to country or those who have just forgotten it." Hitting the play button of the tiny tape recorder the music started.

When the excerpt stopped she said, "In this song he demonstrates the evolution of words from as recent as twenty-five or fifty years ago. His examples included: coke, crack and hoe, among others.

"If you used the word "coke" in a sentence fifty years ago it would have meant a drink and only a drink.   It now can still mean the drink we all enjoy, but it also is a name for a horrible drug.

"The main word I will be focusing on today, although there will be others, is "nice."   In the thirteenth century the word nice actually meant "a foolish or simple person."   In 1616 when Shakespeare used it, it meant behavior characterized by or encouraging wantonness." With each definition she shared an example and spelling. "Later it meant foolish, silly, simple or ignorant; later changing to mean a wicked person, then extravagant, elegant, strange, modest, thin and even shy.

"Other words have gone through similar changes, like nuisance," she said. "Who can give me a definition of nuisance, as we use it today?" Using the same technique she discussed quick, silly and awful.

When she finally finished, she was surprised when the class applauded. "Very well done," said Dr. Jamison. "You handled that very well."

Suddenly embarrassed, and immediately over warm, Melanie retreated to her seat.

As the days turned into weeks, Lee found the use of his arm returning. Therapy demanded he use it more and more until finally his range of motion increased to nearly 75%. "I'll be able to shovel snow on the next go 'round!" he said jokingly one day.

Melanie looked at the notes at the bottom of the grading sheet, "You have a presence in front of a classroom," it read. "You will do well in a teaching environment."

"Wow!" thought Melanie. Still she had one more major hurdle to get over in her Humanities class and she was dreading it.

A week later Melanie made her way to the testing center. This would be the equivalent to the class final. Signing in with the Administrator, she was directed to a computer and told she could start anytime. Breathing a prayer, she pulled up the first question. Exhausted, an hour later she finally clicked the "finish" tab. The test had been grueling and many of the works of art and in particular, the places and specific architecture information eluded her. She knew her grade would come instantaneously and she was worried. When the grade was displayed, her heart sank. It was worse than she anticipated. Only a 75. It wasn't what she wanted, but "at least I passed," she said aloud. With the print out of her grade in hand she left the room.

Chapter 22

Melanie shuddered. It wasn't cold outside, but she couldn't erase the chill that swept through her at the very thought of College Algebra. Panic threatened to control her and she fought hard to resist the urge to walk away. Instead she took a deep breath and entered the room. As usual, she took a seat in the front row. She didn't want any distractions in this class. It was going to be tough enough without that. She leafed through the book while her stomach churned. Everything looked like a foreign language. She'd managed to come away with a low A in both the other required Math's, she was already doubtful that was going to happen here.

As the room filled with students, she acknowledged again that she was the oldest student in the class. She didn't mind that, yet she felt intimidated. Her nerves would not calm. "All these kids are smarter than I am in here. This is going to be just awful," she thought. "They're all going to think I'm so stupid! And the awful thing is, in here, that's not far from the truth!"

"Hi!" said Eva, a young woman she recognized, but wasn't sure from where.

"Hi!" returned Melanie. "Have we had a class together? You look familiar."

"I think maybe in Fitness For Life. Did you have Dr. Kline a couple semester's ago. There was a girl named Stacey in the class and her brother died?"

"I do remember you! That was the very first semester I was here. I loved that class."

"I did too. He's a good instructor!"

"What do you think about this class?" Melanie asked cautiously.

"I don't know yet. I'm not strong in Math and I'm told Mr. Embranthiri is new so there wasn't a lot of information on him. And there weren't a lot of options. I just had to take it."

"Me too and I don't have an Algebra background. I will tell you, straight up, I am terrified!

"So is that how you say his name?" Eva asked. "Em-bran-thir-I"?"

"Oh, I don't know. I was just trying it phonetically."

"His nationality is part of the reason I waited until this semester to take this Math class! I was told they had a new College Math teacher coming in and was hoping he would be American so language wouldn't be a barrier. I was told Mr. Guneta is a fairly decent teacher, if you can understand him. His English is poor at best. I figured I'm weak enough in the subject matter; I didn't need another road block! But as it turns out, Mr. Embranthiri isn't American either and I have no clue about his language issues."

"Me either," Eva said. "Guess we'll find out. Here he comes."

"Good morning, class," Mr. Embranthiri said kindly in only slightly broken English, while coming in the room. Rearranging papers on the podium on the table in front of him, which nearly completely hid the short man, he continued. "This is College Math."

Eva and Melanie exchanged looks of satisfaction. "Maybe this will work," Eva whispered quickly. "I can at least understand him, so far!"

"Indeed!" said Melanie, smiling.

"Let's begin," he said, "We need to go over the syllabus before we get started and I need to do roll call. Please answer with present when I call your name."

Finally he said, "Open your texts to chapter one please. This chapter is just review so we will move quickly through it." And as promised, the chapter one summary was displayed on the page before Melanie could catch her breath. As the class neared its end he said, "We will also review on Tuesday," he said "on chapter two, before really getting into the meat of our class. Note also that Tuesday before we do any review you will be tested on all you should already know about Algebra. This test will count as part of your grade. Everyone in here should pass this test without any problems. I suspect you all have had plenty of preparation for this college class. With that said, class is dismissed."

Melanie sat stunned, panic rising in her throat. "I don't know a lot of algebra, Eva," she said. "What in the world am I going to do? Am I the only one in this class this far behind? I'm toast," she said. "Just toast! The semester hasn't even started and I'm already failing." Fighting tears, she stood and gathered her things.

Making her way to Mackenzie's office, Melanie replayed the scene in her mind. At the sight of her daughter, Melanie burst into tears. "Mom, what on earth?

"There's going to be a test on Tuesday on everything we already know in Algebra and I'm going to fail."

"I wouldn't worry about it. I'm sure it's just a test to see where everyone is in the class."

"No," said Melanie emphatically. "It counts! And it's not fair. He's not testing us on what he's taught us, it's stuff we've learned from before. I'm not strong enough for a test like that. I'm done. I'm gonna fail!"

"Okay, calm down. I'll work with you this weekend and we'll see if we can't get the bugs out so at least you can pass the test. He's really counting this as an actual grade?" Mackenzie asked, frowning.

"Yes! Isn't that awful? It's just not fair!" she said, tears being replaced by momentary anger.

"Wow!" was all Mackenzie could say. "That's tough. You might be in for a hard semester."

"That's an understatement. I'll be lucky if I pass the class."

"You will pass the class. Maybe not with an A but you will pass."

"That remains to be seen," she argued.

Melanie's mood hadn't gotten any better after she arrived home and as soon as she saw Lee she started crying again. "What are you crying about?" he demanded.

Recounting the episode, her tears continued to flow.

"Stop crying!" he commanded. "You're way overreacting. It's just a test. Even if you don't do well on it, you'll be able to make it up."

"You don't understand," she said, hurt by his reaction. "The test counts and I already know I'm gonna fail."

"Well you sure will with an attitude like that!"

Melanie turned and fled the room.

"We're having a cook out later today," Melanie said to Tara over the phone. "Why don't you, Brent and the children come over?"

"Sure, we'd love to. Besides, Brent and I need to talk with you anyway."

"Okay, see you in a while."

As the grandchildren were playing after the meal, Tara looked at Brent and then her parents. Taking a deep breath, she plunged forward. "Brent and I are going to move," she announced without preamble.

"What do you mean move?" Melanie said, feeling her eyebrows coming together and the nerves in her shoulders grow tense.

"Well, Brent got a job in Sioux Falls as foreman of the research shop in the lab at the Sioux Falls University."

"You're kidding? You're really moving to Sioux Falls?"

"Yeah, we are. Brent has already accepted the position. We leave in a month."

Melanie was stunned. Her weekend had just gone from bad to worse. "But the babies are due in three weeks. You're going to leave now?"

"No in a month!"

"But even a month," Melanie said, "How will you do that?"

"We'll manage," said Tara. "Brent is going ahead to make all the arrangements. Housing is one of the perks at a real reasonable rate. So Brent's going with some of the big stuff we don't need just now and get that set up and then he'll come back and we'll go as a family."

"But what if you have the twins while he's gone?"

"That's why he's leaving in a week. He'll get things started and then come back. It's only a day drive and if necessary, he can fly back. They know I'm pregnant and due any time and they're willing to work with us, and we're hoping I don't go early. I didn't with the other three. The first two were both late, and Ethan was born on his due date."

"But you're carrying twins.," Melanie persisted. "How are you going to get things packed in your condition?"

"Mom, I'm pregnant, not sick. Remember? I can still do a good deal and as long as I don't overdo, I'll be fine. Putting stuff in boxes is not difficult. Moving them would be and I'm not going to do that. I've already asked Betsy and Lila if they'd help and they said yes. You are welcome to come help too, and I'd like it if you could. I know with classes and work, you're pretty busy."

Melanie just sat there unable to say a word, her mind was screaming in revolt. She's having twins; my grandbabies and they're going away. They're moving away! Her mind recoiled at the thought. First Kaitlyn and Phil and now Brent and Tara.

"What kinds of things will you be doing?" Lee asked, breaking the uneasy silence.

"A variety of things," Brent said. "I will supervise a work crew, do routine lab record keeping, working with some construction specs, testing and other stuff depending on the project before us. It pays well and I didn't feel I could pass up the opportunity."

"No, of course not," said Lee rising to shake Brent's hand. "Congratulations. We'll miss you around here, but I can't blame you for looking to do better."

"Thanks, Dad," he said. "I appreciate that."

"Mom," he said. "You okay?"

"I'll be fine," she said simply. "I'll be just fine."

When Tuesday finally arrived Melanie was a case of nerves. She and Mackenzie had spent hours going over the math problems, but Melanie was too out of sorts to even concentrate. "I declare," she said as she sat next to Eva, "I don't know if I'm hot or cold today. One minute I'm shivering cold and reaching for a sweater and the next I'm breaking out in a sweat. I am some kind of dreading this test."

"Well, honestly I am too," Replied Eva, the pretty brunette. "I studied all weekend and don't feel I'm much closer to being ready. I don't think we're the only ones feeling this way either."

"Class, let's get started," said Mr. Embranthiri, walking to his podium holding a stack of stapled papers in his hands. "We have much to do. The first forty to forty-five minutes will be spent on your test and then rest will be a continuation of review. Following that will be a short introduction to chapter three." Moving to the front of each row he counted the students, then laid the packets on the front desk.

"Pass them back," he said simply. "You may begin as soon as you have a paper. I'm looking for good grades," he added. "This is old material. Everyone in here should be able to get a solid B, or an A. I'm counting on it."

Melanie shivered, feeling the hair on her arms stand up while goose bumps made her arms rigid. She stopped rubbing them in an effort to get warm and calm herself, when he reached her desk. She picked up the stapled copies, kept one for herself and passed the rest back. Leafing quickly through the five pages, she suddenly felt sick. Looking at the first problem, she tried to organize her thoughts.

$$3x + 2 = 5$$

If I subtract 2 from both sides, then $3x + 2 - 2 = 5 - 2$

$$3x = 3$$
$$x = 1$$

Okay, I think I have that one done. Melanie looked at the next problem.

$$2 + \frac{3(2\sqrt{x} + 3)}{2} = 17$$

Square roots! You've got to be kidding! Melanie tried to lay out the problem in simpler terms. First, I need to get rid of that two, so when I subtract two from both sides I get:

$$\frac{3(2\sqrt{x} + 3)}{2} = 15$$

Then I have to multiply both sides by 2 to get rid of the fraction so that's going to be

$$6(2\sqrt{x} + 3) = 30, \text{ then what?}$$

Melanie moved on and with each passing moment and problem became more frustrated.

Solve for x in terms of y in the equation $3^{\left|\frac{x+2}{3}\right|} = y^2 - 1$

Okay, I've got to do the math inside the brackets first so

$$\left|\frac{x+2}{3}\right| = \frac{y^2-1}{3}$$

Then I have to multiply each side by three. Oh man, I'm lost. I completely don't know how to do this! Melanie looked at the next problem.

If $2x^2 = 72$, then what is the value of x?

If $f(x) = \dfrac{3x}{4-x}$, what is $f(x+1)$?

Solve for x in the inequality $\dfrac{x}{2} - 3 < 2y$.

When Mr. Embranthiri asked for papers to be turned in, Melanie felt the blood drain from her face even as her heart raced and stomach knotted even tighter. She was on page three and she knew she hadn't done well, even on the ones she tried. She heard a collective moan in the classroom. She must not have been the only one having difficulties, she decided. But that didn't ease her own pain. She swallowed hard trying to push the lump in her throat down in an effort to keep tears from flowing from eyes that were welling up with liquid. Fighting for composure she placed her head in her hands wishing she could leave. Still there were fifteen minutes left in the class and she had to wait.

It was difficult to focus and Melanie fought to respond when he asked the class to turn to chapter two in their books. Reading the content right from the pages, he began. He scrawled the problems from the book on the board talking quickly as he wrote. In the remaining time he sped through the chapter and finally the class was over.

Without a word, she picked up her things and fled the room. Hurrying she turned into the first ladies room she could find. It was empty and she was grateful. No one needed to see her devastation and humiliation. Retrieving a paper towel from the dispenser she wet it and held the cool dampness to her face while trying to control her breathing and her emotions. But she couldn't stop the onslaught of tears despite her efforts and simply buried her hands in her hands and allowed the tears to flow with great silent heaving sobs. "It's going to be a long semester," she said to herself once composure had returned. "I am so done. I'm gonna fail this class. I'm gonna fail," she kept repeating. "I'm just gonna fail."

Melanie wiped her face one more time, hoping the residual effects of a good cry didn't show. Picking up her things, she headed to the financial aid office.

She had three hours of work today before she could head home. Her efforts to hide her melt down weren't successful for those who knew her.

"What in the world?" asked Debbie as soon as she came in the office. "You okay?"

"No, but if I talk about it, I'm going to cry again," she said adamantly.

"Okay. Is there anything I can do?"

"Only if you can take my math test again that I just failed," she answered trying not to start a rain storm again.

"Melanie," she said softly. "You're a smart girl. You'll get through this."

"Easy for you to say. You didn't just fail a math test."

Debbie giggled. "Sorry," she said. "I would if I could. You might need tutoring for this class. There's no shame in that."

"That's irrelevant," she started, angry now. "That test was unfair. I know without a doubt, I failed it. But the test wasn't on what he taught. The test was on stuff that he thinks we should already know. It should have been a test, if he was going to give one like that, that gives him some clue where we all are in the class. I'm in a huge hole and the semester hasn't even started!   Errrrr!" She growled. "It's wrong, just wrong. And I failed. I just failed."

"Well, what about seeing the head of the math department."

"I don't know who that is."

"There's a solution for that," Debbie said reaching for a sheet of paper from the stackable file on top of her desk. "It's Mrs. Clendening, And she's nice. She's been here a while and maybe she can help you."

"What's she going to do? It's not her class."

"But it's her department."

"I'll see," Melanie said sullenly. "Let me find out just how horrible my grade is and maybe I will."

The next week Melanie, just before getting ready for bed was surprised by a late night telephone call. "Hey, Mom. It's Brent. Tara's headed for the hospital. You and Dad coming out?"

"Already? She's early!"

"Yup! But at least I'm here!"

"True! We'll be there. See you in a bit," she said.

"Uh, oh," Melanie said before they reached the hospital. "Another call from Brent."

"Mom, would you and Dad mind stopping by a fast food place and bring me a burger. I'm starved. I should have eaten but by the time I got home and then started helping Tara with some packing, I just didn't get it done. Now being in hold mode, I need food."

"Okay," she said laughing. "We'll bring you something. Tara doing okay?"

"Yeah, she wants you two to come on in the room."

"Are you sure?"

"It's fine with the hospital if you're in here during birth, if you'd like. Tara says she's good with it."

"I'll let you know when we get there," said Melanie cautiously.

"You want to go in while Tara has the babies?" Melanie asked Lee.

"You can do that now? I mean I went in with you for ours, but parents? And both of us? Tara isn't going to mind if we're both in there?"

"Apparently it is completely accepted with the hospital and Tara says sure, come on in! I don't think I would want anyone else in the room while I gave birth. But it'd be cool to see our next grandbabies make their entrance into the world."

"Well, we'll start. If it gets more than I want to see, or hear," he added, "then I'll just leave."

"That works!"

Walking into the room, Melanie was surprised with how informal and laid back the staff and room was. There was to her immediate right a sofa and table for relaxing with a selection of books to read, and a large water cooler so those who would like drinking water had it quickly available. They weren't required to wear gowns or mouth shields of any kind, in fact it almost seemed non-sterile.

Tara acknowledged their appearance and then called out for Brent. "I've got another contraction coming," she said. "It's a good one." With that all else stopped except the sound of Tara's efforts.

Taking turns, standing next to the bed, holding Tara's hand and talking with her in an attempt to keep her calm over the next four hours, Brent, Lee and Tara waited for the birth of the new little miracles. At 3:20 a.m. baby Grace made her grand entrance into the world. The dark haired beauty immediately stole the hearts of her grandparents. Five minutes later her brother, Aaron joined the family. Melanie was filled with both joy and sadness. In only two weeks, they would be moving across the state. Her heart ached as she held the tiny package that was Grace, touching each of her fingers and caressing the tiny cheeks as tears fell down her own followed by the little bundle that was Aaron.

Melanie walked into Math class with a rock at the pit of her stomach. She dreaded the return of her math test, yet knew she'd have to face it sooner or later. Earlier in the week when she went to class she expected to get her grade, but Mr. Embranthiri hadn't finished grading them. The only thing he'd said about it was,

"There seems to be some problems with what you know about Algebra. It looks like some of you are going to have to work harder than others. I will have them ready for the next class session."

Standing before the class he said simply. "We have much to do. Here are your Math tests and as I mentioned last time we met, the grades really aren't good. Several of you did quite well, others not so much and some really didn't do well at all. If you have questions come see me. My office is right down the hall."

Melanie paled even as her heart sank with the sound of thunder created by a shock wave. The grade was worse than even she expected. A huge red 44 glared at her from the top of the page. Not only were many of the ones she tried wrong, but not finishing the test added insult to injury. This wasn't a deep hole that needed to be crawled out of, it was a giant chasm that threatened to swallow her from math existence.

As if nothing unusual happened, Mr. Embranthiri opened is text book and said, "Open your text books to chapter five please. We are moving along. You need to keep up because if you don't keep up, you're going to fail. Be aware that each chapter builds on the previous one and if you don't have complete command of it, getting the next one will be more difficult."

Melanie tried to concentrate and take as many notes as she could, but clearly not comprehending the material. She raised her hand. "Could you explain that again please?"

Looking at her like she was a total idiot, he redid the problem just as the book showed but it made no more sense to her the second time around than it did the first. Exasperated by the end of class, Melanie decided not to visit Mr. Embranthiri's office just now. She knew that would only make things worse. "I'll go after work," she told herself. "At least that way I have a chance to calm down."

After work, as planned she walked across campus to the Math building. Taking a deep breath and knocking on his door, she waited. "Come in," said the male voice inside.

"I've got a big problem," she said without preamble. "I bombed that first test and I don't have a clue how I'm going to get out of that hole. Can't you slow down just a bit so those of us who are struggling can catch up? I can't even say it's been a long time since I've done Algebra. I never had it in high school. I did well in the other math's I took, but this is kicking my tail!"

"No, I'm sorry I can't. This is my first semester here and I am expected to get through this entire text during this semester. They are watching me and I have to do well. What you can't grasp in class you will have to go elsewhere to get.

"You are right, Mrs. Carson. You are in quite a hole, but I'm confident you can dig your way out. We have several more tests this semester. You can make that up."

"A 44? That's almost impossible to make up!"

"Make sure you do your homework and get help and you should pass my class."

"I don't want to just pass. I want to do well."

"Concentrate on passing. Doing well can come later."

Melanie looked at him incredulously. "You're serious."

"Concentrate on getting the work and you can get through. I see you as a solid B student.

Melanie looked hard at the man before her. "B is not my style," she said. "But I will attempt to get help. I have daughters who are very solid in math. But I still take issue with you moving so fast. What good does it do the students in the class if we don't even have time to learn the material?"

"I can't help you there," he said matter of factly. "My job is to present you the material and like I said, I must complete the entire text. It will be rapid, but most of the students should be fine."

"What about the ones who aren't fine?" she argued, surprised at her own resolve.

"There's nothing I can do about that," he said. "We must work within the parameters we have. So keep trying and I'm sure you'll do just fine."

Melanie walked out of the office more discouraged than ever. "This is ridiculous," she said to no one in particular. "Absolutely ridiculous."

As planned, Tara, Brent and the babies were leaving for Sioux Falls. "I love you," she said to the infant in her arms and then the other one. Hugging the other grand children, first Ethan, then Dylan and finally Ariana, she looked at Tara sadly and said, "I can't believe you guys are moving so far away."

"Mom, it's only a day's drive. We'll be back. It's not across the country."

"It feels like it," she pouted. "First it was Kaitlyn and Phil, then Gavin, Luke is who knows where and now you."

Hugging her daughter and son-in-law once more she watched them climb into the truck and pull away, unable to pull her eyes away until they were completely out of sight. Lee put his arm around her shoulders. "They're right you know. It really is only a day's ride away."

"I know," she said sadly. "But right now a day's ride feels more like a week's worth."

As the days passed Melanie struggled to keep up with math. Tears flowed freely night after night while doing homework with Kaityln over the phone as they had in semesters past, but frustrated beyond belief. The final was upon her and she was filled with anxiety and doubt. For a moment she recalled a question in passing from one of the counselor's at the college. "Melanie, you have Mr. Embranthiri for College Algebra, right?"

Stiffening she answered slowly, "Yeah."

"How's that going for you?"

Without preamble, she burst into tears and said, "I can't talk about that right now. Please excuse me."

She had visited Mrs. Clendening, the head of the department, as Debbie had suggested, but that wasn't helpful. Melanie described the situation through tears and with genuine sympathy, Mrs. Clendening said, "Melanie, I am sorry for your trouble in that class. If it's any consolation you are not the only one who has been to see me. I heard about the test he gave at the beginning of the semester and while I don't approve and agree that it was horribly unfair, there isn't a thing I can do about it. He is permitted to teach his class any way he chooses so long as no harm comes to his students."

"Does he really have to teach the entire book in this semester?" she argued. "Isn't it more important to meet the students right where they are and teach them from that point?"

"No, he does not have to teach the entire text this semester. That is his perception. And if it were my classroom meeting the students where they are, as you put it, is the stance I would take. But it's not my class. He will be reviewed at the end of the semester, but for now my hands are tied."

Feeling defeated, Melanie left Mrs. Clendening's office. "I've used all my options," she told Debbie later that day. "It'll be a miracle if I pass the class."

"Okay, Mom," said Kaitlyn on the phone one afternoon. "Give me all your grades and I'll figure out what you have to get on the final to at least come out with a C."

Reading the figures Melanie cringed. "I got it. Even if you completely bomb the final you can still come out of this class with a C. You've done it. You got through it. It's not the A or even the B you wanted, but take it and run. You have worked so hard, be happy with it!"

"You're sure. I will absolutely get a C in the class no matter what."

"Right! It doesn't matter how badly you do on the final, you will get a C. Now understand you can't do any better either. You could never do well enough, even getting a 100% on the final and get a B. But you will have the C. Actually, I'm proud of you."

"Really? How can you be proud of me? All I'm getting is a C."

"Mom, I know how hard you've worked. You didn't have the background and you still made it. Deal!" she finally said laughing. "You did good! Your professor was unreasonable! Run with it!"

Chapter 23

Melanie took her usual seat near the front of the room and waited for Dr. Hayden to come in. She had only met her once, but liked the person she knew mostly from the online class. Looking around the room, she recognized some of the students, mostly girls, but there was a young man among them. She was immediately taken by his accent. He was clearly Australian. In his early twenties, blond hair and tanned, he fit the visual she'd always had of someone from "down under."

"I'm an exchange student," the young man said to the young woman next to him just as Dr. Hayden entered the room, pulling a suitcase caddy neatly stacked with crates of papers and notebooks. Instantly the room quieted as the tall brunette with kind eyes stopped at the front of her desk and began unloading the cart.

"Please," she said perusing the room, "don't stop chatting just because I've come into the room. You still have about five minutes before class time. I like my students to know each other." Slowly the chatting that had begun before she came into the room began again. Melanie listened to the different conversations since she was still sitting alone at her table.

At the moments ticked away, Melanie watched Dr. Hayden. The fair skinned, stylish woman was confident and pleasant with what seemed like an unlikely laid back demeanor. It was apparent by the way she would occasionally stop and listen to the conversations, she loved her job and enjoyed her students.

Finally she said, "Okay, I think it's time to get started. We may have another student or so join us. I don't think everyone is here who should be, but that's okay. They'll find us.

"I like to begin my classes with self-introductions. It gives everyone a chance to share a little about themselves and I encourage you to share something no one else probably knows. I'll begin so you get a feel for what I mean.

"I am Alexandra Hayden, married to Kent for 13 years and have three adorable children: Logan, 9 years old, Amber 7 and Natalie 5. We moved here from Wyoming and I have been a professor at Cedar Ridge for eleven years. I love to ski and ride horses."

The first girl to speak sat near the door on the far side of the room. "I am Lenore. I live in Black Hawk. My parents moved here from Texas when I was six years old. And I have three younger siblings."

"I'm Janet," said the next girl. "I live in Rapid City and have all my life. I love rodeo competition and won the barrel racing championship last year. My horses name is Treasure and we plan to compete again this year."

"Congratulations!" said Dr. Hayden. "We have a celebrity in our class."

Looking at Melanie, she said, "Tell us about you."

"I'm Melanie, I have five grown children, seven grandchildren and my husband and I like to summer near Glacier Falls in Montana. In fact we've gone out there almost every year since the middle 80's."

"Where do you stay?" asked Dr. Hayden, clearly interested.

"We stay in Columbia Falls at the Columbia Falls RV Park."

"Wow! My mother-in-law lives in Columbia Falls. It's been years since we visited. Do you know where Pinewood Park is?"

"Sure."

"She lives just a couple blocks from there."

"Oh, my goodness!"

"Kent and I have been talking about visiting again for some time; he really needs to go see his mom, but with my work and his, it hasn't happened in quite a few years. It's beautiful there."

"Yeah, it is. In fact we were just passing through that area all those years ago, when we took the "Going to the Sun" Road. I fell in love with the area and we just keep going back. Our youngest son moved out there to finish college. He loves it."

"So how is it you get to travel? You look really young to be retired."

"Thanks," Melanie said blushing. "Lee is eight years older than I and he's had a great deal of medical issues, but he retired and so we travel. Well, we travel when I'm not in school. His plan on retirement was for us to spend most of our time on the road, but that all changed."

"I just can't wait to tell Kent about you. I think it's wonderful you get to travel. And I need to get on him about taking that trip ourselves really soon. Thanks for sharing."

Melanie suddenly became acutely aware that she and Dr. Hayden had been having a private conversation while all the other students sat patiently waiting for their turn to speak. Attempting to give her full attention to the next student, Melanie pushed aside the "re-run" of the conversation she'd just had with this professor she hardly knew. "I like her," she thought, smiling, hoping no one noticed.

As the days passed she looked forward to her visits to Educational Psychology with Dr. Hayden. Their friendship grew with each class as they exchanged stories about children and husbands. "I'd love to repaint the living room," Melanie said one day, "but Lee likes it like it is and would be real upset if I went ahead and did it."

"Kent can be like that," she said. "I remember once I wanted to buy a new sofa for the family room. He was just certain we didn't need it but I bought it anyway. I figured, 'What's he gonna do, be mad? Yeah, probably for a while, but he'll get over it.' He was and he did and now he loves that chair! Go figure!"

Melanie thought about what Dr. Hayden had said and even looked at colors in the paint department at Lowes. Choosing the color she wanted she set about to buy the paint. "I'd like this color," she told the girl behind the desk.

"Oh, that's a pretty shade of blue. It's almost powdery. What room are you painting?"

"I'd like to do the living room that color," she said, then suddenly realizing the impact of her decision, quickly said, "Never mind. I'm not going to buy it today after all," and nearly ran from the store.

"I don't want Lee mad with me," she scolded herself. "It'd take him forever to get over it, not to mention I'd never be able to paint it myself good enough that he'd be happy with it. I did the right thing," she said aloud consoling herself on the drive back home.

"Presentations will be during our next class," Dr. Hayden said. "These are important because it will demonstrate your understanding of the different situations." Melanie thought about her options. There had been five from which to choose. The first had been on schema processes which is dependent on what knowledge a person brings with him to a learning situation, the second dealt with how a teacher should deal with parents relative to the students she is teaching.

Behaviors in a classroom setting had interested her, but Melanie was sure she couldn't be biased enough to give both sides since she believed behavior issues often stemmed from what was learned at home and the lack of freedom teachers have in disciplining students in a classroom. This particular subject had become quite the topic in one class where other students felt it was more appropriate to ignore any bad behavior and only notice when a child does well. "Student's abuse that," Melanie had argued. "They need and expect guidelines and when the set boundaries are crossed, I don't believe it should be ignored. Nor do I believe that a student has the right to misbehave because he knows he's on medication. I completely believe that the idea of medicating a child has been abused by parents, doctors and teachers and it isn't a problem that can be ignored."

Study habits had been another topic that had produced some conversation, but there was such a distaste for studying, it was easy for her to see why students had the apathy she'd seen in some of her classes and it not only angered her, it frightened her. These were the students who would be in charge of the next generation, whether they were to be teachers, professionals or homemakers. Any of them could be in politics and have a voice in our government. How can they know what's going on and how to handle things if they can't even sit down with a book or other material to study it?

She'd settled on a problem that many teachers were facing in their classrooms that also caused Melanie to become angry with the system. So when she was called the next class period to begin her presentation she said, *"One of the major problems found in classrooms is the need for teachers to be structured so they are teaching for the "test" that has become inevitable in many grades. This has become the number one criteria for teaching instruction in most of our public classrooms. With this pressure put on teachers, they become afraid of "getting out of the box" and changing the way they teach in fear of missing something relevant for the state standardized test!*

"In addition there are those teachers, who have taught for such a long while the "old way" with textbooks and no technology, they become afraid of change. In addition to this scenario the added element of belief that when the children reach Middle School all the efforts of teaching are going to be torn apart anyway creates an attitude just defeats the purpose and takes the joy right out of teaching!"

Melanie continued sharing her ideas of learning centers, teaching with enthusiasm, strategic thinking, confident in her skills and ability to motivate children while recognizing their differences."

Finishing she said, *"Teachers should be able to encourage students to identify problems they wish to explore and then allow the teacher to act as a guide as the students work to answer their questions. She should have what I like to call an "Essential question" time which allows the students to ask why, what, where, when, how much and all the questions that would be relevant to the issue at hand, and then let the students again work on solving the question by thinking the issue through! This is a form of discovery learning and I believe children learn better when they are interested in a topic rather than having them conform to a generalized test which doesn't tap into the natural, God given abilities at all."*

"Well done," said Dr. Hayden. "I can see you are passionate about your feelings. That's a good thing. You'd do well in a classroom setting.

"Comments anyone?"

"Crystal?"

Melanie cringed, recalling other times Crystal gave her critique. "Here it comes," she thought, steeling herself for the onslaught.

"I agree with some of Melanie's presentation but there's a lot of information out there that suggests that standardized testing is a reliable and objective way to monitor student achievement; they are all inclusive and non-discriminatory since all students receive the same test.

"Teachers can focus essential content and skills on what children need to know to do well in our society, not what they want to know which may have no relevance at all on their survival into adulthood. I believe teachers should teach the test. It's what's going to be most important."

"Any other thoughts?" asked Dr. Hayden.

"Lacy?"

"I think Melanie is right. We rob our kids of being creative and I believe the tests are "dumbing down" our schools. Our kids may be good at taking tests, but not preparing them to be productive adults. I think the tests are more a measure of the teacher's performance than the kids she's teaching. How they do on the test is, in essence, a direct reflection of her teaching ability."

"I'm glad to see there are some very strong opinions here and this is a topic we could discuss for hours and probably not really come to any real conclusion. I am looking forward to the rest of the presentations.

"Melanie you have laid the groundwork for the rest of the class. You've raised the bar to what I expect from the rest of your peers. Well done."

"Thanks, Melanie!" said Karla, laughing. "You just had to make it harder for the rest of us!"

"I didn't mean to," she said defensively. "I thought I was just doing the assignment!"

As the days turned into weeks, Melanie worked on her Portfolio assignments in conjunction with the class assignments. The portfolio would be her capping achievement. There was a class designed just for this next semester, but this class opened the door into what would be expected. Once again her name was called to present and although she'd gotten used to presenting, she always seemed to break out into a sweat and have cold hands as she made her way to the front of the room. Nervously she shared an edited version of the first of many portfolio assignments:

Reflection on "Self-As-Learner"

As a learner, I lean toward being a "Tactile/Kinesthetic" learner which means, in the broadest sense, I prefer a "hands on" learning experience. Learning for me, regardless of the subject, is best completed when I can make the lesson tangible and clearly understand the "how and why" an answer given, is the correct one. This learning style suggests I learn best when I can participate in the lesson being taught.

Within the framework of an English or History class, reading is essential to be followed with a spirited and genuine discussion of the given readings. In a Math or Science class, where I tend to struggle more, I find the lab work within the class is helpful whether it's deciphering a geographical map, participating in a science experiment or doing a math problem by way of calculator or working the process out by repeated effort.

In a classroom, remembering my learning preferences can be helpful to students who share my learning style. The greater challenge for me will be to accommodate those children who do not share my preferred learning style. It will be necessary for me to make certain that I have material available that supports the visual, verbal or auditory learning.

While I will naturally gravitate toward my learning style, I will need to be especially aware and considerate of those children who are not Tactile/Kinesthetic learners. It will be my greatest challenge to accommodate these children, equally, to those of my preferred learning style.

Learning, whether it's English, History, Math or Science is fascinating! I just need to keep doing my best in each of the content areas and hopefully, should the opportunity present itself for me to have a classroom, I can be a good teacher!"

As the weeks drew to a close Melanie was actually sad. "I love this class," she told Dr. Hayden one afternoon. "I enjoy the dialogue and the different views from the students."

"Well, I'm glad. It has been a good class this semester. Most of the students are really interested and that helps."

"Is there a chance I may be in one of your classes next semester?"

"Very likely. I'm the only professor for Portfolio. So you'll have me at least for that."

"Okay, Good deal!" she said cheerily.

It was not cheer, however, she felt that afternoon when the phone rang. "Mrs. Carson?"

"Yes?"

"This is Maggie Lewis at Glacier Falls Regional Hospital. We just wanted to inform you that your son, Gavin is here. Although he is eighteen, we see that since he's a student he's still under your insurance."

"Yes, he is. Why is he at the hospital?

"Well, he collapsed while at the sawmill just out of town. We're not sure why. His blood pressure dropped significantly and we still haven't found the cause."

"He collapsed at a saw mill?"

"Yes Ma'am. From what we gather in conversation is he was delivering a photo pack from Glacier Photography, where we believe he works and while he was at the sawmill he collapsed. Please understand he is doing much better, although he still feels pretty rough, and he's groggy from the meds we have given him for pain."

"Is there anything I need to do?"

"Not really. He's covered. We just needed to inform you. And I will ask you. Does he have a history of this sort of thing?"

"This sounds like what he did a year or so ago," she said. "They thought it was Marfan's but ruled it out. We don't know what it is."

"Well, okay. We'll keep monitoring him and probably send him home later today."

"Can I talk with him?"

"I'll make sure that he gets the message you want to talk with him later and ask him to call you."

"Thank you," said Melanie now shaking with fear. "What in the world?" she thought to herself. "I wish he was here. At least then I could take care of him!"

"Mom?" came the call late in the evening.

"Gavin? You all right?"

"I'm better. I have no clue what happened. All I know is I crashed and burned."

"You were making a delivery for work? The lady I talked with said something about a photography packet."

"Yeah. It was a packet of pictures for Glacier Mountain Sawmill they had taken about two weeks ago. My boss asked me to deliver them. When I got there, I felt some pain, but then I remember nothing. They called an ambulance."

"What did your boss say?"

"He felt bad. But what's really bad is Thelma, one of the ladies that work here, isn't crazy about me and actually started this rumor that I was drunk! She says she saw me last night out partying at someone's house and she even went so far to say that I had alcohol on my breath today when I came in!"

"Gavin! Are you serious?"

"Yeah, and as you know, I don't drink. I wasn't at a party last night. I was at Rev. Steele's home having dinner. I don't know who she thinks she saw or where, but she's got the rumor out there."

"Where did you go after you left Rev. Steele's house?"

"Home. I was beat!"

"How's your boss with all that junk going on?"

"He's ignoring her remarks. The hospital can vouch for me that I had no alcohol. It's just frustrating."

"No kidding! That's just wrong!"

"Yeah, it is, but some people just don't care about the things they say."

"So are you all right?"

"Yeah. Mostly. I'm tired. I feel really beat up right now. I wish I knew what it was and what causes the crashing."

"By the time you get home for Christmas I'll have some appointments set up and see what we can find out."

"Well, all right. That'll work."

"Until then you be careful. It's only another month."

"I will. I'll be fine."

A week later on a Saturday, Melanie drove to the college. It had already been a morning and she didn't like the way she felt. She nervously put on the last of her makeup and reached for her earrings. These were special ones; hummingbirds. Lee had brought them to her as a gift on one of his trips away. One earring was in place and picking up the other let it slip out of her fingers and down the drain. Tears rolled down her cheeks as she realized the loss. "How am I going to tell Lee I am just clumsy?" she berated herself. "He is going to be furious!"

Just then Lee walked into the bathroom. "What's the matter?" he asked.

Crying harder now and trying to talk, she sputtered, "I dropped my earring in the sink."

"You did what?"

"I picked it up and I dropped it and I can't get it. It's these," she said taking the other one out of her ear lobe. The ones you bought for me while you were gone. I can't get it," she said again, exasperated.

"Calm down. I'll try to get it for you."

"How? It went down the sink."

"Have you run water since it happened?"

"No, why?"

"It should be in the elbow part of the drain. I'll take it apart and see if I can find it."

"Really?"

"Yes, really! Now would you calm down so you can go take your test?"

Hugging him, she said, "I love you and yes, I'll calm down. I just thought it was gone forever!"

Parking the car at the college, she took a deep breath. This was it. She was here to take the Praxis test. Passing the test was a requirement by the state to be certified in the teaching profession. Passing the test was also a requirement for graduation. All Melanie had ever heard about the test terrified her. Most, she learned, did not pass it on the first try, some not until the third or fourth. And again, the subject matter she feared the most was science and math.

Opening her door she exited the car and was surprised to not see another single student. A momentary flicker of doubt crossed her mind. She was sure she had the right day, but did she mess up on the time? Quickening her steps she headed for the building designated the testing center. She fumbled in her purse when she heard her phone.

"Hello?" she said.

"You don't have to worry about your earring," said the kind, familiar voice on the other end. "I found it and it's safe and sound!"

"Good deal!" she said exuberantly. "Thank you!"

"I just wanted you to know so you wouldn't be fretting about it during your test!"

"Good deal," she repeated. "And thank you! I'll be home as soon as I'm finished."

Entering the designated hallway, she was relieved to see other students. "Hey, Melanie," came friendly voices. "Are you ready for the test?"

"As ready as I'm going to be."

"I don't know how ready I am, but I've been studying a lot. No one passes this the first time around ya know."

"Really? I'd heard that."

"Have you done lots of studying?"

"Some, but not lots. What do you study? I guess I could have put more time into math and science," she said suddenly fearful.

"Students taking the Praxis may come in the room now and take a seat," said a medium height, overweight, gray haired lady.

Sitting down, Melanie placed her bottle of water on the desk along with her three pencils and calculator.

"All water bottles and everything except your pencils and calculators must be removed from the top of your desk," said the gray haired lady, sternly.

Surprised, Melanie and several students around her complied with the command. "Remember," the woman continued. "No one may rise from their seat once we start until time is called on the test. If you finish early I recommend you go over your answers. Once this set of testing is complete you will be excused for seven minutes and we will promptly begin the next series. If you are not in the room when we begin, you will not be allowed to enter."

"Wow," thought Melanie.

The other proctor in the room said, "I'm going to be taking roll based on registration forms. You will need to complete three more forms before we begin the first test." Rising, the blond haired, slender woman with a limp walked around to each desk and provided the students with the forms to be completed.

Once the forms were complete, the gray haired lady said, "Let's begin."

Melanie turned over the packet of papers before her. She looked through the questions. This series was English and she dove in full tilt. Grammar wasn't an issue, although the structural relationship section proved to be a little more difficult. Idiom and word choice was interesting and the essay part of the test didn't seem really difficult.   Literal Comprehension and the Critical and inferential comprehension while not a breeze, was not as difficult as it could have been. She finished, looked at the clock only to realize she had twenty more minutes before the end of the test. She started again, re-reading each question and still finished before time was called.

Taking a drink of her water and standing to stretch, Melanie decided to remain in the room during the break. The last thing she wanted was to get hung up somewhere and not be allowed to finish. Sitting down when directed with her heart pounding, she began the next series of tests. This one would prove to be more difficult. It was math.

Plunging in, Melanie did the first problem and the second, then skipping the next one, moved on. She'd have to come back to attempt the ones she wasn't sure about. She placed an asterisk beside the number to remind her and noted her time. She would have to take a best guess, if she was close on time. At least she'd have a one in four chance of getting the right answer if she couldn't figure it out. Completing what she knew, she still had ten minutes on the clock and began re-computing the ones she didn't know. Looking at her answer, after a third try, Melanie chose a best guess. In this manner she completed the test just as the gray-haired lady said, "Time. Please put your pencils down."

All Melanie could do now was wait. The results would come in the mail in about two weeks. She prayed she passed. The last thing she wanted was to have to go through this again.

"I picked up the mail on my way in," said Luke who was now home from the service. He'd completed his obligation and tour overseas, made the decision to leave the Marine Corps and now was looking at college in the Spring.

Melanie had been surprised with his decision to leave the service, since he'd planned on making it a career. "There's just too much politics involved," he stated simply. "I've seen all of war I want and now I want something more. I'm not sure what it will be but I'm thinking somewhere in a detective agency but more likely in the FBI if I can work it out. I think I'll start in the Criminal Justice Program at the college," he had told her.

"As long as you are happy and safe," she had replied.

"So what's in the mail?" Melanie asked off handedly.

"You've got something here from the Educational Testing Service?"

"Oh my gosh!" she said, her eyes wide and heart suddenly racing. "That's the Praxis scores." Nervously she held the envelope afraid to open it.

"You want me to open it?" Luke asked.

"No," she said taking a deep breath, and walking away from him. "I will." Ripping the envelope open, she pulled out the score report. Looking at the front sheet, she couldn't decide how she'd done. Looking to the inside she saw the line "Total Comprehensive Score: 536 with a required score 527; Passed!"

"I passed, I passed," she squealed! "Oh my gosh, I passed!" She ran to Luke and hugged him. "I passed, I passed," she said again and again. "I can't believe it! I passed!"

Stopping she looked at the back sheet to see how she had really done. In the English, she really hadn't done badly at all. It was on the math test where she could see her greatest deficiency. While she fell into the Average performance range in all three areas, Conceptual and procedural knowledge; quantitative information; and measurement, geometry and formal mathematical reasoning, she still ultimately failed that section by only three points. But because it was a comprehensive score which determine a student's fate, she had passed. Elated, she called Lee, "I passed, I passed," she told him still giddy with excitement. "I really passed and on my first try!"

Chapter 24

Melanie looked at the professor at the head of the class; a well dressed woman in a dark blue business suit. Her medium length hair hanging loosely about her shoulders, and soft blue eyes were accented by her perfectly applied make-up. "Wow, she's pretty," thought Melanie. "Somehow she's not what I expected. She looks like she belongs in a big office building somewhere.

Smiling as students came in, the woman seemed friendly, even as she projected complete authority. "I am Claire Randolph," she finally said. "You should all be familiar with the routine and what is expected from Field Experience classes. I expect you each to make contact with the school administration in whatever schools you choose to work in this semester and then make sure I am kept up to date with all forms and your reflections after each day's visit. This is very important because it allows me to see just where you are in a classroom. It's always interesting to see if your perspective of your interactions with the students and teachers is the same as the final evaluation by your teacher."

As instructed Melanie made the necessary phone calls to Sweet Creek Elementary and was excited as she entered Colleen Garrity's second grade class. The classroom was enclosed without windows so the brightly decorated walls with lots of numbers and letters throughout and, bright bulletin boards displaying the children's work and other themes was very pleasing to the eye.

The children had just begun their reading and writing hour. They were working on letters to their pen pals in fifth grade. The work included prompts, a rough and final draft.

Mrs. Garrity explained to the children that they were all at different stages of writing and they should work from where they were. She asked the children to read their letters to her and then if it met the criteria they were allowed to color the accompanying picture motivating them with compliments on their hard work. The class was orderly but allowed children who were finished to help another if they desired. Jason, one of the nearly thirty students, was really good with the process and was helping two other children at the same time, impressing Melanie with his ability.

Surprised with the diversity of the group, Melanie noted that along with Caucasian and Native American children there was an Asian girl, an African American boy and a set of Spanish twin girls who spoke little or no English and required the help of Mrs. Benson since she could speak their native Spanish. A local family, Melanie learned, had adopted the girls from Belize, South America. Both languages were spoken to the children which aided not only the Spanish children who spoke so little English, but also the other children who by default were learning another language!

Mrs. Garrity explained to Melanie that within her classroom they operate like family. She said "I have taught the children, we are a family and we will disagree, but we're a family first."

"I like that strategy." Melanie responded. "I believe it would give a feeling of belonging, even if you're different."

"Lee! Check this out. I just got an email from Tristen. There is a PTK Leadership conference down in Hot Springs on Saturday, the 29th. She wants me to go."

"What?" he asked sounding exasperated.

"I got an email from Tristen. Listen: *There is a PTK Leadership conference down in Hot Springs on Saturday, the 29th which I am told is a two hour drive from the college. Vanessa is going and it would be great if you could too. I'm driving, so you both can go with me. It's all day, though and we'd be gone from about 8:00 a.m. until about 7:00 in the evening. Let me know as soon as you can so I can get everyone registered.*"

"So Tristen says she's driving and wants me to go. Would you mind?"

"I think it's a waste of time."

"Well, as vice-president with Vanessa, I think I should go. I think it'd be interesting. Maybe this is Tristen's way of putting out the proverbial "olive leaf." We haven't exactly been best buddies."

"No, I don't care. Go. I'll find something else to do or somewhere to go."

"Thanks," she said, eyebrows furrowing, with unease. "I'll let her know."

Meeting at the college on the appointed date, the three ladies headed for Hot Springs. Melanie sat in the back seat since she was the smallest of the three and listened while Vanessa and Tristen made small talk.

"I'm glad Crystal came on board," said Tristen finally. "I think she'll be good for the group."

"Did you know she has a younger brother who is special needs, and lives with her?" asked Vanessa.

"I heard that," said Melanie from the back, "I don't know much about it, though."

"No, I didn't know that," said Tristen, interested. "Is it bad?"

"I don't know the details," said Vanessa. "It's just kind of sad."

"Why does her brother with special needs live with her?" Tristen pressed.

"I don't know the details," repeated Vanessa. "Just that he has lives with her and she's taken care of him for the last five or six years.

"I don't know her well, really," said Melanie. "All I do know, because she shared in another class is that her brother lives with her and her four small children, a set of twin boys and two older girls. And they goes to Denver every once in a while for some kind of treatment. In fact, I even watched her kids once while she took him down."

"You watched her kids and you don't know her well?" asked Tristen incredulously.

"Well, yeah. She needed a sitter and while I don't do that often, she asked and I said I would."

"She has a way of speaking her mind," said Vanessa.

"That is true," said Melanie emphatically, "and that's all I'm going to say about the matter."

Walking into the large foyer of the college, Melanie was struck by the amount of people who had already arrived. Signing in, the girls got their materials for the conference and then set out to get warm drinks. Tristen ordered a Latte from the cafeteria, while Melanie ordered black coffee and Vanessa, hot tea.

"Reggie!" said, Tristen excitedly, rising from where she had sat just moments before quietly drinking her Latte. "I hoped you would be here! You're a long way from Minnesota!" she added, hugging the tall, over weight, redhead.

"Well, it is a Tri-Stare organization," he said, boisterously.

"Vanessa, Melanie. This is my friend Reggie. I haven't seen him in about two years."

"And she looks great," he interjected.

Shaking hands, they each said hello and then while Reggie and Tristen caught up, Melanie noticed how different they seemed. Tristen, dressed in heels and a tailored black and white suit, perfectly manicured and perfect hair looked even more so the model image against the ear ringed, shaggy, long haired, masculine counterpart who wore a long over coat with black boots and chain belt. His thick glasses finished the look which Melanie could not describe.

Looking at the schedule, Tristen said, while curling her arm in his, "Oh my, we'd better get in here and get our seats."

Following the pair, Vanessa and Melanie went into the large room filled with chairs and waited on their guest speaker for this workshop. "Randy!" said Tristen, suddenly on her feet! "You, I didn't expect to see here! How are you," she asked rushing to wrap her arms around him.

"She sure is a lot different here than at the college," said Melanie.

"No she's not," countered Vanessa. "You just haven't seen her in the right place with the right people!"

"Oh!" said Melanie, clearly surprised.

Picking Tristen up off the floor and swinging her around, causing her skirt to rise higher than appropriate, Randy said, "Hey, Tris! I'm good. How are you?"

"What've you been up to?"

"It's time we got started," said the speaker as he walked behind the podium.

"I'll catch up with you later," said Tristen hurrying back to her seat. "I haven't seen him in a long while either. We've been buddies for years!" she whispered to the girls seated beside her.

At lunch the parade of people Tristen seemed to know continued, as did her boisterous reactions and expressions of each. "You sure know a lot of people here," commented Melanie.

"Well, it's the elite group I knew in Minneapolis. It was great."

"Oh," said Melanie with an understanding nod. "I see."

Tristen eyed her warily but didn't respond.

The final speech given by a retired Evangelical minister, stirred Melanie's heart. "You've got to be the best you can be in all things," he said. "It's about developing all of your intelligences. You must work on a continuous, discipline study of education all throughout your life, seek to understand those you are working with and strive for creative cooperation. Maintain your integrity and values while attempting to demonstrate meaning in your life through everything you do."

Melanie was glad to get home. It had been a long day, but clearly she had learned much. While she was surprised at Tristen's behavior at the conference she said to Lee, "I don't know. I really wanted to be president, but honestly I think Tristen was probably a better candidate. She seems to know all the right people and she is smart. She has been working in her father's law office as an intern there. I can't say I think her behavior is appropriate and there is the suggestion that while I haven't seen it, her behavior on campus hasn't been stellar. But that's not my problem."

"Well, I think it's shameful!"

"Maybe. But she's got to live with her conscience, not me. I can look at me in the mirror in the morning and not be disgusted."

As Melanie spoke, the phone rang. "Hey Kaitlyn. How are ya?"

"I'm a wreck. I didn't get a chance to call you yesterday, but I have discovered a lump in my breast and I am terrified. I know Grandma had breast cancer and I'm just sure this is going to be."

"Kaitlyn. Stop! You know no such thing! A lump does not necessarily mean cancer!"

"But Grandma!"

"Kaitlyn! Stop! Have you been to the doctor yet?"

"No, I just found it yesterday. But I did call and make an appointment."

"Good. Now until you know you have something to fret about, don't! You're getting yourself all worked up over something that hasn't even been confirmed! Breathe!"

Monday morning Melanie opened an email from Mr. Parnell:

"Melanie,

"I'd really like to talk with you about PTK, among some other things. I understand there are some...uncomfortable feelings...afoot, and I'd like to hear from you about your feelings and perceptions. I know you told me at the induction that you didn't feel entirely comfortable with the group, and I know that I don't like it when people feel uncomfortable, so... can we clear the air?
Mr. Parnell

"Hi, Mr. Parnell," said Melanie as she entered his office.

"Hi," he said casually. "Have a seat."

"What's up?" she asked nervously.

"Crystal came by and shared there were issues between you and Tristen, and I just want to make sure everything is okay."

"I'm fine," said Melanie.

"Level with me Melanie," he said smiling. "I know you two are very different, and I appreciate that."

"Well, we are different. I suspect she's upset with me because I am not as involved as she'd like. I do have a family, she's single and seems to know all the right people. I don't fit into her world any more than she fits into mine."

"You going to be alright working together for the rest of the semester?"

"Sure," she said.

"You know we have the induction ceremony coming up for the next group coming in. I hope you'll be a part of that."

"I will," she said matter-of-factly. "And," she added, "I will try to pull my weight more. Tristen is just abrasive somehow. It's hard to describe."

"Like I said," he nodded, "You two are very different."

Melanie had a class and then hurried to Sweet Creek Elementary. This was going to be her last field experience with Mrs. Garrity's second grade class. It had been much more enjoyable than even Melanie expected.

Today's Science lesson was a session on insects. Making sure each child had his own insect folder, Melanie watched with fascination as the children drew "their" insect they had collected from outside the day before. Their drawing included labeling the parts of the insect and identifying the kind of mouth part it had.

Laughing, Melanie said, "Mrs. Garrity, I'll be honest, I didn't have a clue about all the parts of the insects! These kids loved this subject and they know their bugs well! This was enormously enjoyable! Thank you for allowing me to work with your children in your classroom!"

"It was my pleasure," she said. "The children and I enjoyed having you!"

As Melanie was leaving the main office, Aurora, one of the little girls in Mrs. Garrity's class said, "Mom, look! This is the one I was talking about," as she pointed to Melanie.

"Hi," said, Mrs. Blakey, Aurora, mother. "Aurora came home weeks ago and said she'd seen someone at school in her classroom sometimes, who was really sweet. She was obviously talking about you."

"How kind," said Melanie. "Aurora is a very pleasant child and in fact Mrs. Garrity has a wonderful class. I have enjoyed my time there.

Arriving home later Melanie checked her email and discovered one from Crystal, who since joining the PTK team seemed to make Melanie her personal charge.

"I just wanted you to know, Tristen and I were talking the other day about participation in general and somehow the conversation turned to you, although nothing negative was really said. I did let her know that I thought that the issues between you two need to be resolved, and that speaking with you regarding matters that she may be stressed about would probably be better than involving Mr. Parnell, although I've already said something to him.

She agreed and admitted that she comes off as very offensive, rude and insensitive. She said this is her down fall. So, I just felt you should know that. And with induction coming up we really need to work together to get everything done. There is so much to do and we may need to re-classify jobs and reorganize duties. It's really going to be important to be able to depend on one another to see it through to success. There is talk that Vanessa may resign as an officer. I hope she doesn't.

I just wanted to keep you in the loop.

Thanks,"

Crystal

Responding, Melanie said, *"Oh, I already know you talked with Mr. Parnell. He sent me an email and I've already taken care of it. I'm sorry if Tristen has issues with me. We are just different. That being said, I do intend on helping with the induction coming up in a few weeks. I know there is much planning to be done and I'll do my part."*

Melanie

Rushing to work the next day, Melanie heard a familiar voice call her name. "Melanie," she heard again. "I need to talk with you."

"Hi, Ms. Spiker! How are you?"

"I'm fine," said her former Psychology professor. "I have something I need to ask you."

"Okay?"

"I am President of our local Women's Professional Group. I'd like you to come and talk with our ladies about your writing."

"Me? You're kidding!"

"No, I've seen some of what you have done and I think you have something to offer the ladies would be interested in."

"How long would I have to talk?"

"About twenty to thirty minutes."

"Wow, that's a lot," she said.

"Not really. Not when you consider what you've done. I'd like you to share a little about your life, and your decision to go to college late in life and how your writing ties into all that."

"Oh my!"

"Will you think about it?"

"Sure. When would you want me to present, and where?"

"In two weeks, on Thursday evening and our meetings are held at the Civic Center in town."

"I'm honored you asked and I will certainly think about it. Thank you."

As the semester continued to wind down, Melanie found herself readying for the latest PTK induction ceremony. Putting on the final touches of makeup and doing a last check on hair and clothes, she heard Lee call her name. "Melanie. It's time to go if you plan to be there on time."

When they arrived many seats were already filled. Lee went to find Mackenzie and Steven while Melanie headed back stage. Spying Vanessa, Melanie hurried over. "Is everything set?" she asked.

"Yes," she said emphatically. "Coming in yesterday and setting up was a good idea. The caterers have arrived and are all ready and the guest speakers are ready."

"Have all the inductees arrived?"

"I'm not sure. Tristen had the list."

"Okay, I'll go find her and see if there's anything else I can do."

When final preparations were completed, Tristen walked out on stage to welcome the guests and begin the ceremony.

Melanie swallowed the lump in her throat and tried to calm her nerves. She was speaking next and wanted to do it right. Her hands were cold and sweaty and she caught herself shivering. "Lord, keep me calm," she breathed as she left her seat and headed for the podium.

"Good evening, ladies and gentlemen, inductees and honored guests. Tonight is a special occasion and we have much to be thankful for." As she continued she found herself relaxing and remembered to slow her speech so she could be clearly understood. Finishing she said, "God has given us gifts and each Phi Theta Kappa member and new inductee has much to offer. We will do our best to use our gifts wisely for our college, our community and beyond. Thank you all very much."

The applause made Melanie blush as she exited. "You did good," whispered Crystal, as she took her seat next to her at the far end of the stage.

"Thanks. Did I sound as nervous as I felt?"

"No. You sounded very confident. Good job."

"Melanie, that was awesome. You would have made Mrs. K proud!" said Heather. "And I'm going to be sure to tell her how well you did," she added laughing.

"I agree, you did great," said Mackenzie, as they made their way to the refreshments.

"Boy, I didn't feel like it," Melanie countered. "I was scared silly!"

"Do you really need me to go with you tonight?" asked Lee the next night as they prepared to leave for Mr. Parnell's home for dinner.

"Yes, I do! We were both invited and I know it's an unofficial PTK meeting that includes some of the higher officials in the organization, but I don't want to go alone.

"Crystal, the girl whose brother is special needs is considering becoming president next semester and Mr. Parnell wanted an informal meeting and dinner with everyone who might be involved."

The house, decorated in multicolored Christmas lights welcomed the pair, even as a gentle snow started falling. The yard glowing with lighted reindeer and Santa's sleigh reminded Melanie of when she was a child. The porch wearing tresses of elegant Christmas garland and large red bows looked like it was dressed for a celebration.

Once inside the Christmas decorations continued as each room seemed to carry its own Christmas theme from around the world. The large family room boasted Christmas from Europe decorations, while the dining area was the setting for an early American Christmas. A Christmas in Bethlehem warmed the hearts of those in the formal living room and a Christmas on the Polar Express could be experienced in the game room.

"Hey! Melanie," said Crystal as she entered the dining area where she and Vanessa were chatting. "I'm glad you brought your husband. Lane didn't want to come, but I coerced him into coming anyway. He was sure he would be out of place. He's outside with Mr. Parnell, who is cooking the turkey out there in the deep fryer."

"It's awful cold for that!" said Lee, laughing. "I'll go keep them company."

"I think you should go with me to Regional's in February," said Crystal later.

"I don't know, Crystal. I went to the Leader's Conference and I had a good time, but I'm just not into it like you and Tristen."

"Well, will you at least think about it?

"Yes, I will, and I'll talk to Lee about it. You okay?" asked Melanie in the same breath, sensing something was wrong.

"Honestly, I am. It's just that Lane has tests this weekend. And I'm worried. He's been so good for the girls and the twins since Howie walked out three years ago. He is the only "dad" they really know. Oh they know he's their uncle, but he's just always been here for us. I can't imagine what I'd do without him.

"His "special needs" aren't as bad as the illness that comes with it. His cognitive abilities aren't nearly as bad as they could be, and I'm grateful for that. But he's also got muscular dystrophy and his just happens to affect his heart along with his muscle mass breakdown. The tests this time will include the normal electrocardiography but this time they are doing a nerve test called electromyography. It gets complicated and seems worse every time we go. He hates it and I hate taking him."

"What happened to your folks?"

"They were killed in an auto accident about ten years ago and I inherited Lane's care. I could have put him in a home, but I couldn't. Actually, that's part of what broke Howie and me up. He couldn't handle the stress. Lane had a real bad time when Mom and Dad died."

"Anything I can do?"

"No. Just keep us in your prayers."

The day before Melanie was scheduled to give her presentation to Ms. Spiker's Women's Professional Group she found herself practicing her speech over and over again. "Lee, what if I make a complete idiot of myself?" she asked him.

"You won't. It'll be fine. You can do the presentation and then we'll go out to eat to celebrate."

"Well, I'll do my best," she said pulling out her speech to practice it one more time.

Reaching the civic center, she and Lee exited the car. "Do I look alright?" Melanie asked nervously.

"You look fine! Now quit fretting," he commanded.

"Melanie! It's so good to see you. Thank you for coming. I think you'll find the ladies warm and interested in your subject. Relax and share."

"Okay," she breathed

"Good evening ladies," she began. "I heard once that it takes twenty years to become an overnight success. Well, I've been writing for about twenty years and yes, I've had success, but hardly the 'overnight' success that brings wealth and fame.

"I started writing when my youngest of five children was still an infant. I'd journaled for years before then, but actually writing for the idea of publication didn't come until then. It's been an interesting journey that I hope you'll allow me to share."

Fifteen minutes into her presentation, a lady wearing a lavender silk blouse, perfectly matching the lavender in the plaid suit she was wearing with short, blonde hair neatly framing her friendly face in the third row raised her hand.

"How long does it take you to write something?"

"That depends entirely on what I'm writing," Melanie answered confidently. "If I'm writing a devotion, generally by the grace of God, it usually only takes fifteen or twenty minutes. If I get stuck after that, it makes me wonder if I'm listening to what God is trying to have me write!

"If it's a book, it may take me several years since I work on so many projects at once. If it's a puzzle, usually the puzzle creation only takes about fifteen minutes, but getting it into the computer becomes problematic because I tend to get a little creative with my codes!" The ladies laughed.

Getting back to her speech, Melanie continued, when yet another lady asked a question. Forty-five minutes later Melanie finished having answered a myriad of questions and displaying some of the published work she'd brought.

"You make me want to go right home and begin writing," said a lady in a black pantsuit with a teal top beneath.

"You should!" said Melanie. "It's a wonderful thing knowing you can write something someone else would like to read. That in itself is motivating."

At the end of her presentation another middle aged woman asked a question without even waiting to be recognized. "So do you ever sleep?"

"Sure," laughed Melanie, "but granted sometimes, not as much as I'd like."

"Actually, she just shuts down," interjected Lee who was standing off to the side of the room, inciting a round of pleasant laughter.

As the evening finally came to a close, Melanie was overwhelmed with the kindness each woman showed her. "Thank you," she kept saying.

"Melanie, that's one of the best presentations we've ever had," said Ms. Spiker as the women continued their visiting.

"I agree," said several of the other ladies.

"Well, you're all very kind and I'm grateful," said Melanie. "Thank you again for inviting me," she added as she and Lee put on their coats. "I've had a wonderful time."

Two days later Melanie took a call from Crystal. She was exhausted and crying. "Lane has Becker muscular dystrophy."

"What does that mean?" asked Melanie.

"Well, it's not the worst kind but it's still bad. The muscle weakness in the legs and pelvis area gets slowly worse and by the time he's 25-30 he might not even be able to walk. I can't imagine what I'm going to do. He's convinced he's just going to die."

"He's wrong about that, though, right?"

"Well, remember, he has heart issues too, so no, that's not out of the realm of possibility and he's not handling the whole thing well at all. He's horribly depressed and the kids don't understand what's going on. I don't know how else to help him.

"We do have insurance and I'm glad for that. I could never afford his care on my own."

"I hadn't even thought about that," said Melanie.

"Its' been tough."

"Know that I'm here for you, if you need me. And, of course you'll be in my prayers."

"Just having someone to talk with, helps. Thank you for that."

"No problem!"

By November, the winds had claimed most of the leaves from the trees. Still, even with the barren foliage, the hills were a breathless deep forest green from the Ponderosa Pine. White patches could be seen on many peaks and even on the sides of hills where afternoon sun was blocked. It was cold and blustery the day Melanie got the call. "Good morning," she said cheerily.

"Mom,"

"Steven?"

"Hey. Just wanted you to know Mack and I are headed to the hospital. She's gone into labor."

"Good deal! Another little one; perfect for Thanksgiving and Christmas. Tell Mack her father and I will be down directly. Keep me posted if you can, on how she's doing until we get there."

"Will do," he said.

Eight hours later, Raven, a beautiful dark haired baby girl was born, the image of her mother.

"Mack, she's beautiful," Melanie said.

"Well, I think so, but then I'm just a little prejudice," Mackenzie quipped.

"What a gift," Lee added. "Good job, Mack."

"What about me?" asked Steven laughing. "I'm the dad!"

"Good point," said Melanie joining in the laughter. "Good job to you, too!"

Final exams were finally over and Melanie was glad for the break. Putting the finishing touches on the house, she heard the door bell ring. Mackenzie had come over early to help with the preparations. "I'll get the door, Mom," Mackenzie said, as she laid tiny Raven back in the bassinet.

"Kara, look how big you are!" Melanie heard Mackenzie say. "Oh and Jackson, aren't you the cutie? Kaitlyn, Phil," continued the chorus of names. "Come in, come in."

Entering the room, Melanie was swept with emotion as she saw her daughter. It had been far too long. Holding her close, she said, "It is so good to see you! Look at these babies!"

Hearing the doorbell again, she turned to see Tara and Brent, the new twins, Grace and Aaron along with Ariana, Dylan and Ethan walk in the door with Gavin just a few steps behind. It was going to be a good Christmas and it wasn't even here yet! All of her children were here. It was almost too good to be true. Luke walked in with Steven who had gone to town to complete Melanie's shopping list. "Hey, everyone," he said, as hugs were given and handshakes were exchanged.

"Okay, announcement!" said Melanie, talking so loudly she felt like she was screaming. "Dinner will be ready in about an hour and then don't forget we have church tonight. Jackson is getting dedicated."

Scurrying off to the kitchen, she turned to see Gavin close behind. "I just came out for some chocolate milk," he said grinning.

"I have missed you so much," she said suddenly overwhelmed with tears.

"Mom, don't," he said, softly.

"I'm sorry," she said. "But I can't help it. You have no idea." Gavin embraced her and never spoke.

"I'm okay," she said. "I really am. I'm glad you're home. Now get your chocolate milk and get out of my kitchen," she scolded, while laughing.

"I'm going, I'm going," he said, feigning a pout.

As everyone gathered around the table, Melanie's heart was full. Lee reached for her hand setting the tone for everyone there. Holding hands around the table, Lee spoke, "Gracious Lord, we are thankful for this bounty before us. We are also filled with gratitude that our entire family has been able to come together again to celebrate your birth. Grant that we remain strong in our devotion to you, living according to your laws and remaining in the center of your will. Amen."

"I need the bread," said Gavin rising from the table. "And the mayo."

"You still do that?" asked Tara laughing.

"Absolutely! It's only the best way to eat Christmas turkey! I love my turkey sandwich with mayo and Old Bay seasoning."

Melanie could only smile as she took in the sight. There were so many conversations going on at once she could barely make out what was being said. Stories from the past year were shared as were tales about adventures and problems. When finally everyone had their fill, the females of the group rose to clear the table while their male counterparts fled to the garage and outside to avoid being called upon to help.

The church was decorated with candles adorned with red ribbons surrounded by evergreen branches. A large Christmas tree stood in the foyer covered with brightly colored ornaments depicting the birth of Christ. A large star sat on top of the tall tree while a manger scene sat humbly nearby reminding each person that Christ is the reason for the season.

"Let's get our seats near the front," said Melanie leading the entourage down the aisle. "I want to be able to see and to get pictures." When all the family and guests of the family had finally filed in and were seated, three entire pews were filled. After the opening remarks and first hymn were sung, Pastor Henderson said, "Kaitlyn and Phil Brennen are here from Grassley Texas and are going to have their new son, Jackson dedicated. So Kaitlyn, Phil I'd like to invite you to come up along with Kara and little Jackson and whatever family is going to stand up with you."

Midway through the dedication, Pastor Henderson reached for Jackson. Taking him in his arms, the small baby looked at him with complete trust. Moving again toward the pulpit and mike so he could be heard, Pastor Henderson continued, but was interrupted when Jackson began reaching for the mike. The quiet child suddenly became very animated and with solid determination began squirming and reaching for the mike, while babbling the entire time. Ripples of laughter could be heard throughout the congregation.

"Well," said Pastor Henderson. "We have a busy one."

As the giggles continued, Jackson reached for the open Bible. "Sorry Buddy," he said gently, backing away a bit so Jackson couldn't reach it. "But good for you. Looks like we might have another preacher in our midst!"

As the year came to a close, Melanie counted her blessings; another semester complete. Earth Science had been challenging but interesting, while the Humanities class stretched her and developed her teaching abilities. College Algebra had been trying, but she had prevailed and her Educational Psychology class had netted her what was sure to be a lifelong friend in Dr. Hayden.

Her kids and grandkids, including three brand new ones, had all been nearby for the Christmas holiday and it had been a wonderful visit. Still she had a heavy heart. Gavin's heart issues remained and the blood work and EKG which had been scheduled showed no concrete answers. He would be returning to school in just two weeks and still there were unanswered questions to the incessant heart pain he endured. Melanie bowed her head in prayer. "Lord, thank you for the gifts of my children and grandchildren. Please send answers regarding Gavin," she said. "Please free him and us from this burden. You are the Great Physician. Help me to just trust you. Amen."

Chapter 25

Melanie walked into the already filled classroom. Gratefully she took one of the two remaining seats on the front row and waited. There wasn't a single student she knew in the class. All were in their late teens and early twenties. These were business students. Her entire curriculum until now was specifically focused on education. She needed one class to fill the slot to still remain a full time student and opted for a Business 101 class. She'd heard it was challenging, but she wondered, how challenging could it really be? It was business after all, she considered. And as long as it wasn't business math, she should be able to wade through it rather well.

Moments later a tall, fifty-something, perfectly groomed, Italian man, dressed in a three piece business suit walked into the room pulling a cart filled with a large black briefcase and another oversized black bag which he parked next to his desk. Without saying a word the man with dark, wavy locks, retrieved a large black notebook out of the oversized black bag and laid it open on his desk. Setting his brief case on the desk beside the large notebook and opening it, he pulled out a set of stapled together papers. Wearing a pleasant smile with perfect teeth and gentle green eyes, he said, "Good morning, class! I am Nickolas Rafaelle. I will assume that each person in this class is here because he or she chooses to be. This is Business 101 and in this class you will work very hard and earn every point you acquire. I will add you must pass this class to pass within the business curriculum. If you are not willing to work, then you may as well leave now." He paused. "Good! No takers!" he said, soundly. "Let's get started."

The rest of the class was spent pouring over the syllabus and expectations of the class. Cramping from writing so much and so fast, at the end of class, Melanie shook her hand to ease the pain. "He's right," she remarked to the curly brown haired boy on her left. "We are going to have to work hard in here."

"Who cares? He's eye candy," quipped the red headed girl to her right.

"I'm told the class is good, though and he's supposed to be the best," said the boy, ignoring the red head.

"Well, I guess we'll find out!" she replied smiling. "I'm Melanie."

"I'm Evie," said the red head.

"Hi, Evie! Melanie said.

"Hi! I'm Cody. Glad to know you!"

"Thanks!" Melanie said picking up her books. "Me too!"

"Cody, do you think you and I could work together sometime?" Melanie heard Evie ask as she walked away.

"I don't know. Maybe," was all Melanie heard of the continuing conversation.

"I am never disappointed any day I walk into my business class," she said to Lee one evening. "I am amazed at all the stuff you learn in there. And Mr. Rafaelle is an amazing professor. "He is so knowledgeable. It's weird though. He tells us to read the chapters in the book, but he never goes over it. He may mention it in passing, but he has his own set of notes he seems to work from. And I love how he gives so many good examples about what he's talking about. He makes it applicable to everyday living and totally relatable. I hear his tests are a bugger, though. I guess I'll find out!"

Three weeks into the semester, Mr. Rafaelle addressed the class before removing his large black notebook in his usual manner. "Along with the tests you will be taking in this class, one of which will be in two weeks, you are required to do a project. This project is directly related to the commodities market.

"I want to introduce Peggy Smith who is my Supplemental Instructor," he said pointing to a short woman, poorly dressed compared to Mr. Rafaelle, with short, curly, light brown hair. Ms. Smith is here to help you outside of class with any holes in your notes, study aids and help on the project which I am going to tell you about. Make use of Ms. Smith. She is here to help you and some of you will likely need it."

The woman stood and waved to the class then sat back down.

"I don't know how much any of you know about the commodities market but this is one sure fired way you will get some understanding of how it works. Each of you will be given on paper a theoretical $100,000 to spend in the commodities market. You must spend your money judiciously and wisely. You will choose no less than seven commodities and no more than ten to invest your $100,000. There are a variety of commodities to choose from," he said while writing on the board, stressing the different categories, "including Agricultural which includes grains like corn, wheat, oats, and soybeans; Energy which includes crude oil, propane, natural gas, etc; Metals, both precious and industrial; Softs which are usually defined as commodities that are grown rather than mined like cocoa, coffee, sugar, or lumber; and Livestock and meat. Within each of these categories the commodities are further broken down into specific elements, some of which I named, but not all. So do your research well.

"Once you have chosen your commodities, you must write each company, literally, not figuratively, and request information just as if you were actually investing in their company. Of course, inform them this is a required project in a college setting and usually they are very accommodating. They accommodate partly because there is the chance you may one day actually invest in their business so it is in their best interest to be helpful and give you as much information as they can. You, of course, may also use the internet and whatever other sources you like for informational purposes.

"I expect you to record the ups and downs daily from the commodity index on your individual commodities to be turned in at the end of the semester, as part of your project. Additionally, each student will write a report on each company he has chosen. Further information regarding information to be included, is in the packet I will be handing out. If you have questions, please see me. And enjoy the project. It is work, you will learn a lot, but it can be very interesting. How you set up your report is entirely up to you as long as each element required is included.

"The optional part of the project includes a trip to Minneapolis to visit the Minneapolis Grange Exchange. You will have the opportunity to actually be there during trading hours."

"Yes, Landon?"

"Are you saying we actually get to go to Minneapolis, not via satellite or something like that?"

"That is exactly what I am saying. And while the trip is a bit costly, I have tried diligently to get the best prices available. I've done the trip many times and know many of the business owners there and they are willing to work with us to give us the best possible opportunity. So if you can, I encourage you to go. We will leave early on a Friday morning and take a bus into the city. It will be the second weekend in April, so plan accordingly. You may bring a companion even if they do not attend this class. All rooms are double. And there will be planned dinner meals and activities all weekend. That being said, more information will be forthcoming as the dates approach.

"If you are interested, at this point and think you might like to go, I have forms available for you to fill out, so I can begin assessing how many to expect and be able to provide the required packets of information."

"Wow!" said Melanie, giddy with excitement. "What do you think, Cody? You think you'd like to go?"

"Are you kidding. I'd love it. I just don't know if I can afford it!"

"I would love to go! Wonder if I can talk my husband into it? That would be just amazing! Think of it! Minneapolis and the commodities exchange!"

"Now back to the matter at hand: the Commodities Project." Reaching into his now opened briefcase, Mr. Rafaelle picked up a stack of papers. "We need to go over these just briefly before we continue with today's lesson."

Feeling overwhelmed, Melanie tried to explain her assignment to Lee at dinner. "It sounds really complicated to get the money to work out just right.

We're not supposed to have more than $25 left when we are finished investing. I have no clue how I'm going to do this, but ya know, I really find this kind of exhilarating. I've never thought of myself as more than a possible teacher. I really kind of like this whole business thing. Who would of thought? Maybe someday I'll be some kind of business woman!"

"Yeah, right!" Lee scoffed. "This from a woman who doesn't like math!"

"It isn't that I don't like math," she protested. "I'm just slower at it until I get it."

"Yeah, maybe! But it takes you a long time to get it."

"Never mind!" she quipped. "I still like this and I'm going to enjoy it!" Turning on her heels she went to the kitchen carrying the dirty dishes.

"So what do you think about the Minneapolis trip?" She asked coming in the dining area for more soiled dishes and the remainder of the food. "Do you think we could go? I filled out the "interested form" cause I'm surely interested. I'm not sure we can afford it, but I sure would love to go. Imagine. That would be just amazing."

"Well, it's something to think about. Get the packet of information and we can at least check it out."

Melanie began pouring over newspapers and internet sites to determine which commodities she would invest her theoretical monies in. "Mackenzie," Melanie said later in the week. "You want to help me do this? I am having a ball looking at all these commodities, but I feel like such an idiot trying to decide which ones to choose.

"And then I would love it if you would help me set up my spread sheet so it makes sense. Mr. Rafaelle said we could set it up any way we wanted, but it's got to at least have some kind of order so it works. I declare, I'm still trying to learn this whole computer thing. Gavin keeps telling me I need to take a computer class."

"Sure, I'll help you. How many commodities do you need?"

"No less than seven or more than ten."

"Tell you what. You choose twelve and then we can narrow down from there."

"Thanks! Maybe this weekend we could get together and go over this stuff, maybe Saturday night after dinner."

"Works for me!"

"Well, I have about fifteen commodities I'm interesting in," Melanie said to Lee at breakfast the next morning. "Mackenzie said she'd help me narrow my list down this weekend."

"I think I'm going to take off for Arizona for a few weeks," Lee said without preamble.

"Really?" she said, surprised.

"Yeah. I just need to get away for a little while. I think the trip to Minneapolis in April is going to be doable, but I'd like to go where it's warm for a while before then."

"Well, alright. I'll miss you. When are you planning on leaving?"

"I figure the end of next week. I have a doctor's appointment on Tuesday and then I could leave on Wednesday and then be gone for two or three weeks."

"Wow," she said pausing again. "Okay. If you really want to go, then you should go. At least I graduate this year and then next winter I can go with you, like we planned before I started school."

"Yeah, no kidding," he grunted.

"Come on now. That's not fair. You encouraged me to go to school. I know it wrecked our travel plans. But honestly, I've loved it. I've learned a lot and the experience as a whole proves that I'm not a dummy."

"Who ever said you were a dummy?"

"Well, no one. But I felt like it. I felt like I couldn't do anything that required any amount of intelligence. I didn't know it at the time, but I needed to go to school. I'm really grateful for the opportunity. I don't know about going for the Bachelor's degree, but I am grateful for the AA degree."

"Well, I'll be glad when it's done. I'm ready to go on the road for a while and not be stuck here all the time."

"I know. I'm glad you're able to at least go to Arizona for a while."

The days leading up to Lee's trip were difficult for Melanie. Facing a test in Mr. Rafaelle's class had her nerves taunt. Reaching for her Business book right after dinner one night, Lee barked, "Give it a rest! All you do is study. How hard can this professor's tests be? I've seen you stressed before, but this is ridiculous."

"I just want to do well and everything I've ever heard about his tests is that they are hard. They include the stuff from the text plus the stuff he gives you in class, most of which isn't even in the book!"

"You'll be fine."

"Well, I appreciate your vote of confidence, but it scares me a little."

"But me leaving doesn't bother you, does it?" he accused.

"Yes, of course, it does. But you've left before and I guess I'm used to it. That doesn't mean I like it. Me asking you not to go isn't going to change your plans, so I've just adjusted to your decision, that's all."

"Yeah, right," he said sounding wounded. "I'm going to go finish packing. You just keep studying."

Melanie sighed. "Lord, give me patience and understanding," she said while turning to the next marked page in her text.

The next morning, tears slid down Melanie's face as she watched Lee drive away. They hadn't really fought, but somehow she felt like a huge hole in her heart was deepening with every tear that dripped down her face. "Stop it!" she commanded. "This is ridiculous. He's left before and he'll be back in two or three weeks. I've got this test today and I need to focus!" Turning quickly on her heels she turned from the door to finish getting ready for her day.

Taking her seat in the classroom, she noticed she wasn't the only one apparently concerned with this test. While a few of the students sat chatting with little concern, most were deep into their notes or textbooks.

"Good morning class! We have much to do today. When you receive your test, do not turn it over until everyone has theirs. There are 35 multiple choice, 25 short answer and five essay questions. I have supplied the little blue books for the essay part of the test this time. The remainder of the semester you will be required to buy them.

"Be aware that you need to finish the test. If you have a class directly following this one raise your hand and I will make sure a message gets to your professor indicating you are still taking my exam if you need more time. I do not have a class directly following this one and this room is not needed for another class, so take as long as you like. I want complete answers for the essays. Include everything relevant to the question."

"Wow!" said Melanie just above a whisper to Cody seated next to her as papers were being laid on individual desks. "Glad I don't have another class after this one. This is gonna be hard!" Two and one half hours later she put her pencil down beside her test paper and glanced over it one more time to make sure all questions were answered before turning it in. There were eight other students still working.

"It wasn't that the test was so hard," said Melanie to Mackenzie later. "It was just long. He said he wanted complete answers and I gave him all I could remember, it just took forever to write!

"Thanks for your help on the commodities. I like the ones we've chosen. Now I just have to get all the research done!"

"No problem. You okay? Any word from Dad?"

"No not yet. I expect later tonight he'll phone."

Melanie wasn't surprised when the phone rang at 9:00. "Hey, Melanie," said Lee.

"You okay? You sound really tired."

"I am. It's been a day! About the time I got to Colorado Springs I ran into a full blown blizzard!"

"You're kidding!"

"I wish I was. There was white out conditions. Snow was falling about three inches an hour!   You could barely make out the outline of the mountains on either side of the road as I drove through the pass. And then a truck pulling a trailer jackknifed and all traffic was stopped. They closed the interstate!"

"No way! So where are you now?

"Well, I didn't make it much past Colorado Springs. I had to turn around and go back because I couldn't get through. So I'll stay here tonight and then leave in the morning, hopefully, and go on down to AZ.

"Sometimes I wonder if we shouldn't just live in Arizona. At least we wouldn't have to worry about cold weather."

"Lee! You're not serious! I can't imagine living down there. I know we have to deal with weather. But I love it here."

"Well, I do too. Just sayin'."

Melanie stayed busy doing research and getting some quilting done while Lee was away. She hated it when he was gone, but it was quiet and she knew keeping busy would make the time pass more quickly. She was home when he pulled in the yard two weeks later. "Lee!" she said, running out to the car, despite the cold rain falling.

"Hey, Mel! Do I have news for you!" he said smiling broadly.

"What kind of news?" she asked hugging him tightly.

"I'll tell you in the house," he said while retrieving his luggage.

"Okay, I'm dying, here. What news?"

"Well, I bought property in Arizona," he said simply.

"You what?" she asked stunned.

"I bought some property. It's in a development area that isn't totally developed yet and probably won't be for a few years. It's in Cochise county near the Chiricahua National Monument. I figure it's a start. Who knows? Maybe someday we'll have a house down there."

Melanie blanched. "You're kidding, right? You're just kidding me," she repeated.

"No. It was a good buy and so I bought it."

"Wow!" was the only way Melanie could respond.

"Maybe the next time we go down together, I'll take you to see it. Like I said, it's not much now, but you just never know!"

"Okay," said Melanie quietly, still not sure what to say. "If you say so.

"I'm glad you're back," she said changing the subject. "I've stayed really busy, but I sure missed you."

"I'm not sure I'm glad to be back, yet," he countered. "I heard on the radio coming back that next week we could get more snow. I'm tired of cold and snow."

"I went to see your mom while you were gone," she said trying again. "She's just a shell sitting there in that wheelchair now. It's so sad. There is absolutely no recognition now, not that there has been in a while, but she's gone. Her body is there, but that's all. It's just so sad."

"I'll get in to see her in the next day or two."

"I'm excited about going to Minneapolis," Melanie suddenly gushed. "I got the packet and it looks like so much fun!"

Melanie scanned the places they were visiting in Minneapolis one more time. They were to meet at the college by 5:30 a.m. to begin the ten hour trip. "This is an awful hour," complained Lee.

"I know, but I am so excited," replied Melanie.

"Do you really think everyone who is supposed to be here will be on time?"

"Sure, why not?"

"These are young people," Lee reminded her. "They don't like getting up early!"

"It'll be fine," Melanie reassured him. "Everyone's paid money for this trip. I can't see anyone not being here to get on the bus. You don't get your money back now. If you don't show up, I guess you lose it."

"True. We'll see," he said, not convinced.

Lee wasn't disappointed by his prediction. "I told you we'd have to wait on somebody," he said sarcastically.'

"Well, as long as they got here," Melanie said finally taking their seat in the very front of the bus behind the driver, fifteen minutes past the time they were supposed to leave.

"Now for a nap," said Cody. "What an awful hour!"

Melanie laughed. "That's exactly what Lee said!" she told him.

The next three hours on the bus were virtually silent. It wasn't until they stopped for breakfast in Chamberlain that anyone seemed to have anything to say, and even that was minimal. Crossing the Missouri River was always a treat, whether in the spring when the land was just re-awakening or in the dead of winter when everything was white and the river was iced over. Admiring the scene while walking to stretch legs and grabbing a breakfast sandwich or other breakfast item, seemed a quick forty-five minutes before everyone was herded back on the bus so they could be on their way. Melanie loved the ride across South Dakota. She had hoped they would stop at Wall, but that would have been only an hour past the time they left and wasn't practical.

Wall was one of her favorite places. She and Lee would drive there on Saturdays for their famous coffee and donuts and then stroll the old town that is just outside the Badlands. Wall, known for the infamous Wall Drug only boasted about 780 residents most of the year, but during the summer months it welcomed thousands to their town with great western hospitality.

As the beautiful rolling hills gave way to expansive prairie, Melanie could only drink in the sight. She never tired of the prairie grasses and was delighted as she observed Spring planting beginning in earnest. While signs of large ranches could be seen along the highway, Melanie was always surprised that the cattle always seemed so sparse. Lee assured her there were large herds and they just had plenty of grazing area.

Once back on the bus, Melanie, curled up against Lee, drifted off to sleep. Waking, she found they were just arriving into Minnesota where they would stop again at the accommodating rest area for a brown bag lunch which everyone had been required to bring.

Back on the bus once more, Melanie pulled out the information packet. They would have one more stop before reaching the city. Once there, they would get a hotel room and settle in for the night. First thing the next morning was a visit to the Grange Exchange building. The closer they got, the more nervous Melanie became. "Would you just settle down?" said Lee becoming annoyed. "You are antsier than a bed bug. What is the deal?"

"I don't know. I'm just excited."

As they made their way onto the bridge crossing the Minnesota River, Melanie commented, "Wow! Would you look at that traffic coming out of the city? They even have one lane on this bridge open going the other way. I haven't seen that since I was back East. Glad we're going in rather than coming out. Still," she said, "there's a lot of traffic going this way too."

As she spoke, she noticed the bus slowed. "What are we slowing down for?" she asked.

"Got me," said Lee as they watched the driver shifting gears.

"Is something wrong?" asked Mr. Rafaelle from the other front seat on the bus.

"Yes, sir. I think there might be," the driver answered, clearly concerned. "Give me a couple of moments and I'll see if I can figure out what is going on." The bus completely stopped now in the center lane allowing only a trickle of traffic maneuvering around it. There was quickly a backup and jam in the flow. The oncoming traffic continued and the traffic behind the bus was attempting to merge into the right lane to continue on.

Watching the action, Melanie quickly pulled out her camera as the traffic snarled. "Central dispatch," said the driver picking up his two-way radio, "this is bus 791 on the I-35W Bridge crossing the Minnesota River. I have lost power to the bus and, all attempts have failed to restart. Congestion is heavy and traffic has snarled quickly."

"Clarification please," said his radio. "You are on the I-35W Bridge inbound to Minneapolis?"

"That's affirmative," the driver responded. "And we're not moving."

"Well," said Mr. Rafaelle, to the bus passengers, running his hand through his hair in an attempt to calm his nerves. "It seems we've run into a bit of a problem and it will be taken care of shortly." Melanie watched at the usual composure of the professor teetered on high agitation.

In just five minutes help arrived, but making the already snarled traffic even worse. In the far left lane traffic had been stopped coming out of the city and re-routed onto the other bridge so the tow truck could make its way to the bus. Once the tow truck arrived, all traffic stopped as the truck made a U-turn on the bridge. Carefully backing up to the bus, Melanie watched and snapped pictures as quickly as she could while watching the tow truck being hooked to the bus. Slowly the tow truck pulled the bus across the bridge allowing the rest of the traffic to continue.

Once across the bridge and safely out of traffic, the tow truck stopped. Mr. Rafaelle stood once again and spoke, "Everyone needs to disembark this bus and load onto the other bus that has just arrived," he said. "Do not worry about your suitcases. They will be delivered to our hotel and we can pick them up there later. Remember that dinner this evening will be right at our hotel, so all we need to do once we arrive is check in and get our rooms. You may want to freshen up just a bit before dinner. Our luggage should be in our rooms once we return from dinner."

As everyone rose, Mr. Rafaelle spoke again. "Do not," he paused, "do not," he repeated, "leave anything on this bus." Moments later sitting on another bus, Melanie said, "Boy that was weird, but how fun!"

"What do you mean how fun?" asked Evie who found the whole situation unnerving.

"I thought it was great! What an adventure," Melanie said. "How often are you going to be on a bus during rush hour traffic that breaks down on a bridge going into a large city, that has to be towed across the bridge and ties up traffic?" she asked breathless!

"I think it was awful!" said Evie.

"No, it was great," Melanie restated. "What a memory!"

Just as Mr. Rafaelle predicted, luggage was delivered to each room by the time their dinner meal was finished. "I just want to crash!" said Lee.

"I'm tired, too," said Melanie. "I wouldn't have thought so, but I am. I'm excited too," she continued. "We go to the Grange in the morning."

The Grain Exchange didn't disappoint. Walking to the Grange Exchange the group spread out in clusters of six or eight, and exchanged information. When they entered the main building, Melanie gasped. Far from what she expected, she saw the intricately designed stonework in marble, brass and brick, with tall columns in terra cotta stonework. Following Mr. Rafaelle, the assembly climbed a staircase to obtain a bird's eye view of the traders on the floor.

"Wow!" said Melanie. "This is pretty cool."

"Yeah, it is," agreed Lee.

After thirty minutes of observation the company was invited into a large board room with a table that seemed to reach from end to end, with enough chairs for the entire group to sit on. After a five minute delay a distinguished, well-suited man came into the room. "I'd like to thank you for your visit," he said. "It won't be too many more years before we won't be able to accommodate visits like these because there is discussion that the Exchange will do away with the operations of the open outcry you witnessed today on the trading floor. Our daily futures trading operations will continue but via an electronic trading platform.

"I trust you enjoy your stay in our fine city. It's a wonderful place to visit and to live. Are there any questions I can answer?"

As everyone sat in silence, one hand was finally raised. "Yes, young man. You have a question?"

"What do you consider the benefit of trading futures over stocks?"

"Good question," the man replied. "From my perspective one good reason is futures traders have the opportunity to trade early, usually before 9:30 a.m., so we get a head start on making a profit for the day. This gives us an edge over stock traders."

Another hand was raised. "Yes," he said.

"What kind of edge?"

"Since most economic reports are released early and are cyclical, meaning they come out the same time of day, every day, we have information early. The stock traders cannot benefit from this same information since it opens an hour later than when the reports are released."

Melanie listened with interest. As they walked out of the building, she said, "I really find this interesting. Confusing, but interesting. The futures project we had to do helped me understand some, but I still find it a little overwhelming."

"I do, too," said Lee. "But at least the gentleman who came to talk with us put his information in what I think was simplest terms. There's just so much to absorb. The way I see it, it is not simple at all. And of course, the biggest issue from my perspective is you have to have money to invest! If you don't have money to invest and that you can afford to lose, then your best bet is to stay out of investing!"

"I suppose you're right," Melanie agreed. "I'm hungry. I'm glad it's lunchtime," she said, changing the subject looking at the eateries before her. "Which one should we try?"

"From what I see as choices, I think I'd like Italian. What about you?"

"Sounds great," she said walking in the direction he pointed.

"This isn't bad," Melanie said. "Wonder what's next," she said as they ate their lunch pulling out their schedule. "We're supposed to meet back at the hotel at 1:30. We're supposed to visit the Foshay Tower. There's supposed to be an observation deck up on the 30th floor," she said.

"The 30th floor?"

"Yup! The view should be awesome! And dinner tonight is at Manny's which is a steakhouse that is in the downstairs. How cool is that?"

"Well, I don't know that I'm excited about going up to the 30th floor, but dinner sounds good!"

Melanie collapsed on the bed. "I'm exhausted," she said. "And my feet are killing me!"

"I told you to wear more comfortable shoes!" Lee scolded.

"I know. I'm wearing my sneakers tomorrow for the Skyway. It's supposed to be amazing."

After a quick breakfast, the next morning, the group started their journey on the Skyway. As Melanie, Lee, Cody and his girlfriend, Alexis walked the twists and turns around the city, Cody said, "You know, this is fantastic. If you lived here in the winter you wouldn't need all the coats, boots and other gear necessary for hard winters. This skyway system makes it possible to walk, depending on where you lived, to work! You'd never be exposed to the elements!"

"And don't forget the shops" said, Alexis. "Speaking of which, I want to go in here. Look at these cute shoes."

"Really?" said Cody laughing, all the while following her.

Melanie and Lee continued their walk for another half hour when Melanie asked, "Where in the world are we?"

"I have no clue. I feel like we've walked for miles and made so many turns, it's hard to say."

"Now might be a good time to get a map," laughed Melanie. "Look, there are some over on the wall. I'll get us one and you can figure out where we are. We have to be back by 6:30 to go to the Theatre in the Round."

"Then I guess we'd better figure out where we are and how to get back!"

Sunday morning Melanie and Lee rose early and made their way to the nearest Protestant church while Mr. Rafaelle and those who chose to accompany him went to a historic Catholic church nearly a mile away.

After lunch the group congregated in the lobby of the hotel. "We're headed for "Uptown" for a brief visit this afternoon," Mr. Rafaelle said. "I suggest we stay together because we will board the bus about a mile up to go to the Mall of America in Bloomington at three, where we will spend the rest of the afternoon and have dinner. This is considered the "hip" part of town where you will find all kinds of interesting shops, as well as, some high-end chain stores. I know some of the shop keepers and they are eager to sell you their wares."

Melanie found the walk "Uptown" interesting. She was surprised, although she didn't know why, of the amount of people. "It's so busy," she said. "I like the city, but I sure wouldn't want to live in one. I don't think people in cities ever rest!"

"You could be right," Lee agreed.

"Oh, Lee, look. These scarves are beautiful! I think I "need" one," she laughed.

"Need?" he said. "Or want?"

"Well, it can be both," she replied

"How much?" Lee asked.

"Fifteen dollars," said the little black haired lady.

"Too much," he said. "Ten."

"Twelve fifty," came the counter offer.

"Twelve," said Lee.

"Done," said the lady.

As the group waited for the bus, Melanie observed the people walking by. "Everyone is in their own little world," she mused aloud.

Just then the bus pulled up and everyone boarded and they made their way to the Mall of America. Once there Melanie again felt overwhelmed with the sheer vastness of the place. Watching the roller coaster in the indoor park, Melanie said, "I can't believe it! I just can't believe it!"

"Wait until you see the Nickelodeon Universe," said Mr. Rafaelle, overhearing her comments. It's the nation's largest theme park and all indoors! And there's an American Girl store and the Lego area is phenomenal, not to mention the Sea Life Aquarium and the Dinosaur Walk Museum. It's a grand place!"

As they strolled through the Mall, Melanie felt lost. "It's too big," she said finally. "I like it, but I wouldn't want to shop here, at least not alone. How in the world do you find your way out? It is so confusing! I'd never be able to find my car."

"Well, you have to remember where you came in, that's all," said Lee.

"I wouldn't do it," she said adamantly. "I just wouldn't! I rather like our little mall that isn't so busy or big that I feel lost. Who needs this many stores to shop from anyway? Everything is a specialty store, which of course means it's going to be more expensive. No, it's not for me," she said as they walked toward children playing in the Lego section.

"Oh my goodness! Now I will say this. Our grandkids would love this! Can you imagine them playing in something like this? Look how big it is! Look at all the rooms and how the different things move! How cute! I wonder how many Legos it took to build this? Amazing! Absolutely amazing!"

Monday morning Melanie was glad to board the bus for the return trip home. It had been a wonderful trip full of exciting adventures, but she was ready for quiet and rest. "I am absolutely exhausted," she said laughing "and it's only 6 a.m.!"

The uneventful trip home was good for both Lee and Melanie and each napped along the way. When nearly home, Melanie said, "You know I really enjoyed our trip. We were the oldest ones there, but I think we did good, and we did so much!

"What might be fun sometime would be to take the same trip again, just you and me. We wouldn't be able to get in the Grange to observe like we did this weekend, cause that's special and they said they're thinking on doing away with that anyway. But to visit the places in a slower, low keyed kind of way. It's a fun city. I wouldn't want to live there, but it is fun to visit."

"You might be right. It probably would be fun. Course it'd probably be really expensive, too. I'm glad we had the breaks on prices for what we did this weekend. I'm sure it would cost more if we went alone. Even the rooms would be more expensive."

"Well, we could go and just do the "free" stuff. Sometimes that's as much fun or even more enjoyable than the stuff that costs so much."

"Maybe we will."

Melanie squeezed Lee's arm. "I love you," she said, smiling broadly.

"I love you, too," he responded.

Chapter 26

Melanie walked into the classroom and immediately spotted Victoria, who she called her Hawaiian princess friend, sitting in the front row. Her long, straight jet black hair, hanging around her shoulders and past the top of the seat reminded her of her own long hair when she was that age, although hers was brown. Melanie set out to claim the empty seat on the end and to Victoria's immediate left. "Hey there, friend!" she said as she sat down.

"Mrs. Gavin's mom!" she responded with soft brown eyes that shared the smile on her face. "I didn't know you were going to be in this class."

"I didn't know you'd be here, either! And I am so glad you are. Biology and I are not friends!" Melanie said laughing. "I didn't have this in high school and I expect it to be a tough class."

"Well, this is my second time at it. I took it a few semesters ago, and I passed it, okay, but I really want to bring up my GPA so I'm taking it again. So maybe we can work together."

"I'd love that! Thank you!

"Oh goodie!" said Melanie sarcastically. "Look who else is in this class. This should at least make it interesting."

"Who?" asked Victoria, her eyebrows furrowing.

"Tristen Cadby. She's the PTK president and I declare she and I just don't see eye to eye!"

"Oh, her. I've seen her around campus. I don't know her well, but then, from what I've heard, that's just as well."

"So why aren't you in PTK?" asked Melanie, changing the subject just a bit.

"I choose not to be. I could, but that would just put on more stress to get higher grades and I'm just not that competitive. Even re-taking this class; being in PTK would make that look bad and I don't need it. And besides that, I am not crazy about the politics that go with it."

"There is that," Melanie agreed. "Still, I'd love to see you in the group. I'd sure feel more comfortable!"

Just then a medium sized, well dressed man, with light brown hair and wearing glasses came into the room carrying a stack of papers. "Oh, here comes Mr. Parnell. I've never had him as a professor. I know him from PTK and in that he seems very kind. We've had several really nice conversations." said Melanie.

"He's fantastic. I've had him for Botany two semesters ago and I loved his class. I think I would have done better the first time in Biology if I'd had him. He's real clear and patient. He wants all his students to do well."

"Good deal. Maybe I can pass this class, after all!" Melanie said quietly as Mr. Parnell made his way to the desk.

"Hello, class!" he said. "You are in Biology which can be trying for some who don't have much background in it, but you should know right up front, we do have Supplemental Instructors for this class and I encourage you to use them.

"Let's begin with the syllabus and preparing for your first lab. All labs will be across campus in the Lakota Science building even though we meet here for all lectures. The first lab will be in two weeks on Enzymes. The first eight pages in your lab workbook are designed to familiarize you with all equipment and procedures in the lab room. Make sure you complete all the questions because you will need to turn it in before you can participate in the lab itself. If it is not finished, you will not participate. Every class day that it is not turned in, is an additional ten points off your first lab. It's to your advantage to get it done before class.

"That being said, I urge you to also make sure you follow the proper procedures for reports. I have an interactive web site that accompanies this class with plenty of information regarding what we cover in class and other helpful information. Use it.

"There is something else I am introducing for the first time this year," Mr. Parnell continued as he passed out a packet of papers stapled together. "I think it will enhance your learning in my class and it counts as 20% of your grade, so do your best. I am implementing a "metacognitive portfolio." What I am handing out now is information regarding this new feature for our class. I believe it will not only aid your progress in this class but across the board in all disciplines."

Melanie leafed through the papers as he spoke and stopped to look at the page detailing the information to be included in the portfolio. Each category had its own list of particulars including the requirement of writing a reflection:

- A Writing sample demonstrating paragraphs
- A Novel Response or Book Report
- A sample Creative Writing exercise
- A Computer activity sample
- A Math assignment demonstrating progress (need not be a test)
- A Science experiment, project, or assignment

Then Melanie saw the next section and cringed: What I Have Accomplished in Science Class: Each question should be answered with examples and reflections. Noting the list she turned the paper over and saw more than twenty-five objectives. Flicking the sheet back she read the first twelve.

- Can I understand the basic principles of the cell, cell processes and functions, identify the chemical compounds found in a cell and solve problems in biological cell areas?
- Can I recognize discrepant events?
- Can I articulate a clear hypothesis?
- Can I collect appropriate data?
- Can I enter data into an appropriate spreadsheet/statistics program?
- Can I correctly interpret data?
- Can I retain or reject hypotheses based on the data?
- Can I revise my research to follow-up new information?
- Can I present my findings in a clear, concise and logical manner?
- Can I identify and describe the scientific method?
- Can I name the two great unifying theories of biology and understand their significance?
- Can I list the properties of water?

"Wow! A lab already?" said Melanie after class, wincing. I am so not into the whole lab thing. I'm clueless! And I've never created a portfolio, although I'm working on one for my EDU classes. This somehow just looks even more complicated than that one!"

"As for the lab, once you do the first pages in the lab book, you will be fine. And you and I can work together along with whoever else is at our table and we'll get through. Don't worry!" assured Victoria as they exited the class. "You'll be fine. You'll see!

"Now I can't comment on the portfolio. That's new for me too. But Mr. Parnell has always been fair and is willing to work with you and answer questions. So I guess if we have questions we'll just have to go see him!"

"Well, if you say so," said Melanie, clearly doubtful.

"I don't know about Biology," Melanie said to Mackenzie one evening while eating dinner. "It looks awful complicated and without the background, I'm lost. And then when you add this whole portfolio thing, I'm afraid of how my grade will look at the end of the semester."

"Mom, would you just not worry about it? I will help you. And you said Victoria said she would help you, right? You'll be fine!"

Melanie walked across the campus ready to attempt her first lab. The workbook pages, which she immediately laid on the "hand in" pile, had been helpful in familiarizing her with the names of all the equipment she would be using, but she wasn't excited about the lab itself.

After signing in, a requirement in the lab room, Melanie took her seat and looked over the upcoming assignment. When Victoria, Chase and LeAnn arrived they set out to acquire the necessary instruments: goggles, test tubes, droppers. In turn they received the warm rennin, boiled rennin, refrigerated rennin, warm milk and refrigerated milk. Then following the directions they carefully marked their test tubes and filled them with the milk and rennin and placed them in the incubator and then waited the required fifteen minutes before continuing. "We need to work on our paperwork while we wait for the temperature of the milk to change the enzymes," said Victoria. "So let's start with our intro and purpose and then we can create our hypothesis."

"We have to have a hypothesis before it finishes, right?" asked Melanie.

"Yes, because we are attempting to prove our hypothesis is correct."

"And we need to make sure we're specific on our method, too," added LeAnn. "And remember he wants all measurements in the metric system."

"Ugh!" said Melanie. "I hate the metric system. This whole process is so specific,"

"Well, that's how they figure things out," said Chase. "I'm not a scientist, but at least this is interesting."

"I guess," Melanie conceded.

At the end of class, Mr. Parnell said, "Make sure you have all your data recorded so you can create an appropriate data sheet to be turned in with your lab report. Make sure your lab report has an Introduction, a Purpose, Hypothesis, Method, Results, any necessary Tables, Discussion and Conclusion. Remember you are college students and I want clear, complete, logical sentences."

"Wow," said Melanie to LeAnn as she turned in all her equipment. "I hope I come close to doing this right."

"Well, if you follow the format he gave us, you should be fine. Just write it like you were talking to him, that way you can share your thoughts. It'll show you participated and maybe even show you thought it was interesting, but mostly that you understood what you did."

"But I'm not sure. Even though we did the experiment and I saw the whole thing, it still seems foreign to me. I'm not scientific at all. What makes that worse is, I really am not interested in what makes it work. Just that it does. I don't have to know why one enzyme does one thing and another does something else. What's sad is this class is required for my Education degree. I have no interest in

Science at all and I plan on working with young people who will not be doing Biology!"

"I like Biology. I find it interesting. I actually want to be involved in Clinical Research."

"Well, all I can do is the best I can and hope for the best."

"Think of it as a "maybe someday I'll use it class." At least that way you can see some reason for taking it. Maybe it will turn out you end up working in a high school someday and need it."

"I can't picture that, but you're right. The better attitude I have about taking the class, the better off I'm going to be. Thanks! I appreciate that advice."

"You're welcome, although I hadn't thought about it being advice," laughed LeAnn.

"Well, it was and I'm grateful. It certainly changes the way I look at this class." Feeling better and resigned to a changed attitude, Melanie left the room and headed for the urgent, impromptu meeting Tristen had called for PTK that afternoon, via a text message on her phone.

"What's so urgent?" asked Melanie when she saw Crystal on their way to the meeting.

"I'm not sure, but I guess we'll find out."

"Vanessa has resigned from PTK," Tristen announced without preamble. "I have a replacement," she added. "Jennifer Robbins, who joined us in the Fall, said she would be happy to take her place."

"Is that legal?" asked Crystal.

"Well, she may not have the title until she's voted in, but I think we could do that now, don't you?"

"Well," said Crystal, "I guess."

"Whatever!" said Melanie rolling her eyes.

"Okay, then it's done. All in favor? Passed!" said Tristen without further discussion. "There is lots to be done. We need to have phone calls made and a food drive set up and we're supposed to have a guest speaker at our meeting next month.

"Melanie, will you see to the guest speaker? We'd like to have Owen Paxton who teaches History. Would you see to it? And then in two months we would like to have Nickolas Rafaelle from the Business department. I'd like you to ask him to speak, too."

"Sure," she said without emotion. "I'll take care of it."

"Tristen drives me absolutely nuts!" complained Melanie to Mackenzie one afternoon. "She is so assuming and demanding. It's like she is the only one who can make decisions and she bosses people around like she owns them!"

"Stand up to her."

"I can't. Somehow that just doesn't seem right. Besides, it's probably just me."

"No, from what I've heard, others feel the same way."

"Are you serious?"

"Yes, and she isn't well thought of with all the faculty either. She uses people. She has an agenda. Besides, I know Vanessa. Why do you think she resigned?"

"No way!" said Melanie. "Vanessa was good. I'm sorry she left. It's a shame Tristen's like that, but I'm glad to know it's not just me!"

"You want some other news?" asked Mackenzie.

"I don't know. Do I?"

"Crystal is leaving. She's moving to Belle Fourche."

"But she's only lived here a little while. Why is she moving? I thought she was going to do the whole President thing for PTK next year."

"Well if my information is correct and I believe it is, Crystal is going to be going to Laden Peak College. From what I am told, she's gotten a scholarship there and is transferring in two weeks."

"Wow! Things just seem to be going from bad to worse where PTK is concerned. I hope Jennifer Robbins who is taking Vanessa's place is up to dealing with all the junk the rest of us have."

Dreading the test results later that next week Melanie walked in to Science class. It had been a difficult test and she was sure she wasn't getting an A or B and hoped only for a C. Along with fifteen fill in the blank, five definitions and ten matching questions, they had been asked to name all the parts of a cell structure, both for an animal and a plant. Although they were similar, there were distinct differences and she wasn't sure she got them all right. To make matters worse Mitoses phases were also included on the test and she was certain she had mixed those answers around.

"Well," said Mr. Parnell, as he walked to his desk. "This test was really a struggle for many of you. There were only three B's in the entire class and one person received an A. I'll pass out the papers at the end of class. For now we need to move on to today's lesson."

"Oh man!" said Melanie. "Only one person got an A? It's not going to be me. Sure hope I at least got a C and didn't do any worse than that!"

"I'm right there with you," said Victoria.

A long hour and fifteen minutes later Melanie's fears were alleviated. "A C!" she said with relief. "At least I passed. It's a low C, but I can deal with that," she added as she pulled her things together to get ready to leave.

"I got the A!" came a loud voice Melanie immediately recognized. "I hoped it would be me, but I didn't know it would be." Melanie watched as Tristen waved the test paper in the air as she spoke to Ellen, a plain girl in the second row. Ellen, whose dark curly hair was pulled back in a half pony tail, smiled without saying anything.

"Can you believe it?" Tristen continued, laughing.

"Good job," Ellen finally said. "I got one of the B's. I'm happy for that."

"Well, I sure am happy," Tristen said, then added, "Are you in PTK?"

"No, why?"

"If you got a B on this test, I'll bet your grades are fantastic in your other classes, too."

"I do okay."

"Well, I think you should join PTK. Let's go to lunch and we can talk about it."

Mackenzie met Melanie in the cafeteria a half hour later when Jennifer walked up to their table. "I am so mad right now," she said. "I'm absolutely fuming."

"Why?" asked Melanie.

"I just overheard Tristen go on and on with that girl she's sitting with at the table over there about all "she's" done for the chapter…and how "she's" the only one who does the work and carries the load. It was all I could do to hold my tongue."

"I'm not sure I would have," said Mackenzie. "Someone needs to put her in her place! She's downright disrespectful to Mom, but Mom won't let me say anything to her!"

"No, you can't!" Melanie said, laughing. "It wouldn't be right."

"But you won't stand up to her," Mackenzie accused

"I know, and I should, but I don't like doing that."

"Well, somebody needs to."

"So, who is the new girl?" Jennifer asked suddenly, looking puzzled.

"A girl named Ellen from our Biology class. Tristen was telling her about how well she did on our Biology test and found out that Ellen got a B; so now it looks like they're gonna be best buddies," Melanie answered with a touch of sarcasm.

"Interesting," replied Jennifer. "It's gonna get interesting."

Melanie and Lee rode out to the nursing home to see Flo. Each visit was getting more and more difficult. It had been so long since they had seen the mother they both loved. She never spoke, hardly ate and stared straight ahead without any emotion. Melanie watched saliva dribble down her chin and felt the urge to cry.

"I wonder if they will ever be able to cure Alzheimer's," Melanie said softly stroking the woman's hand.

"I don't know," said Lee.

"It's such an ugly disease. It just steals your loved one from you while you watch and there's nothing you can do," she said sadly.

"I just had a thought," said Melanie abruptly. "We have to do a paper on a new gene discovery. I think I'll see if there is anything for Alzheimer's patients."

Lee said nothing. Melanie retreated within herself, unsure what to say next. Unable to think of anything, she like Lee, said nothing else.

The next several weeks were spent scouring medical journals and the computer searching for new Alzheimer's information. Could there really be something that could help these patients?   Then she saw it! "Lee," she yelled with excitement. "Look! According to this article, they have discovered a new gene that gives hope for Alzheimer's victims. It says there is some gene called a SORL1 that may open new possibilities to discover the cause and possible treatments for Alzheimer's Disease. How cool is that?"

"It'd be great," Lee responded only half listening, "but it's not going to do Mom any good."

"I know, but at least there could be hope for our generation and for our kids. Who knows, maybe it'll be figured out before your Aunt Martha gets any worse. I'd hate to see anyone else in your family have issues and what does that say about you and your siblings? How at risk are you?"

"What are you trying to say?" he asked suddenly very interested.

"Nothing!" Melanie said laughing.   "Just wondering how far down generational lines it goes. How does it affect other family members? You'll have to admit between your mom and Aunt Martha; and even your Aunt Sylvia said she asked the doctors what her risk was, with already having two sisters fighting it and he told her she was at very high risk and essentially to expect it."

Lee just stared at her.

"Anyway the author suggests the disease needs to be controlled since it is estimated in the next twenty-five years the frequency of late-onset of Alzheimer's is likely to increase substantially.   But he also says the research is only the tip of the iceberg.   Imagine! Maybe they can really do something about this disease. Wouldn't that be wonderful?"

"Guess it would, at that," Lee agreed.

"The article does add that there is still a lot to learn, but the disease is at least in part a genetic structure.

"It at least looks like I have the information I need for writing my paper for Biology class and with Mom being personally involved I can qualify my interest with personal reactions and feelings." Melanie put the magazine she was reading down and reached for note cards. She hated note cards, but Mr. Parnell preferred seeing this method used for research. She began writing.

"Mr. Parnell," she said walking up to him after class near the end of the semester. "You got a minute?"

"Sure, what's on your mind?"

"This has nothing to do with Science but I just want to say I'm sorry about the way this semester has gone with Tristen," Melanie said. "I don't feel like I've been very productive. Tristen and I have just had our difficulties and I have had a hard time working past that. That being said, I'll admit that she was probably the better choice for President of PTK."

"Oh, I completely disagree," said Mr. Parnell. "You bring something to the club that Tristen does not. You are compassionate, kind and just as smart as she, just in different areas. Don't let her make you think otherwise.

"And I think it is I who owe you an apology."

"Why?"

"Well, I think I am responsible for the way things turned out with president in PTK and I put you in a very uncomfortable position. I wanted you to stay on so I asked you to be Vice President and didn't even consider how different your personalities are."

"I thank you for the thought, but it's not your fault at all. I just wish I'd have had what it takes to work with her and honestly, I just don't."

"Melanie, you've got to stop putting yourself down. You are a good student and wonderful person and our lives are better for it."

"You are kind and I appreciate it." Feeling better about herself, Melanie exited the room.

"We get to dissect a frog today, Melanie," said Victoria obviously excited.

"Oh, yuck! And you want me to be excited about that why? I wasn't crazy about the bird or the fish if you'll remember. I feel cruel and just plain mean when we cut it open like that!"

"But it'll be great to see all the insides of it."

"Well, you can enjoy it all you want. I will again participate, but only because I am required and need the grade. You can do all the slicing and dicing you want. It's not my idea of a good time!"

Victoria and Taylor, the newest member at their table, laughed. "No problem. You take the notes and record everything and Taylor and I will be the surgeons again!"

As the three of them peered at the tiny body laid open, Victoria and Taylor were completely absorbed into the makeup of the frog. "There's the heart," said Taylor, "and the lungs."

"Oh, and there are the kidney's," added Victoria. "It's weird to see the similarities and differences between the frog, the fish and the bird. I think I like the frog better than the fish!"

"Why?"

"Because frogs are amphibians and can stay on both land and water because it has lungs, and a fish has to stay underwater with the help of gills to breathe since it doesn't have lungs. Besides that," she said laughing, "I like frogs!"

"I like the bird best," Taylor said. "They are really similar to fish, except for some external differences. Birds and fish share most of the same organs and cellular structure, like backbones, hearts, and brains. But the birds have feathers and fly, while fish have scales, swim in water, and have to get oxygen from their gills. What really surprises me though is how the bones in a fish fin are very similar to bones in a bird's wing. It amazes me how they fly."

"What about you Melanie? Which is your favorite?"

"I don't have one. I will admit that it's interesting to study, to a point. But slicing and dicing and all this just does not appeal to me. So I'll just be content to record thoughts and procedures and all the stuff we need on paper and do the write up for the group. Fair enough?"

"Fair enough," Victoria and Taylor said in unison.

"You are too funny!" added Victoria. "But I won't say it surprises me. I can't imagine you ever doing anything like this just for fun or even for research. It doesn't suit you."

Melanie was looking forward to the end of Biology class. She hoped she would get an A knowing the grades from tests and quizzes would be close. But she couldn't be sure, she figured it would more likely be a B and while it wasn't what she wanted she'd take it and run.

Chapter 27

Melanie saw the small, dark skinned woman behind the desk poring over papers. The petite woman whose hair was slicked back into a tight bun on the back of her head wore a business suit with matching heels. Looking up, she smiled a smile that flickered into her warm brown eyes making her whole face shine.

"Welcome to my class, everyone. I am Addison Conner. Special Education is an amazing field, if your heart is in it. This semester we will have some wonderful guest speakers who can identify with the immediate problems facing teachers in the class room, as well as, someone who as handicapped person has succeeded despite his handicap.

"There is much to learn so I hope everyone will do their best to attend every class. That being said, I will be giving a ten question quiz every class period to see if the material you are reading resonates with your understanding."

"Ugh!" came an audible sigh from the class.

"Don't get too alarmed. The quizzes represent a very small percent of your grade. Read the material, do your best and we'll all be just fine."

The days passed quickly in the class and Melanie discovered she enjoyed the lively discussion. Reading another situation to be discussed in class, Melanie was surprised at the anger she felt. "So," said Ms. Conner, "what do you think? Should the prisoner who is also a convicted murderer get the heart transplant or the child?"

Raising her hand, Melanie answered, "The child hands down," she said.

"Why?"

"Because a child has their whole life ahead of them and the prisoner didn't show any consideration of life."

"But what gives you the right to decide which one gets the transplant? Whose life is more valuable?"

"I still think the child," Melanie argued.

"I'm not saying you're wrong," countered Ms. Conner, smiling. "Suppose the prisoner was really innocent. He wouldn't be any less worthy than the child." Pausing for just a moment, she asked, "Melanie, what would Jesus do?"

"Oh, wow! I'm not sure I considered that," admitted Melanie. "My heart just goes toward the child."

"I can tell you, I'm glad it's not me who makes those kinds of decisions," Ms. Conner said. "But it's to demonstrate there will be times in your classroom, whether you are teaching handicapped children or not, where decisions must be made and sometimes being fair becomes a difficult slice of the pie. Neither side is more fair than the other, but you have to make a decision based on the information you have available."

"My reaction to the question makes me feel horrible," Melanie said after class to Ms. Conner.

"I don't want you to feel horrible. I just wanted to make a point and you made it easy!" she said again smiling.

"I still feel awful," she repeated. "I just didn't think about both sides of it, I guess."

"Lee, look! I've been invited to participate in an Advocacy Delegate Meeting in Pierre. How amazing is that?"

"I get to go listen to current legislation being submitted, problems, solutions, and ideas that our state leaders are discussing."

"You actually want to listen to that?"

"Well, yeah. I don't see me as political, but I am interested. They will be discussing ways to balance the state's budget, the issues with all the cuts to educational funding, and other issues."

"How do you get there? It is over a three hour drive there, you know."

"I do know. And there are about twenty of us who received the invitation, so the college provides the transportation. We'll be gone one day. We have to leave really, really early and we get back late, but I'd love to go. Do you mind?"

"No. If you'd like to go, then by all means, go!"

"Thanks, Lee. I am so excited!"

Two weeks later, around dinner time, Melanie looked outside at the falling snow. A foot of the intricate, soft, white, icy crystals had already fallen. They were scheduled to leave at 5:00 a.m. the next morning for Pierre, for the Advocacy Delegate meeting. Chances were excellent the trip was canceled.

"I am so bummed!" said Melanie. "I love the snow, but why now? There's no way we'll get to go tomorrow. I already heard the news cast say classes were canceled."

"Are you really that upset about it?"

"I'm really disappointed. I think it would have been really interesting.

"The snow is beautiful though," she mused. "I never tire of a good snow storm. I love the thick blanket of whiteness. Everything looks pristine and the air is clear and clean."

"You can have it!" declared Lee. "I'm tired of snow. I think we should move to Arizona."

"Lee, you're not serious! I love it here."

"I'm just tired of hurting, that's all," he said giving her a hug. "But I wouldn't mind living down there. It's warm all the time. I could have a tan year round."

"It's hot in the summer and I'd hate it."

"Well, you come up here in the summer."

"I'm sorry the cold hurts you, but this is where our home is. We'd be so far away from all the kids and grandbabies."

"They're not all here now."

"I know that, but some of them are and I cherish the moments we have with them!"

A week later when classes resumed the students were introduced to Stacey Livingston.

"I've been teaching fifteen years and am currently a Special Education instructor. I was a substitute teacher for three years and an instructional assistant for two. Because my background is Latino I was able to be an interpreter in a class room for two years while my husband and I lived in New Mexico. I have my *Bachelor of Science* degree in Early Childhood Education and Special Education Pre – K through 12 and I'm dually certified. I have a Masters of Education degree in English and I have an Educational degree in school administration and supervision. I am qualified in special education to teach Social Studies, English, and Mathematics. I am currently co-teaching in an English eleven class and two History nine classes."

One of the questions Ms. Conner wanted me to answer today was "why I became involved in special education. To answer that I begin by saying ever since I was a child I knew I wanted to become a teacher. I started a little later than most of you. When I was 26, I found myself working as an instructional assistant in the class with students who are deaf. I hadn't planned that, but it was what was available. I was pleasantly surprised to have found my focal point at that time. I saw the yearning my students had to learn and my heart went out to those children. I discovered I loved them and loved seeing them develop and take steps forward. It's more of a struggle for these children but they have such heart and I identified with them for some reason. I knew it was where I belonged.

"The greatest challenge when working with special needs children is probably best described in terms of stamina. It is critical for me to stay current academically and learn a variety of strategies and techniques, since all my students are different and have such a variety of needs. It is imperative for me to stay healthy, since students count on me for accommodations and modifications. In some ways the most demanding part of my time is spent doing paper work.

Everything must be completely documented since the State Department of Education still believes that students are numbers with dollar signs and not people!

"Technology is becoming more and more important in the classroom. We use PowerPoint presentations for notes which makes it much easier to make copies of notes for students with writing difficulties. We have assistive technology tools like literacy software that helps with inclusion classes; and while I believe that all students can learn; and need to be exposed to content area material from instructors who know the material, I disagree with the idea of inclusion classrooms being the only way this can happen.

"There is much more I can share with you, but I wonder if there are any questions?"

"What advice would you give first year teachers who are about to step into special education?" asked Dana, a short, robust girl with chopped hair seated in the back of the room.

"Know your content, but get to know your students better. They rely on you and the better informed you are about them and their issues, the better you are equipped to handle whatever situation arises."

"Are there special considerations necessary in working with parents of special needs children?" asked Lacy, a well dressed, blonde haired girl seated in the third row.

"To a point," she began. "There are obvious special considerations needed for your students but sometimes also for special needs children's parents. They are not really any different than any other parent but it is different in the way they approach their children's education. Special needs parents will either be advocates for their children's education, or you have those parents who are resigned to their situation and feel like there is no hope, or you have parents who are apathetic and choose to do nothing regarding their child's education. Mostly, I've discovered stressing their child's strengths, like with any student, is the best way to first approach parents or guardians."

Melanie raised her hand. "What was the worst experience you had to deal with in a special education situation?"

"I hate to say it, but my worst experience could be described as horrible. The day started out pretty normal but one of my bigger boys, Lyle had already had a stressful morning in a situation that actually involved his mother. Normally, he's well behaved, but this morning he was agitated. One of my other students, Raina, made a remark to him about something benign that normally wouldn't have been an issue, but this particular morning it really sent the ball rolling.

"He began cursing and kicking Raina. When I spoke to him, he started cursing me, and flailing his arms around. He knocked Sidney's glasses off, who was just a bystander, and as I am trying to get things under control, Lyle actually attacked me. He beat me unmercifully. I had broken ribs, a black eye and I was pretty bruised up. I've since healed physically, but emotionally, I still have a ways to go."

"Being a Special Education teacher requires a certain amount of fortitude and determination," said Ms. Conner after Ms. Livingston left. "I admire her courage and resolve to help these children and continue teaching in light of what she has experienced. I would encourage you to consider Special Education since there is a real need for qualified teachers, but make sure your heart is in it. It's the only way you will succeed and remain in this field."

Later that night Melanie shared Ms. Livingston's story with Lee, as he played a game of Solitaire on the computer. "I came away with a whole new perspective," Melanie said. "I don't know if I could do it."

"I don't want you to," said Lee.

"Seriously? You'd be opposed if I wanted to do Special Ed?"

"Just what I need; you to get caught up with some kid who wants to bully you."

Surprised with Lee's reaction, she said, "Well, I have my field experience in Special ED and so far, that's not been bad, just interesting!

"So, I think I'll go work on the presentation, Ellie, Ruth and I have to give in this class. It shouldn't be hard, but I declare, Ruth and Ellie are just having issues! We are all working on a power point, and written presentation on being deaf and mute. Oh my goodness. These two ladies disagree on everything! It's nearly finished, but Ruth has decided since we've seen some of the others and it's not like theirs, we need to change it. Ellie wants no part of it and honestly, I don't see the need. But it's like they have this private battle going and I'm stuck in the middle!

"I think if we each edit a little, maybe all sides can be happy. We have a boatload of information and it is long. I suppose what might have helped was to have a more narrow focus so we didn't have to cover so much information. But we planned on three topics, one for each of us and then we each had three points to cover.

"And to make matters worse, Ruth isn't real computer savvy so she's having issues with that and thinks Ellie is criticizing her. Ellie even offered to take her information and create the power point. Anyway, it's just been real frustrating hearing first from one and then the other. They are to the point of not speaking in class. All exchanges are done via email. It'll be interesting on the day of the presentation, that's for sure!

"Oh and I meant to tell you, Mackenzie and I are going shopping on Saturday and I'm going to be a mute person!"

"What?" Lee asked for the first time since Melanie had started speaking.

"Well, we all have to do some kind of real live participation in being disabled or handicapped, and then report on how it went. We could be in a wheelchair for a day or any number of creative things, and I decided I was going shopping without the ability to speak or hear. That being said, Mackenzie is going with me to help me."

"What a weird idea!"

"Well, it's to give us a connection, however small, with the child who is handicapped. Those of us who have none, can't really relate. I think it'll be interesting."

"That's one word for it," Lee said rolling his eyes.

On Saturday, Melanie and Mackenzie headed for town. "Do you have everything you need?" asked Mackenzie.

"I have my little notepad and pen. That should be all I need. I'm kind of nervous," Melanie said.

"Why?"

"I don't know. Do you know how hard it is for me not to talk?" They both laughed.

"Actually, I do," her daughter commented. "But it'll be okay. Just remember to use your pen not your voice!"

"Oh, speaking of using my voice, I wanted to tell you about Mr. Hanby's visit to our class the other day. I never did tell your dad about it."

"Mr. Hanby? From the college?"

"Yeah. He works in Student Services. He's handicapped and gave a presentation in our class this week."

"Cool. How'd it go?"

"It was really good. He gave a presentation about the problems facing the handicapped but then told us that he's leaving the college after this semester and actually moving to Washington DC to work for handicapped rights."

"Really?"

"Yeah, how amazing is that? He's going all the way back East. He says he doesn't have any family there, but they contacted him through the work he's done here and offered him a job."

"Wow! That's pretty exciting. Oh, here we are. Now make sure you're ready and we'll go shopping!"

Mackenzie and Melanie walked into the Christian Book store in Rapid City. Beginning her search for a pen that is designed to underline the thin pages in a Bible without going through to the other side, Melanie wrote a note to Mackenzie saying

"I'll ask for the pen." She carried the refills of the pens she wanted to the girl near the checkout and wrote on her sheet, "Do you have the pens for this?"

The girl's immediate reaction was to answer Melanie verbally, until she pointed to her ears, shook her head no and handed the girl the pen and paper. Taking it, the girl wrote her response. "We are out but will have some in soon."

Melanie wrote "thank you" on the paper and held it up so the girl could see. The girl smiled and said "you're welcome."

The next segment of their journey was a trip to Staples. "I want to get the numbers we need for Portfolio and ink for my printer, but in refill bottles," Melanie told Mackenzie before leaving the car. Again, Melanie opted to again get help from one of the employees. Writing her question on paper, she handed it to the young man before her: "Do you have sticky labels with numbers on them to number pages?"

His response, like the girl before him, was a verbal answer. Handing him the paper and pen, he responded. After searching for the specific item and finally deciding they didn't have what Melanie wanted he reached for the tablet and wrote: "Try Office Depot or a craft store. Sorry."

Melanie's next request was ink. Writing again, she put her need on paper since she and Mackenzie couldn't find it. After a few exchanges of the paper writing back and forth, the young man again motioned for Melanie and Mackenzie to follow him. When they approached the ink area, he picked it out and handed it to Melanie and then made a point of showing that the one he gave was black and the color one was near it. His first instinct was to talk verbally, but then motioned until he knew he was understood. In both cases Melanie was surprised at the kindness she had been shown.

Proceeding to the Mall, Melanie and Mackenzie shopped, always making sure they used pen and paper to communicate. Finally it was time for lunch. Walking to the fast food court the two "chatted" via pen and paper before making their decision on which "fast food" place would best be suited for lunch and then had to decide what to order.

Walking up to the counter, Mackenzie told the waiter, "I'd like a number seven." Observing their "conversation" before approaching the waiter behind the counter

said, "is that for her?"

"Yes," Mackenzie answered.

Forgetting quickly what he'd just seen, asked, "Do you want regular fries or curly fries?" And as quickly recovering, reached for Melanie's pen and paper and wrote his question. Pointing with the pen, she shook her head yes to the regular fries.

Once the order arrived and the ladies had taken their seat, it was all Melanie could do not to begin chattering with her daughter. So she wrote. "I am amazed at how kind and accommodating everyone has been. I didn't expect that."

"Me, either," Mackenzie wrote. "When you're ready we can head out of here and then we can talk," she wrote grinning.

"I'm right there with you," Melanie responded on paper. "Let's finish eating and go!"

Once in the car, Melanie said, "Honestly, from the stories of the students who had tried this same project last semester, I expected people to be rude and non-caring. I don't know what made the difference between their experience and my own. I think we did really good by asking questions via paper and pen and emphasizing my inability to hear. That's bizarre, though! Glad it was only a temporary "disability!"

Chapter 28

Melanie walked into the second grade classroom. Standing in front of the class of eight girls and seven boys, she saw Mrs. Pippin, a tall lady with medium length, brown hair dressed in a gray baby doll pantsuit. "She's pretty," thought Melanie, as she approached the desk.

"Good morning!" Melanie said extending her hand. "I'm Melanie Carson. I talked with Mr. Adkins, and he said you agreed for me to complete my field experience in your class."

"Oh, yes. I thought he'd mentioned you would be in today. I am Sandra Pippin, and these are my children. We are a busy bunch. As I understand it, this is for your Special Ed field experience, correct?"

"Yes,"

"Well, five of my fifteen children are special education, while two don't quite qualify and some others who are just behind. There are, however, several children who are advanced in my class for their grade level. So it is challenging in a variety of ways."

"I'm looking forward to my time here," Melanie said as she examined the busy room. Shapes and designs covered the walls with neat bulletin boards for new words, behavior tracking, calendar, a work board, a clothes pin board for special work for her students, the alphabet and a writing board. The desks formed a U around the room with an "island" in the center (four desks facing each other) that served as the main table for supplies or a work area for games or activity for the children. Additionally, the U had breaks in it, enabling walk area between some of the desks.

"We will begin this morning with Math time," Mrs. Pippin said as she began calling each child by name, corralling them into their separate work centers. "I would suggest you observe the children with their shapes and ask them if they remember about symmetry. Some forget symmetry and that is what they are supposed to be doing in groups," she said as much to the class as to Melanie. "I will begin with this group and you work with the group there near the back of the room."

"Okay," said Melanie walking to the children to which she had been designated.

"Can you remember what symmetry is," Melanie asked the little red headed boy in front of her.

"I can't remember," he said.

"Well, when you can fold a shape in half, and one half exactly covers the other half, then we have symmetry. So let's take this shape and see if we can put the shapes together to show symmetry."

"I don't remember how to do it," he said.

"I'll show you," Melanie said as she picked up two shapes and placed one on either side to cover the larger solid one."

"I do remember!" said the boy suddenly excited. "Can William help me do it?"

"Sure! Why don't you work together as a team? And you two can be a team, she said to the little Asian and Indian girl who had been sitting quietly waiting their turn.

"Mrs. Pippin! Look," said Drake, the little red headed boy, Melanie had been working with. "William and I did it. We got it all done."

Midway through the class period Mrs. Bailey, an aide, came into the room. Enthusiastic about her work, Mrs. Bailey shared Beginning School Math program with Melanie explaining the different levels. After Math the children wrote in their journals sharing what they thought was most interesting in math. Taylor, a sandy haired boy was so busy chatting during journal time, he hadn't written anything, so he was going to miss going to Mrs. Rae's class for Social Studies.

Melanie watched as Mrs. Rae shared about Helen Keller. To the children's delight she produced a Braille book and allowed the children to run their fingers over the raised letters. Carrying the lesson further Mrs. Rae taught a few words in sign language and included an activity which included using your finger to write a letter on your partner's back and guessing what the letter is.

"What an amazing class you have," Melanie commented before she left.

"I like it," Mrs. Pippin said. "Like I said, it is challenging because of the different levels of learning. But the children with learning disabilities are challenged by those without disabilities and the children without disabilities have the opportunity to show compassion and understanding to those who struggle."

"Parents of non-disabled children are okay with a classroom this integrated?"

"The ones that are in here were required to have parents willing to sign a statement saying they understand and in agreement with our learning environment. It's been a joy to have both these students in my class and to work with these kinds of parents."

"What a wonder," Melanie shared with Lee later. "It's an interesting classroom, but I still think it takes a real special person to teach Special Ed. Mrs. Pippin is very good at it, but I don't know that I would have the patience. The children are so very busy."

Hearing the phone, Melanie said, "Hold on. It's probably just a solicitor.

"Good evening," she said in the standard way.

"Hey, Mom. How are you?"

"Phil! How are you?"

"Just fine, thanks. Just wanted you to know Kaitlyn is in labor."

"Really? She's early. Is everything alright?"

"Oh yeah. She's about three weeks early, but the doctor says she and the baby should be just fine."

"Okay. Well, keep me posted. How are Kara and Jackson?"

"They are fine. We have them with some friends from church."

"Well, okay. Call me as soon as you can after the baby is born."

"You know I will."

"Lee," said Melanie excitedly. "We're about to have another grand baby. Kaitlyn is in labor."

"Good deal!" he responded with pleasure. "Everything okay?"

"Phil assures me all is good. All we can do now is wait!"

The next morning Melanie called Phil's cell phone. "What in the world?" she said. "Is Kaitlyn still in labor?"

"She is and it's been a long night. But she's finally dilating and the baby should be born in the next little while."

"I have class this morning and then field experience this afternoon. Can you let me know what's happening about 11:30? That'll be after class, but before field experience."

"I can do that. Worse case scenario, I'll send you a text."

"That works."

Agitated and clearly concerned, Melanie left for class. Concentration was beyond her but at least she was there in body. Gladly exiting the room when the clock struck 11:20, she headed for her car. Pulling her phone from her purse, it startled her when it vibrated. "Hello," she said quickly.

"Hey, Mom," said Phil. Melanie could hear him smile. "You have another grandson."

"How's Kaitlyn?"

"She's fine, and so is the baby. We've named him, Garrett."

"Oh Phil, that's beautiful! Thanks for calling and letting me know. Tell Kaitlyn we love her and I'll call her this evening."

Elated with the news Melanie made her way to Mrs. Pippin's second grade. Signing in at the office, Miss Temple, the office secretary said, "Strep Throat is going around! We are not letting any visitors in, but students doing field experience are being allowed to stay. You are required to make a visit to the nurse to make sure you are okay, with no sore throat, etc."

Leaving the nurses office Melanie walked to the classroom. Opening the door she immediately noted that the children were all eating at their desks and Mrs. Pippin at hers, who responded to Melanie's silent question of confusion. "The cafeteria has been shut down and all classes are sequestered for the lunch hour," she said. "The bizarre thing is we still go outside and share recess time and all the children will be together on the busses going home! I guess this is just a huge precautionary measure."

"Well, I saw some teachers in the hallway with masks on."

"There are classrooms that have really been hit hard by this virus, and there are teachers who are even wearing masks during teaching! One classroom had eleven of twenty-two out for today. I heard fifty children were sent home from our school alone today! This creates issues not only for the children who are sick, but for us teachers trying to teach a half empty class! How do you start a new lesson when half the children are missing? You would have to redo the entire lesson again!" she said clearly agitated.

After lunch, Mrs. Pippin asked the children to break into groups, and Melanie gravitated to the center where most of the children with learning problems had gone. Billy, a little blond headed boy fascinated her. "You are doing a really good job!" Melanie told him. "Some of those shapes on the Geo Boards can be very difficult and you have it figured out! Fantastic work!" she said.

Changing centers, Reese, a large boy with dark hair looked at her after being particularly difficult with another student and said, "I haven't had any medicine today. That's why I'm mean."

"Oh my," said Melanie, "there's never an excuse for bad manners."

Julia, a dark skinned Asian girl, looked at Reese and sounding older than her years said, "No, you control yourself. The medicine doesn't control you!"

"Mrs. Abbott will be in our class for the next hour," said Mrs. Pippin, to her class. "I need to step out for a bit. I want everyone on their best behavior and want no reports of bad behavior," she admonished before leaving.

At the end of the day, after Mrs. Pippin returned, Melanie shared with Mrs. Pippin her observation about Billy. "I was really amazed at his skill on the Geo boards. He has great special discrimination! He seems to have the process down pretty well!"

"Oh I wish I'd known that sooner! I just came from an Individual Education Meeting with his Mom and it would have been great to give her some good news. She was so upset and crying."

"That's horrible. I wish I'd known, because that happened before you left, but I didn't know who your IEP meeting was with and it never occurred to me to ask and I don't think it would have been proper to do that anyway!"

"Oh, don't feel bad. It wasn't your fault. You had no way of knowing. I'll just phone her later and tell her. Not a problem."

Feeling like she let Billy and Billy's mother down, Melanie left the room and headed home.

After dinner, Melanie called Kaitlyn. "So tell me about Garrett," she said smiling through the phone. "I want all the details!"

As she hung up the phone, Luke and Leslie, a petite, soft-spoken girl with a friendly smile, warm eyes, and brown hair pulled back into a pony tail, walked into the room. "Leslie and I are going to spend some time in her friend's woods to prepare for hunting early tomorrow morning."

"Really? Leslie, you really like to hunt?"

"Absolutely! And I'm good at it!" She said, without sounding arrogant. "My dad took me hunting when I was just eight and I love it! I killed my first deer when I was ten. My mom was in the deer stand with me, although Mom is not a hunter. She always went because she believes self-provision and self-reliance are important aspects of life. Mostly we hunt just to put food on the table. But I'll admit I love the tranquility of the woods and the early morning, waiting. It's awesome to see deer just amble where you are.

We go to a family friend's place who has some beautiful, beautiful acreage. On one side is a wooded hillside with hardly any undergrowth and the other side has two different angles opening into a large field. And there are several great scouting places that run on the opposite side of the creek that runs through there.

"We've been out already on a four-wheeler putting out corn and salt licks for the deer. We've already seen some fairly fresh tracks, markings, bedding places, some scratched out areas and even a couple trails into thickets. I am so looking forward to getting my first rack this year. It's always a very exciting time. The adrenaline just flows!"

"Wow, that sounds exciting. It amazes me that you are such a deer hunter.
Lee enjoys it
although it took him a long time to get past Vietnam."

"I guess I didn't think about something like that," Leslie said thoughtfully, looking at Luke who hadn't said anything.

"You okay with going?"

"Sure," he said gruffly. "Why wouldn't I be?"

The next week Melanie was back in Mrs. Pippin's second grade working with Amber, a frail looking child with hair all askew, wearing clothes that reeked of cigarette smoke. "How are you doing, Amber?" Melanie asked as she watched the child struggle to finish copying the required material from the overhead projector.

Frustrated and angry she said, "I'm going to die or just kill myself."

"Amber, you don't mean that. You're just copying words from the over head. Calm down and concentrate. You can do this."

Worried and slipping away from the child, Melanie walked over to Mrs. Pippin. "Amber is frustrated and talking about dying and killing herself."

"I don't think Amber even knows what she's saying. I wouldn't worry about it."

"Aren't we supposed to report stuff like that to the authorities?" Melanie pressed.

"Yes, we are, but I don't think this is a legitimate case of personal harm so I'll just keep my eyes open and see what develops."

As the field experience hours neared their end, Melanie considered her time spent in the class and spoke of it to Lee. "You know, I really admire what Special Ed teachers can do. I admire and am fascinated by their tenacity and dedication to these children who need so much. But honestly, as much as I'd love to have a classroom, it wouldn't be with Special Ed. I just don't think I have the special qualities it would take."

"That's okay," Lee said. "There are things I like watching but wouldn't or couldn't do. There's no shame in that. As long as you recognize it for what it is and then focus on what you do well, it's just fine."

"Thanks!" she said, pleased with his response. "I appreciate that!"

"Mom, Dad, do you think it would be horrible of me if I don't go hunting with Leslie?"

"Did something happen when you two went scouting the other week?"

"No, not at all. And I even enjoyed being out there. It was great. In fact, we actually did see some deer. But somehow the thought of killing, right now feels revolting. It's just something I don't want to do."

"No, I wouldn't think it would be horrible at all," said Lee. "I know what I went through when I came back from the war. You're no different. And if you are uncomfortable with hunting, then wait it out. Have you told Leslie how you feel?"

"Honestly, not yet. I'm kind of afraid to. She is so sports oriented and especially hunting. I'm just not there. I'd much rather be studying. I think I'd like to become an architect. That was my interest before I went in the service. But that's so boring next to Leslie."

"Son," said Lee, "If you are going to have any kind of relationship with this girl, then you had better be honest."

"I know, but we really are so different. I'm not sure it's going to work."

"Give her a chance," said Melanie. "You're not being fair to her if you don't tell her how you feel. I guess the question is going to be, how do you feel about her hunting? Does that upset you to the point of not being able to deal with it? Will that detail have an effect on your relationship with her, especially since she seems to be such an avid hunter?"

"I don't know. I don't think so, but I really don't know."

"I think you need to find that out before you go any further with your relationship."

"I guess," said Luke thoughtfully. "I'm just not sure I'm going to like the answer."

Chapter 29

Melanie took her usual seat at the front of the room and waited for Dr. Hayden to come in. She had come to look forward to her meetings with the tall, brunette who had become a cherished friend. As students came in one by one, she could name them all now since this class only held ten students and their paths had crossed in a variety of classes over the past three years.

"Hello, everyone!" said Dr. Hayden as she entered the room. "We have a good deal of work to do before we end today and then we don't have to meet again for two weeks, unless any of you have questions and by all means be sure to contact me.

"I'm handing out the Portfolio packets which detail everything you will need in your portfolio and for your portfolio presentation. I hope you've been saving stuff from all your classes. You will need it for the portfolio to be complete."

Melanie began leafing through the packet. There were to be five sections with a specific list of requirements for each. Melanie read Section One: Biographical sketch, philosophy of education, resume, professional qualities inventory and a profession qualities inventory reflection.

Section Two looked to be a list of work samples in various classes and reports, while Section Three had to do with pedagogical, or teaching, reflection materials, Four was the printed version of the power point presentation, and technological work samples and finally Section Five included the praxis scores, high school transcript, field experience log sheets, community service sheets, awards, and finally a goal sheet which would outline what each student would like to do with their education degree.

"Wow!" said Melanie barely audible except to Sage who was sharing her table. "That's a lot!"

"Your work for your Portfolio will mostly be done outside of class. We will meet about every other week, to answer questions," Dr. Hayden said. "Your grade will be determined by the content of your portfolio and the presentation."

"Can you tell us a little about that?" asked Libby

"I can, but I'd rather wait until later after you start pulling your things together. I will tell you that each student will have an assigned date and time for their presentation because it will be given over in the White Buffalo Auditorium. I will reserve it for different days, so you each will have a time slot to work in.

"You will need to prepare a power point, and will be encouraged to invite guests. This is your capstone for all the work you've done. So do your best.

"Any other questions?"

"What exactly is a reflection?" asked Ruth. "Why are there so many?"

"A reflection is your thoughts on whatever paper or project you are writing about. You should be able share how you viewed the project, why you liked it or not; what you learned from the project, or why you thought it wasn't worth the effort and lastly what you could have done better. Did you grow from having done this project intellectually, emotionally or even socially?

"There are quite a few required because each project is an opportunity to grow. As you "reflect" on what you've done, you need to be able to say why and perhaps even how much. You should be able to see where this might take you. And besides all that, it's a great writing exercise and no one ever has too much writing practice! Each of you will have plenty of opportunity to present your writing skills to parents, other professionals and even your students. Writing is very important."

Opening the mail, Melanie said, "Oh my goodness! Lee look! I didn't realize I had done quite so well in high school."

"What are you looking at?"

"I had to request my transcript from high school to include in my portfolio. I did better than I remembered."

"I always knew you did well."

"I knew it to a point. I remember thinking about going to college and thinking that I couldn't and not only because I wasn't smart enough. I knew mostly Mom and Dad couldn't afford it. Course I can see now where I might have been able to get at least a partial scholarship."

"Yeah, but then you met me and all your plans changed."

"You're right, they did. College wasn't important then. All that mattered was getting married and having a family, although I am still amazed that I got pregnant so soon. Who would have thought?"

"It was just meant to happen," Lee said matter-of-factly.

"I think you're right. When I see the young people at the college now, just out of high school and how many don't want to be there, I wonder if that could have been me if I'd had gone right after graduation.

"It's sad, though, to see kids you know have the ability, waste this most precious time in their life and they don't even know it. They hate where they are and think going to work in a fast food restaurant and partying is all that matters.

"Sometimes I feel bad because the instructors will say, straight up, that I am responsible for raising the bar on a project or a test. I love the classes. I love learning. There aren't a lot of young people who share my enthusiasm."

"I agree, it's a shame," said Lee. "I expect a lot of kids are told they either go to college or get a job and it would seem easier to just go to college."

Placing the transcript in her notebook, Melanie sat down to write her last reflection. Finally finished, she printed it, situated it in the clear protector sheet and finally added it to her portfolio. All that remained was adding a few specialty items, and preparing her presentation.

Three weeks before her graduation, Melanie rode with Lee to the airport. Gavin was flying home for the summer and she was filled with both excitement and anxiety. Gavin had attended a concert at the college just four nights earlier and had passed out. He had been taken, as before to the hospital via ambulance and by the time they arrived, his heart and lungs were all functioning normally and all the other tests were inconclusive. "I am so frightened for him," said Melanie trying to calm her nerves.

"He'll be fine," Lee said. "He's in God's hands. We've already made the appointment with the cardiologist for next week. We'll just wait and see what comes up."

Standing in the airport waiting for her tall, thin, dark haired son, Melanie's own heart pounded. Gavin was special. He had stolen her heart from the very beginning. All her children were exceptional, but Gavin tugged at her heart strings even more than the others. Probably first, because he was her last; her baby. He hated that expression, even though it was true and Melanie found herself smiling at the thought.

She remembered when he was just four years old when a violent flu bug hit the family. All five of the children in turn, had been horribly sick and even Lee had been down a day or two. She had been the only one who had warded off the virus. The other four children had finally all gone back to school and Lee back to work. When she finally did get a touch of the virus she only wanted to sleep. Gavin, was sitting on her bed reading a book while she lay there. Finally she had said, "Gavin, go play in your room. Momma just wants to rest."

"No, it's okay," he said. "I'll stay."

"No, Gavin. It's okay. You can go play."

Again, he said. "No, Momma. I'll stay."

"Gavin," she tried again. "Remember when you were real sick and just wanted to rest?"

"Uh huh."

"Well, that's how I feel now. I just need to rest, so you can go play."

"But Momma," he insisted. "You stayed with me when I was sick."

Melanie nearly broke out into tears. This sweet child, too young to realize the depth of love he had just displayed and profound understanding well beyond his years, tied the cords of love that much tighter. And stay he did, reading his book while Melanie rested. This was typical of the insightfulness demonstrated throughout his young life. Is it any wonder Melanie loved him so?

"Hey, Dad. Hey Mom!" came the cheerful voice, breaking her reverie.

Smiling, Melanie gave him a hug. Looking at her quizzically, Gavin reached out to shake Lee's hand and then hugged him, as well. "Welcome home, Son!"

"Thanks, Dad. It's good to be here."

"You doin' alright?" asked Melanie.

"Sure. Excellent, actually!"

"Would you tell me if you weren't?"

"Of course not!" Melanie and Gavin laughed together.

The following week Lee and Melanie took Gavin to the cardiologist as scheduled. He would have a stress test on the treadmill first and then have a "tilt test." Melanie's hands were cold, yet she found herself sweating. Taking her jacket off, she felt cold and put it on again. Pacing the floor nervously and rubbing her arms to keep from shivering, she finally picked up a magazine to pass the time. Unable to concentrate she put it down again.

After only fifteen minutes the doctor came into the waiting area. Standing quickly, Melanie and Lee waited expectantly for an explanation. "Gavin is sitting in my office sipping on a drink. Can we go into my office for a few moments?"

Sitting, next to Gavin who just looked up and smiled, Lee and Melanie waited for the doctor to begin again. "Gavin has what is known as neurocardiovascular syncope. His heart rhythms were irregular when we took him off the treadmill for the stress test. And when he did the tilt test, his blood pressure was 120 and crashed down to about 50! He was only on it less than twelve minutes and he nearly passed out. So we stopped and took him off! Basically what all this means is his heart and brain don't always communicate! The symptoms include fainting, difficulty breathing, chest pain, and heart racing, to name a few.

"But the symptoms are not consistent, so treating is an issue although there are medications for it, and it's entirely likely he will go on something within the week. All the "right" doctors have to read the tests and then we can write the prescription."

"Will this ever get better?"

"That depends on who you talk with. It can completely disappear, or not be visible for months at a time. For most patients with this problem, it means taking better care of themselves, eating right, and oddly enough, often ingesting a greater intake of salt and fluids because it will help the blood flow from the heart to the brain to work more expeditiously. We'll send home material for you to read. Of course he will need to come back and will need to be monitored. He may not have another symptom or attack for months, but we want to keep a watch and make sure the problem doesn't worsen."

"Gavin, you feeling okay, now?"

"Excellent!" he said grinning, in his normal fashion.

"Yeah, okay!" said Melanie, returning the smile.

The next week during the portfolio class, Dr. Hayden said, "I want to talk about your presentations. As I told you, I encourage you to invite guests. There will be guests from the college attending. Portfolio presentations are vital to the Education department and there are many interested parties. Dean Phillip's will be there, as well as, quite a few professors. After your presentations, the guests are invited to ask questions. So be prepared to answer thoughtfully and completely."

"People really ask you questions about your presentation?"

"Yes, they do. They may ask you something directly related to what you have spoken about or perhaps your feelings about something in education. Be prepared to answer."

"Melanie you are up first. You are scheduled for one week from today. Are you almost ready?"

"I think," she replied nervously. "I'm not sure about talking in front of all those people."

"You did it for PTK."

"I know. And I have to do that again next week for the new PTK inductions, although it's just reading names, so that's not too bad. Somehow this just seems more difficult. So we'll see."

"Does anyone have any questions?"

"I am so frazzled," Melanie said to Tristen.

"Why are you frazzled? I've done most of the work."

Here we go again, thought Melanie. "I think we all worked hard," said Jennifer who walked up behind Tristen.

Tristen shot her a glaring look. "Just sayin'," Jennifer added, shrugging her shoulders and slightly smiling. "I think everyone deserves the credit."

Taking their assigned seats on stage, the ceremony began. Each candidate was called up, given a certificate and a rose. The guest speaker for the evening was Eric Anthony, one of the Communications professors. Dark, shiny hair, bronze skin, and warm eyes, complimented the man of only five feet four inches.

Walking up to the podium, he began. "Life is a journey, and should not be taken lightly. I admire each of the students who have joined this organization tonight because it demonstrates their character and how hard they've worked."

In conclusion, he said about ten minutes later, "moments need to be remembered and life treasured. I started something while I was in college as a reminder of this." Picking up a large clear jar that looked very nearly like a fish bowl he continued. "In this jar is a match for every single day I am alive. There is so much to celebrate and so much to be thankful for. Of course there was the one time when I dropped the bowl once and the matches spilled everywhere. I felt like my whole life was lying in front of me!" Giggles could be heard from the audience.

"Seriously," he said, "Cherish the moments you have. Be grateful for the opportunity to learn. Grab onto life; make it important. Make a difference." Applause continued for several moments as the weight of all Mr. Anthony said impacted the entire audience. It was the pinnacle of the evening and everyone there seemed to know it.

The next day was warm and beautiful, perfect for Mackenzie's graduation from Rushmore State University. She had attended night school for months, but after becoming pregnant with Raven, had to take the Fall semester off until the baby was born and then finish during the Spring semester.

Lee, and Melanie who held Raven, took their seats next to Steven and waited for Mack's name to be called. As Mackenzie crossed the stage, Melanie filled with tears. "I am so proud of her," she said. "I don't know how she managed to keep up, not to mention graduating with honors. Between work, classes, helping me in classes when I needed it and being pregnant, I am just amazed. And to think, I graduate in just a couple weeks. It doesn't seem possible!"

The next week Melanie looked at herself in the mirror one more time, not sure the simple dark blue skirt and white blouse looked dressy enough. "Are you sure I look alright?" she asked for the third time. "I'm afraid if I wear a jacket my nerves are going to cause me to get hot up there and then I'd start sweating. Should I wear different shoes?"

"Your shoes are fine. You look great. Stop fretting."

Walking into the White Buffalo Auditorium, Melanie was surprised by how many people had already arrived. She double checked her watch. She wasn't late, but hurriedly she took her place in the front row and waited for Dr. Hayden to take the stage.

Lee took a seat near the top of the bleachers. Mackenzie came in just moments later. Mr. Parnell came in and took his seat right beside Lee.

"Our first presenter this afternoon is Melanie Carson," Dr. Hayden said. "I'd also like to announce that she will be receiving the "Graduate of the Year award for Education.""

Melanie stopped as the crowd applauded. "Thank you," she said as she reached the podium. "I am very honored." Nervously she began, timing the power point with the verbal part of the presentation.

"Good afternoon! I am Melanie Carson, a non-traditional student, married to Lee Carson with five grown children and nine grandchildren. I am from the East Coast, have a strong faith and wonderful family. I am described as warm, bubbly and pleasant, with decent people skills, relatively organized, a willingness to work hard with high ethics and values.

"My strengths socially lie in my faith and my personality and academically it is in History and English. By having five children, I nurtured the innate teaching skills I had, long before I recognized them. In this way, education has been an important component of who I am for many years. I had perhaps, my first inkling of interest in being a teacher, in ninth grade, but life had different plans and I ended up married and had five little people.

"Mostly, I was a full time mom and housewife over the past thirty years, but education was still an important part of my life. I worked in the public school system for three years as an Instructional Assistant and three years as a substitute. Additionally, we decided to home school when my boys, Gavin and Luke, were going in to seventh and tenth grade respectfully. This was hugely successful and an incredibly wonderful experience.

"After they finished high school, circumstances came together that allowed me to begin my college education. I was terrified. It had been over thirty years since I was in an educational setting where I was the student! With my family's help, I have been successful.   In addition to this adventure, I continued my journey in freelance writing which also was a huge part of my life for the past twenty years and in this genre I have also been successful.

"In closing," Melanie said a full fifteen minutes later, "I have a ridiculously long list of people I need to thank. Since that's impractical I will name only a few of those folks who have made an impact on my education here at Cedar Ridge.

"I need to begin by thanking God for getting me through the last three years and helping me reach my goal. I need also to thank the faculty at large here at Cedar Ridge, for all they have done: Professors like Mr. Rafaelle, Ms. Spiker, Mr. Anthony, Mr. Parnell and so many others who have been so helpful and kind. I thank you.

"Specifically, I'd like to thank Dr. Kline. He is pure sunshine! He has been incredibly kind, one of my biggest cheerleaders and accepted me just for who I am. For that I am grateful.

"Secondly, Dr. Vasser. He is awesome. Dr. Vasser believed in me even when I didn't, and gave me the courage to tackle those subjects (Science and Math) even when I didn't think I could do it. For him I am also hugely thankful.

"Dr. Alexandra Hayden. She's become a dear friend and I cherish her. She's always been there whenever I've needed to whine when things have just gone badly and she's listened to my concerns and my issues, whether they were class related or not. For her, I am also grateful.

"Lastly is my family." Melanie felt emotion overwhelm her as tears welled up in her eyes. Pausing and taking a deep breath, she continued, as tears ran down her cheeks. "They have been hugely responsible for getting me through these last three years. My husband, Lee, who has been patient with my exhaustion when I just wanted to curl up and go to sleep, my endless chatter about school and all the stuff that happens in my world here, my complaints when things didn't work out like they should, and my tears when I didn't do good enough on a test."

Unable to stop the flow of tears, Melanie backed away from the podium to compose herself and then began again. "My children, who made it possible to get through classes I would not have conquered without their help." Fighting for composer, Melanie continued, "Each gave of themselves at different times to accommodate me when I was absolutely certain "I just wasn't going to get it." ….from homework via telephone, states away, to sitting down with me and working through a math problem….over and over and over again, to patiently demonstrating how to use a scientific calculator! These things may all seem silly to one who has the know how and ability to do them. But when you honestly don't know, it's encouraging and reassuring to have this kind of love demonstrated over and over again and words cannot express my gratitude.

"Thank you, you have been a gracious audience," she said stepping away from the podium.

Dr. Hayden stood and applauded with the rest of the audience while tears trickled down her cheeks. "I can tell you," she said addressing the crowd. "Professors like myself appreciate students like Melanie. She has been a breath of fresh air and I will miss her!

"Are there any questions from the audience?"

Dean Phillips stood. "Mrs. Carson I would just like to commend you on the clarity of your presentation. Very well done!"

"Thank you," said Melanie, clearly surprised.

"I have a question," said Dr. Hayden when no one else from the audience stood. "Considering public education what do you see as the biggest problem?"

Laughing, Melanie answered. "Discipline, hands down! I believe children are much too aware of the power they hold over teachers or any authority in the school. They realize they cannot be adequately punished for bad behavior. It's become the student against the teacher and I think the teacher loses. The child has lost respect for teachers and authority in general and it's a shame. I believe it's one reason we have such a high rate of teenage crime and bad behavior. Children know they have the upper hand.

"When I went to school I knew if I got in trouble in school, I was going to be in trouble at home, as well. And what's more, my children grew up with the same philosophy. Children need to learn respect and that can't happen when children are in control and a teacher or principal's hands are tied."

Melanie found it difficult to fall sleep that night, still giddy from the evening's events. "That was just amazing!" she said, before giving in to sleep. "Absolutely amazing."

"You did a nice job," Lee affirmed. "I think it's great you got the award, too. I'm proud of you."

"Thanks," said Melanie still in a daze. "It never occurred to me I'd even be eligible for something like that. Imagine!" she said, finally beginning to get sleepy. "Me! Student of the year!"

Graduation was the next big event on the calendar and that included rehearsal. Making her way to the South Dakota Building where the graduation would take place, the graduates, like her were still filing in.

"I need everyone to take a seat," said the woman with the microphone. "We need to get this rehearsal underway." Once quiet reigned, she continued. "I do have an announcement to make. Each year Cedar Ridge College gives one student a full scholarship to the college of his or her choice within the state of South Dakota based on nomination and academic ability. The winner this year of the Cedar Ridge Outstanding Student Award is Tristen Cadby. Tristen, you will receive your award the night of graduation, but in the mean time, congratulations."

After the rehearsal, Melanie went to visit Mrs. Simon who had been her Nature of Knowledge professor, but was also the head of Student Services. "Hi, there!" Mrs. Simon said when she saw Melanie. "Are you ready for graduation?"

"I think so," Melanie answered. "I just came by to say hello. I will miss you."

"I will miss you, as well."

"Tristen Cadby received the Cedar Ridge Outstanding Student Award. I'm not quite sure how I feel about that."

"Well, I share your sentiment," said Mrs. Simon. "You might be interested to know you were in the running for that."

"I beg your pardon?"

"You were in the running for that award!"

"I was? You're kidding?"

"No, in fact, I nominated you."

"Oh my goodness! Thank you," she said dumbfounded. "I certainly didn't expect that!"

"I also know I wasn't the only one who felt you deserved it. So from that standpoint, I congratulate you!"

"Thank you so much," Melanie said again, hugging her friend and fighting emotions. "My college experience has been amazing. I had no idea when I began this journey three years ago I would have such a feeling of accomplishment.

"I have made wonderful friends, realized a dream, and recognize now that I can now do something more than just be a mother and wife. I feel like I have the potential to do something constructive with my life. I didn't feel that way before. It's been an amazing journey."

"Well, I can tell you, there are many here who are grateful you decided to embark upon this journey."

Again fighting tears, Melanie said, "thank you."

Sharing her story with Lee while on the way to Rapid City the next morning, Melanie said.   "I am amazed with how nice people have been at the College. What an experience. You know I think that if I ever went to work, I'd want it to be there, or at least in that setting; there in the Student Services area or in the main library where the Supplemental Instructors work.

"I think being a Supplemental Instructor would be interesting," she continued as Lee listened in silence. "Ms. Spiker has told me she'd love for me to be able to tutor some of her kids on Wednesdays and Mrs. Jansen has said she wanted me to work as a tutor in English. I know they have supplemental instructors for Biology and for Mr. Rafaelle's business class. I just think it would be interesting.

Lee sat quiet for a while and then finally said, "You'd be good at it!"

"You mean that?"

"I do," he answered and then fell silent again.

"I've been thinking about it," Lee started again. "It would take some rearranging of plans, but if you want to work, I'd support that!"

"Seriously? Wow! I didn't expect that. I just thought it'd be interesting."

Excited, Melanie went to see Ms. Simon first thing on Monday morning. "Do you think Mr. Rafaelle could use another Supplemental Instructor?" Melanie asked. "I was talking with Lee and he said if the position is available he wouldn't be opposed to me working. And then if I could get some hours here in Student Services tutoring, that would be just amazing," she gushed, unable to contain her excitement.

"I am delighted with the idea of you being Mr. Rafaelle's SI, and I believe getting you work here in Student Services would not be a problem. But you would need to talk with Mr. Rafaelle since he has to "recommend" you, since he is who you would be working with! I know there have been some issues with Peggy, the SI he has now, so you getting hired might certainly be an option. He isn't here today, so you'll have to wait until tomorrow."

"I'd say I'd be willing to be a Biology SI, but I don't feel strong enough in that subject, even though I got a decent grade. I just struggle with all the particulars there."

"That's fine. Maybe you can do that later, when you're more comfortable."

"Okay, that works! For now I will plan on visiting Mr. Rafaelle in the morning."

Nervously Melanie knocked on Mr. Rafaelle's door. "Come in," came the pleasant reply.

"Can I talk with you a moment?" asked Melanie warily.

"Sure. What's up?"

"I was talking with Ms. Simon and told her I'd like to be your new SI if you would be interested."

"Okay," he said.

"But, Mr. Rafaelle, you have Peggy."

"I know," he said. "Come back to my office about noon and we'll work it out. I have a class in about ten minutes."

"Okay." Confused at the seemingly simplicity of getting the position, Melanie left.

When she entered his office at the appointed time she said, "Did you understand what I said?"

"Yes, you want to be my SI! This is good. I can use both of you. Peggy can be at the Blackhawk Campus. So, what's next?"

"Well, if you are serious, Ms. Simon said you would need to recommend me."

Without hesitation, the next instant, he picked up the phone and called Ms. Simon. "Melanie Carson is here. I want her to be my SI and I'll keep Peggy too, but have her on the Blackhawk Campus."

"Oh really? Melanie, would you excuse me for a few minutes?"

Melanie waited outside his office until he came to the door and asked her back in. "I've been enlightened about a few things! And with that said, you are now my new SI and that is the end of it!"

Melanie went back to Ms. Simon's office. "That was bizarre!" she said. "It looks like I'm actually going to be working at Cedar Ridge in the Fall. How cool is that?"

"I think it's wonderful. You need to go visit Mr. Hanby about tutoring," she said. "He will be leaving us in just a few weeks and moving to Washington DC, but for now he is still the person in charge of tutors."

"Mr. Hanby visited our Education Psychology class. He's nice. I had heard he was leaving. Course I didn't know at the time that he was in charge of the tutoring services. I only knew he worked in this area."

"Go talk with him. He's expecting your visit. If there is no student in his office already with him, just knock on the door."

"Okay."

"You come highly recommended!" Mr. Hanby said enthusiastically, just moments later. "I believe we can use you. Welcome to the staff!"

Melanie was overwhelmed. So much, so fast and now it was graduation night. Most of her family would be there. Tara and Brent would make the trip across the state, Gavin was home from college, Luke was there and always Mackenzie and Steven. The only ones not able to attend were Kaitlyn and Phil. There was no way they could make it up from Texas, especially with newborn, Garrett. Still having the others there along with Lee, Melanie's heart was full.

Filing in the auditorium with cap and gown, Melanie could barely contain her emotions. She kept swallowing so she would not cry. Taking her seat and breathing deeply, she regained control. Finally she heard her name, "Melanie Carson, winner of the Outstanding Student Award in Education."

Walking up the steps, she stood before Dr. Phillips, Dean of students. "Congratulations!" he said, shaking her hand, and handing her both her diploma and Outstanding Student award and plaque. Pausing a moment longer as the cheering continued, he added, "You have quite a cheering section!"

"Yes, I think I do!" laughed Melanie. "Thank you so much!" she added before walking across the stage.